Gucci Mamas

BANTAM
SYDNEY AUCKLAND TORONTO NEW YORK LONDON

GUCCI MAMAS
A BANTAM BOOK

First published in Australia and New Zealand in 2007
by Bantam

National Library of Australia
Cataloguing-in-Publication Entry

Kendall, Cate.
Gucci mamas.

ISBN 978 1 86325 565 3 (pbk).

1. Social values – Fiction. I. Title.
A823.4

Transworld Publishers,
a division of Random House Australia Pty Ltd
100 Pacific Highway, North Sydney, NSW 2060
www.randomhouse.com.au

Random House New Zealand Limited
18 Poland Road, Glenfield, Auckland

Transworld Publishers,
a division of The Random House Group Ltd
61–63 Uxbridge Road, Ealing, London W5 5SA

Random House Inc
1745 Broadway, New York, New York 10036

Typeset by Midland Typesetters, Australia
Printed and bound by Griffin Press, South Australia

10 9 8 7 6 5 4 3 2 1

For Kelly, sister extraordinaire – MH
To Ian with love – LB

~Prologue~

Mascara Epiphany

I could be happy, really happy, if I had an arse like that.

Mim sighed as she caught sight of a taut, toned butt in Calvin Kleins reflected in the chemist's mirror. Lucky bitch, I'll bet her bloody life is perfect, you can just tell, she thought ruefully, sneaking another glance at the tight cheeks and making a silent promise to fit in another yogalates class that week.

Funny, she had those jeans on today too . . .

Oh Jesus.

That was ***her*** *reflection.*

That was ***her*** *arse.*

But how could that be?

That was the arse of a truly happy woman, a woman who was 'there'.

Mim wasn't anywhere. She wasn't happy. She was still striving and fighting to get somewhere even near 'there'.

This presented a dilemma. How could she be seen out in public with an arse that boasted such confidence? One that sent such a message of taut smugness? When there was so little else to back it up?

It was disconcerting to have one's buttocks move ahead in social status before one had all the other necessary accoutrements for a better life.

Perplexed, she paid for the mascara she had rushed in for before dropping the kids at school. Then, stealing one more backward glance in the mirror, she headed back into her life.

~1~

Trouble in Paradise

Present Day

Mim stared daggers at James. Then her fight-or-flight response kicked in. With Mim it was always flight. Get the hell away, escape, just hide. She grabbed her bag and keys and turned to storm out.

'That's right, as always, run away, Mim. You've been doing it your whole life.'

She spun angrily back towards her husband. He stood there in an aggressive male stance – hands on hips, legs astride. He glared at her, daring her to call his bluff.

'What else do you expect me to do?' she screamed at him. 'I can't stay here and put up with this shit another second, I just need to get the hell away!'

'What you need, you spoilt little princess, is to stay here and resolve this. You need to stop hiding for once. Now put the fucking car keys down.'

'How dare you, you utter shit,' Mim responded, throwing the keys at James's head. He ducked just in time, and the keys clipped the corner of the wall behind, leaving a nasty rip in the plaster.

'Oh, nice one,' said James as he turned to survey the damage. 'Domestic violence a new strategy with you, is it?'

'How dare you turn this around!' Mim was almost hysterical, her high-pitched tone revealing her frustration. 'This isn't about me, James, it's about us, our family. You haven't been home from work in time to see the kids in weeks! You're out at dinner meetings every weekend. Charley was crying the other night because he misses you so much. And now you're off to London for God knows how long.'

James glared at her and, as he drew a sharp intake of breath to thwart her tirade, she jumped in with more to stop him from speaking.

'And take a look at yourself, for chrissakes, you look fucking awful. You haven't exercised in months, you're gaining weight, you're drinking and eating out so much, you've got bags under your eyes, your skin's playing up again. You're under so much stress and it's completely poisoning this family.'

'Oh, so it's my fault, is it?!' James strode to the kitchen, yanked open the fridge and practically snapped the top off a beer. 'I'll drink and eat what and when I like, Mim. I am under so much fucking pressure at work and yes, at home! When do I ever get to have a social life?'

Mim scoffed as she threw her bag onto the leather sofa and followed him, listening to him rant.

'Going out with Japanese business men and schmoozing them is not my idea of fun, Mim. It's not something I choose to do. I have to work my arse off to keep up with the fancy fucking lifestyle that you insist we live.'

'What the hell are you talking about? I haven't chosen this . . . this . . .' Mim threw her arm around vaguely, attempting to illustrate her home and lifestyle. '*We* made the decision to live here; to renovate; to send the kids to Langholme Grammar, not me.' She turned her back on him to hide her tears.

'Mim!' James flung the breadboard onto the granite bench with so much force it split savagely down the centre with a loud crack like a gunshot.

Mim spun around in shock.

'When we made those decisions we knew that we were going to have to keep the belt tight. We agreed on a five-year plan to live frugally so we could have all the things we wanted.'

'Oh yes, of course, the middle-class poor.' Mim circled one hand in a regal wave.

'That's what we decided,' he shouted in frustration. 'But now all this doesn't seem to be enough for you. We have the house, the cars, the holidays, the schools and every fucking designer-labelled toilet seat and toothbrush known to man – what more do you want from me?'

'I just want you to be around, to be a part of this family. I don't want to do it all alone any more.'

'How in the hell am I meant to do that and provide all this? Maybe *you* could do more than that freelance shit that costs us more than you earn. Maybe *you* could get a real job?' he shouted, wild with anger.

'A job?! How dare you tell me what to do! I am not getting some hideous nine-to-five office job – how would I mother my children properly if I'm completely exhausted?'

'Well, I'm sure it wouldn't be any worse a job of mothering them than you're doing now,' James spat back, aware that he'd gone too far, said too much, but so hyped on adrenalin and stress that he was powerless to stop himself.

'YOU ARSE!' Mim was gobsmacked. He actually thought she was a shit mother?! Her hands went to her hips.

'How the fucking hell would you know what kind of a mother I am when you're never even here?'

'Well when I am here you're short-tempered, you've got half a bottle of wine under your belt, you're snappy, you never want to do bedtime for them. You used to fight me for bedtime, but now you try and get out of it.'

'Okay . . .' (*you complete fuck-knuckle*, she added in her head) '. . . one,' and she held out one finger in an accusatory manner, 'of course I'm short-tempered and snappy – I am freaking exhausted.'

'Oh, puulease!' said James, cutting her off before she could continue, 'midweek tennis wearing you out, is it? Or is it the Prada sale that's causing you stress?' His voice was mean with sarcasm.

'Surely you don't really believe that?' Mim stared at him in bewilderment. 'Have you any idea what it's like raising three little children? How much pressure they put me under? The constant squabbling, the demands on my time, the need for attention. Making food all day that's just thrown right back at me. Never any sense of being appreciated? Do you have any concept of that?'

'Should I bring out the violins?' James asked viciously as he crossed the room and threw himself down on the couch, angry with her, angry with himself, hating the sheer ugliness of his life at that moment.

'You are really a fucking self-centred son-of-a-bitch and I have no idea what I saw in you in the first place.' Mim picked up her bag and walked across the room. It was time to collect the children from Liz's house.

As she was about to close the door to the garage she swore she heard James mutter under his breath, 'Fuck you too, princess.'

~2~

Same Old, Same Old

Mim's satin Simone Pérèle robe flapped wildly about her legs as she jumped awkwardly, groping blindly above her head to reach for a handful of leaves from the imposing 100-year-old oak in their front garden. She gazed around the lawn in frustration. Surely there must be some leaves on the ground, it was autumn for God's sake. But the gardener had been the day before and had left the turf in pristine condition.

She tried again, slipping on the muddied ground and scratching her arms on the lower branches, but missed the leaves entirely. After a few more vain attempts she decided she needed extra propulsion. Taking a determined run-up, she leapt and finally tore a few leaves loose.

'Woo hoo,' she puffed in triumph.

'Doing some early morning gardening, Mrs Woolcott?' sang a smug voice.

Of course Mrs-bloody-Lacey from the huge mansion next door would be enjoying Mim's early-morning antics from her breakfast wing.

'Hello Mrs Lacey,' Mim managed through bared teeth. She glanced down at her muddy boudoir slippers and stalked back to the house.

'Right, here are the autumn leaves for your project, Charley. God forbid that you should be late with a Grade One project. Who knows how it could affect the outcome of your academic career.' She hated the sarcastic tone in her voice, but really, how much pressure was Langholme Grammar putting on her six-year-old if he was too frightened to go to school without finishing his homework.

'I'll put the autumn-leaf collage together in your homework book, Charley,' she said, reaching for his school bag. 'Oh look, I . . . I mean *we* . . . well, I mean *you*, darling – you got an A for the gastro-intestinal system diagram we drew . . . I knew all those hours on Google would pay off.'

She glanced up at the clock. Oh bugger! They were running late, as usual.

'Come on, children, we've got thirty minutes to get dressed, finish breakfast and get to school and ELC before the warning bell – and I do not want another demerit point, thank you – I've already got more than all the other mums put together!'

She banged a jug of frothy green liquid on the table, ignoring how much it resembled pond scum. 'I've made carrot and wheatgrass juice. Here's a glass for you, Chloe. Please don't spill it on your new PJs, they were the last Country Road pair in your size.

'Jack, please take your tie off your head and concentrate on gobbling up your mung beans; they'll give you a significant protein advantage.'

Jack made gagging noises as he sniffed the beans suspiciously, while Chloe accidentally knocked her juice over, creating a slimy green river on the linen tablecloth.

Mim sighed. 'At least eat your yoghurt and muesli, you

know how hard Saffron works to design these diets for optimal brain stimulation and physical stamina . . .' She couldn't believe she was actually worried about the bossy dietician rebuking her for straying from the organic, high-energy, low-carb diets she had tailored for the children.

Of course, Mim really wanted them to eat well, but right now a speedy resolution seemed a better option.

'Oh for God's sake! Here.' Mim took a box of Coco Pops from the hiding place at the back of the pantry and slammed it on the table. She left them pouring huge bowls of sugary cereal as she headed upstairs to dress. She tipped her glass of wheatgrass juice into the labradoodle's bowl on the way past – at least someone in the family would enjoy its health-giving properties.

Stepping into the calm sanctum of her bedroom momentarily soothed her. Last night's fight with James had left her feeling drained and anxious, with a headache that throbbed with the intensity of a bad hangover. They had never fought so viciously before and now he had left the country for a week with nothing resolved between them.

She gazed at her wedding picture on the wall. God, we look so happy, she thought as she flicked on the music system. Tears pricked the backs of her eyes and she hurriedly shooed them away as she set about the important business of selecting the day's outfit.

Thank God for the healing balm of fashion.

She decided on white-cropped Calvin Klein jeans and a crisp Pucci shirt and stepped gratefully into her pastel Todd loafers.

She caught her (natural) glossy brunette locks in a barrette at the nape of her neck and dotted on her favourite La Prairie face cream, neck cream and eye cream. She smoothed on Elizabeth Arden foundation, lippy and concealer (for her imagined problem eye area), eye shimmer, lip-liner, and eye-liner.

She reached into her Louis Vuitton cosmetic case and then the horrible realisation hit her.

Oh no, surely not!

She couldn't believe she'd forgotten to buy a new mascara yesterday. She usually had a stock of two or three of each cosmetic lined up in her cupboard, each tailored for specific occasions. It was a sign of how stressed she'd been lately that she hadn't thought to replace an essential item in time. Now she'd have to stop at the chemist on the way to school.

It would be better to be late than to arrive with naked lashes.

Frantic now, with her marital woes suddenly overshadowed by more immediate concerns, she quickly chose a chunky rose-gold bracelet and matching necklace, her Prada sunglasses and her taupe Hermès bag. A generous spray of Bulgari and she was ready for the day.

Ducking into the children's room she gathered the dozen or so uniform components they had forgotten; plus sports gear, art apron and hat for Jack, recorder and reader for Charley.

Mim caught sight of the clock as she headed downstairs. Christ, it was 8.10 a.m. She tutted in exasperation as the phone rang. Typical, at the most stressful time of the day. It usually rang either just as they were leaving for school or at 5.30 p.m. (also known as hell o'clock).

'Yes, hello,' she spat into the receiver, not trying to hide her impatience.

'Hi honey, sorry, I didn't realise what time it was,' James said on the other end of the line.

No, you never do, she thought, but wisely held her tongue and said as brightly as she could muster, 'Just the usual morning frantic pace. Are you at the airport?'

'Just kicking back in the Qantas Club with a coffee and a newspaper. The flight boards in half an hour,' he replied. She rolled her eyes at the thought of how different his morning was from hers.

'How are you this morning?' he enquired with what sounded like genuine concern.

'Fine,' she said shortly as she reached the kitchen and leaned across the bench to wipe up a butter smear, simultaneously picking up a knocked-over cup and kicking the dishwasher closed.

'Listen, honey, I'm really sorry about last night. I really think we need to talk about it. Have you got a minute?'

In her mind, Mim sighed in frustration at her well-meaning husband as she glanced at the evil clock whisking her morning away.

'James,' she said, in what she hoped was a well-modulated, patient voice, 'of course I would love to talk about yesterday afternoon's "discussion" but I have to get three little people in the car and to school in six and a half minutes.'

'Oh,' said James in a quiet voice, 'okay then, if you haven't got the time . . .' he drifted off, letting the accusation dangle unsaid.

'James,' she said, very impressed she wasn't screaming as she noticed the minute hand click over, 'honey, I'm very sorry too, a lot was said that was harsh and unfair, but really, right now isn't a good time. Perhaps when you land in Hong Kong you could call me then and we can talk further?'

'Sure, honey,' James replied, slightly chastened. 'Listen, is there anything special you want me to get you at Harvey Nicks?' he asked, hoping to smooth Mim's obviously frayed nerves, 'or should I just get the secretary to pick you up whatever?'

'Whatever,' Mim replied. 'Look, I have to go. Have a good flight. Bye, honey.'

The kids had taken advantage of her phone call and were watching television in the playroom. She flicked it off angrily. 'You know there is to be no visual stimulation before school,' she said. 'Right, get your uniforms on properly now. Jack, get me the hot-glue gun from the art-and-craft cupboard. Chloe, put the guinea pig back in its cage, you are not sneaking it to kinder again. You know Mrs Casey has pet issues. Charley, get me the lunches from the fridge. Let's get MOVING.'

'Aw Mum, can't we buy our lunch, this stuff sucks,' Charley moaned.

'No way,' she answered, plugging in the hot-glue gun and assembling the autumn leaves on a piece of gold card, shuddering at the thought of the tuckshop menu and the effects the preservatives would have on her children's post-lunch learning potential.

She darted into the front room to get her calligraphy pen to write the headings. As she entered the room, Mocha, their chocolate-brown labradoodle, vomited wheatgrass juice theatrically on the flokati rug.

'Fudge!' yelled Mim as she trod in the warm puddle. 'Fudge, fudge, fudge.' They'd instigated a no-swearing-in-front-of-the-children policy, but right now she was regretting it. She surveyed the damage to her Todd loafers, kicked them off and dropped them angrily in the bin. Now she'd have to rethink her whole outfit. 'Shit!'

'Mum, that's five dollars in the swear box,' Jack said gleefully. 'We've got about fifty bucks already!'

It had been a stressful week.

'Pay up,' Jack grinned.

'I don't have any cash right now, Jack,' she retorted angrily. Maybe they were taking their plan to teach the children fiscal responsibility a bit far. 'Look, we'll work it out later, now get the assignment and get in the bloody car, for God's sake. I have to get changed.'

'Muuuummmm.'

'Forget it, you're not getting another cent!' she yelled. 'Get your brother and sister, get your shoes on and GET IN THE CAR!'

Damn, she thought, only 8.20 a.m. and I'm shouting already.

She wasn't the mother she wanted to be. Vexed and angry; rushing and tired. Always running late for something; always behind and never in control. What had gone wrong?

She'd had it all planned, she'd read all the books. She knew exactly what sort of parent she wanted to be. She and James had even attended pre-parenting classes and discussed at length their parenting policies before she'd become pregnant. They would never smack, avoid shouting and reason logically with their offspring. There would be no television or other forms of visual anaesthetic, no junk food and definitely no arguing, drinking or swearing in front of the children.

But all their best plans had been torn asunder once the children became a reality, and Mim felt she had been chasing her tail ever since.

In a new taupe, sleeveless, ribbed twin-set to coordinate with the Prada slides she'd been forced to change into since the canine vomit incident, she hopped into the driver's seat of the black Mercedes 4WD and revved it out of the driveway. Then she stopped abruptly to jump out, run around to fling open the passenger door and strap Chloe into her child seat.

Off again, she sped to the pharmacy and then on to school and Chloe's Reggio Emilia centre, while hastily coating her lashes in the rear-view mirror.

Her mobile rang and she grabbed to answer it, skilfully juggling it against the mascara wand and the steering wheel. 'Mim Woolcott,' she said breezily, gesturing threateningly at the children to be quiet in the back seat.

'Latte, darl?'

'Ellie, sweetie, I'd love to,' Mim answered, plucking a stray glob from her eyelash. 'Just have to deposit the demons from hell and I'll be with you.'

~3~

Good Morning

LJ groaned as sunlight assaulted her sleep-swollen face.

'Morning, cherub,' her husband sang.

Bloody Philby, why was he always so bloody chirpy in the mornings?

'How are we feeling this morning?' he enquired, knowing full well that the equation of two bottles of champagne plus too few hours of sleep would equal an unpleasant result.

LJ inched slowly into an upright position, pushed her eye-mask into the brittle nest of red hair atop her head, and screwed up her eyes in disgust at the daylight streaming through the plantation shutters.

Philby placed a chai tea by her bedside and planted a kiss on her forehead before heading into the shower.

'Bono's had breakfast and is ready for school,' he called over the sound of the water. 'He was just getting up when I came in from my run.'

LJ had the body of a praying mantis – all stick and no figure. She stretched in an effort to get some blood flowing through her tiny frame, admiring the red-painted toenails that emerged from under the red and black oriental-design duvet. She'd copied the look from an Akira Isogawa piece and it fitted perfectly in her Asian-inspired bedroom.

Philby's inconsequential prattle washed over her as she sipped her hot tea and felt its soothing effects. She leaned forward to examine the daily papers that Philby had dutifully left on the end of the bed, flicking through the pages keenly.

'Oh FUCK!' she spat, spilling tea on the duvet.

'What's wrong, sweetness?' Philby was braced for the worst.

'The social pages from last night's Dan Dandrews exhibit!'

Philby tensed; from the tone of her voice he could tell it was more than just a bad review.

'No shot of you, love?' he ventured warily, wishing he'd checked the papers first and made an early break for work.

'Well, of course I'm bloody in it. But it's absolutely tiny and they don't even have the journalistic integrity to use my name. It just says "the gallery owner's niece", like I was some two-bit accessory. But what's worse . . .'

Philby could tell she was building up to a crescendo. LJ stalked into the bathroom, her flimsy red silk negligee barely skimming the flat expanse where her bottom should have been.

'Look!' she screeched, shrew-like, flattening the offending page onto the glass shower screen.

Philby sighed inwardly, turned from his therapeutic hydro-massage and, wiping the steam from the glass, he looked, as ordered.

His brain ticked over quickly. There was no time to waste. If he didn't identify the problem and sympathise within the next three seconds the episode would escalate to a Code Red domestic alert and it would be days before the damage was rectified, and then only by serious sucking up and brown-nosing on his part. He was under pressure, sweating despite the shower. He scanned the full page of socialites parading in their finery . . . but, damn it, for all his experience with such imagined slights, with all his rigorous drilling from his wife, he just could not see the problem – and that was his undoing.

Sensing his hesitation, then spotting the brief look of confusion that slid across his damp features, LJ snapped.

'LOOK HOW BIG THE PHOTO IS OF ELLIE FUCKING ASHCOMBE! It's practically a quarter of the page!' she screamed at the imbecile who was her husband.

This was now a full-blown situation and Philby swung into immediate damage control. A PR guru, he was well-versed in the fragile emotional state of creative types, and although he'd failed the first test of the day, he was damn sure he wasn't going to stuff up another.

'But cherub, Ellie is an attractive woman and it is wonderful PR for Nev's gallery,' he said, stepping from the shower and roughly towelling his blond-streaked hair. 'He's lucky that she even attended the event. Beautiful people – people like you, *ma chérie* – are what sells papers and, in turn, advertises his gallery.'

'She's not that good looking! She always gets better press than I do! She's always in the social pages, and she often gets to go to better things than us!' LJ stamped her foot on the white tiles and pursed her collagen lips, vaguely conjuring up an image of Mick Jagger in drag in Philby's mind. He suppressed a smile, relieved now that the domestic alert seemed to be decreasing.

'But darling, you invited her,' he pointed out.

'That's not the point,' LJ whined childishly. 'Of course I invited her. It's very important to invite her. I obviously couldn't have not invited her, now could I?'

Philby was having difficulty following both the syntactical trickery of the sentence and the intricate social politics at play.

'But how come she has to be more important than me! I'm Nev's niece, and I look good too,' she whined, drawing out the final word over several annoying seconds. She angrily tore up the paper and let the scraps fall carelessly about her on the carpet for someone else to pick up later. Philby made a quick retreat to his wardrobe to dress.

LJ flung open the double doors of her walk-in robe and selected her day's outfit.

Black.

It was her 'thing' to wear black and accent it with the colour she was 'feeling' on the morning.

Today's accent was to be black – all Ellie's bloody fault.

LJ decided on a black skin-tight singlet mini dress, black knee-high boots and a black wrap. She piled what to her mind were her luxuriant curls (but actually looked more like frayed strands of old rope) into a loose bun, then flew downstairs, the wrap flapping like a crow's wings behind her.

'Bono, get in the car, we're late.'

'Sure, Mum.' Bono jumped off the couch, grabbed his bag and nipped down the corridor to the garage. He sensed his mother's mood and knew there was no point in arguing or dilly-dallying, it just made her shittier.

LJ grabbed a banana from the fruit bowl to keep her hypoglycemia at bay, wrote a terse note to the cleaner to work harder on getting the white-tiled family-room floor to sparkle, and followed her child to the car.

'Five more minutes; just five more minutes; just four and a half; not long to go, keep going, girl, you can do it.'

Tiffany's chunky, Lycra-clad legs pumped as she chanted

to the end of her daily sixty-minute workout. She talked herself down to sixty seconds, then twenty, then ten, then stepped off the treadmill, holding the supports until she steadied herself.

Many women glow after exercise; but not Tiffany. She sweated; her face turned bright red; she puffed alarmingly and had been known to groan mid knee-bend. All of which was why she'd insisted on a home gym, so she could wage a battle against her thighs in private.

If Tiffany could change a single thing about herself it would be her thighs, she had decided many years ago. Looking in the mirror every morning she scowled at the saddlebags she carried on her legs, like a pack mule loaded for a long journey.

It wasn't that she didn't work hard. She'd just drawn a short straw in the genetic lottery of life. During her twenties she'd enjoyed the figure that usually accompanied petite women, but since child-bearing her hips and bottom had ballooned until her Peter Pan shape had gone pear-shaped.

Still panting for breath, she walked down the corridor into her huge kitchen. The pristine grey granite benchtops gleamed, the bright red-tiled splashback a striking contrast. She peeped through the glass door of her most recent appliance acquisition, the full-sized wine fridge, to ensure the supplies were up – champers for cocktail hour this afternoon, she decided.

Jana, the smiling French au pair, had surfaced unusually early today, and was busying herself with cereal and bowls, combining Kellogg's with Wedgwood and Weet-Bix with Mikasa. The children not only had different tastes in breakfast, but also in china patterns.

Jana crammed some oranges down the throat of the juicer as it whirred into life, and sliced some melon.

'Kids, breakfast,' Tiffany called up the stairs. While she

waited for the morning parade to begin, she swapped her trainers for high-heeled Miu Miu thongs. At a diminutive five foot tall, Tiffany felt awkward in flats, even while padding around the house. In fact, years of high-heel usage had shortened her hamstrings to the point where it was almost impossible for her to walk barefoot.

'Morning, gorgeous,' she greeted Sophie as she swung her daughter from the third-bottom step, 'who's nearly six then?'

'ME!!!' said Sophie in glee as she ran off to the breakfast table.

'Hiya, handsome,' she said to the ruffle-headed Edward. 'Good sleep?'

'Yeah,' came the tired reply, and he walked down the hallway ahead of his mother towards the breakfast table.

What is it with eight-year-olds? Tiffany thought in wonder as she followed her pyjama-clad son. I'm sure they're made of plasticine, he's grown five centimetres this week, I swear.

As the children crunched noisily, Tiffany nibbled at a piece of melon.

'Hi Dad,' the children sang out in unison as Cliff sauntered in, shirtless, fresh from the shower.

'Hi guys,' he returned from the side of his mouth, on a desperate mission for coffee. Tiffany had tried tempting him with the espresso machine but he was old-school and preferred the drip variety. She shuddered at the thought.

'Good morning, sweetheart, I didn't hear you come in last night,' Tiffany said.

Cliff's naked, hairy guts spilled messily over his pants, his belly-button a tangled black eye of wiry fuzz. Tiffany worked hard to keep her eyes on his face.

Cliff grunted as he deposited his weight into a kitchen chair in their sunny breakfast nook. 'Yeah, it was a late one,

I tried to be quiet.' Before she could question him further he distracted her: 'So, how was your night?'

'Oh, it was fine. The artwork's meant to be good, at least that's what the reviews say . . . most of Langholme Grammar turned up, so there were plenty of people to talk to. It's a shame you couldn't make it, you would have enjoyed it . . . Bryce Ashcombe was there.'

'Great bloke, Bryce, really good man.' Again to avoid further interrogation, Cliff placed his shaggy paws on the table and pulled himself up. 'Well, best get dressed, I've an operation first thing.'

Forever attempting to show an interest in her husband and his dreary work, Tiffany asked, 'What type of procedure?'

Cliff, never missing an opportunity to talk about his chain of orthodontic practices, turned on his way out of the room and explained, 'Strange really, her teeth are perfect – the woman wants them all scraped back and a complete set of porcelain veneers put on! Very dramatic and an expensive operation for a very minimal end result – could have advised her against it but it's what she wants – says it's because of that Hollywood starlet, whatsherface, who had it done.' He turned to leave and threw over his shoulder, 'Oh well, ten grand for a morning's work is nothing to be sneezed at.'

Finally dismissed, Tiffany turned to her children and, after instructing Jana to establish the status and location of homework, readers, library bags, sports uniforms and show-and-tell, she sent them off to get their school uniforms on.

She finished her melon, flicking through the latest *Vogue*, interested to see that snakeskin was in (her favourite), then went upstairs to face her daily struggle with her wardrobe and mirror.

* * *

Ellie floated into the Italian marble kitchen in a floor-length white silk feather-trimmed robe and blurted a raspberry on the necks of the kids sitting at the kitchen bench tucking into their porridge and Vegemite toast.

'Hi Mum,' giggled Paris.

'Muuuuum,' said Rupert, flicking her away like an annoying mosquito.

Ellie responded by giving him another raspberry and this time he scrunched his neck and laughed.

'Ursula, darling, how are you?' Ellie flopped onto the overstuffed white couch and plumped the down cushions behind her head, kicking off her feathered slippers.

'Very well, Mrs Ashcombe, and you?' the au pair asked, handing Ellie her regular morning latte.

'Tired. I'm afraid I had a late one last night.'

'Oh, I know, look, I've put the paper out for you on the coffee table.'

Ellie glanced over at the social pages. 'Nice pic of LJ. Look, doesn't Liz look sweet next to the artist; she was so interested in his work with underprivileged children. I don't think she once talked to him about his exhibition.'

She sank back into the sofa and studied her children. 'You could probably use a hair-wash tonight, Paris darling.'

Paris pulled an unimpressed face.

'Yes, Mrs Ashcombe, I was thinking the same thing. We'll be sure to do that, won't we, Paris sweetie?' Ursula said.

'Oh you're divine, Ursula, thanks lovey,' Ellie drawled, draining her latte and leaving the cup on the table, the paper scattered and her slippers on the floor as she padded back to the master bedroom. She pushed open the heavy floral curtains that draped luxuriously onto the thick carpet. The sun bathed her naked husband, half-asleep and half-covered in the king-size bed, and filled the white and raspberry room.

Ellie had been just twenty-three when she fell heavily

for the international media mogul, and to this day she couldn't quite decide what had finally won over her heart. She knew Bryce was the most exciting and yet gentle man she had ever met, and when they were together their twelve-year age gap just melted away.

Society decided the beautiful model Ellie Fitzpatrick had married down in the looks department, and way up in the finance department. But Ellie had ignored the whispers. Sure, Bryce was no oil painting with his thinning hair, expanding waist and large nose, but Ellie saw so much more. So much, in fact, that she was happy to leave her successful and high-profile modelling career behind to be with him.

Bryce had swept her around the globe immediately after the wedding on an international adventure of exotic locations, experiences and glamour that lasted eight years until they'd decided to settle back in Australia and start a family.

'Mmmmmm,' murmured Bryce and reached out his arms to his wife as she came to prise him out of bed.

She deftly slipped out of his grasp. 'No you don't, big guy,' she smiled. 'Once a morning is enough for you.'

'Oh, am I on rations?'

'You most certainly are. Time for work,' she said sternly, her eyes laughing.

'Oh, you're mean,' he grumbled, climbing out of bed and staggering into the ensuite. Ellie slipped out of her robe and joined him in the double shower, where his rations were very quickly increased.

A little while later, Ellie contemplated her wardrobe thoughtfully. This was her art – fashion – and her body made the perfect canvas. She had the poise and shape to make any outfit look great.

The Guess jeans and her new little Tommy Hilfiger white top would be just right for today, she decided. She had always had the knack of grabbing any old (designer-label) bag and shoes from her vast collection and by calling it 'eclectic' and wearing it with aplomb, she easily got away with it. It was so much less effort than stressing about matching accessories, like her best friend Mim always did.

'Ursula, I think the school run is just a tad beyond me this morning, love,' she called down the corridor. 'Would you be a darling and take them for me please?'

'Certainly, Mrs Ashcombe,' Ursula responded. She quickly had the two children dressed, organised and, after farewell cuddles with their parents, in the car headed to school.

Fresh from her regular five-kilometre power walk, Liz stepped into her minimalist foyer. She preferred an uncluttered entrance in order to highlight their collection of Australian art. She was particularly proud of the Albert Namatjira piece, which filled the main wall.

She unclipped Strauss, their white standard poodle, and he rushed to his water bowl. She followed him into the kitchen and flicked on the music system that piped classical music throughout the house. It was her gentle way of alerting the children that the day had begun.

Sebastian entered the light-filled room, his long, grey hair messy on his shoulders. His gaze was fixed on the score in his hand and he was muttering to himself.

'Good morning, darling,' Liz said brightly as she started to get the breakfast things out. 'Big night tonight?'

'Hmmm, what, oh, yes . . . morning,' Sebastian said absently as he sat at the bench, continuing to mutter and wave his hand. As second conductor of the Melbourne Symphony Orchestra, Sebastian was preparing for the opening night of a new piece – a tribute to Beethoven – and he was understandably distracted.

Roman entered the kitchen and climbed up onto a stool at the breakfast bar. With his dressing gown tied about his waist, his slippers on and his glasses folded neatly in one hand, he resembled a little old man.

'Good morning, darling, how was your sleep?' his mother asked as she started boiling eggs and cooking toast.

'It was all right but I had a song in my head all night. I think I have to write it down. Have you got a pen?' he asked, tapping one finger in time to the music in his head.

'Certainly, darling, here you are.' She handed him a pen and a sheet of music paper and he started scribbling madly. She stood back and smiled at the sight of her husband and eldest son, bent over side-by-side, immersed in their music.

Hubert ran in and threw himself into his mother's arms. 'Mummy,' he yelled out, his words muffled against his mother's legs.

'Hello ragamuffin,' she said, and gave him a squeeze. 'Eggs for brekkie?'

'Mmmmm, yes please,' he yelped, and clambered up onto the stool in between his father and his brother. He didn't bother greeting the other two males in the room, he'd learned from experience that they wouldn't hear him.

Liz doled out four serves of egg and toast and opened the paper to the cultural section. She was hoping to catch a recital at the Windsor Hotel next week and she needed to find the details.

The social pages caught her attention and she looked with distaste at the photo of LJ, with too much make-up and too much wine under her belt. What a nasty piece of work, Liz thought. So NOCD (Not Our Class Darling), as she and the girls said. LJ's top plunged almost to her navel and her tiny skirt left little to the imagination.

There was a gorgeous photo of darling Ellie too, and she looked as divine as ever. It had been a fun evening. The artist was perhaps not her taste, though. Although she prided herself on being a lover of contemporary art, Liz felt that Dan Dandrews was perhaps still an amateur and yet to develop maturity in his subject choices.

She put the paper away, efficiently stacked the dishes into the Miele dishwasher and removed all evidence of breakfast. The cleaner was coming today and she certainly didn't want the place to be in a mess.

In her ensuite, Liz removed her navy blue legging track pants and white tee and splashed cold water on her face. Soap and water was the beauty regimen to which Liz attributed her translucent complexion. She never used products on her skin and rarely wore make-up. She twisted her long blonde hair into its trademark chignon and went into the robe to choose her outfit for the day.

Understated elegance was Liz's traditional look, to the point of almost being a uniform. Most days she teamed tailored trousers with a unique blouse. Today's choice, however, was a lot more understated than usual.

Slipping on trainers and transferring her wallet, keys, mobile and diary into a basket-weave handbag she walked back into the family area. A testament to contemporary minimalism, low white couches accented by cushions in orange, yellow and red squatted on recycled timber floors. Modern sculptures stood tall in each corner.

The boys squatted at the low timber coffee table, dressed and ready for school. She interrupted their game of chess, 'You're all ready then I see. Have you done your homework?'

Neither boy deemed the question worthy of a response and both merely shot her a look of disdain.

'Of course you have,' she corrected herself. 'Okay, in the car then. I guess being ten minutes early to school won't kill anyone.'

As she followed her two little men down the hall to the garage she couldn't help but wonder at their seriousness. Of course she was thrilled with their gift for music and academia, what parent wouldn't be? But sometimes she almost wished they'd muck about a bit more, play in the mud, get dirty. She quickly corrected herself as she reversed the Volvo down the driveway. She was very fortunate to have her boys.

~ 4 ~

Running the Gauntlet

Dropping the mobile into her lap, Mim nudged her way into a parking spot at the front of Langholme Grammar. She grabbed Jack's autumn project, which was rapidly shedding debris through the car, nagged the boys into their blazers, straightened ties, hastily dabbed at stray cocoa spots on their cheeks and wet their hair with a discreetly licked hand.

'Mum, gross,' Jack complained, pulling away.

'Well we don't want another uniform demerit, do we? And pull your socks up too. People will think your mother doesn't care.'

She quickly unstrapped Chloe and, dragging her by the wrist, shepherded the whole bunch toward the entrance just as the final bell sounded.

The Car Park Mafia (CPM) was in its usual spot at the front gate. First to arrive and last to leave, this group of fashion victims never set foot in the school yard or classrooms, yet they always had their over-manicured fingers on the pulse of all the gossip.

The CPM was easily identifiable in their dress code of spiky stilettos and flared designer jeans for school drop-off; Reebok tennis-dress combo for social mornings; or tight Lycra crop tops and bike shorts for meetings with their personal trainers. They were the new money. Footballers' wives, rock stars' wives and ex-models past their prime. They flaunted their wealth with flashy accessories. Lashings of gold was a must, but diamonds were the ultimate fashion statement. These chicks were hooked on bling. Ever since the thrill of their first diamond hit, they'd become desperate junkies pursuing the next glittering high.

Body diamonds were the ultimate trip. Their taut midriffs sparkled with them; manicured pinkies dangled dainty rocks, and you could catch a glimpse of the occasional incisor sparkler if you were lucky. Their acrylic nails were a dazzling spectrum of hues and designs, from Hawaiian sunsets to glittering silver shooting stars for special occasions – such as Brownlow night and the Logies.

They had produced offspring only because there was little else to do once the wedding was over. Of course, any evidence of pregnancy had now been erased by the local plastic surgeon – the same guy, coincidentally, who had straightened their noses and homogenised their breasts to an unrealistic 10DD.

Mim bustled past them with a tight smile, feeling their appraising eyes on her back. She wished she'd had time to properly blow-dry her hair this morning. She muttered a quick hello to the Triple Ds (divorced, desperate and dateless), with their bloodshot eyes. The Triple Ds were career divorcées, women who married for money and status, drained their men of money and affection and then headed on to the next conquest. They were jaded, shallow souls who had lost their looks to vodka and the sun. Most of the Triple Ds had started out as nannies, screwing the husband on the sly and eventually making off with him and the house, leaving the wives and kids to sink or swim. Invariably they'd then play happy families for a few years, even producing a kid or two, but they'd soon get bored and move on to bigger bank accounts.

When they weren't marrying or divorcing, the Triple Ds were popping over to Hong Kong to find shoes small enough for their tiny feet. Their little-girl figures were maintained by careful adherence to a host of eating disorders of which they were inordinately proud. Their expensive manicures did little to disguise the nicotine stains on their fingers, and the litres of French perfume they were doused in never quite covered the smell of stale cigarette smoke and alcohol.

The few lines of coke the Triple Ds snorted every now and then helped them kick-on at all-night parties and still be glassy-eyed and conscious to take the kids to school (once the nanny had them ready). School drop-off was a must-do event each day: a chance to be seen; brag about their latest boozy exploits; and eye off any new prospects among the dads. These creatures of the night then dragged themselves home to bed and the daylight hours of misery when the harsh reality of their empty lives seemed too great to bear. But there was always the night, and the hunt for a new victim to look forward to again.

Having run that particular gauntlet, Mim kissed Jack absently as he headed for his class, and attempted to steer Charley into the Grade One room where another group of mothers barred her entrance. These were the Mothers Superior, a formidable bunch of mothers who made parenting their career. They were self-sacrificing, self-important women who suffered from empty-cot syndrome and now made the school the centre of their lives. Any well-intentioned mums who came to help were quickly shunned by this powerful group, who made life a misery for the teachers. They read all the latest pop-psychology books and education texts and had a better way to do everything. They regularly voiced strong concerns about education styles, parallel learning, discipline and stimulation issues. They relished the challenge of a detailed school note, attended every assembly and supervised every excursion. They invited the reluctant teachers home for dinner, emailed snappy letters of thanks to the principal and ran all the committees.

This was the inner-core of school mums. They always looked right, always finished their homework on time, always had a beautifully presented home-baked cake for the fete and knew the ins-and-outs of all the school families. A huge team of nannies, au pairs, housekeepers, personal assistants and lifestyle coaches worked behind the scenes to give their lives the façade of seamless perfection.

'Late again Mim?' said Hortense Mathews, a long-standing member of the Mothers Superior.

Hortense was originally from Surrey, England, and despite having moved to Melbourne when she was eight years old she had maintained her plummy accent, which resulted in a most disconcerting affectation. She had a horse's laugh and a face to go with it, and the entire package had Ellie and Mim convinced that she thought she was actually Princess Anne. None of the teaching staff was excluded in her determination to impress. The senior and junior school headmasters had both learned to look busy whenever she approached, to avoid her waxing lyrical on what a wonderful educational institution Langholme Grammar was.

'Slept in, did you, darling?'

Mim acknowledged them with a brief smile as she edged past the tight-knit group, but determinedly ignored the question.

The women slid their eyes over Mim, registered her hair, shoes, outfit and (thank God) professionally applied mascara. They avoided full eye-contact, however, and subtly angled their bodies away from her as she passed.

Mim popped her head into Charley's class and mouthed a silent 'sorry' to Mrs Keith, who nodded sternly at her.

Hurriedly unpacking Charley's bag by the door she rummaged through the flotsam of contents. 'Charley, where's your reader?' she asked frantically.

'I dunno,' he mumbled.

'I put it in your bag, where is it now? Did you take it out in the car?'

'Oh yeah, that's right, I took it out so I could look for my PSP.'

Mim stamped her foot in annoyance. 'Why can't you be more responsible, Charley? Stay here in the corridor with Chloe and I'll get it.' She stormed off back to the car in irritation, and once again ran the gauntlet of the CPM.

'Love those jeans,' LJ Mahoney said, still smarting from seeing Mim's best friend Ellie trump her in the publicity stakes. 'They look fab on you.'

'Thanks,' said Mim, surprised.

'Yeah, I wore mine to death – last season.' The stick insect took a satisfying pull on a fag and smirked at her clan.

Mim hurried away and almost threw Charley's reader into the circle of Mothers Superior, who were set for action in the corridor. They wore holier-than-thou expressions of patience and tolerance and held big red pens for marking mistakes.

'Forgot our reader, did we, Mim?' one mum said, smiling at her nastily.

'Actually, Charley forgot it,' she spat back. 'Where's Chloe, Charley?'

'She went into the playground,' he said, one finger searching keenly in his nostril.

'Stop that, and get into class.' Mim pushed him toward the door and then, remembering, added: 'I love you; you're special and unique, make good choices today'.

'Reading today, Mim?' asked Mother Superior Mary, lifting her perfectly shaped eyebrows and making not a crease in her botoxed forehead.

'Oh, sorry, I can't. I've got to put together a proposal for a new client.' Thank God she had work for an excuse.

'Shame. You always seem to be so busy these days, Mim. We miss your input into the literacy program. It's so important for the children to have parental support in their educational endeavours, don't you think?'

Guilt nibbled at Mim. She had helped out in first term, but the sheer boredom of listening to kids stumble helplessly over words had been more than she could bear.

'I'll see what I can do next week,' she offered weakly.

Christ, she thought to herself as she escaped into the autumn sunshine, I hope Charley and Jack like this place better than I do. I can't stand to be here for more than a few minutes.

The disloyalty of the thought startled her. After all, this was one of the country's best junior schools, and the boys had been enrolled when they were still just foetuses.

And the bloody fees could probably go a long way to reducing Third World debt too, Mim thought grimly. Shame it was such a bloody awful place to spend time.

She found Chloe drenched from the drinking taps. 'Come on,' she said through clenched teeth. 'Time for kinder.'

She dried the child as much as possible with the beautiful Armani towel that had somehow been relegated to car towel, and pulled out of the car park behind the other shiny black European SUVs.

Chloe's Reggio Emilia kindergarten, TJs (Toorak

Juniors), had originally been a Victorian cottage. Mim loved the fairytale cuteness of the place. The storybook feel of the centre had remained even after extensive renovations. Vibrant red geraniums spilled from the timber window boxes and with the picket fence and white shutters it wasn't inconceivable that the three bears were on the other side of the little red front door grousing about the temperature of their porridge.

Mim led Chloe into the front foyer, which opened on to a roaring fire flanked by mini armchairs and a mini couch. Perry, the centre's vivacious director, greeted all parents and children personally with warmth and smiles and the stark contrast to the boys' school was not lost on Mim.

'Good morning, Mim,' smiled Perry, 'and good morning to you too, Chloe, are you both well today?'

'Yes thanks, Perry, good weekend? Did you go boot-scooting?'

'I did, as a matter of fact,' replied Perry, with a quick little two-step, hands on hips. 'It was so much fun, I just love it!'

'It sounds great. I'll have to find out more about it from you one day.'

Perry's much-loved teddy bear collection smiled benevolently down at the trio from every shelf and bookcase. 'I'd love to chat right now, but today I'm going on the Phar Lap excursion,' she said with a smile. 'The children decided they were really into horses, so we've extended their interest. Ellie's actually volunteered to drop off their pony Dumpling for an afternoon – won't that be exciting!'

'You're kidding, the children will love that!' Mim said with a laugh. 'Trust Ellie, she's absolutely mad!' She often wished she could drop off Chloe in her classroom and stay by the fire to chat with Perry all day. The woman had so much passion for children and education and her dedication was inspiring and infectious.

Mim and Chloe continued down the brightly decorated narrow corridor, which boasted bright artworks and were of course, in the Reggio Emilia style, not just displays of talent but also included documentation of the process behind the art.

Mim was amazed to see that the room for the four-year-olds had been transformed yet again. The staff was always keen to play around with the space to find new ways to engage and inspire the children. Today a massive eucalyptus bough festooned with pea lights and children's artistic offerings dominated the room, creating an out-of-season Christmas feel.

Chloe's teacher, Maureen, immediately came to greet her. She crouched down and looked up at the little girl. 'Good morning, Chloe,' Maureen said with a smile. 'Did you have a nice weekend?'

Chloe, suddenly dumbstruck, stared at Maureen in silence. Mim, keen to get on with her day, answered on Chloe's behalf. 'Yes she did, didn't you, darling? She visited her little friend.'

Maureen ignored her and continued to look at Chloe. 'Funny Mummy thinks we're talking to her,' she said, without looking up at Mim. 'I think we'll get Chloe to answer this one, Mum.'

Mim swallowed the rebuke; after all, she really should have known better by now. Answering for a child was a definite no-no in this joint. She held her tongue and quickly felt redundant, so went to hang up Chloe's bag on her hook while Chloe finally answered Maureen's question.

Maureen flashed Mim another meaningful look and she knew she was in trouble again, but wasn't sure why this time.

'Mum,' said Maureen, 'how about we give Chloe an independence opportunity and encourage her to carry her own bag and hang it up on the hook herself?'

'Of course, yes, silly of me. Here, sweetie.' Mim handed the offending item to her five-year old, who busied herself at the hook.

Mim indicated to Maureen behind Chloe's back that she was going to sneak out so that Chloe didn't get teary at separation, as she had done lately.

'I think it's best for Chloe's development if you say goodbye to her and let her know that you have confidence in her resilience,' Maureen gently chided her.

Oh Christ, that's three strikes this morning, Mim thought. Maureen must wonder how I actually managed to mother for all these years without her.

'Yes, yes, of course,' Mim repeated, and bent down to cuddle Chloe goodbye. Naturally, Maureen's advice was right on the money, and after a quick squeeze the little girl skipped off to home corner.

Mim stood there, suddenly not wanting to rush away, gazing after her free-spirited daughter, both grateful and slightly sad that the separation-anxiety period had obviously passed.

'It's probably best if you leave us to it now,' Maureen said, with one hand indicating the door. 'I have other little ones about to arrive and we need to keep our foyer clear.'

'Yes, of course, sorry.' Mim left the room, determined not to make as many early-learning faux pas tomorrow.

Back in the car she laid her head on the steering wheel for a few minutes while her mind cleared. What a morning! Thank God for Ellie and the promise of caffeine. She fired up the Mercedes and headed to Lorenzo's for a well-earned slice of 'me' time.

~ 5 ~

Caffeine Hit

Mim tried to massage away her headache as she stepped into the café, almost colliding with her dear friend Liz, who looked unusually casual in jeans and T-shirt.

'Mim, darling, how are you?'

Mim immediately dropped her hand from her forehead and smiled brightly at Liz, who was one of her Mothers' Group mums.

'I'm just fiiiine,' she said, stretching the word out for extra emphasis. 'How are you? Time for a latte?'

'Can't, pet, got something on. Are you sure you're okay? You look a tad strained.' Liz insisted.

'Oh? No, I'm just great, couldn't be better.' Mim widened her smile and wondered if she could forcibly make her eyes sparkle.

'Okay, gorgeous, must head off. Call me! Ciao!'

Mim glanced back at Liz briskly striding towards her Volvo.

On the surface Liz appeared to be someone who – financially – had it all; a wealthy lifestyle, Portsea house and an international party schedule. Her domestic duties were outsourced to an army of staff who kept her mansion and gardens immaculate, a nanny kept her children clean and well-fed, and a personal assistant managed her busy diary of travel and social engagements.

It was easy to assume that little depth lay beneath Liz's rich socialite demeanour. Yet it was rare for her friends or neighbours to bump into her in the shopping precincts of Toorak, Malvern or South Yarra, and the way in which Liz chose to spend her days would have raised many a well-shaped eyebrow if it got out.

Most mornings, after her mandatory five-kilometre power walk through the leafy streets of Toorak, Liz swapped her designer clothes and diamonds for flat shoes, jeans and a simple white T-shirt.

Liz volunteered regularly at a homeless mission in Grey Street that catered largely for drug-addicted young people. She chopped veggies, served up soup and support, and listened when the kids wanted to talk. She'd been helping out for years and sometimes wondered if it was worth it. No matter how many hours or thousands of dollars she spent, there was a seemingly endless stream of troubled and confused kids every day.

But she couldn't, wouldn't, stop going; stop helping, stop looking. She just knew that one day she'd find what she was looking for.

Mim moved into the chattering café throng. Sidestepping tables full of business meetings and gossiping women she felt triumphant. Yes, I am fine, she thought. It's going to be a lovely day and I feel just great.

She popped into the ladies and locked herself into a cubicle, sitting on a closed toilet lid. It wasn't her bladder that needed attention, she just wanted a few minutes' solitude. She took a deep cleansing breath in, but suddenly it turned into a ragged, gasping sob, and before she knew it she was engulfed in a surge of despair. The ugly walls of the cubicle blurred through her tears as she clenched her teeth and rocked back and forth on the toilet. She folded her arms across her body and dug her nails into her arms in a desperate bid to pull herself together.

'God, oh God, it's just all too much,' she whispered desperately. James's angry face flashed into her mind and she remembered his words: 'Fuck you too, princess.'

This morning's phone call had done little to erase the image.

No, I'm not a princess, she thought bitterly. Just because I want standards for our family; want the best for our family. Doesn't he understand that?

Hiccoughing back a sob, she clutched herself tighter and fought for control.

Suddenly her mobile beeped with a message. It was just the jolt she needed. With sheer will she swallowed down her panic and quietened her sobs. This will all work out, she told herself. She exited the cubicle, washed her hands at the basin and restored her foundation. We've had bad fights before.

Not as big as this, though, her mind whispered.

It's so much harder than I'd imagined, she thought to herself as she remembered her wedding day. It's fascinating how much money, time and effort goes into that one day of splendour, yet nothing is invested in preparing those two young people for a lifetime together. If I'd spent as much time researching the male psyche as I did at dress fittings I wouldn't have been stumbling along blind for these last ten years, surprised and sometimes horrified at every male quirk that comes out of him.

Back then I actually cared about what china was going on the registry, what style of silverware. Did I think I was embarking on a life of endless glamorous dinner parties? Now my mission in dinnerware is to find the perfect plastic tumbler that is narrow enough for little hands yet not tippy.

And the amount of money and angst spent on feeding those two hundred people that night at the reception, half of whom we haven't seen since. I can't believe I cared so much about whether to serve quail or not. If I'd known the reality of entering a lifetime of preparing three to five meals a day for the fussiest individuals on the planet I may have cared less about the wedding banquet.

But we were so much in love. The world was all about finery, silk gowns, white Rolls Royces and an endless honeymoon that was hour after hour of surf, sand and sex.

It's very easy to be in love when there are absolutely no worries in your world, she reflected. The most controversial issue in her life at the time was whether to wear ivory or white.

James had not had a care in the world. He laughed at absolutely anything, he was relaxed and he had the most magnetic personality. Everybody enjoyed his company, but she most of all. She remembered with a smile the long lazy lunches down at the Portsea pub with their mates.

Now when he walks in he just represents more work for me. No, that's crazy, she corrected herself. He's still fun. We've just been so busy we've both forgotten who we are, or who we were. It's all so hard, nothing comes easily, nothing is exciting any more, it's just all about trying to keep my head above water – financially, emotionally, as a mother and as a wife. I didn't know it would be this hard.

She took a deep yoga breath and cleared her mind. A liberal spray of Bulgari momentarily cheered her. Distracting herself with a quick lippy fix and a few strokes of mascara, she then headed back to the welcome distraction of the bustling café.

Her coffee, complete with fleur-de-lys swirled foam, enticed her as she checked the message on her mobile.

The message was from her mother, Julia, via her preferred method of communication. A brief SMS was about as deep as Julia ever got. She was, after all, a very busy woman. Mim replied and a quick conversation ensued.

How's things?

Gr8. U?

Fab. Kids good?

As always, Dad?

At squash. Dinner?

Love to. Will call.

Must dash, meeting.

No point worrying her mum about the tiff with James. Personal issues only made Julia feel uncomfortable, but Mim knew she could count on her if there was a real crisis.

Julia Jones was a tough businesswoman who dealt better with facts than emotions – a lesson Mim had learned early in her childhood. Julia had efficiently produced the pidgeon pair: Mim's brother Raymond and then, four years later, Mim. The junior school years had been a mild inconvenience until they were both tidily dispatched to boarding school.

Mim constantly felt that she fell short of her mother's expectations. Julia had been dux at school, whereas Mim, although she'd always worked very hard, had fallen just short of that honour. She remembered the first time she'd felt that she'd let her mother down. Mim had been very young, perhaps three or four, and had decided to surprise her mother by dressing herself. Her mother's reaction had been extreme: 'What AAAARE you wearing? For God's sake, you look like a bag lady!' and Julia had stripped her daughter off and laid coordinating pieces on the bed for Mim to right herself.

Mim had been very careful to ask what exactly went with what from then on to avoid making such a dreadful mistake again.

The instances continued. Julia never appeared thrilled or excited no matter how great Mim's achievement. Once, when Mim excitedly brought home first prize in an art contest, Julia's response was brief:

'First? In the state?' she'd enquired, looking up from her desk.

'No,' Mim had replied, 'the district.'

'Oh, the district.' And Julia had turned back to the newspaper.

Lost in her thoughts, Mim sipped her lukewarm latte, flicked through an *Architectural Digest* and glanced discreetly at her Omega as she waited at length for Ellie.

Finally, Ellie breezed in, flicking her pashmina over her perennially tanned shoulders. Her mission in life was to find a pair of jeans small enough for her tiny size-six body, but long enough for her six-foot-one frame. It was, as she had sighed to Mim many times, 'a hell I have to bear'.

Ellie leaned over to envelop Mim in a cloud of air kisses and Chanel No. 5. A slave to fashion, she always looked as if she had just stepped out of *Vogue*. Today she was immaculate in flared-leg, faded denim Guess jeans, a white lycra capped-sleeve, Tommy Hilfiger tee over which she'd carelessly (well, painstakingly, actually) thrown a pink pashmina. Pastel pink strappy stilettos and frameless pink-tinted sunglasses completed the look.

Ellie was never on time for anything, and considered tardiness her personal trademark. She thought it made her appear unpredictable and mysterious. But today after trying to look cool and content with her own company for twenty-five minutes, Mim was distinctly peeved.

But, as usual, her best friend immediately unleashed an

entertaining and highly caffeinated torrent of gossip and chatter that quickly washed away Mim's annoyance.

'I am soooo sorry, darling, I got caught up with that dreadful Jennifer Gowrie-Smith from tennis. I had to listen to her go on and on about their Noosa trip. Such a poser. I'm sure she had an affair with her masseuse. She kept going on and on about this woman's "magic fingers" – I mean really! Ever since she saw Madonna and Britney pash she's been dying to try out the lesbian thing. And she lost two kilos with gastro in the first week. Lucky bitch, I never get sick. But never mind, I've heard there's a flu going around. I purposely didn't get the injection.'

'Did she mention Sophie's party tonight?' Mim asked.

'No, thank goodness. God forbid her brat's going. If I have to listen to her sing "Happy Birthday" in Japanese one more time I'll scream . . ' She paused for a breath. 'Have you sorted costumes for the children? At least the Carnivale theme leaves plenty of room for imaginative costumes. Paris has decided she wants to go as a horseback dancer. I've had the most divine little costume made for her – it's v. Kylie – from her Showgirl phase. I'd love to take Dumpling with us, though I suppose that would be a bit OTT! I think it's so important to accessorise a fancy dress outfit, don't you?'

Ellie stopped to sip her chicory soy latte, and Mim took a deep breath to prepare for the next onslaught.

'Annnnyyhooo,' Ellie continued, stylishly wiping latte foam from her newly Restylaned lips. 'Rupert wants to be the ringmaster – well of course – he is such a natural leader, isn't he? Like his father! So Mr Nguyen ran him up a stunning three-piece suit and custom-made top hat, and I had my hair stylist make him an authentic hair moustache from the trimmings at his last cut – what a hoot! Mr Nguyen is such a treasure, what those Chinese can't do with a needle!

Such a clever people, don't you think? So, darling, what will your spawn be wearing?'

'I thought maybe I could put together some pirate costumes for the boys with bits and pieces from the dress-up cupboard, and Chloe can just wear her old fairy dress.'

'Oh,' Ellie looked aghast. 'Isn't that a bit, you know, Martha Stewart of you darling? I mean, who just "puts things together"? No, look I'll give you the number of this divine costumery on Malvern Road, you still have time to pop in there before the party tonight.'

'Bit exxy?'

'Oh darling, don't even consider the price; it's all about having the right look,' Ellie advised.

Mim chewed the inside of her lip and tapped at her latte glass; this was shaping up to be an expensive outing. She'd already bought one elaborate gift online from F.A.O. Schwarz in the States, but had received an email yesterday to say it wouldn't arrive until next week.

'I can't believe I wasted all that time and money on a gift for Sophie that won't even be here today.'

'What was it again?'

'I designed a one-of-a-kind, custom-made Barbie dressed in Sophie's favourite Gap cowgirl dress. You can do it on the web.'

'Couldn't you save it for another party?'

'No, they stamp the child's name on Barbie's instep. She's the world's 1225th Sophie Barbie, so she's unique.'

'Darling, you're over-thinking it all. Just dump the bloody Barbie at goodwill somewhere, grab another pressie and be done with it.'

Mim sighed. The invitation to Sophie's party had come as a beautifully wrapped gift-box delivered by courier to Mim's front door. Although it was addressed to Miss Chloe Woolcott, Mim knew its main purpose was to impress the invitees' parents. She'd torn open the satin ribbons and the box exploded in a cloud of confetti and streamers. A helium balloon burst from the centre of the decorations, trumpeting an invite to Miss Sophie Mason-Jackson's sixth birthday party, a Carnivale to be held in the extensive grounds of her parents' Malvern mansion.

'Damn it,' Mim had said in dismay as she'd surveyed the festive fallout on her hall carpet.

There was no getting all that back in the box – she'd have to come clean with Chloe.

A gift registry card had been thoughtfully included with the invitation. It appeared Miss Sophie was registered at David Jones and several small, exclusive toy boutiques.

Ellie broke into her reverie.

'How are Chloe's prep interviews going?'

'Oh God, it's hellish,' Mim sighed. 'The competition is so intense for five-year-old places at all the good schools. We're committed to a single-sex environment, although we're not adverse to parallel learning and we might consider a Steiner approach. She's thriving under Reggio Emilia at ELC, but we're not sure if it's too unstructured for her needs into the future.'

'Mmmm, it is such a dilemma, darling. How did the psychological assessment go?'

'She had her second last month and it's still off-target, so we've booked at a new centre for this Thursday.'

'Oh I know, it's so tough to get someone who knows what they're doing. We had to take Rupert to six before we found a psychologist who truly understood him and gave us a result we were happy with. You have to work at these things.'

'We've got an interview next week at Barlyn. I've made a PowerPoint résumé for Chloe, but I worry that we haven't provided enough educational opportunities for her. Her list of extracurricular activities is a bit thin – just conversational French, interpretive dance, swimming, choral enrichment and violin. I wish I'd stuck with the Essential Breath Meditation class, but it clashed awkwardly with Jack's Testosterone Time – you know how important it is for the boys to generate a healthy testosterone level in a structured environment. Can you imagine if I let them self-express physically at home – my *objets* would be under constant threat!'

'Sweetie, Chloe's résumé will be fine, there's always time to add a few enrichment classes before she starts primary school. You know what Prue Watson did? Remember her: she was a Thornbury – old money? Anyway, they hired a feature film director – just an Australian – to put together a really stylish DVD of their daughter, Lillianna (they call her Lola – like Madonna's girl) – anyhoo . . . that's what you need to do, everyone's doing it. Lola was gorgeous, they had her singing – she has a beautiful voice – doing her ballet, some jujitsu, babbling away *en Français*, and just interacting within her environment – you know? Playing? And the highlights in her hair came up a treat under the studio lighting. Anyway, she was accepted straight into the three-year-old room at Milton, no questions asked, which was a really lovely coincidence given that it's part of the new Thornbury wing.

'Oh, and remember Prue's sister? What was her name, Melita . . . no . . . Melina, that's right, I knew it rhymed with ballerina, which is a hoot, because she is in fact a ballerina, or she used to be,' Ellie lowered her voice and leaned towards Mim. 'Weight issues,' she whispered. 'Couldn't get bulimia, no matter how hard she tried; no gag reflex, poor love.'

Mim nodded sympathetically and steered the conversation back to the school issue. 'I haven't got time to get a DVD together before next week. Do you think our PowerPoint presentation will be okay?'

BC (Before Children), Mim had been a graphic designer at a busy advertising agency and now kept her hand in by doing occasional freelance work from home. She'd pulled together all her skills to produce the slick PowerPoint résumé for her five-year-old.

She suspected she was being a tad too over-the-top about the whole school thing, but nevertheless she'd hired a tutor to prepare Chloe for the Barlyn College prep entrance exam. What choice did she have when all the other mothers were doing it? She had to give Chloe every opportunity to excel, and Barlyn was one of the best girls' schools in the state – although that sort of excellence didn't come cheap. The junior school fees were up to $20,000 a year and then there were the extras: a mandatory laptop, two camps a year and a $450 blazer for starters.

The boys' fees were already exorbitant and increased at each year level. Then there were music lessons, sports uniforms, cadets, excursions and incursions. Sometimes she scared herself by adding all the numbers together and then her chest got so tight with fear that she couldn't breathe.

Sometimes Mim woke in the middle of the night with the feeling that her life was spiralling out of control. Maintaining the lifestyle was overwhelming. They were just scraping by on James's IT income as it was. It was so important for the children to have the best start in life and every opportunity money could buy, but somehow it was all unravelling and after last night's fight, things seemed to be getting worse.

Ellie interrupted her thoughts again. 'Where are you, sweetie? You seem miles away today.'

Caught out, Mim blushed slightly, reluctant to relive the whole scene with James. She felt exhausted just thinking about it.

'Oh,' she sighed deeply, 'James and I had a bit of a stoush

last night. It was pretty ugly and now he's gone off to London for the week.'

'Oh love, that's awful,' Ellie sympathised. 'Things have been a bit tense for a while, haven't they?'

'I guess so. I suppose I just thought it was always that he was tired, or I was premenstrual or whatever, but actually I think it's more that we're just not connecting any more.' Her eyes filled with tears. 'I'm really frightened about our marriage, Ellie.'

'Sweetheart,' Ellie reached across the table to take Mim's hand. 'You guys are such lovebirds, I'm sure it will be okay. You just have a lot of pressures with the kids, and your jobs, and James being away all the time – does he have to take so many business trips?'

'Well the stupid thing is I encouraged him to change roles to the international department because it meant more money – and with Chloe at school next year God knows we'll need it. I thought it would be best for the family. The trouble is we're never actually a family any more because he's always away.' She wiped her eyes carefully on her napkin and gave herself a small shake, pulling her cardigan tighter around her shoulders. 'Anyway darling,' she managed a smile, 'we'll be fine, you know how these things seem so dreadful at the time and you think divorce is on the cards and then the next day he brings you flowers and it's all forgotten – this will all blow over soon enough.'

'You're probably right, sweetie,' Ellie soothed. 'But it would be nice if he was home a bit more. Anyway, my love, I must away. You sure you're okay?' she questioned, fishing in her Prada sac for her Porsche keys.

'Absolutely, darling, thanks for listening,' Mim replied.

'Well then, *ciao, bella*,' Ellie called as she swept out.

On her own, Mim was seized by a wicked desire to order the Chocolate Orgasm Cake and lose herself in the passion of the moment. Shaking her mind back to reality she allowed herself a tiny nibble at the edge of her fat-free, low-cholesterol, high-fibre biscotti. That would do for breakfast.

~ 6 ~

The Present Dilemma

It was a sparkly pink princess doll, dressed in shiny satin and lace, with happy blue eyes and a smiling rosebud mouth. She was named Bettina and her smile held the promise of a special secret that she would whisper quietly to only the little girl who took her home to love and treasure her.

Mim wanted her badly, she wanted to cuddle the doll's squishy body to her and hear those secrets again, the secrets she had heard as a little girl and had truly believed existed just beyond her own life – in a world of uncomplicated froth and prettiness.

She seemed a long way from those days now. Everything had become so complicated and confusing. She rubbed distractedly at her forehead again, her headache by now an expected companion.

Mim smoothed Bettina's shiny acrylic hair and stroked her soft synthetic body lovingly. She was so perfect, so soft and pretty. Something inside Mim yearned so strongly for the doll that she was halfway to the counter before she realised what she was doing.

'Oh good gracious,' Mim breathed out loud, attracting looks from several other DJs shoppers. Reddening, she placed the doll carefully back on the shelf. 'I almost bought a mass-produced, foreign-made toy for a very discerning little miss,' Mim said with a brittle laugh to those around her.

She shook her head as she returned the doll to the shelf. Yes, it was a crappy made-in-China piece of rubbish, complete with hideous cheap scratchy lace and horrible butter-wouldn't-melt expression on its over-painted, over-cute face. But who was she buying the gift for, for heaven's sake. This was the kind of glitzy, pink and frothy shit that little girls absolutely loved. The more tizz, the better! It takes a lot of growing up to appreciate the beauty of beige. But in the meantime, little girls only have eyes for the tacky spectrum. Sophie would love this present; she should get it, but it just wasn't worth the weird looks Mim would get from the other mothers at unwrapping time.

So far the trip had been a failure, not a single unique piece to be found, and certainly nothing that would compete with the European Babushkas, the Hong Kong electronics and the artisan-crafted timber educational toys Sophie would unwrap this afternoon. She would have to go to Malvern Road now, and it was already 1 p.m. – there was no time to even fit in a Pellegrino at the food court. There were still the children's costumes to find, as well as the present – and all before the 3.30 p.m. school pick-up.

Mim power-walked through the store, pressing her palm to her chest as a cold wave of panic surged through her. What if she couldn't find the right gift in time? How would it look to turn up at the party without a gift and with inappropriately dressed children?

She stopped in front of Estée Lauder and allowed herself to breathe in the comforting air of tranquil beauty that radiated from the pink cosmetics. She caught her harried reflection in a make up mirror and quickly whipped out her Chanel Rouge Noir and lightly bruised her lips with it. Better, she smiled to her reflection.

She looked over to see Deidre Munroe, a school mum, admiring her own reflection at MAC Cosmetics. Deidre was in a wrappy, drapey shawl thing over a long-swing crushed-velour skirt and long boots that suited the successful film and television actress persona that she desperately tried to display.

'Hello, Mim!' Deidre said excitedly at seeing Mim standing there. 'Kiss kiss, sweetie,' she effused. 'So, I suppose you're here preparing for Saturday night too?'

'Saturday night?' Mim muttered vaguely.

'The Production!' squealed Deidre. 'It's opening night in two weeks!'

Mim's heart knocked wildly in her chest. Christ, how could she have forgotten? She still had costumes to make for the annual production and neither of the boys had learned their lines yet.

'. . . so I explained, as patiently as I could, to Mrs Forbes . . .' Mim tuned back in to Deidre, who had yet to take a breath. '. . . Samuel is a trained performer, he has a voice coach. I have been working with him since Prep to ensure he was prepared for a lead this year, and to pass him over like that, well, I was mortified. And the pathetic reason they gave me is that he's too short for Father Time's costume. I mean, really, what kind of production is this anyway?'

'Well, absolutely,' Mim said refreshed by Deidre's approach. 'After all, it is just a primary school play, isn't it?'

Deidre looked at Mim strangely, then threw her head back and pealed with theatrical, diaphragm-assisted laughter.

'Oh, yes, it's just a . . .' she made air-quotes with her

heavily jewelled fingers, '"primary school play". You're so funny, Mim. Of course we all know it's soooo much more than that. One of the prep parents is a NIDA director, can you believe? I just know he would have noticed Samuel's incredible luminosity and stage presence if only he'd been given his rightful chance to shine. I'm sure he will be scouting for future talent.'

I'm sure he'll be bored shitless like the rest of us, Mim thought.

'Any idea what you're wearing yet? I've been searching for a month. It's worse than Spring Carnival, don't you think? The whole thing will be splashed all over the social pages . . . so generous of LJ to organise Philby's time to do the PR for the school. My goodness she's a go-getter, isn't she? Have you seen her lately?'

'Yes, last night at the Dan Dandrews exhibition – she looks well.'

'Of course she does, she's been chasing the sun around the Bermudas, such fun! You know how LJ likes an authentic tan all year round, not a cheap shop-bought spray-on.'

I know that LJ should not be crossed no matter what her pigment, Mim thought to herself. But a non-committal 'Mmmm,' was all she said out loud. Despite her vicious streak, LJ had a lot of friends among the Langholme mothers.

'Excuse me,' came an ancient voice at Deidre's elbow.

Deidre beamed and rolled her eyes at Mim indicating the challenges she faced as a star, and she turned to the older woman.

'Did you want an autograph, love?' Deidre groped in her bag for a pen and projected her voice in the way many people reserve for the elderly.

'No, I just need to know where the lift is,' the woman said.

'Over near the back wall,' Deidre spat at her. And the woman moved on, throwing Deidre a strange look.

'All the old ducks pick on me,' she said conspiratorially to Mim, who was fighting to keep a straight face. 'Just because I'm a celeb they think I'll know everything. Honestly, I wonder if it was worth doing that SBS series now. My life is just not my own any more.'

'Oh, was it shown again recently?'

'No darling, but you'd be amazed – even after four years people feel as if they own a piece of me.' Deidre shuddered, pulling her throw tighter around her bony shoulders.

'So, where are the twins, Deidre?'

'Oh, they're right here,' she said, glancing into the two empty seats of her McLaren double stroller. 'Oh bugger it.' Deidre glanced about wildly then leapt over to the Clinique counter where her ADHD twins were scooping expensive samples from the eyeshadow display and painting their faces in a rainbow of colour.

'Othello! Leopold! Look at your faces, we'll have to go home and get washed and changed before your headshots this afternoon. *Adios*, Mim, see you at pick-up, oh, and you look gorgeous!' Deidre tossed over her shoulder as she steered the stroller madly toward the car park.

Mim made her way back to the car, cursing Deidre for holding her up and still racking her brains for a suitable gift idea.

'Thank you, parking angels,' Mim said out loud as she pulled up in a killer parking spot right in the middle of Malvern Road. She swung her legs out of the car (two feet at once, then standing up, just like Princess Di), pulled up her hipsters, tugged her sweater's waistband down and bipped the locking system on the Mercedes 4WD.

Moving quickly through the shop door, she knocked her

head on the jangling bells hanging inside the Fairyland Costumery and was confronted by a sour-looking woman dressed as a somewhat faded elf princess.

'Was there something you were looking for?' the princess asked in a monotone, scratching at her wig vaguely.

Twenty years ago the shop's vendor had been the pretty and enthusiastic Princess Evelyn, delighting in sprinkling fairy magic and glitter on her beloved customers, but she had seen too many fights over fairy dresses between too many pretentious parents to care much any more. To add to her malaise, Princess Evelyn had gotten high the night before and had another savage argument with Kevin, her ex, so today what little interest she might have had for fairy mummies had dissipated.

'I'd like costumes for my children for a Carnivale party tonight.'

'What, the Mason-Jackson party? Left it a bit late, haven't you? I doubt we'll have anything left, all the good costumes have already been snapped up.' The princess wound her acrylic hair around her finger and stared at Mim as if daring her to push the point.

Fabulous, thought Mim. She had no choice but to persevere with this jaded fairy. 'Perhaps you could just point me towards the fairy dresses, please,' she asked, peering into the half-lit gloom of the fairy grotto. The mist of smoke at the back seemed a nice touch, except it smelt more like a public bar than a woodland grove.

'If you must,' sighed the tarnished princess. 'There's a rack out the back, but like I said, all the good stuff has gone.'

Mim poked around in the half-light and easily found the perfect rainbow fairy dress with a matching purple sequined cardigan and the sweetest little rose-coloured glitter slippers. She couldn't wait to see Chloe dressed up like a little doll. After a bit more digging she found a fabulous jester's costume for Charley and a lion tamer's outfit for Jack. This was too easy.

'Well, maybe there is magic after all,' Evelyn scoffed as Mim placed her items on the counter. 'Sure, the whole world is just one big ball of glitter,' she laughed hollowly, her laugh quickly turning to a hacking cough that went on for some minutes and finally subsided in a heavy wheeze. 'All that magic for just $397,' she announced still wiping her eyes and breathing raspingly.

Mim pretended not to hear the amount, otherwise the income from the freelance work she had squeezed in for a few hours yesterday would have silently gurgled down the drain and she really didn't want to be a witness to that.

Out on the street, Mim began wildly scouring the boutique windows for the bloody gift.

An Esprit outfit – no, too ordinary. A hand-sewn patchwork quilt – too babyish. A charm bracelet – too personal.

The thump of her racing heart was by now competing for attention with the throbbing in her head as Mim strode from one shop to the next. Then, thank the designer gods above, she found it – an object that achieved all criteria: it was tasteful, brand conscious, original and très, très elegant. It was even educational – if you counted fashion nous as education – and of course everyone did.

It was a teeny Gucci handbag – the same one as Sophie's mother, Tiff, had. Mim felt faint as she surrendered her credit card yet again, but what price social acceptance, she thought in a bubble of relief at having scored such a winning gift. She didn't even blink when she was charged $20 extra for voluminous pink wrapping. It was worth it for the time saved, and a bonus to have the store's exclusive label stuck to the ribbon.

She swung her shopping bags gaily as she headed back

to the Mercedes. Everything would be all right after all. She was a good mother, with impeccable taste, beautifully attired children and a gift that would be the envy of all the other mothers.

Life was sweet.

~ 7 ~

A Troubled Teen

May 1998

Damien Thompson was shit-scared.

Just a week out of the academy his uniform was still crisp and his gun a cold, new weight against his body, reminding him of his power and responsibility.

His first few days at the Moe cop-shop had been spent making coffee for the senior sergeant, shuffling paperwork and cruising the town's main drag in the divvy van. But now here he was, enveloped in the black syrup of a moonless night, creeping down the side of a shabby brick-veneer house on the ragged edge of town.

His size ten boots seemed to magnify his every step and he cursed inwardly as he tripped awkwardly over broken toys and empty cans. The fog of his breath swirled around him in the bitter air, clouding his view. He could hear only the thrumming of blood in his ears and the clatter of his nervous teeth.

The call had come in five minutes ago as he and Senior

Constable Harbour trawled the main street waiting for the pubs to spew out their usual collection of Friday-night drunks, brawlers and bitch fights. In a small town there was little else to do at the end of the week than try to out-drink your mates.

Now, as Damien waited with trembling hands, he heard his companion shout, 'Police, open up!' Harbour never got tired of saying that. After fifteen years in the force, he was a power junkie who loved the authority of his uniform. He had consistently followed a clear model of policing – punch first; ask questions later. Of course nowadays he had to use the namby-pamby capsicum spray first, but he usually managed to get a few good solid belts in with his ASP on most arrests. Anything else was too good for the low-life scum he dealt with. If he started acting like some of the soft cocks in the city he'd soon lose respect in the town.

In the backyard, Damien's pale face was vivid against his dark uniform, and he knew that he was a beacon, an unavoidable target for the shooter that might be lurking in the house. Then he saw the point of entry: the bathroom window jimmied open, the torn lace curtain.

Adrenalin surged through him as Harbour's shout echoed around him. He knew the strategy. Just like dropping a ferret in a rabbit hole. The terrified bunnies always ran out the back-door and into the hunter's nets. Sure enough, seconds later a wiry figure exploded in a flurry of arms and legs out of the bathroom window, and Thompson, not sure whether to vomit or piss, decided instead to dive toward the offender, arms outstretched.

The suspect nimbly avoided him by weaving to the right and sprinting full pelt through the yard.

'Aw, shit!' Damien cursed, knowing he'd be a laughing stock at the station. 'HE'S GETTING AWAY!' he bellowed to Harbour as he gave chase.

The suspect, in black beanie and hooded sweats, ducked easily around the patio furniture and over a pile of bricks. Thompson was close behind until he caught his ankle in an unfilled hole, stumbled and then managed to right himself with the help of a rusty Hills Hoist. He threw himself at the paling fence as the offender began to scale upwards, lunging forward and grabbing the climber's upper body to pull him down.

'Fuck me! Tits!' he yelled. Thompson was a shy lad who had seen few live breasts in his time, and touched even fewer, so his first reaction was to release the young lady and apologise for his lack of decorum.

'THOMPSON, WHAT THE FUCK DO YOU THINK YOU'RE DOING? NAIL THE BASTARD!' Harbour screamed as he watched the newbie releasing their perp.

Suddenly remembering who he was and what he was doing, Thompson grabbed again at the offender, holding her tightly by the hips as they both fell to the ground.

'Name?'

'Fuck off, pig.'

The station's harsh fluorescent lighting emphasised the pale cheeks and dark-circled eyes of the young girl as she slumped on the hard bench seat, scowling from behind her black dreadlocks.

'Now Mikaylah, why do you have to be like that? What's gotten into you lately? Come on, you know I've got a job to do here.' Sergeant Higgins sighed as he dropped his pen and leaned his beefy arms on the desk to appraise the sullen young teen. 'Now come on, let's try it again . . . name?' He picked distractedly at the dry, flaking skin on his elbows while he waited for the response he knew wasn't coming.

Ready to chuck with disgust, Mikaylah turned away. Ian

Higgins had always been a tosser, ever since he'd dobbed on her when he'd sprung her ditching school in Grade Five.

'Okay, I'll do it then . . . Name: Mikaylah Boomhauer, Address: Is it thirty or thirty-two Old Mill Road?'

Given the full force of her ugliest stare he sighed once more and went back to his form. 'I'll just put thirty-two Old Mill Road, Moe. I'll double-check with your dad when he gets here.'

'Dad? Oh, man! What'd ya have to go and call that dick-head for?'

'Mikaylah, these are serious charges. It's not just shop-lifting or truanting this time. Breaking and entering is heavy stuff, and, as you're a minor, your parents need to be informed.'

'Fuckwit,' she muttered under her breath, sullenly sliding her eyes sideways.

'Yes, well, I'll pretend I didn't hear that.' And he went back to his paperwork, licking the end of his pencil with gusto.

'Look, in view of how unhelpful you're being, I'm going to ask you to go and wait in the lunch-room, get yourself a coffee and I'll fill in the paperwork without you.'

Higgins fired a final shot to her hunched shoulders as she left. 'You're a real worry, Mikaylah, I don't know how such a bright kid like you has fallen into this crap.'

Mikaylah slunk off to the room at the back of the station. She knew where to find it; this wasn't the first time she'd been a guest of the boys in blue.

She picked up a plastic spoon thick with old coffee and sugar grains and shovelled three heaped loads of International Roast into a Styrofoam cup. She dumped in three – no, what the hell – four sugars and smelt the milk from the fridge before adding a splash. Then she sat grimly, scowling at the steam that snaked from the cup – she needed this hit now, not in ten fucking minutes, she thought, blowing at it to cool it faster.

She was jumpy and itchy. She rifled through a stained and scratched Tupperware container of Arnott's Assorteds and hit paydirt, finding two Monte Carlos at the bottom. She plucked one out and prised it open to get to the creamy filling and the sugar fix she was desperately craving.

Sighing, she munched on the bickie and considered her awful position. Like, hello?? She didn't make a habit of knocking off other people's gear. It's not like she didn't have a reason. It's not like she wasn't totally desperate.

Desperate to get that fucking Tony Marecci off her back.

He and his custom-painted panel van had been a regular fixture at the school gates as long as anyone could remember. A vulture waiting for the fresh young things to fall so he could feast on their demise. His patter was polished: his free Mars Bars; hot chips on cold days and his thin guise of mateship were welcome balms to troubled souls. He made a fortune from the shit he sold cheap to kids who didn't know any better and couldn't stop once they'd started.

But of course, nothing's really cheap, and when Tony had urged his newest customer, Mikaylah, into more debt than she could hope to afford, he offered to let her 'clear the books' with a small gesture. His ugly knuckled hands had karate-adjusted his package to illustrate his idea of the sort of gesture that was required. 'I wouldn't touch that poxy cock with a barge pole,' Mikaylah had hissed at him, her throat constricting with fear.

Tony was a little weed of a bloke; stunted, scrawny and mean. The sparse black fibres of his mo did little to disguise his cruel lips, which constantly housed a smouldering Peter Stuyvesant. His head was permanently tilted to the side as his eyes squinted through a coil of ciggie smoke. His weak chin was a battleground of acne scars, punctuated with piercings. Lurid satin boxers hung from his bony arse, atop baggy jeans that sagged to his knees. He jingled about the school gate each afternoon as the chains linked through his belt loops slapped in time to his loping walk.

He was the worst kind of travelling salesman, peddling his wares strictly to the vulnerable teenage market and spending no longer than necessary in the town. He'd laughed in Mikaylah's face when she'd refused the sweet deal he'd offered her – she'd be back, he thought as he watched her stride away. He'd adjusted his cock in a well-practised motion and run his tongue over his festering teeth – they always came back.

In the coffee room Mikaylah shook off her tough-girl veneer and leaned forward on her folded arms. Her clear blue eyes filled with desperation, her bottom lip began to tremble and suddenly she looked more like a sad eight-year-old girl than a wayward teen.

What was she going to do? It was two hundred and eighty-five bucks. For chrissakes, how was she going to get it by the Monday deadline?

The door slammed open and the mask was slapped back on. Her mouth became hard and cold and her eyes steely as she met her stepfather's ugly look.

'Right, moron, get to the car. You're in so much strife, you stupid little tart.'

Mikaylah walked past him through the doorway. As he turned to follow her she instinctively flinched and pulled herself out of his reach.

The fight reverberated around the fibro shack for hours after Mikaylah stormed past her grim-faced mother and slammed her bedroom door. With her head jammed under her pillow the words were muted but the anger swelled in the walls and filled the house.

Mikaylah eventually drifted off into a troubled sleep, waking just before dawn, parched and momentarily confused about the heaviness in her head and the pain behind her eyes. Her gut twisted as she remembered her predicament.

Seeking water, she opened her door and heard her parents still muttering in the lounge.

'She's your fuckin' kid, Darleen, why can't you do something about her?'

'Listen, Carl, she's been your kid too for the last twelve years, so go easy on the blame.' Darleen lit a fresh Alpine off the dying butt in her nicotine-stained fingertips. Thank Christ she'd bought another packet that afternoon after her shift at Ritchies. She'd have bought two if she'd known she'd be still smoking in the wee hours.

Her pink 'Funky Mummy' T-shirt nightie, the glitter long washed away, hung over her saggy breasts and fell to her knees, her legs bare and fuzzy with winter regrowth – why bother shaving when you were in jeans all day, she reckoned. Her mauve moccasin slippers covered bright-orange-painted toenails. 'She's weird, you know, ever since Johnno died. I know she was only a kid but she kind of went into a shell.'

Carl leaned back in his Jason Recliner, scratching the expansive gut that escaped over his belt and fell onto his thighs. He was concentrating hard on ignoring her.

'It's like she doesn't fit in,' Darleen went on. 'She never just hangs out at the shops like the other girls; she doesn't have blokes after her. I mean why would she? It's not like she dresses like other girls.'

'You're right there,' Carl said. 'How's that Christie from over the road? The little tops and the short skirts . . . Phwoarr!'

'She's fourteen, you sick perv!' Darleen puffed out a

cloud of smoke in disgust. She was getting tired of listening to Carl putting her daughter down and decided to end the conversation. She picked up her smokes, her treasured Crown Casino lighter and her empty glass, the pungent aniseed scent from the last several ouzo-and-Cokes still wafting from it, and headed for the kitchen. 'Look, I don't know why she's acting this way. We know she's a loner, but her marks at school have stayed really good. It's just bloody lucky she hasn't got my genes.'

'Shit, yeah,' Carl agreed, flicking through the channels for some sport or a bit of that wog porn on SBS. 'She'd be in real serious trouble if you were her *real* mum.'

Down the hallway, through a slight crack in the door, the clear blue eyes opened in shock as the impact of that statement hit home.

~ 8 ~

Party Princess Present Time

Present Day

'I don't want to go to Sophie's dumb party,' Chloe shrieked. 'She smells bad and she's mean to me.'

In the frothy fairy dress Chloe looked the picture of angelic innocence, except for her angry red face.

'Darling, I told you, Sophie's mum gives her a special medicine called fish oil that sometimes smells a bit funny, but it's not her fault, it's actually quite important for her store of essential omega-three fatty acids.'

'Don't care, she's just a stinker, and how come she gets the beautiful pressie and all I got was this dumb dress?'

They were late. Mim had already gone three rounds with Charley, who had flatly refused to put on the spangly tights and leotard of the jester's costume and was now sitting defiantly in the Mercedes in his everyday clothes. Mim had given in for peace, but now Chloe? This was too much.

'But if you don't come you'll miss out on the lolly bags

– remember last year you got a Strawberry Care Bear in your bag? I wonder what they'll have this year?'

'Don't care.' Chloe stuck out her bottom lip and crossed her arms defiantly. She pointed with her chin at the elaborately wrapped gift. 'Want that.'

'But sweetheart, that's for Sophie. Mummy spent all day trying to find it, we can't just give it to you – but how about I promise to get you the same thing for your birthday?'

'Not going,' Chloe answered as she started to shred the netting on her fairy skirt.

Mim dragged her hands through her hair in frustration. She should just punish Chloe by making her stay home. It was no skin off her nose – except the other mums would think she couldn't control her own children, and how would it look to not turn up now after she had RSVPd weeks ago. Her stomach tensed in tight knots. 'For fuck's sake,' she whispered under her breath, and then looked Chloe in the eye and spoke desperately. 'I will get you the same gift tomorrow if you get in the car right now and be a happy, friendly little girl at the party, okay?'

'Okay, Mummy,' Chloe sang, then kissed Mim on the cheek and ran to get in the car with her brothers.

Mim shot a desperate look at the Pimm's bottle through the glass of the kitchen cabinet and prayed for patience.

The Mason-Jacksons' Georgian mansion was gaily festooned with coloured flags and festive bunting. Catering vans, amusement floats, an ice-cream truck and several animal trailers stretched around the gravel driveway and the Hooley Dooleys were singing up a storm on the front lawn. It looked like the circus had arrived in the centre of Toorak.

Mim parked in the first spot she could find, and did a harried last-minute check of the children's costumes. She couldn't believe Charley had refused to wear his costume, but she was almost past caring now. Where had she gone wrong with this child? Why wouldn't he simply join in like the others? Why did he have to be so damn uncooperative? Now she had to walk into the party with an inappropriately dressed child. Some days were just too hard.

Charley's therapist had encouraged her to provide dress-up opportunities at home, as a window to imaginative role-playing, but no matter how she tried, Charley had just never gotten into it. He kept drifting back to his *Tintin* comics and the other countless favourite books he kept under his pillow. It was obviously inappropriate for a six-year-old boy to have his nose stuck in a comic book all the time, but no amount of therapy had managed to stem the problem.

So there he was, her 'recalcitrant one', dressed in white Bermuda shorts, tan OshKosh sandals, Country Road checked shirt and sleeveless sweater-vest in stone with a pale blue trim.

Shepherding the children, juggling the gift, her Chanel bag and the children's props (whip and fairy wand), she made her way up the wide stone steps to the ballooned entrance. The day had been drizzly on and off, creating small puddles at the foot of the steps. Charley couldn't resist. Seeing Mim distracted by Chloe's tiara, he let out a whoop of joy and stamped in the biggest puddle, splashing mud onto the white steps, the perfect white roses and his pristine outfit.

Mim looked up to see Charley's guilty, mud-specked face and soaked clothes, but found herself incapable of speech. As she opened her mouth only a faint guttural noise came up.

Blood rushed hot and fast through her head, white spots of rage danced before her eyes, and she silently counted to ten in French, German and finally Mandarin.

Still feeling homicidal, she began reciting her emergency

mantra over and over in her head: 'It's not happening, it's not happening, it's not happening,' and moved away from a still-dripping Charley and into the party. Jack and Chloe immediately joined the cacophony of sound and activity, but Charley stayed close behind, now guilty and bereft with his head down and thumb firmly in his mouth.

In the centre of the hall a massive table dazzled with shining wrapping paper, metres of curling ribbon and dozens of gifts. Mim laid her gift on a wedge of free space and looked up to see the mother of the birthday girl, Tiffany, teetering towards her in a leopard-skin lycra top and leopard faux-fur stiletto pumps. 'Darling!' She bestowed two generous kisses in the air above Mim's cheeks.

Their friendly greeting was suddenly ambushed by Tiffany's poisonous mother-in-law. Dressed head-to-toe in Louis Feraud with impeccably polished nails, pumps, diamonds and freshly sharpened dentures, she moved stealthily towards Mim.

'Mim, you know Cliff's mum, Beatrice,' Tiffany asked with an apologetic look, moving reluctantly away to greet other arrivals.

'Of course,' Mim said, hiding a grimace.

'We thought you must have had a better offer,' Beatrice rasped in her crow-like voice, looking ever-so-subtly at her Cartier.

Mim could have slapped her. 'Oh no, you know us, so much to do, so little time to fit everyone in,' she replied cattily.

'Anyway, you look just fabulous as always, Mim. I don't know how you manage to make all your little eclectic pieces work. I feel so much safer just sticking to the designer's vision.' Beatrice smoothed the lapel of her puce silk suit.

'It's not happening, it's not happening,' Mim's mind recited.

'Well, you look great too, Beatrice,' she said, tired of the bitchy undercurrent.

'Thanks. And this is . . .? Which one again?'

Charley glared at the woman from behind his fist.

'Charley.'

'Aaahh, of course, your eldest is called James after his father, isn't he?'

'Yes, we call him Jack for short.'

'Darling, I hate to intrude but aren't you concerned about the . . .' Beatrice lowered her voice and mouthed in a loud whisper: 'psychological ramifications of the . . . well . . . thumb issue?' She gestured meaningfully at Charley. 'Not to mention the hideous dental implications you'll be facing. What a *shame* for you, darling. Of course, my son's an orthodontic surgeon when the time comes.' Without waiting for a response she continued, 'He's a bit S.H.Y., is he, poor love. He might have felt more comfortable in a costume like all the other children, rather than those,' she paused for effect, 'soiled clothes.'

'Oh no, no, I had it all planned . . .' Mim began.

'Of course you did,' Tiffany interrupted as she re-joined them. 'It's okay, Charley, I provided extra costumes for just this reason. They're hanging on a rack in the hall. Now, there's a circus in the garden, *Star Wars* in the home theatre, food in the dining room and a quiet reflection space in the morning room if you feel the need for downtime.'

Beatrice sauntered off to find a little man to refill her brandy and water, and Mim breathed a sigh of relief, feeling rather battered from the social onslaught. She looked over at Tiffany, who was settling Charley by showing him a first-edition copy of Tintin. It was easy to believe that she swanned around town as a typical Toorak housewife, enjoying a life of bridge mornings, manicures and cocktail parties. But Mim sensed some sadness lay beneath Tiffany's bubbly over-privileged exterior; she knew her friend's life wasn't all diamonds and roses.

Mim wandered into the domed function room where a nervous looking balloonologist was struggling to make the more-and-more-elaborate creations the assembled children were demanding.

'I wanna replica of the *Titanic*,' Digby Symes whined, grabbing the balloon man's elbow.

The poor man twisted and bent his balloons into a ship-like shape and handed it to the child, who immediately screeched in horror and exploded the rubber work of art between his pudgy hands. 'You moron,' he shouted at the ship's hapless creator. 'Don't you know the *Titanic* had four funnels?'

Felicity Symes teetered inside from the garden, bits of turf dangling like ornaments from her Manolo Blahniks. 'Possum, what's all the noise about?' she enquired of her now hysterical son.

'He stuffed up the *Titanic*, he got it wrong. I hate him,' Digby screeched.

'Now, treasure, what have I told you before?' Felicity scolded lightly. 'Not everyone has had the educational advantages you've had, my sweet. We must learn to make allowances.'

With that she steered him outside to heckle the clowns.

Mim saw Ellie in the corner of the room trying to re-attach Paris's tailfeathers. 'Well, what did you expect you silly girl, this is not a costume you can SIT in,' Ellie reprimanded.

Looking stunning after her day at the stylist, Ellie's hair was sleek, highlighted with a fourth colour, blow-waved and straightened. The down-lights positively bounced off it. Her chiffon black Alannah Hill top, off one shoulder, contrasted perfectly with the wide-leg white Merivale and

Mr John pants. Black closed-toe mules with a kitten heel completed her elegant ensemble.

Pushing Paris back into the party, *sans* tail feathers, Ellie caught Mim's eye and moved over to her. 'Darling, thank God, you're here. What a nightmare.'

Grabbing glasses of sparkling burgundy from a passing waiter they appraised the scene.

'Did you see Tiff?'

'Yes, when we arrived.'

'Gorgeous.'

'I know . . . she's divine.'

'So sweet.'

'Sweet, just so gorgeous. Love 'er.'

'LOVE!'

'What a do!'

'Ohmigod, so OTT. But, they can afford it, I suppose.'

'She's paying back Cliff for being in Tokyo for the past three weeks; he only got back yesterday.'

'Another pharmaceutical junket?'

'With geishas laid on, no doubt.'

'Apparently he's flying in today for the party.'

'God, he's cutting it fine.'

'I know. Tiffany's furious, she's had to supervise the entire management of this event by herself!'

'No thanks,' the girls said in unison to the waiter offering a tray of arancini.

'Liz coming?' Ellie asked, scanning the room to assess the standard of attendees.

'No, she's got something on as usual,' Mim said, following Ellie's gaze. 'She wouldn't say what of course, she never lets on much, does she?'

'I know what you mean,' said Ellie, staring wide-eyed at her party ally, 'what's going on? I mean, I love her, absolutely adore her, she's so elegant and obviously very well-connected, but we're her closest friends and we don't even know what she does with her days.'

'Yes, I know what you mean,' offered Mim, desperately trying to avoid the tacky habit of bitching about a friend. 'She can be distant.'

'Distant! Hah! That's a polite way of putting it,' finished Ellie, smoothing a polished finger over an equally pristine eyebrow.

A flustered Fairy Fanny flew into the room and rushed up to Tiffany, who'd been about to join Mim and Ellie.

'Fairy sorry I'm late, fairy mummy, but my fairy car's fairy engine wouldn't fairy start.'

'Well you can kiss ten per cent of your fairy cheque away,' Tiffany muttered as she ushered the fairy out to the big top.

Mim wandered around the mansion to check on her kids. The boys were busily engaged in a pinball tournament, but Chloe was nowhere to be seen. Heading upstairs, Mim heard giggling coming from a bedroom and found Chloe and little Willow Arbour playing with Sophie's elaborate doll's house. The house, an exact replica of the family home, was a gift for Sophie from her maternal grandparents. The little girls were in heaven playing ladies and gentlemen. They were in the middle of reconstructing a dinner party when Mim spoke.

'Hi, girls, what a beautiful dinner party.' She sat cross-legged on the floor, for once not caring about her white pants, to admire their little scene.

'I show you, Mummy. This is Mrs Lady and this is Mr Lady and they run this house, except for Mr Lady who goes to work all the time. And this is Mrs Lady's friends and they are all here for a dinner party and they're having, ummm . . . some meat and vegetables – but not Brussels sprouts – and lots of strawberries and they're drinking champagne . . .'

As Chloe prattled on in her sweet little-girl voice, Mim

gazed at her pink chubby cheeks and remembered the baby girl she had so recently been. Although Mim had long since accepted the foibles of her own mother's parenting skills she didn't want to be that kind of mother, coolly detached and distant. Soon there would be a day when Chloe wouldn't let her sit on the floor and join in her games.

Mim leaned forward and released a blonde curl that was stuck to Chloe's cheek with a red sugary stickiness. She was filled with love for this little person and vowed to spend more quality time with all her kids, listening to them and playing games with them for as long as they'd have her.

'The banquet is served,' intoned the deep voice of the head waiter from downstairs.

The girls shot out of the room, leaving Mim to tidy up the mess they had left in their wake. Maybe we won't do interpretive dance next term and I could schedule time to play with Chloe while the boys are at soccer, she considered as she headed back downstairs.

'Where's my princess?' a booming voice suddenly filled the entire house.

'Daddy's home!'

Sophie, flanked by hordes of partygoers, flew down the hall and into the huge arms of Cliff Mason-Jackson, his face ruddy from exertion, his thinning hair dishevelled.

'Daddy!!! What'd you get me, what'd you get me?'

Cliff stood back proudly from the doorway to reveal a toy silver convertible Mercedes Benz parked beside Tiffany's in the driveway.

'See, it's just like Mummy's, and it's electric so you can really drive it.'

'Daddy, Daddy, Daddy, I love it, you are the best daddy in the whole world.'

Cliff, puffed up with self-importance over his winning present, never doubted for a moment that he was, indeed, the world's best father. He caught Tiffany's eye and gave her a leery wink.

Tiffany shook her head and stalked back into the party.

An hour later the food had been pawed at, spilt and thrown around the room – a small amount had even been eaten, but it didn't really count because most had come back up again in the garden and on the front steps, in vibrant pools of artificial colour.

It was almost time to go. Mim hunted around the back garden for Chloe's fairy wand and Jack's whip. Passing the scullery she spied Fairy Fanny bent over to pack up her fairy handbag and fairy parka. She was about to stop and commiserate with the poor girl over what had been a horror afternoon when she heard a deep voice from behind the scullery door.

'Well, hello there, Fairy Fanny, tell me . . . what's at the bottom of your garden!' Cliff's massive paw grabbed at the girl's dainty rear.

Embarrassed and shocked, Mim quickly moved away and moments later saw Cliff stumble past nursing a red cheek.

'You go, girl,' Mim thought with satisfaction. But poor Tiff, no wonder she's so highly strung. She must have a rotten life behind the scenes.

After bee-sting kisses and promises of 'must-do-lunch' all round, they finally headed home. The kids were overwired and overtired. Their costumes were bedraggled and torn – except for Charley, who had grabbed a cowboy outfit, complete with noisy guns, from the Mason-Jacksons' rack five minutes before they left. In his miniature Stetson and kerchief he re-enacted shoot-out scenes from his favourite westerns.

Mim fantasised about adopting him out.

It was a challenge to calm the children down. Even the ylang-ylang/lavender combo in the oil burner was fighting a losing battle. They finally succumbed to sleep after several guided meditations and some whale music.

At 9 p.m. the house was finally quiet. Mim was exhausted; too tired even to sink into the hot, essential-oil bath she'd been promising herself all day. Instead she slipped into her favourite man-style silk pyjamas, crawled between the Egyptian cotton sheets and let out a groan of relief. 'Please let them all sleep through the night,' she muttered as she leaned over to turn out the lamp.

Damn, forgot to phone James, she thought as she drifted off to sleep.

~ 9 ~

Mother's Group

'I deserve a bloody medal,' Mim thought with satisfaction as she glanced around her immaculate home. There were still five minutes to spare before the Mothers' Group girls arrived and everything was in order.

They'd all met in the exclusive birthing suite at the private Toorak Hospital eight years ago. Of course, there were a couple of duds that the girls had soon ditched, but this core group of five had remained close friends ever since.

Mim had immediately recognised a soul-mate in Ellie. She'd seen through her languid, lazy, rich-girl-about-town act and identified her as a woman of substance. She also enjoyed Tiffany's bright company, Monique's dry wit and Liz's sensible, conservative manner, which kept them all grounded when they started to get a bit silly.

Of course they were still very competitive; vying for smartest, best-dressed kid or most elaborate party – but they were also a genuine support team. On the journey from acquaintances to best friends the ladies had helped each other in times of need. In fact, they were really a refreshing and well-dressed take on the tribal society. Because they all had children of similar ages they had an innate sense of each other's needs. Each woman knew that they could call on each other over anybody else in times of crisis. More than once, Mim had whipped around two litres of milk for Tiffany during a migraine episode; Liz had taken Mim's children to the park during a last-minute work emergency; and Ellie, well Ellie was pretty useless really, but great at tolerating a long phone whinge while offering the appropriate platitudes.

Mim had groaned out of bed at 6 a.m. to bring the house up to Open-for-Inspection standards. Yesterday her cleaner had washed the windows and floors till they sparkled and put huge triangular vases of lilies and grasses on the altar table and flanking the fireplace. She'd polished Mim's precious mirrors to enhance the positive chi, and had the bathrooms glistening with hygienic cleanliness. The gardener had come in to rake out the fire and re-set it for today, and ensured the stainless-steel water features were algae free. Then Mim had carefully arranged her favourite Sheridan ecru Egyptian-cotton hand towels beside the glass basin in the upstairs bathroom and the sable Country Road towels beside the Porcher Vallo basin in the powder room. She'd spent an hour in Plane Tree Farm choosing organic soaps, and then another hour at Aura selecting new aromatherapy oils for each bathroom.

She'd managed to get the children to school early, giving her time to pop into the chic little French patisserie to buy morning tea. Of course, none of the girls would so much as inhale the dangerous, calorie-laden aroma of the dainty pastries she had bought – such behaviour could lead to a nasty outbreak of bingeing – but it was important to offer them all the same.

With everything done, Mim took time to enjoy some cleansing breaths and spend a few seconds in her happy place. As she opened her eyes she caught sight of her new

Saeco Espresso machine. Such a satisfying purchase at the time, she reflected, moving to fill the stainless-steel jugs with skim and soy milks.

The espresso machine more than justified its $1400 expense, Mim felt. It ground the beans to just the right consistency, made an excellent *crema* and frothed the milk itself. The result was a café-quality latte or espresso. It used to make her feel so happy when she looked at the machine, so full of smug consumer satisfaction. It was the latest model, everyone else had one, but not the top-of-the-line one like theirs. But now she just stared at it blankly. Where had the thrill gone? The high of ownership? Hmm, she pondered, maybe she'd better go out and buy the internet fridge she'd had her eye on. Something that high-tech would be bound to give her that elusive buzz.

She smoothed down her stone, straight-leg pants with satisfaction. She knew she was looking good today. She had felt a tad crampy this morning so she'd carefully factored in comfort along with style and triumphed beautifully with the pants, a black Eugenie cashmere turtleneck and her favourite comfy black Gucci loafers. She felt chic, yet cosy.

She didn't have to open the front door to know that it was Liz who had rung the bell.

'Hello, Mim, you look fabulous as always. Am I the first one?' she said, handing Mim a bakery box. The smell of freshly baked banana bread filled the hall.

'As always! Come on in.'

Liz strode into the house with the usual long-legged elegance to her step. Her whippet physique was clad in chic workout gear as she'd just come from a spin class. Her glowing cheeks further enhanced her youthful complexion. Her blonde long hair was in a pony-tail for once, a break from her usual French knot.

'House looks great, Mim,' commented Liz, casting an

appraising glance around the hall and into the formal living room.

Mim followed her gaze with a critical designer's eye. Yes, she thought, it did look great. But it would be better as soon as they could put the media room cabinetry in the front living room. Perhaps that was what was missing – that would definitely cheer her up.

The two friends made their way into the open-plan kitchen. Mim shifted the Alessi fruit bowl and Philippe Starck 'Salif' citrus juicer to make way for Liz's offering on the mink limestone breakfast bench.

Liz perched on the edge of the white leather stool as Mim busied herself with the Saeco.

'Latte?'

'Loooove one. Haven't had the caffeine fix yet this morning. So, how's work?'

'The usual frantic pace. I swear, as a working mother, I do more in three days than I ever did in five – and a lunch break, what's that? Working from home is so tricky, but I just have to keep my hand in, keep the CV up-to-date,' – and make a bit of extra cash, she added silently. 'Work keeps me sane, you know, it makes me feel like I have some worth in the real world.'

Liz nodded, fully aware of the difficult reality of being a working mum.

Mim realised she was going on too much about work. 'And how are the boys?'

'Fantastic! Roman entered his first inter-school chess tournament the other day and won four out of the seven matches.'

'What a smart cookie,' Mim said dutifully. 'And how's Hubert? Still practising that violin?'

'He is – we're absolutely amazed with his dedication. Ever since he fell in love with the Violin Classics CD he got from Santa he has genuinely been intent on mastering the instrument. His violin teacher can't believe the ability he is displaying for such a young age. We're so chuffed!'

'Good on him! Looks like we've got a child prodigy on our hands then?'

'Oh, I doubt that, he'll probably just toss it away and go back to the Dungeons & Dragons again next week. And how about you, Mim? Are you well?'

'Well, I don't know, I'm just a bit frazzled. I suspect I'm overdoing it a tad.'

Liz put her hand on Mim's arm and said, 'Well, if you need any help with the kids at all you will let me know, won't you?'

'Thanks, Liz, you're a real friend.'

The doorbell rang again and then Monique let herself in. Her blonde Suzi Quatro hipster haircut suited her cutting edge dress sense. So on top of the fashion trends she was usually two years ahead of the other girls. Today she was wearing unbelievably gorgeous boots.

'Monique, they are unbelievably gorgeous boots,' Mim squealed.

'You're such the fashion-guru, I swear it's in your blood,' Liz said with a smile.

'Well, after ten years as a fashion buyer it should be,' Monique laughed, dropping her Prada sac on the breakfast bench and twirling around to show off her new footwear. 'The trouble is that these days I have to use my own money. It was so much more fun when I was spending someone else's,' she lamented. 'But I'm getting such a buzz out of setting up the shop. High Street is such a to-die-for location and can you believe it's only two weeks until we open – ohmigod, I'll never be ready on time!' She paused for a moment, lost in thought, then said, 'Anyway, how are you, Liz?' while skimming her lips over Liz's cheek.

'Fine, lovey, how are you?' Liz returned the butterfly graze.

'So busy, I can't believe this shop thing is actually going to happen. Thanks, sweetie,' she took the skinny latte from Mim and fixed her grey-green eyes on Liz.

'What sort of things will you stock?' Liz asked, as she made herself comfortable on Mim's chocolate-brown leather couches.

'Lots of gorgeous loveliness. Retro pieces, vintage things, all with a contemporary edge, but definitely with a design flair,' Monique answered, stretching out her leg to admire her new boots again.

Mim placed a plate of biscotti on the coffee table and sat down. 'That's so fab. How are you fitting it all in with the children?'

Monique was seriously in line for a supermother award, or maybe some extended care at a mental facility. She'd been a stay-at-home mum since her first child, Mitchell, was born and Sienna had followed two years later, but now with her retail project she had returned to full-time work and the guilt was making her overcompensate at home.

'It's working so far,' Monique said, crossing her fingers. 'I've set up a parenting timetable and it seems to be functioning quite successfully. I do reading twice a week at school, I have thirty minutes of structured together time with each child before their bedtime, a shared bedtime story ritual, and we like to fit in blocks of unstructured time if we can, just to allow for spontaneity.' Even as she was saying it Monique was looking for flaws in her plan, wishing she could do better and hoping her kids wouldn't end up in therapy in twenty years' time – like their mum.

'And while they're at school I sort out the shop. It's just a matter of juggling, I guess.'

'Oh I know that one,' Mim cried. 'All my balls seem to be in the air all the time!'

They laughed. Liz eyed off the biscotti, extended then withdrew her hand. 'Oh I can't, they look so naughty – but fabulous,' she said skimming her hand over her greyhound-thin highs. 'Oh, Mim, I just remembered,' she said, looking up from the biscotti with a start, 'I heard some playground gossip from the Car Park Mafia today.'

'What?' Mim said, looking over.

Monique stopped admiring her new boots, this sounded tasty.

'LJ is furious with you, apparently,' Liz said.

'Me? Oh, shit, that's all I need. Why?'

'She is mad that you had the idea for the very best stall at the fete. She's fuming. Hortense says she's trying to do an aggressive takeover and take it on for herself,' Liz explained. 'I spoke to Hortense at drop-off.'

'But that's stupid! It's only a few of us girls with espresso machines, for heaven's sake. She can have it if it means that much to her!' Mim said in disgust.

'Oh, don't do that, Mim,' Monique protested. 'We're all going in on your stall with you. I don't want to spend the day with LJ – I'll get toxic shock syndrome!'

'Why can't she just think up a different stall?' Mim asked. 'She's totally over-reacting.'

'Of course she is. Don't worry about it, it'll all blow over by Saturday,' Monique placated her friend.

'Yes, of course, you're right. I can't help feeling nervous though – she's just so . . . scary!'

Everyone murmured in agreement.

'Are Ellie and Tiff coming today?' Monique asked.

'Yah! As if they'd miss it, they'd be too worried we'd talk about them,' Mim laughed. 'But I am so worried about poor Tiffany. Did you hear about Cliff's performance at Sophie's birthday party?'

The other two had missed the party – Monique had

been in Hong Kong on a buying trip and Liz had been on one of her mysterious outings.

'I heard about the OTT present, a mini-Mercedes. Good God, what will they give her for her eighteenth, at this rate she'll have everything!' Monique sniffed.

'Well, that's not all.' Mim told them about the Fairy Fanny incident.

'Oh no, that's shocking. Did you tell her?' asked Liz.

Mim frowned. 'No, I didn't, and I'm in a bit of a quandary about what to do.'

'He is such a sleazebag, so creepy. I can't stand the way he grabs my butt when he says hello,' Monique shuddered. 'Surely she must know her husband is a complete lech!'

'Well you'd think she would,' Liz reminded the girls. 'Tiffany was his affair, remember, He ditched his first wife for her, so she really has first-hand evidence that he is a complete dirtbag.'

'I don't think she recognised it for what it was at the time – love is blind and all that,' said Mim. 'Maybe it's only just dawning on her now. You should have seen the filthy glare she threw him when he arrived at Sophie's party. I assumed it was because he hadn't helped at all with the preparation, but now I'm thinking it must be something more. Maybe she thinks he's having an affair.'

'I wouldn't put it past him,' said Monique. 'Did you see him looking down Ellie's top at school sports day?'

Mim nodded. 'Yes!! What a pig!'

'He'll be in a world of pain if Fairy Fanny decides to slap a sexual harassment suit on him,' said Monique.

'I doubt she'd do that,' the sensible Liz said. 'She's cash only, so no union and also, it would create publicity and her little lucrative business is not something she'd want the ATO to find out about.'

'So the bastard can just hit on any poor innocent girl and get away with it?' Mim said in disgust.

'I know,' agreed Monique. 'Although I reckon Fairy Fanny can look after herself, but poor *Tiff.* What do you think she'll do if it's true? I'd leave Malcolm in a heartbeat if he so much as looked at another woman. But it's my theory that if you look after the boys at home, they won't stray.'

'Oh, for heaven's sake, you're not still putting out once a week, are you?' asked Mim. 'You're a sexpot!'

Monique smiled demurely and turned to Liz. 'What about you, Liz, what would you do?'

'Well,' said Liz, 'I'd have to be sure, you know, the evidence would need to be fairly strong, but I guess my first course of action would be to take Sebastian to marriage counselling and see if we could work it out.'

'What about you, Mim?' The girls turned to get Mim's opinion. 'What would you do?'

'I don't know – it's a tricky hypothetical, isn't it. I guess it depends on what kind of sex James is having.'

'What do you mean?' asked Liz. 'Sex is sex, isn't it?'

'Not necessarily. Obviously if he fell in love and left me for her then that's the end of it and I'd have to move on, but if it was sex like meeting a mate for squash, then I'd probably be more lenient. I wouldn't castrate him immediately, at any rate.'

'Jeez, lucky James,' commented Monique.

'Well, don't tell him, obviously!' Mim said, laughing. 'It's not like he's got a leave pass to screw around on me!'

The women were laughing at this when the doorbell rang.

'Bugger,' said Mim getting up to refresh the coffee. 'Well that's put a downer on that conversation!'

The doorbell rang again and Mim went to answer it.

'Hello beautiful lady,' Mim said to Tiffany, giving her close friend a hug and wishing she could share her pain.

'Hi Mim,' said Tiffany breezily. Her bouffant, blonde mane bounced about her shoulders and highlighted her recently acquired Noosa tan, which was offset by a white silver-studded denim jacket and tight white jeans.

'Sorry I'm late, girls,' she squeaked, throwing her arms out in greeting.

'Tiff!' Monique and Liz said in unison as they burst into a quick round of 'love-your-outfit, have-you-done-something-new-with-your-hair?' exclamations.

'Ellie not here yet?'

'As if,' said Mim. 'She's only half an hour late, it's too soon yet! Caffeine pick-me-up, sweetie?' she asked, moving into the kitchen.

'Kill for one, darling. Can you do me a soy macchiato with low foam? My lactose intolerance is flaring again and I've just bloated like a pig.'

'How was Noosa, darling?' Monique asked. 'Did you stay at the Sheraton again?'

'Oh, God no. We were going to but Cliff had to cancel coming with us at the last minute – work commitments – so I said, stuff him, and booked us into a stunning house on the riverfront with a pool, and took Jana with us instead.'

'Fabulous, take the nanny and you've got yourself a real holiday,' Mim said.

'I know, it's a nightmare with them on my own. The kids have a grand old time, and *husband* usually skives off from doing anything remotely associated with parenting because apparently it's his holiday. But for me . . . well, it's just same shit, different location.'

They all nodded knowingly.

'Did you go out much?' asked Liz.

'I ran into Jennifer Gowrie-Smith – unfortunately,'

Tiffany grimaced. 'What is with that woman? She's so pretentious.' Tiffany sipped her coffee. 'So I went out one night with her and her husband to Berardos. It was worth it, though. The food is absolutely divine.'

'And how was Hastings Street?'

'Oh, the usual, see and be seen. Aromas for coffee every morning. And as usual the place was teeming with Victorians. Although it wasn't anywhere near as "Little Melbourne" as it is in the September hols. I did run into Carla Johnson though, just back from a cruise and off she pops to Noosa. Life's a bitch, ain't it?'

'Oh, how did she find the Diamond Cruise Line?' enquired Mim.

'Oh who'd know, all she could do was rave about Davey the cabin boy, how hot he was, how sweet he was, what a great body he had, the tattoo on his shoulder . . .' Tiffany let the sentence drift off and raised her eyebrows over her coffee cup.

The girls all squealed. 'How would she know about the tat unless she . . . ohmigod, you don't think she . . . but she's married!' squeaked Mim with barely concealed delight.

'I don't know anything, I'm not saying anything, but what I do know is that he was twenty-eight years old!'

'Twenty-eight!' The girls screeched in unison,

'Oh Jesus, half her luck. I'm very jealous!' said Monique, fanning herself with a napkin. 'Look, I've gone all hot under the collar just thinking about it!'

As the ladies twittered and tittered and filled each other in on the latest inane gossip, Mim was suddenly struck by the shallowness of it all. When was the last time she'd had a truly deep discussion: an esoteric, spiritual, meaty dialogue with someone? She fondly thought of her uni days: hours spent over bottles of cheap red and flickering candlelight in crappy student housing, wrestling with fellow students on the questions of the cosmos. She'd been dirt poor at the time, but somehow she felt that her life had been richer.

The doorbell finally announced Ellie's presence. 'Greetings, gorgeous girls,' she sang, gliding in on a cloud of Allure. She bestowed noisy air-kisses all round before seating herself regally like the rightful Queen Bee of their group and carelessly spread her designer accessories around her.

Mim couldn't help but smile. Ellie really was a parody of herself. She took the whole society thing to the nth degree and was probably laughing on the inside the entire time. You couldn't help but love her, no matter how pretentious she seemed.

'Hello, Ellie, sweetie,' said Mim. 'Latte?'

'Mim, darling, you life-saver, I am DYING for some caffeine stimulation! Make it a double. Liz, looking resplendent. Monique, stylish as ever. And Tiffany, what a sweet little pure white thing you've got going on there, love the tan.' Ellie immediately assumed centre stage and spread her charismatic glow among them.

If anyone was to ask Mim to define the elusive X factor, Mim knew exactly what she'd say: Ellie – whatever it was she had, it was what all the minor celebs in Hollywood needed. Stylish, beautiful and with perfect white teeth, Ellie lived the golden life – and to top it all off she was actually a nice person too.

'So what have you been up to, Ellie?' Mim asked.

'Oh sweetie, it's been such a bore with Bryce away again, my bed is just too big without him.'

'You guys are such a love story,' Monique laughed. 'After fifteen years, how do you do it?'

'Just lucky, I guess,' Ellie smiled.

'You met him when you were modelling, didn't you?' Mim asked.

The Mothers' Group had intermittently badgered Ellie to show them her modelling portfolio, but she insisted it was in storage and too difficult to find. They had to be content with the few snippets of her hey-day and the deliciously romantic details of her wonderful years spent overseas with Bryce. Although she was extremely vivacious and chatty, and could quite frankly talk the leg off an Eames chair, she remained evasive about the details of her life pre-Bryce. The other girls, self-involved with their own busy lives, didn't seem to notice, but it always struck Mim as curious how she'd remain tight-lipped when the others would reminisce about their private schoolgirl days of hats and gloves, trams and boys.

The conversation swelled around Mim as she cradled her latte and watched Ellie carefully. She seemed her usually glowing and chatty self, but Mim had detected a slight edge to her voice in the past few weeks, a subtle shadow in her best friend's eyes, and twice when she had questioned Ellie about it she'd been fobbed off.

'So Mim, how's life as a single mum?' asked Liz.

Mim sighed. 'Oh, the same as always really. Even when James is home it's not like he's ever home before bedtime or anything. I had to send him an email with a photo of Charley's lost tooth last week.'

'That's crappy, Mim. Have you told him how you feel?'

'Well, I haven't as such. We just don't seem to be connecting lately. Our only communication seems to be brief phone calls and emails about domestic stuff – it's not exactly how I thought marriage would turn out.'

'Work must be intense for him if he's so busy. He must be under a lot of pressure – not that we care really, because we're on your side,' Tiffany laughed.

'Well, absolutely. Anyway, we'll cope,' Mim said, rubbing absently at an invisible mark on her pants. 'With all the retrenchments in his company he's keeping his head down and his bum up. He leaves by 7.30 a.m. every day and never gets home before eight in the evenings.'

Liz frowned, leaning forward to pat Mim on the knee.

'I know exactly how you feel. Remember when Sebastian got that huge job last year? I can't believe we actually celebrated it! Sure, the money was great, but he disappeared overseas for months. He missed Hubert's first recital and when he eventually came home he was at the piano the whole time.'

'I remember, you were at the end of your tether,' Tiffany sympathised.

'What we did was to make a standing booking with a babysitter and go out together once a week on a date,' Liz said.

Mim shot Liz a quizzical look.

'I know what you're thinking: why go out when you're at home together most nights, and sometimes they're the last person you want to be with, particularly with you feeling the way you are at the moment. But it really works. It gets him away from the desk, the phone and the television and gives you two a chance to talk. Think of all that empty space to fill in between ordering and entrée!'

Tiffany nodded enthusiastically. 'Yes, it worked for us a couple of years ago too. You get all the boring household stuff out of the way in the car en route and then in the restaurant you discuss topics that can't be discussed over the children's dinner or on the weekend.'

'So, Tiff, why did you guys stop this date routine then?' Mim asked.

Tiffany rolled her eyes. 'It worked fine for the first few weeks, but then he kept being called away for an emergency, and once he didn't even show! I felt like a right twat sitting at Florentino's by myself nibbling breadsticks.'

'I didn't know that cosmetic orthodontists were on call,' Mim said subtly.

'Oh, yes, well, apparently it's the way the whole medical profession is going now. Even a colleague of his, a plastic surgeon, had to do a house call recently when a patient's boob job suddenly dropped during a particularly strenuous tennis match.'

'Ohmigod, no way,' said Mim as they all laughed – except Monique, who looked at her chest nervously.

'Our house at Portsea has always been a great spot for romantic getaways, too, you know,' mused Tiffany, never missing a chance to mention their new beach house.

'God, I love Portsea, so relaxing. Have you seen the Trevallys' new place?' Mim asked.

'Isn't that in NQP?' said Liz.

Mim looked at her enquiringly. 'NQP?'

'Not-Quite-Portsea, you know, Sorrento,' finished Liz. They all laughed at the sheer bitchiness of the comment.

'What's on for tonight, girls? Usual Monday night blah?' Mim asked as they all started to make moves towards leaving.

'Same old, same old,' said Liz. 'Violin lesson, then tae kwon do, homework, dinner, bath, bed, ho, hum.'

'I've got the out-laws coming over,' said Tiffany. 'Hideous man, Cliff's dad, he's such a creep.'

'Oh, poor you, what are you serving?' asked Monique.

'It doesn't matter what I serve, she always turns up her lip as though it's chuck steak,' Tiffany moaned.

Mim leaned in eagerly. 'I know what you mean. James's mother is the same and she sniffs my food constantly. It's truly odd.'

As the women gathered at the door, swapping kisses and goodbyes, Tiffany's mobile trilled an incoming SMS. She flipped it open and read the message.

'DAMN!' she cried out and looked up at her group of friends. 'That was Cliff, he's cancelled on me again! That's the third time this week. I'm going to have to deal with his parents by myself!'

As each of her friends murmured words of sympathy to Tiffany there was no longer any doubt in their minds.

Cliff was clearly having an affair.

~10~

The Stress of Life

September 1998

Half-wits and morons – that's what I have to deal with, Liz thought in exasperation as she bustled along the high-ceilinged hall of their newly-built modern, streamlined home. Good Lord, what a day she was having already. Why could nothing go right? What with the nanny whingeing about baby Roman keeping her up at night and the nightmare of their move a few weeks ago, it was all too much. No matter how hard Liz supervised the cleaning team, removalists and unpacking specialists, none of them could get anything the way she wanted it. No wonder people in the suburbs did things for themselves, she thought wryly, as one of the little men from *Moveurs* – the unpacking firm – placed her objet d'art in completely the wrong light yet again.

And tonight she'd decided to host a small soiree, just a casual get-together for the other mothers she'd just met last month at the upmarket private hospital where seafood, fine wine and vaginal bypass (aka caesarean) were all on the menu.

She'd met a few of the other mothers at the postnatal manicure morning provided by the hospital and, deciding it was never too soon to start acquiring the right sorts of playmates for her newborn, had planned tonight's dinner. Parchment-printed invitations had been sent out with spearmint-coloured teddies in cute boxes to some of the most promising prospects. That lovely Mim Woolcott who had been so friendly in the maternity ward, and Monique, whose husband ran the family business importing bottled water from Europe and seemed to do very well out of it.

She wasn't quite sure about that Ellie, married well, of course, and the figure had snapped back almost immediately post-birth – naturally can you believe? But there was something a bit flashy about her that Liz couldn't put her finger on.

Tiffany had amused the women greatly because she had chosen the birthing facility largely for its comfortable approach to cosmetic caesareans – after the money she'd spent on labioplasty to acquire a designer vagina she was hardly going to have it mashed out of shape by giving birth the old-fashioned way, thank you very much. Liz didn't hold out much hope that she'd become close friends with the woman – her idea of classical music was 'Hooked on Classics', for heaven's sake. However, she had invited her and her husband Cliff as the other women seemed fond of her.

With the plans made, invitations sent and caterers booked, Liz was hoping for a smooth day, but so far it had been a nightmare. She fiddled nervously with her three-carat brilliant-cut diamond ring and tried to blot out Roman's wails from the nursery.

The front doorbell rang and she opened the grand,

timber and opaque-glass door by its long, stainless silver handle and tutted to find the caterer standing there.

'Yes, hello, I'm glad you've finally arrived,' she said to the young woman obscured by a huge load of foil trays. 'I did make it clear to your company, however, that I expected you to unload your van at the service entrance around the back.'

'Oh, I am sorry, I didn't get that message,' the girl said with an exasperated sigh. 'While I'm here, do you think I could drop this lot off and I'll drive the van around the back for the rest of the unloading? It's just that it's very heavy.'

'You'll find the rear entrance is off Sandford Lane,' Liz replied, closing the door firmly in the girls' face.

She immediately regretted being so rude, but it had been one hell of a day. Her exclusive dry-cleaners had not managed to clean and press her Dior silk blouse by this morning, which meant she'd have to send someone back there to pick it up this afternoon, and if they didn't have it done by then, well, she may as well call the whole evening off. The blouse, in its gentle taupe, was the centrepoint of the evening's colour scheme, and nothing else in her several wardrobes would suffice.

Then the florist had phoned, to explain they didn't have any of the Stella roses in the beige that matched the dining room and her outfit perfectly – they only had white. White, honestly!

Experience told Liz not to depend on Sebastian – these creative types found it so hard to live by a schedule, so she'd booked a waiter through Dial-an-Angel. It was too much to expect that Liz could also pour guests' drinks. She'd be flat-out mingling, making small-talk and supervising the catering staff as it was. She was only one woman after all. And then, just to put the icing on the cake, she'd broken a nail. Really, what more could life throw at her today? Her eyes filled with tears as she surveyed the torn cuticle. I mean honestly: this morning, ten perfectly manicured fingers, and now this. She wondered if Larissa would make a house call, after all it was an emergency.

Her eyes scanned the room for faults, alighting on the timber Indigenous sculpture inside the front door. She sighed heavily as she noticed the dust resting on it. She must get Lenore on to that when she'd finished polishing the cutlery.

She glanced anxiously into the formal dining room. The Minotti glass-topped table and steel chairs had been shipped from Italy, arriving only days earlier. It had been an extravagance, but the gallery-style dining room was a space that afforded such a striking piece.

She sped her way back to the kitchen and pressed the garage door remote to allow the caterer entry through the rear four-car garage when the front doorbell summoned her again. She nearly screamed in exasperation. If that bloody florist has had the nerve to come to the front door I'll spit, she fumed, retracing her steps, her Chanel loafers muffled by the Persian runner.

She flung open the front door, ready to snap, but was caught off-guard by the bizarre sight that greeted her. A hideous-looking creature stood there, startling blue eyes peering up at her through a horrifying wild nest of black hair.

'Yes?' she said officiously, immediately relieved that it was clearly nothing that concerned her. The child had obviously got lost or come begging, though one would have thought the council would have taken better care with such things.

The creature simply stood and stared. Her jaw dropped open, then closed.

'Yes, whatever is it? I am a very busy woman.'

'Are you Elizabeth Munroe?'

'Yes, I am, what can I help you with?' Liz was getting

very impatient and folded her arms in front of her, contemplating a glare – although tempting fate for future wrinkles, it could well be worth the cost in this situation.

The child paused and then said, 'Were you Elizabeth Hepburn?'

'Yes, I was,' said Liz suspiciously. 'What's going on here?' The stench from the child was starting to seep into the front hall and an odour issue was the last thing Liz needed today.

The phone began trilling and she just knew that it was that damn florist with another excuse, and she really had to get a wriggle on if she was going to apply a face-mask before the evening's function.

The girl anxiously looked past Liz and into the house within. She took in the stark interior and warehouse-style foyer. Her eyes followed the clean lines of the sweeping staircase up to the second floor.

'Look, child, if you want money I'm afraid you've come to the wrong place,' Liz said, shooing her off the front step in frustration. 'I'm not in the habit of making doorstop donations to beggars. Now please leave.' She moved to shut the door.

The girl, who had recoiled at Liz's words as if she'd been slapped, stepped forward, took a deep breath, shook her dreadlocks from her face and said:

'I am Mikaylah Boomhauer. I am your daughter.'

~ 11 ~

Day of Reckoning

September 1998

Liz paled. Her manicured hand, the one with the five perfect nails, fluttered to her pearl choker. She opened her mouth to speak, closed it again, then opened it, but could only manage a sharp intake of air.

Mikaylah stood trembling, frightened she might black out at any moment. She'd rehearsed this moment many times on the long hitchhike from Moe, but the reality of it was much more intense than she could have imagined.

Liz's mind was blank, empty, groping for information, for a way to process this scenario.

Then it was full, buzzing and spinning wildly.

Oh God, it was true. Well of course it was true. It's just that, well, she'd buried it so deep, almost convinced herself that it had never happened, but it must have, because the proof apparently now stood on her doorstep.

She'd worked so hard to seal over the damage from her hideous mistake fifteen years ago and moved on – fast. Her life had been full and busy – and, well, perfect, really. How dare this dirty child turn up and spoil everything she'd worked so hard for.

Liz felt her world slipping out of her grasp: her marriage, child, lifestyle, the reputation she'd fought so hard to maintain. No way was she going back, she would not go back to that awful time when everything was so ugly and hard.

Girls from the exclusive Catholic school, St Bernadette's, just didn't go and get themselves knocked up. It was not the done thing. Most of the junior-school girls still believed in the Immaculate Conception, for goodness' sake. And the senior school girls, although they knew better, would hardly have dreamed of squandering their virginity before marriage. An intact hymen was a valuable bargaining chip into the best families.

In particular, one should not be deflowered by the gardener – no matter how green his thumb.

But to fifteen-year-old Elizabeth, succumbing to the masculine charms of Thomas was irresistible. An only child whose parents were often on extended overseas work commitments, the impressionable teen was attention-starved and ripe for the picking that summer. Her lonely hours led her to the garden, where she soon struck up conversation with Thomas, only two years her senior. At first she had hung around watching him work, but eventually she was compelled to kneel beside him in the dirt as he tenderly bedded seedlings and whipped unruly weeds into submission.

He ignited a passion for literature within her, recommending the books that would always remind her of that summer; *Hamlet*, *Catcher in the Rye* and *Moby Dick*. Her intrigue with his large dark forearms and torn denims, his clear laughing green eyes and shock of unruly hair, was only heightened by his obvious love for and knowledge of books.

The day of her sixteenth birthday simmered with languid heat, which had her glowing with sweat before she even stepped from her bed. She showered and put on a bikini top and denim cut-offs and went to find him.

Possibility buzzed in the air, and now, officially a year older, Elizabeth felt emboldened, as if she might just do anything today. She slapped away a mosquito that was droning lazily around her long, tan legs and searched for Thomas in her mother's rose garden, where the David Austins were already swollen and drunk with heat.

He worked quietly and efficiently, snipping the best blooms for the house. Choosing huge cabbage-like heads in pinks and mauves musky with perfume. His calloused fingers held each bloom tenderly as his secateurs snapped the woody stems of the roses. She watched as he carried a fragrant armful into a shaded gazebo to keep the blooms cool.

Elizabeth followed him. And soon the heady perfume of roses and summer-sounds of clicking sprinklers, strumming crickets and children shrieking in a neighbour's pool formed a gentle backdrop to their love-making.

She went to him eight weeks later. His hands were grimy with fertiliser, his face masked when she told him her news.

'Our love can survive this,' she smiled at him, caught up in the tragedy and romance of the moment. She clutched her battered copy of *Romeo and Juliet* to her heart and swore, with teenage naivety, to run away with him, to leave this 'shallow world' and be with him forever.

His eyes above the mask were still and shuttered. But he smiled his slow grin, kissed her cheek and told her that he loved her.

Her parents were annoyed when they discovered that

their gardener had walked off the job without a word, but they quickly found a new boy and life returned to normal.

But something ended for Elizabeth; there in the garden, something died amongst the weeds and the compost.

Too stunned to even think clearly for several weeks, and still holding to some faint hope that he had simply gone ahead to set up their new life and would contact her soon, Elizabeth was too far gone by the time she confessed the truth to her family. She spoke from somewhere far away from her body, somewhere a long distance from her father's shouts and her mother's slap. They couldn't touch her – neither they, nor the child blithely growing inside her, ignorant of how unwanted it was.

Elizabeth was sent away until her 'little problem' resolved itself. Her parents publicly announced a six-month stint in a European 'finishing school', anxious of the need to keep up appearances.

They'd called her Liz at the unwed mothers' hostel and the name had stuck. When she came back she insisted everyone adopt the more casual address. Elizabeth was gone. That name had been extinguished with the hopes of the innocent girl who'd believed the romance of the classics was possible; who'd believed true love was possible. She'd been pregnant, given birth and given the baby away in a tidy, sanitised manner and now it was time to knuckle down to her studies and let those vulnerable parts of her heal over forever, lest she be hurt again.

She would never again forget that there was no stronger force in the world than the expectations of society.

'Look, I just don't have time for this,' was all Liz could splutter.

Mikaylah's pale face turned even whiter and then quickly went red as she was suffused with anger, disappointment and confusion. It wasn't like she'd expected this strange woman to wrap her into her arms or anything, but to be dismissed like some kind of annoying bug was too much. She wanted to scream at the woman, to lash out at her, to just crawl up and die with humiliation on the spot.

She did none of these things. Instead she turned around and ran down the sweeping driveway.

A tiny, buried seed of compassion uncurled itself from Liz's core and rushed up into her consciousness.

'Wait!' she called out, and ran down the front steps after the child. She rushed into the street and wildly turned left and then right, but the black-clad figure had disappeared.

She stood there by the kerb in stunned silence, staring at nothing, numb of mind.

The sound of next-door's garage door opening stirred her.

'Oh goodness, what will the neighbours think?' she murmured, and she turned on her heel and slunk back into the house.

~12~

Body Maintenance

Present Day

Mim was busting. The gurgling of waterfalls and rushing of rivers on the rainforest CD was playing havoc with her bladder. She gripped the edges of the therapy bed and willed herself to be calm; to ignore the demands of her body and to just bloody well relax, for God's sake. James would be home tonight in time for the school fete and she wanted to be buffed and shiny – and hopefully reasonably serene – for his return.

It had been two weeks since her last visit to *Moi*, her favourite St Kilda day spa, and knowing how stressed she'd be after a week of single parenting she'd planned this visit well in advance. Not to mention how bristly certain parts of her had become in the past fortnight.

Her regular *Moi* visits were usually sublime. Hardly an indulgence, she reassured herself, but a necessity for maintaining her wellbeing and body-hair-free status.

As she headed toward her forties she appreciated more

and more the benefits of a good ear-candling or lymphatic drainage to manage stress and sagging skin tone. But today nothing seemed to be working. Lying tense and naked under a towel, she wished she'd listened to Ellie and Tiffany and got a nanny in to help out while James was away. She'd had too many freelance projects on deadlines, too much going on with Sophie's party, the fete and the production to manage the children and the house alone.

Not that James was home much when he was in the country, but she had to admit he was a great dad and would play and romp with the children while she got dinner underway or take over the bedtime routine so she could hide out in the office.

After a week of juggling alone she was a frazzled mess incapable of relaxation.

'Now, Mrs Woolcott,' crooned the sleek beauty therapist with tattooed eyebrows as she swept into the room, 'we're grinding our teeth again.'

Are *we*? Mim thought. I know I am, but you seem just fine, pet.

The therapist dipped an applicator into the hot wax and began spreading it on Mim's legs. Giving up on the fight for calm, Mim tried to distract herself as layers of wax, hair and skin were shredded from her body.

No pain, no gain, she reminded herself as the therapist moved on to Mim's more delicate regions. Suffering for beauty was a small compromise at her age, she figured, fighting the urge to shriek as a particularly sensitive area was stripped.

With the wax treatment over, she tried again to relax as the therapist began rubbing granules of desert-salt and oil into every inch of Mim's body to stimulate circulation, drain toxins from her lymphatic system and leave her skin exfoliated and glowing. A day at *Moi* could be like stepping back to the womb. From the tranquil sari-clad girls at the front desk to the comfortable day beds and herbal teas in the waiting rooms; the entire experience was usually very special. But not today. Mim had salt in her mouth and oil dripping in her eyes. She spat delicately, hoping the therapist wouldn't notice.

She tried to clear her mind, but instead found herself thinking, God, my pores are huge. What happened there? she wondered, staring at the mirror above her. Where did the peaches-and-cream look go? Now I'm more 'pizza-with-the-lot'.

The young therapist interrupted her thoughts as if reading her mind, 'You have lovely skin . . . for your age,' she smiled.

Exactly, thought Mim, for my age.

When did I stop being twenty-two?

When did the last fifteen years happen?

What is going on with my pores?

Oh God, what am I doing?

Is this that 'transference worry', like I read in Sahara Sheldon's *Me-time and a Half*?

Am I wasting my time worrying about petty, meaningless issues and avoiding the real problems in my life?

Or am I really worried about my pores?

Ohmigod. I've turned into someone who worries about their pores.

'Just relax,' cooed the therapist as she attempted to wrestle Mim's arms back onto the bed.

I'm not shallow, I care about lots of serious things, I only ever worry about my pores in my own time . . . really.

She began to compile a mental list of really important worrying issues. The children; James; their financial situation. Then she really gave herself a good dose of reality and decided to worry about the Middle East situation and world hunger.

'Seriously, if you would just relax, your lymphatic system will purge the toxins with greater intensity,' urged the therapist with concern.

It's not happening, it's not happening, Mim started to meditate. The therapist started the oil drip on her forehead to realign her chakras and Mim's worries finally began to recede.

The insistent chirruping of birds snapped her back to reality. 'Sorry,' she apologised to the girl, rummaging in her Louis Vuitton for the mobile. 'Kids . . . can't turn it off . . . just in case . . . you know.'

As Mim pushed the receive call button she caught a look from the carefree, single therapist that said, no, she didn't know.

Driving to the GP, Mim's initial worry over Charley's mysterious rash began to dissipate. Stupid school. That's a whole day session at *Moi* wasted. And they hadn't even started to work on her pores.

'Mrs Woolcott,' the school nurse had boomed into the phone, 'Charley appears to be displaying the early symptoms of a nasty little infection.'

Clasping the towel around her, Mim had held the phone away from her ear and wondered why the woman hadn't simply shouted to her from the gate of the school – with that massive voice she'd certainly have heard her.

'He has a peculiar rash on the backs of his hands and we urge immediate medical attention from your chosen physician.'

Mim sighed. This was the fourth time this year she'd been called to school for a 'medical' issue. Langholme Grammar was paranoid about its legal position should any child infect another with anything worse than a computer virus. Last year the Tonkon-Websters had won an undisclosed settlement for breach of care when their young son, Gordy, had missed his cello exam due to a savage dose of chickenpox picked up in the Early Learning Centre.

Mim took one look at Charley when she arrived at sick bay and, apart from the angry red rash on his hands, she felt that it wasn't serious. Best to have it checked out, though.

Luckily, Dr Winterbottom was able to squeeze them in; there was some benefit in paying an extra sixty per cent per consultation.

The doctor took one glance at Charley's hands and asked the crucial question: 'So where have your hands been, Charley?'

'Well, we were in Art class and Lochie Williamson painted them with PVA glue.'

'And why did he do that, Charley?'

'Cos my gloves kept falling off.'

'Why don't your gloves fit you, Charley?' interrupted Mim.

'Cos they're Dad's.'

Oh, Jesus, thought Mim. The new leather, fur-lined driving gloves James had bought on his last trip to New York were obviously goners.

'He's fine, Mrs Woolcott,' Dr Winterbottom assured her. 'It's just a reaction to the glue. This Aloe Vera gel will have his skin back to normal in no time.'

The doctor applied the gel. Mim paid the hefty bill.

'Sensational,' said Charley, 'what a ripper way to get off school. And it's not a wasted day cos I'm not too sick to enjoy it!'

'Think again, champ!' replied Mim. She frog-marched him back into his class and went to discuss the incident with the art teacher – one of her least-favourite people.

In fact, Mim had decided she had serious issues with Mr Maurice. Whippet-thin and waxed to within an inch of his life, Mr Maurice had all the charm of a rattlesnake and about as much artistic ability as far as Mim was concerned. If there was one thing in life Mim was sure of, it was that she knew art, and appreciated it in all its forms, from the works of the masters hanging at the Louvre to a pre-schooler's interpretation of Van Gogh's *Sunflowers*. She was passionate about nurturing and encouraging a love of art in children and allowing them to express themselves freely.

Which made having Mr Maurice as her boys' artistic adviser hard to swallow.

Mr Maurice was teaching art only temporarily while he waited for his painting career to take off. It had been thirty years so far and as each year passed, with his talents as yet unrecognised by the art community, Mr Maurice became increasingly bitter.

He was critical of those students who couldn't create and jealous of those who could. There was no joy to be had in his art class and there was certainly no room for creativity. He ran a tight ship of controlled art activities with clear parameters that went well beyond colouring within the lines.

'Mr Maurice, Charley's back after his brush with PVA,' Mim said, walking into the art room and quietly congratulating herself on her clever opening line.

'Oh, Mrs Woolcott,' Mr Maurice simpered, 'I do hope that disfiguring rash is not contagious, I really can't be compromising the other children's safety.' He pressed a paisley hanky to his mouth as if to protect himself from dangerous germs.

'Don't panic,' Mim said smoothly. 'It was a simple reaction to the glue one of your boys painted all over Charley's hands. Now, I'm not adverse to body art, but may I suggest something a little less toxic next time?' she added sarcastically.

'Honestly, Mrs Woolcott, it's all I can do to keep the Grade One boys quiet, let alone have them produce the required pieces. I turn my back for one minute and they get up to all sorts of shenanigans. Those boys are well aware that we have a very strict glueing policy in this room. The rules and regulations are to be adhered to. If it was up to me I wouldn't have Lower Primary in art class at all. They're just too silly, they have no concentration span and their minds are too unformed to appreciate any of the nuances of the syllabus anyway.'

Mim was outraged. She took a deep breath, folded her hands in front of her and smiled sweetly at Mr Maurice: she was going to enjoy this.

'Mr Maurice, might I suggest if your art classes were a little more stimulating, offering a more age-appropriate program, you wouldn't find these "shenanigans" occurring so frequently. If the boys weren't so damn bored by your inane, dull, so-called artistic offerings then they might have a bit of fun and surprise you with their abilities. You completely underestimate children's imaginations and as an art teacher you are a disgrace.'

Mr Maurice recoiled in horror and small balls of spittle sputtered from his thin lips.

'And,' Mim continued, 'in future please ascertain the cause of any "distasteful" rash before you send my child to isolation.'

With that, Mim turned and stormed out.

As she sat in the carpark clasping the steering wheel with her chipped nail-polish (another casualty of the aborted *Moi* day), she felt drained and fractious as her adrenalin rush petered out.

But, honestly, that self-important little man was personally responsible for destroying all those young people's potential for art appreciation! Someone had to set him straight.

She drove quietly home. She felt like having a Bex and a good lie down, as her nanny used to say. If the best school in inner-city Melbourne wasn't good enough for her boys, where else could they go?

~13~

It Must Be Fete

A snowstorm of steaming milk sprayed over James, spotting his starched black apron and the pristine black trestle-table with white droplets. An angry hiss of steam sent more milk flying as he wrestled desperately with the controls of the espresso machine.

'James! What *are* you doing!' Mim squealed, shielding her face from the spray of milk with her hand. 'Christ, you're lucky there are no customers yet, they'd all be drenched.'

'Oh, cripes, sorry, honey. How do you work this bloody thing?'

'Give it here,' Mim said patiently, 'I'll show you. It's a disgrace that we've had this machine for two months and you've never even used it.' She gently elbowed her husband aside and showed him how to effectively froth the milk with their new appliance.

It had been her idea to pool the espresso-machine resources of several families as their contribution to the Langholme Grammar Fete. The other mums clamoured to be on her stall, where the smallest amount of effort would no doubt bring the highest kudos – who wanted to be popping corn or stirring fairy floss all day when they could be kicking back with a double decaf macchiato? Besides, the coffee stall was bound to be the most popular, given the caffeine dependency levels of most of the Langholme parents.

Jennifer Gowrie-Smith was in charge of the cake stall and had decided she'd do something different than simply gathering home-cooked goodies made by the nannies and housekeepers of Langholme families. She certainly didn't want to have to cook anything herself; her state-of-the-art kitchen was more aesthetic than functional and she shuddered to think of dirtying her Gaggenau appliances. And what with trying to balance the dietary needs of the lactose-intolerant, wheat-intolerant, gluten-intolerant, diabetic, preservative-intolerant, fat-free, fibre-enhanced, vegan and nut-allergic pupils, home-baking was just too hard. The last thing Jennifer wanted to do was to kill some wretched child, for God's sake. She wasn't even sure her public-liability insurance would cover accidental poisoning, so it was best to stay on the safe side and outsource the whole thing. Through her connections on the tennis circuit Jennifer organised for a delivery from Patersons Cakes, reputed to be Melbourne's best cake shop. Which meant all she had to do was mark up the price tags and take the money – or at least her housekeeper could.

There was little of the traditional or home-made at Langholme's fete: the quilts-and-craft stall merchandise had been flown in from Pottery Barn in the States, and there was nary a jar of chutney or jam in sight, save the raffle hamper donated by Tangelo, of Malvern Road, Toorak, the only place in town to get home-made.

The Devonshire tea stall was outsourced to Lorenzos. The freshly squeezed juice stall was also a well-known franchise whose owners were school parents. The crêpes Suzette stall, decorated in red and white gingham, dispensed delicate, air-light concoctions sprinkled with a lacework of icing sugar; produced by a St Kilda Esplanade Market regular roped in by a friend. The barbecue stall (the Butcher Boys of Camberwell) did a great trade in Steak Diane but found it hard to push the preservative-free, gluten-free, free-range chicken and semi-dried tomato sausage in bread line. The traditional second-hand book-stall was superseded by two mothers signing copies of their latest bestsellers and selling them at full retail. Even the garage-sale stall was more treasure than trash, selling largely antique and vintage pieces from a well-known High Street retailer.

The Langholme parents were not the types to parade broken toys and discarded clothes in front of society. Toys were thrown away the minute interest in them waned; or their batteries wore down; or they created too much clutter in minimalist interiors, or their various noises gave the adults of the house a migraine. Wardrobes were savagely cleared out every season to ensure no child would be caught wearing a Fred Bare or Oililly past its prime.

Most families simply bundled these items up for throwing on the tip, but Mim and her friends were solicitous about ensuring the cast-offs went to charity. In fact, Ellie liked to justify her over-consumption of all things material as really only a clever way to help out the less fortunate.

On the morning of the fete all Mim's Mothers' Group girls were rostered onto the coffee stall. By the time Mim and James arrived, Liz and Sebastian were, of course, organised and already serving the few early-birds, Monique and Malcolm were struggling across the carpark with their machine, and Ellie had, naturally, yet to turn up, and would probably send Ursula in her place.

Much to Bindi Munt's annoyance, her navel-piercing-stall idea had been turned down, due to occupational health and safety regulations, so she was forced to be a last-minute entrant into the coffee stall. As Bindi scanned the thin early-morning crowd for likely punters (husbands, not customers), Mim took in her incredibly inappropriate ensemble of black stretch calf-hugging jeans teamed with silver court shoes and plunging black singlet filled to brimming with her latest cosmetic enhancements. Mim was certain Bindi had dragged herself straight to the fete after a big night out, and could see that she was already tucking into her own contribution to the stall – whiskey shots to liven up the cappuccinos and long blacks.

With ten minutes to go until the fete officially opened, Mim patiently went through the coffee-making procedure with James again to ensure that he knew what he was doing.

'Take the ground coffee, pack it into here – but not too tight mind – then it slots under the machine and a sharp pull to the right fits it fast.'

James followed Mim's instructions to the letter and acted as interested and focused as any student could be. But he had managed to trap Mim in between his body and the machine. His right hand went through the motions as directed by Mim, but his body and his lips followed a very different agenda.

'Now, James,' said Mim, grinning and ducking away from the impromptu nape-nuzzling.

'Are you watching? The coffee drips into the cups, only about one-third full. Keep your eye on the *crema*, it should be thick and rich. It's a slow stream and should take about thirty seconds,' she continued.

James, thoroughly enjoying the proximity to his wife's body, whispered into her ear, 'Thirty seconds – what on earth will we do for thirty seconds?' and he leaned in even closer to indicate his suggestion.

'James!' Mim giggled, and wiggled her hips, enjoying the sizzle his hot whispering ignited on her skin.

'MUM!'

Mim jumped a mile.

'Yes, yes, what is it?' she said, quickly stepping away from James.

'C'n I've some money?' demanded Jack, hand outstretched.

'Please may I . . .' Mim corrected, hands on hips.

'Please?'

'Oh, all right,' Mim caved, handing him fifty dollars. 'That has to last all day, you know,' she called to his back as he scarpered towards the fairy floss machine.

'Dad, Dad, Dad,' yelled Charley and Chloe, running to the stall where they jumped up and down on the spot, 'please, please, please, please, pleeeeeeasssse do mini golf with us!' Chloe added some more pleases for extra emphasis.

'Hey guys, what's going on?' James leaned over the front counter to smile at his two youngest children.

Bindi scowled at the family group and slammed down her Jackie O sunglasses as if bringing children to the fete was just sheer bad taste.

'You HAVE to!' insisted Chloe. 'It's got a clown face and a windmill and even a scary skeleton one.'

'Yeah, come on, Dad, you'll love it, seriously!' said Charley.

'But guys,' stage-whispered James, 'I can't. I'm trapped here like a slave, working. You know your mum is so meeeeann!'

'No she's not,' Chloe retorted with her trademark cackle at such a ridiculous notion. 'She's not mean!'

'Mum,' said Charley, using his serious negotiation face and his very best manners. 'Can Dad please come and play mini-golf with us?'

'Hmmmm,' said Mim, resting her lips on her fingers and affecting to take the request seriously. 'We're going to be pretty busy . . .'

The children clasped their hands in a begging motion.

'. . . and we're short-staffed as it is . . .'

The children's eyes switched to puppy mode.

'But your dad did spray the milk everywhere and make a great big mess, and I don't think he's much good at making coffees, so . . .' Mim trailed off as the kids bounced up and down in anticipation of her answer. '. . . I guess it's okay.'

'YAYYYYY!!!!' shouted Charley, Chloe and James (the latter almost more excited than the kids, Mim noted). James whipped off his apron and leapt over the front counter and weaved through the colourful bunting, melodious rides and gaily-draped stalls, hand-in-hand with his children.

Jack, finishing up his fairy floss, caught sight of them running off and, whooping in delight, ran to catch up.

Mim smiled at the four of them, tears welling in her eyes. There was her whole life in that little group. Suddenly a cold wind bellied out the canvas wall at the back of the stall and chilled Mim's neck. She pulled up the collar of her sleeveless pink quilted vest-jacket and zipped it up to her chin. The few clouds scudded across to momentarily cover the sun and turn the once sunshine-filled morning dull.

As if on cue, LJ Mahoney came stalking across the playground with Langholme mums Carleen Osborne and Melody Waite in tow. Carleen and Melody were new to LJ's entourage and hoping desperately to claw their way to some social status through the new association, after each had committed the sin of rising from family nanny to step-mother. LJ would let anyone into her inner sanctum if they sucked up enough, laughed at her nasty comments and fetched and carried like well-trained poodles.

LJ's accent of choice today was sea-green – a hoody track-top that she wore over black wide-leg track pants and tight black tee. Her Adidas runners had complementary green markings.

Mim, dealing with an increasing line of customers, watched the group stop, smile and chat with the principal and his five-year-old daughter.

LJ's friendly countenance and bright chatter indicated thorough enjoyment at the interaction, although Mim knew it was as fake as her acrylics. She even went as far as squatting down to the child's level and asking her a few questions about her outfit, to the principal's obvious pleasure.

The principal moved on but the little girl ran back, obviously taken with LJ, and tugged at her sleeve. The transformation was striking, Mim thought in shock. LJ stared down her nose in disgust and pulled her arm from the child. The little girl, in confusion, forgot what she wanted to say and ran back, face crumpling, to her father.

Mim closed her eyes and prayed for strength as she noted her stall was in fact the trio's target. She plastered a smile onto her face as they approached. 'Morning, LJ,' she said as brightly as she could, over the heads of the customers.

LJ had been bitter since failing in her bid to wrest the coffee stall from Mim, so had instead decided on a chai-tea latte stall as direct competition. Of course she'd hired a lackey to run it, but Mim had noticed earlier that the teenage girl was more interested in flirting with the older Langholme boys than selling LJ's wares.

'One skinny double decaf latte with NutraSweet, please, Mim,' said LJ, pushing her way importantly to the front of the queue, much to the irritation of the other parents.

'Coming right up,' said Mim. She moved proficiently at the machine and quickly presented LJ with a perfect coffee, complete with ironic love-heart pattern in the foam.

LJ's top lip curled up and she peered at the coffee as if it was infested with leeches.

She tentatively sipped it and looked up with her verdict. 'Bit weak, Mim. Shame you couldn't have outsourced like the other gourmet stalls, it would have been so much more professional to have a barista making the coffees.'

'Oh, well,' smiled Mim, determined not to let LJ wreck her good mood. 'I felt it was more personal for the mums to be supplying the coffees. How's the chai-tea latte stall going? Good business?'

'Hmmm, yes, great,' murmured LJ. 'We're just on our way to check on the stall now. Ladies, shall we?' and she stormed off before Carleen and Melody had a chance to get themselves coffees.

As the three walked off together LJ hissed, 'I hate her. She thinks she's so good, but an espresso machine, how pedestrian! Chai-tea latte is the latest hot drink, doesn't she know that?' She continued to mutter about Mim, declaring her outfit 'naff' and her hair 'dull' as she rounded a corner to see her chai-tea stall unattended. She peered around the back of the tent to find her young stall-keeper with her tongue down the water-polo captain's throat.

'Adriana!'

The hapless teen jumped. 'Oh, sorry, Mrs Mahoney, it's just that there were no customers and I was having a five-minute break.'

'You're fired.' LJ pointed a red finger away from the stall.

'Cool,' said Adriana, and the two teens grinned and ran hand-in-hand towards the hedge bordering the football oval.

LJ turned to Carleen and Melody. 'You're hired, get your aprons on.'

The two women knew better than to argue. Anyway, it would be a relief to work the fete rather than trail after LJ all day, so they willingly donned their aprons and started cleaning up the mess Adriana had left.

LJ had had the chai-tea mix made by a Chinese tea emporium in Little Collins Street, but the mix was too heavy on the cinnamon, and the overwhelming scent of the heated spice was repelling customers. She was fuming. She was determined to beat Mim no matter what it took. She'd hiked the price of her oriental beverage up to a lofty six dollars a cup, hoping that would make it appear more exclusive.

But with no customers keen on chai tea and a steady swell of caffeine junkies lined up for Mim's stall, LJ knew it was time for desperate measures. If she was going down, Mim was going with her. Leaving Carleen and Melody waiting for customers, she slipped across the oval toward the school building with just one thought on her mind: sabotage.

The school's gleaming commercial kitchen was empty; with the fete largely outsourced it was only needed for storage. Many of the stalls' supplies were piled up in boxes along the stainless-steel benches.

LJ snuck around the island bench to ensure she was alone, then sidled over to the walk-in refrigerated room. She pulled open the heavy door and snapped on the light. The shelves were lined with smallgoods, dairy products and a box of meat for the barbecue stall.

She found her target sitting on the ground: an open box full of bottles of special foaming milk for coffee machines. Smiling evilly to herself, she reached in her pocket for her key chain. The sterling silver unit opened out to reveal several useful tools, including a nail file and a bottle opener. But the small lethal stiletto knife was the one LJ needed today.

She pulled out the plastic two-litre bottles one by one, and stabbed savagely into each base. Milk began quietly emptying into the waxed cardboard box.

She stood back and surveyed her handiwork with satisfaction. That'll show that little upstart, she thought, when suddenly she heard the fridge door open. She spun around, preparing for a swift getaway, and came face-to-face with Mim.

'Hello LJ,' Mim said warily, immediately catching sight of the now milk-filled box. 'Oh, no!' she exclaimed in horror, while LJ inwardly grinned with joy. 'What's happened to your milk?'

'*My* milk?' LJ spluttered, 'What do you mean?'

Mim, in one stride, reached the site of destruction and flipped over the box lid. Clearly marked in black texta on the top it read 'CHAI-TEA STALL – LJ'.

'You poor thing! That's just such rotten luck!' Mim said in genuine sympathy, not thinking for one minute that LJ would stoop so low.

She went over to the top shelf at the back of the room and lifted down a large box marked 'LATTE STALL – MIM'. 'I'm glad I thought to put mine up out of harm's way. Probably the year eights, they're a bugger of a group this year.'

She carried her box from the kitchen away to her bustling stall, as LJ watched her profits snake from the corner of the box, across the small room and down the drain.

~14~

It's All About the Shoes

Mim and Tiffany burst into the ladies' room at Crown Casino after nimbly skirting the gaggle of fashionistas, minor celebrities and society types who were mingling with intent in the foyer of the Crown's Palladium ballroom. It was the Child Victims of Landmines Lunch, and Mim and Tiffany needed a chance to check their reflections and swap crowd observations. It was clear that this was the year of the boot – and everyone who was anyone was boasting a pair under the ubiquitous wrap dress. High boots, low boots or ankle boots – boot-mania had obviously struck.

'Thank God I wore my boots!' said Mim with a sigh of relief, fondly surveying her outstretched leg clad in calf-height pale suede. The boots were teamed with a pale-blue silk wrap dress with a tiny charcoal print that enhanced her neat waist.

'I know! Same here!' squealed Tiffany, bending down to stroke the chocolate-brown, knee-high footwear that she wore beneath her kimono-style red wrap dress.

Monique sailed into the ladies' room, distributing air kisses all round.

'Thank God you're here,' she breathed. 'I just did two laps of the foyer looking for you and trying to look content with my own company, but I was dying a thousand social deaths out there alone! And I almost wore pumps, can you imagine?'

Mim and Tiffany burst out laughing.

'Pumps! Monique! Really!'

'Don't stress, Mim, they were slingbacks,' Monique assured her, banishing the thought that she was actually suggesting a court shoe this season.

The women giggled loudly as they touched up their lippy and headed back to the pre-lunch drinks. Snapping up glasses of bubbly from a passing waiter, they found a vantage point to appraise new arrivals above the teeming sea of 500 women pretending to talk among themselves, but who were actually talking about other women, who were talking about them.

The Mothers' Group girls were happy to keep together, as none of them really minded each other gazing distractedly over their shoulder mid-chat to subtly scan the room for important faces and questionable fashion. After all, the measure of a successful function was not who sang what, or what was served for lunch: the only true barometer of success or failure hinged entirely on Who Was There. After that the need-to-know information was: who was she wearing? Where was she sitting? And how close was your table placed to hers? If you were at least five tables away you might as well pack up your Gucci bag and go home because you were clearly a social failure. If, however, you were a mere two-to-three tables away, then you could bask in the glow of social acceptance.

Monique lifted her champagne flute to mask her lips as she passed comment on a nearby fashion victim – a tactic that would have been much more effective had the flute not been made of glass. Her eyes locked with Mim's and slid pointedly to the left.

'That's Belinda Purcell, you know, wife of Andrew Purcell? Daughter-in-law of Lindsay Purcell? I heard that she's flown in from Sydney simply for today's function.'

Mim casually glanced toward the woman in question. 'Oh, she's beautiful!' She turned back to Monique. 'Where does she get those highlights done?'

'That is the thing,' Monique declared triumphantly. 'No one knows. It's a secret.'

'And over there,' Monique continued with her up-to-the-minute social gossip, 'Lady Penelope, you've heard about her, of course?'

'No, what?' Tiffany and Mim had sadly neglected to do their homework in the social pages lately.

'Well, the rumour is that while she appears to live a wealthy aristocratic life, floating between England and the 'colonies', in truth she works undercover for a private global security company committed to ridding the world of evil.'

'NOOOO!' The ladies were amazed and somewhat incredulous.

'So I've heard,' said Monique, draining her glass. 'Of course, it's just a rumour.'

A waitress wandered past in a futile mission to offer a tray of salmon and caviar hors d'oeuvres to groups of women who simply glared in amazement at the insinuation, while the drinks waiter rushed back to the bar to re-fill his fifth tray.

Fashion designer Katie Davenport walked by, the violet of her chiffon shirt-dress a stunning backdrop to her long, raven tresses. A striking brunette woman accompanied her. Her dark hair and open, friendly smile were so similar to the younger woman's it was obviously her mother – internationally renowned designer Liz Davenport.

Monique nudged Mim excitedly. 'Look who just walked by,' she said.

Mim followed Monique's eyeline. 'Oh, isn't that Liz Davenport?'

'Yes, well done, but she's with her daughter, Katie – you know her label, Show Pony?'

'Oh I LOVE Show Pony – I'm considering a piece for the races.'

'You'll look stunning, her stuff's amazing,' Monique assured her.

'Did you check out the table plan?' Mim asked Tiffany as she sauntered back from a 'wander'.

'Yes, I did – we're number twelve, it's very good. We're right next to Lillian and two over from Sarah Murdoch.'

'Excellent. I knew Mildred wouldn't let us down.' Mim smiled in smug satisfaction. The day hadn't been a waste of fashion after all.

'Have you seen her yet?' enquired Tiffany.

'Who? Monster-in-law?' said Mim.

'Yes, this is a big deal for her to have done on her own,' Tiffany said generously, although she felt sure Mildred's motives were more about raising her own profile than helping children from war-torn countries.

'She does have that committee of hers, although most have never worked or studied a day in their lives and couldn't organise a manicure, let alone an event.' Mim said flicking her eyes past Tiffany's to check out the women mingling behind her. 'Oh, sorry, Tiff, I hate it when people do that to me, always searching for someone more interesting to look at. You know that wasn't my intention.'

'Don't be daft, Mim, of course I know, but you do realise that's about the tenth time you've done it,' said Tiffany with a smile.

'Oh, God, how awful,' Mim said, and slapped a palm to

her forehead. 'Pinch me the next time I do it so I know. It's a frightful habit.'

'Where's Liz?' Monique asked, deftly claiming another full glass from a nearby waiter.

'Oh, she's got a thing on. She was a bit vague about it actually so I'm not sure, but she is coming, she'll be here after entrée.'

'Ladies!' a bright voice called out.

The three women turned and smiled as one at Ellie. She pranced her way towards the trio, not unlike a dressage horse. Her hair, as a change from the usual straightened look, was bouncing with large curls. The Donna Karan empire-line, sleeveless dress in taupe was accented with a black velvet bow under the bustline. The look was completed with elegant, strappy velvet sandals in black and taupe, the two-inch heel tapering to a killer stiletto.

Every woman in the room surreptitiously clocked Ellie's arrival and wished they'd worn a strappy shoe.

'Oh look, girls, just in the nick of time,' Ellie pointed, as three huge double-doors were drawn back to display the elegant dining room, awash with the colours and fragrance of spring. A dainty vase of spring blossoms bloomed at each place setting and more flowers burst from the walls, threaded on invisible lines. The chairs wore pretty skirts in a rainbow of soft pastels, and two-foot tall cylindrical centrepieces were stuffed with citrus immersed in water and topped with Magnolia branches.

As they threaded their way to the table Mim couldn't help asking, 'Ellie, I love your shoes, but what made you choose stiletto strappy numbers for today's lunch?'

'It was sunny, darling, I was feeling cheeky,' Ellie replied, completely confident in her look regardless of the fact that she was the only woman in the room not wearing boots.

The four friends found their assigned table and immediately dipped into the supplied goody bags at each place. No function was complete these days without a top-notch goody bag.

'Ooooh yum, Aveda Hand Relief, I love this stuff!' squealed Tiffany. 'And there's also a sample of Ralph Lauren's new fragrance, Pure Turquoise.'

Mim, not above scrabbling for a freebie, added: 'And there's two different colourways of Revlon's Top Speed Nail polish, and neither's crap – they often stick in the non-sellers in these bags.'

'Revlon?' said Monique screwing up her nose.

'Monique, if you're still using Chanel nail polish you're crazy!' said Mim sternly to her friend. 'Revlon, in my humble opinion, is the best.'

'Really?' Monique looked doubtful. 'Okay, then I'll give it a whirl.'

The ladies looked at the patterned stockings, the vouchers for facials and the scented soaps, then tucked the bags under their chairs. 'We don't want them nicked by the goody-bag grabbers,' warned Tiffany. 'Such a tacky habit.'

Goody-bag grabbers were a cheap bunch of opportunists. They'd collect as many of the bags as they could from vacant spots and then either sell them off on eBay or hoard the stuff for themselves. So while everyone pretended to be nonchalant about the freebies – some women didn't even touch the bag until they carelessly picked it up as they were leaving – they all took them very seriously and guarded them jealously.

'Two o'clock, Mim,' Monique murmured, and turned on an enormous social beam directed over Mim's shoulder.

'Oh crap, it's Mildred, isn't it?' Mim replied, and looked over her shoulder, forcing a smile onto her face. 'Mildred!' she exclaimed, and pushed back her chair to stand, turn and greet the other woman, desperately trying not to sound as phoney as she felt.

Mildred made such little effort in leaning forward to deliver the obligatory social kiss that the gap left between her and Mim was wide enough for a fit-ball. 'Mim, darling, glad you could make it, you look . . .' (having started the standard line Mildred was trapped with having to finish it, but, after giving Mim the speedy once-over decided she certainly couldn't say 'lovely or gorgeous' as one normally would) '. . . like you're having fun,' she ended creatively.

Mildred Woolcott had a single raison d'être – to be seen as a tireless fundraiser for charity. As such it was crucial to keep oneself on the A-list. The more glamorous her functions were, the more well-known and wealthy the attendees, the more likely it was that Mildred would remain top-of-mind (and top-of-list) when the invitations were sent for the most prestigious functions in Melbourne.

Mildred could readily whip up 500 or 1000 guests willing to fork out $500 per head and then part with another $100 or so for the obligatory raffle and auction.

The funds raised today would pay for a life-saving operation for little Prewitt Gahungu, a child from Burundi in Africa who had been flown to Melbourne from his birthplace only days before.

Mildred had pulled off the ultimate PR coup, arranging for the current affairs program *The Hard Word* to film a documentary on the boy during his stay.

To have the child at the luncheon, complete with television crew, would draw even more newspaper and magazine photographers. The publicity of this one event was destined to spread far and wide and last a good month or more, and Mildred would feature in every photo, newscast and article. It was the stuff of which socialites' dreams were made.

Mildred had seen a photograph of the child, and he was perfect. Cute little nose, bright sparkling eyes and huge smile. The low lighting in the ballroom was going to prove problematic, of course – he was very black. Never mind, she was sure the professionals could Photoshop the images later.

And just think how philanthropic she was going to appear, how generous and giving. She was bound to be asked to all the right Carnival Marquees this year, and of course the Hamilton Mid-Summer Ball in Sydney. Only the best Who's Who were invited to that.

Mildred had been darting around nervously all morning, ensuring the right tables were close to the runway, relieved to note that the right people were socialising with the right people and ensuring that the unattractive, unconnected people were placed up on the back tables, in the dim light. But her eyes had continued to nervously flicker at the door, awaiting the arrival of her little celebrity (and the all-important accompanying camera crew).

Mim could tell at a glance that, beneath the icy-cool demeanour, Mildred was in a dither. It was the way she kept flicking her acrylic nails and twisting the Belcher bracelet that gave her away. The only way to hold Mildred's attention when her mind was on the million details of the function was to tell her how good she was. 'I was just saying to the ladies how good you are, Mildred, raising money for the poor children in the war-torn countries,' raved Mim, fervently hoping that the girls wouldn't pick up on her sarcasm and start giggling.

Mildred turned her attention to her daughter-in-law. 'Yes, of course, Mim, but it's so necessary, don't you think? I mean we do live in the Lucky Country, and it's so hard for those little poppets with landmines left, right and centre, don't you agree?'

'Oh definitely,' said Mim, and with a wicked sense of irony she moved swiftly into, 'and I love your hair!'

Mildred's hand automatically moved to pat the same steel-grey back-combed bob she'd worn for decades. 'Thanks, darling, I thought I'd try something a bit different in honour of today,' and she smiled at the compliment – at least it would have been a smile, but she'd had $2000 worth of dermal filler last week and her face was completely immobile. Her icy eyes continued to flicker around the room and caught sight of something infinitely more important than Mim.

'Must away, my girl, I've just realised that Prudence Hargreaves is endeavouring to take a seat next to mine when I gave Amy strict instructions to seat her opposite me. Honestly, social seating can be a minefield if not handled appropriately,' she muttered under her breath, then flew off like a witch astride her broom, to chastise her personal assistant.

~15~

On the Nose

The entrees had been served and the trio of salmon – carpaccio, roe and mousse – was being nibbled daintily. The room was a cacophony of chinking cutlery, brittle laughter and staccato chatter.

Mim, Monique, Ellie and Tiffany were busily ignoring the other women who'd joined their table (they weren't from Langholme Grammar or Barlyn so what was the point really?) and having a grand time giggling among themselves.

A flurry of activity caught their attention as the little boy and his entourage arrived.

'Oh God, no, you can't be serious,' Mim said as she realised what was happening. 'That's the poor little kid who's here from Africa to have an operation. I saw him on the news last night. Surely Mildred's not using him as her own personal PR vehicle?'

Monique turned back from the media circus and looked in horror at Mim. 'She wouldn't go to those depths, would she?'

Mim raised an eyebrow at Monique and said in resignation, 'Obviously you don't know Mildred.'

At the first sight of the television crew Mildred catapulted herself from her seat and across the room as quickly as decorum and her girdle would allow. She recognised the 'talent' immediately in reporter Mike DeLuca, and made the error of presuming he was in charge.

'Hello Mr DeLuca, I am Mildred Woolcott. I spoke to your station yesterday. I am delighted you and little Prewitt could make it today.'

'Hello Mrs Woolcott, this is my producer, Annie, you'd better talk to her. I have no idea what I'm doing here.' And he turned to help himself to a glass of chardonnay from a nearby table.

'Mrs Woolcott, I'm Annie Westlake. I am grateful for your generosity in taking the time to meet Prewitt, his mother, and his doctor.'

Once Mildred struggled to understand that this very young woman in denim jeans and a felt tunic was in charge, she half-smiled and replied, 'Yes, of course, my pleasure.'

'If you would like to go with my PA, Rachel, and meet Prewitt, get to know him, perhaps put him at ease a bit, we'll set up our equipment and start shooting.'

Mildred preened her hair and moistened her lips, frustrated that she'd left her compact and lipstick on the table. Rachel steered her to the back of the room where half a dozen people huddled nervously, awaiting further instruction.

'Prewitt's very self-conscious about his condition, Mildred, and extremely shy,' Rachel explained. 'He's a great little guy once he feels comfortable, but this place is freaking him out a bit, so anything you can do to settle him down would be greatly appreciated.'

'Of course,' said Mildred, slightly affronted, 'I had a child once, you know, I am accustomed to . . . them.'

Prewitt sat in a wheelchair, his eyes saucers of shock as he took in the opulent room, the flowers, the hundreds of blonde-haired women and the plates of food being casually distributed. Until two days ago he'd rarely seen a white person and never left his village, so the scene before him was more than his small mind could process.

His mother, a painfully thin woman, looked down at her son and managed a watery smile. Prewitt felt his nerves failing him, even though he'd promised himself he'd be brave.

As Mildred clacked triumphantly towards her 'little project' she was suddenly and grotesquely assaulted by a thick wall of stench emanating from their direction. She stopped mid-step, her fingers flying to protect her nose. The putrid odour was more than her sensitive nostrils could bear.

She grabbed Rachel's arm. 'What is that unbearable smell? We're about to serve lunch, for heaven's sake.'

Rachel looked blankly at Mildred. 'Did no one explain the nature of Prewitt's injury to you, Mildred?'

'No, why, what is it?' Mildred snapped.

Rachel looked evenly at her, and, attempting to keep her voice level, explained, 'When Prewitt's older sister was killed by standing on the landmine, Prewitt was standing ten metres away.

'The shrapnel embedded in his lower abdomen. His intestinal tract was shredded and had to be removed. The doctors here intend to rebuild his bowel and his intestinal tract. In the meantime the child requires a colostomy bag.' Rachel searched Mildred's stony face for a response.

'Oh, right, oh, dear me.' Mildred was at a complete loss, she couldn't possibly go over there, not one centimetre closer. The odour was threatening to overwhelm her and she knew she'd faint clean away and that simply wouldn't do. She glanced desperately around at the nearby tables but thankfully none of her guests appeared to be affected by the stench.

'You see, I have a highly heightened olfactory sense, it's quite a unique condition,' she explained weakly. 'I smell four hundred percent more than the average person. I simply can't continue the interview under such extreme conditions . . . But wait! I know someone who can.'

Mildred wasn't going to watch her golden PR opportunity fade away completely. 'Mim, quick,' she shrieked, sprinting across the room to accost Mim, grabbing her upper arm and hauling her to her feet just as she was about to taste a tender piece of lamb bathed in a merlot jus.

Mim, dropping first her fork then her napkin, was shocked at her mother-in-law's sudden lack of decorum. 'Why Mildred, whatever is it?' she managed as the woman dragged her across the room.

'It's the little boy, Prewitt. I simply cannot sit next to him and be interviewed for *The Hard Word* so you'll have to do it for me.'

'But why not, Mildred, is something wrong?'

'Prior commitments,' Mildred gasped, and thrust Mim towards Rachel before turning on her heel and practically racing to the Chanel No. 5 atomiser in her handbag.

Rachel and Mim quickly introduced themselves as Rachel outlined the requirements for the piece. Mim was to sit next to Prewitt and Mike DeLuca would interview her about the function and the fundraising committee. The camera crew was all set up and nearly ready to go and poor Prewitt looked like he was about to burst into tears from the pressure.

'Hello there,' Mim knelt down to Prewitt's eye level. 'How are you doing today?'

Prewitt's mother leaned down. 'No English,' she

explained. 'He only talk French.' And she indicated the translator in earnest discussion with the camerman.

'French, hey?' said Mim, and wracked her brain in an attempt to dredge up her finishing school French. '*Bonjour*, Prewitt,' she started again.

'*Bonjour, madame*,' replied Prewitt.

'*Comment ça va?*' said Mim.

'*Ça va bien*,' replied Prewitt, relieved to be speaking in his familiar mother-tongue.

'*Comment vous aimez l'Australie*?' asked Mim

'*Australie est très belle*,' said Prewitt.

'*Et des kangourous, ne sont-ils pas drôles?*' asked Mim.

'*Oui, madame, ils sont très drôles!*' Prewitt returned with a giggle, remembering how funny the kangaroos were at the Melbourne Zoo yesterday.

Mim smiled at the poor little boy caught up in this ugly media frenzy. Prewitt, now visibly more relaxed, reached out to pat Mim's hand in an effort to say thank you. Mim smiled in return and pulled over a chair so that she could sit and continue her chat with her new friend. Her French was rusty but she struggled on as she and Prewitt got to know each other. On camera Mike DeLuca asked a few questions of Mim while she and Prewitt sat side by side.

Mim had first-hand knowledge of Mildred's committee, having been a member until she could use her children as an excuse to wriggle out of the commitment. As such she was able to answer the questions easily and painted a picture of a truly benevolent organisation.

After the camera stopped rolling Prewitt was able to relax again, and told Mim how scared he was about the operation. He didn't understand what they meant about putting him to sleep and he was worried that he might die.

Mim explained to him what a western hospital was like, what happened during an operation, and how lovely and helpful nurses were. She explained that it would hurt a little bit but that he would feel better in a few days.

Then it was time for the entourage to head for the hospital.

Prewitt looked up at Mim as he was being wheeled from the dining room. '*Vous veuillez me rendre visite dans l'hôpital?*' he asked.

'*Oui, mon petit chou, bien sûr!*' she replied with a smile. 'Of course I'll come and visit you in hospital.'

Once Prewitt and the TV crew had left, Mim turned her attention back to the dining room. The luncheon was set to reach its conclusion with the drawing of the mandatory raffle. Tickets had been sold for $50 each or three for $100. The first prize was a $75,000 diamond pendant, the second prize was a trip for two to Tahiti, business class, and the third prize a twelve-course Menu Gastronome at the chicest, newest restaurant in town, Vue de Monde on Little Collins Street.

Mildred, suitably recovered from her near miss of earlier, had floated onto centre stage in a waft of Chanel No. 5. All eyes were on her as she started to draw the tickets out of the velvet bag.

'Purple ticket, everyone, B-15, Collette Wright!' she announced, and looked over the top of her reading glasses at the crowd. It was the only time all day that anybody on the stage had the complete attention of the group. Even the performance by the world-renowned Debra Scorch had been largely talked over and ignored by the group of chattering women.

A squeal went up as the raffle number was called and a bouncy, buxom woman jiggled her way around and about the obstacle course of chairs and tables to reach the stage, her hand waving her little purple stub the whole time.

'Now for the trip to Tahiti, orange ticket, C-34!'

The room murmured as everyone shuffled through their tickets. Then the incredible wealthy and well-connected Jeannie Curlew called out from the crowd, 'It's me, darling!' An almost imperceptible mutter could be discerned coming from the core of the crowd. How unfair, the wealthiest woman in Australia had picked up the second prize.

'Re-draw!' Jeannie called out, and the room burst into applause. Ridiculous really, Mim thought, everyone being so grateful that Jeannie had tossed her prize back in for another draw, when the woman owned property in nearly every glamorous location in the world and certainly wouldn't have flown business class anyway.

When the prize was re-drawn, the winner's table all leapt up screaming at once. The table had been donated to the hospital's paediatric nursing staff, which would have been a generous act on Mildred's behalf – except it was really just a good way to cover the embarrassment of not having sold enough tickets. The winning nurse had been through a difficult time personally, so when her ticket number was called out she was stunned and promptly burst into happy tears.

Then the big one. The diamond pendant. Mildred rummaged around in the bag.

It was a black ticket. A-1. Uh-oh. Mildred's mind raced a mile a minute, processing what she was looking at.

Mildred always bought the first $500 worth of tickets to kickstart the buying and demonstrate the level of generosity that was expected. And because she was always on table one she always got tickets A1-A15.

The ladies' eyes were all on her, breath bated. Everybody in the room wanted this prize.

Mildred certainly couldn't say that she'd won. How would that look, she'd been the one to draw the ticket, after all.

She could make the generous re-draw call, à la Jeannie Curlew, and win everyone's admiration.

But the necklace was very beautiful. It was four carats. She really, really wanted it.

The split second was up, she had to make a decision.

'A-1!' she called out, 'Martha Fitzgerald! Martha?' Mildred made a show of shielding her eyes to the spotlight and looking around the room. 'Martha, where are you hiding? Oh, that's right, I just remembered. Martha made her apologies earlier, she had to go to a meeting. I'll be sure she gets the prize.' She waved the velvet box in the air and called out, 'Goodbye, and thanks for coming, everyone, and for your generosity.'

Mildred's PA, Amy, still smarting from the bollocking she got earlier over seating arrangements, was the last one left on her dimly lit table at the back of the room. She fiddled with her napkin and tilted her head thoughtfully to one side. Something about that last ticket draw puzzled her. She'd been up to 2 a.m. for the past three nights, drawing and redrawing the table plans, and she couldn't remember anyone named Martha Fitzgerald at the function. The only Martha Fitzgerald she knew was Mildred's poodle's pedicurist – and she knew for a fact that Mildred was the only one with A tickets.

Half an hour later, she wandered over to her boss's table. Mildred was at the double doors farewelling the last of the guests. After looking around to ensure she wasn't being watched, Amy peeped into Mildred's bag . . . sure enough, there was ticket A-1.

Amy dashed up to the stage. The velvet bag was there, the four drawn tickets crumpled underneath the podium. She knelt down and un-crumpled Jeannie's, then the nurse's, then the third prize winner, Collette something. There was one ticket left. Amy slowly unscrewed it . . . *Mildred Woolcott.* She gasped. Oh, this was great.

Amy grabbed her bag along with the evidence, and left hurriedly before Mildred could collar her for any last-minute jobs. As soon as she got to the carpark she rang an acquaintance who worked at the trashiest of the gossip mags. Oh, this was better than great. This was AWESOME!

~16~

Home Front

Mim printed out the final mock-up for Taylor's Tarts new bakery brochure with a sigh of relief. It was 3.10 p.m.; she'd finished just in time for school pick-up.

Taylor's Tarts was her biggest client, but also the most disorganised. This morning they had decided to set up snap meetings with all their sales reps and rang Mim for more than a dozen different pieces of print material, asap. After she'd returned from visiting her new little friend, Prewitt, in hospital, she'd spent the remainder of her day at the keyboard, fielding email briefs, whipping up mock-ups and trying to get Taylor's to decide on a design direction. At last they were happy.

She hurriedly changed from her work clothes of wide-legged hipster tracky daks, Bonds singlet and her secret ugg boots that were so comfortable but too embarrassing to be caught dead in, into a caramel suede A-line skirt, matching suede boots and Marc Jacobs western-style shirt in teal and caramel.

After pick-up she ran Charley to his orthodontist

appointment – he needed a new retainer, $1500 – Chloe to her violin lesson – she was ready for a larger instrument, $750 – and Jack to swimming.

'He's showing great promise,' his instructor said as Mim groaned inwardly. Compliments like that only ever meant one thing – more money.

Sure enough: 'So we'd like him to come an extra afternoon a week and receive some specialised one-on-one training from our pro. Of course it's pricey, but you can't deny talent, can you, love, eh?'

Biting her tongue, Mim smiled and practically threw her credit card at the pretty blonde receptionist. 'That will be $50 extra weekly, but we only accept six-monthly block payments, so is that what you'd like to do?' she breathed in a little-girl voice.

'No,' said Mim, just to be difficult, 'it's not what I'd like to do.'

'Oh,' the girl blinked blankly, 'but, that's the only payment plan we accept.'

'So why did you ask me if I wanted to do it then?'

'Ummm . . . should I get the manager?' The blonde now looked close to tears.

'No, I'm sorry.' Mim was shocked at her own rudeness. 'Here, just charge the six months,' she said, picking up a pen to sign the charge and trying hard to ignore the tension building in her head.

A few thousand dollars later they were home. The children quickly demolished their tabbouleh and crudités snack, and parked themselves in front of the television (ABC only in the afternoons).

Mim was left clearing up the detritus they left behind. Chloe had upended the sugar bowl during her baby-cino construction and grains crunched under Mim's feet as she moved around the designer kitchen.

She loved this house, she thought as she paused, Enjo mitt in hand, staring out at the open-plan design. They'd snapped it up five years ago, moving in just before Chloe was born. With her design flair and eclectic taste for interiors, Mim had seen the potential of the grey-brick 1970s flat-roofed home.

She'd wasted no time renovating, getting the builders in on settlement day. They'd knocked out arches, opened up walls and stripped off the flocked wallpaper (to be replaced with more fashionable and up-to-date retro flocked wallpaper). She had spent hours scouring op shops and groovy vintage stores to find the perfect accents. She'd discovered a genuine Eames chair that looked stunning down-lit with a Nelson pendant light in the corner of the sunken living room.

The house was a testament to minimalism: lots of stainless-steel beams, floor-to-ceiling windows and white-painted floors, which had seemed a great idea at the time, but were quite challenging to maintain with three children attacking them on a daily basis. White painted floors and roller blades weren't exactly best friends.

As Mim reached for her Dyson to vac the sugar up, she heard the garage door open. She stood up, her heart beating quickly. James's unexpected arrival instilled the same young-girl-in-love anticipation she'd always felt, even though their marriage was into its tenth year.

The children, also attuned to the sound of Daddy's arrival, came barrelling out of various rooms of the house.

Mim quickly prepared her greeting, smoothing her hair and checking her outfit. Too often within seconds of his arrival their banter deteriorated into sniping and subtle one-upmanship. But she hoped that tonight would be different.

As usual, Mim was the last to reach James. She planted a

broad smile on her face as she watched the children squealing and climbing over him.

'Monkey bars, monkey bars, Daddy,' squealed a beribboned and tu-tued Chloe, begging her beloved father to turn her upside-down in their traditional muck-about greeting.

'Sure, sweetie,' he said, and threw her upside-down – too roughly, Mim thought anxiously.

'Dad, check it out,' interrupted big-boy Jack, 'my new watch has a stopwatch on it.'

'Cool,' responded James dutifully, trying unsuccessfully to rumple Jack's carefully gelled and styled hair.

'Dad, Dad, look at me, look at me,' Charley insisted, but all he could muster was a weird face and a clumsy dance.

Mim waited patiently for her turn, but after the children had run away to play, James simply bent to pick up his briefcase and headed towards the kitchen, already mid-conversation.

Mim's smile faded as she followed him.

'We clinched the deal quicker than we thought, so I thought I'd ditch the rest of the afternoon,' James explained.

Mim looked at him standing in the kitchen, her tall, handsome husband in his crumpled Hugo Boss suit. She perched on the kitchen stool as he went through the familiar motions of removing his tie and jacket, revealing his powerful frame.

They'd met twelve years ago, when Mim was a crew member on a yacht that sailed out of the Sandringham Yacht Club. During the once-a-week training and all-day Saturday sailing, Mim revelled in the freedom of being at one with the sea, flying through the bay, slicing through the chop.

A crew of six manned the Farr 50, a sailing boat owned by a friend of Mim's father. The moment James stepped onto the deck to join the crew, Mim was transfixed. His boyish freckled face, sandy tousled hair and ready smile had Mim smitten from day one.

James quickly became a popular crewmember, with his easygoing personality and willingness to muck in. It wasn't long before he had fallen for Mim's refreshingly relaxed and open manner, but he hid his feelings for months before asking her out.

After years of dating Barbie-doll women, James was blown away by Mim's carefree sailor persona. With her relaxed ponytail and no make-up, she didn't give a damn about waves drenching her or ruining her manicure. Her ready laugh made him smile every time he heard it. She was a good sport, a good mate and drop-dead gorgeous.

It hadn't taken long for them to find many common interests. They loved going to the races, the MCC and trying crazy cheap-and-cheerful restaurants, like the mad Senegalese eatery in Brunswick Street. Mim smiled at the memory of James attempting to order in his year-ten French.

Their romantic scuba-diving holiday in Sulawesi was one of her favourite memories. They'd spent hours exploring coral beds and ocean wrecks together. On their last day Mim had caught the sparkle of the diamond engagement ring James had placed on top of an enormous clam-shell, weighting it with a chunk of coral. She'd almost drowned laughing and smiling through her regulator while madly nodding 'yes' to James.

She'd love to rediscover their passion for sailing, Mim thought wistfully, now that the children were old enough, but there never seemed to be enough time.

'Well it's fantastic you're home early,' she said, dragging her thoughts back to the present. 'So you'll still be able to get off early for the school production tomorrow night as well?'

James looked sheepish, his deep green eyes downcast. 'Uh, unfortunately not. I've got a meeting.'

'You can't be serious,' Mim said in a stunned voice. 'You promised the kids.'

'I know, I know, it's not ideal. Hey kids,' he called, 'wait till I show you what I brought you guys home.' The kids came rushing through and their smiles were easily bought with the promotional writing kits he told them were waiting in his briefcase. They raced after James squealing with pleasure as he headed upstairs.

Mim paced the flokati rug, fighting the urge to chew at her French-polished nails. James's early day could have provided the opportunity for them to connect but it wasn't the relief she had been hoping for. Instead he just seemed to bring more problems and disappointment.

It took almost two hours before the kids calmed down enough to go to bed. Of course, James revved them up until Chloe almost vomited and the boys were out of control. But now they were finally asleep and she and James could talk.

As he came downstairs from his shower, Mim noticed how tired and grey her husband looked. He was ageing, she realised with a start.

'So how did the day go?' she asked.

'Usual. Yours?' he responded by rote.

'Oh, fine. Got that client brochure off this morning.'

'Mmmm,' he said, unbuckling his briefcase on his desk.

'Honey, we need to talk.'

'Oh, Jesus, Mim, do we have to?' He turned to look at her. 'I'm absolutely knackered, the kids have done me in, and I've still got these papers to go through. Plus I have to prepare for tomorrow night's presentation.' His fingers swept his fringe back till it stuck up straight, then he sighed and came over to her, putting his hands on her shoulders.

'I'm so sorry, darling, it's just that I'm really under the

gun at work at the moment . . .' he gave her a brief squeeze before stepping back and looking into her eyes. 'Now, what's for dinner?'

Bloody hell, thought Mim. Dinner. She'd been so preoccupied lately that food hadn't even crossed her mind. In fact, she thought a few minutes later, as she tossed a piece of eye fillet onto the Gaggenau steak grill, the last thing I ate today was some tofu for breakfast. She opened a pre-prepared Caesar salad and threw it onto a plate, squeezing dressing out of a sachet. James came in and opened a bottle of red, pouring them both a glass. When she presented him with the meal, he muttered sarcastically, 'How do you do it, whip up a gourmet meal like this? Been slaving over a hot stove all day again, have you, love?'

Mim gave a fake smile. 'Very funny.' She pulled out a dining chair and sat opposite him. 'Seriously though, James, we do need to talk about the situation we're in.'

'And what situation's that, honey?' he said distractedly as he flipped through a *BRW* as he ate.

He glanced up, 'Aren't you eating?'

'I ate with the kids,' Mim lied, moving on quickly. 'It's the money situation, James. When are we going to get that bonus of yours?'

'Oh, yeah, that.' She'd finally got his attention.

He slid his eyes down to the floor. 'Today we were told that the company didn't make budget this year so we aren't getting the bonus.'

'What!!' Mim's face was aghast. 'But James, we've budgeted on that bonus! It was for the Land Tax bill, and we've got the rates due, not to mention overdue school fees – and every one of our credit cards is over the limit.' Mim's throat tightened as she gulped for air. 'James . . .' she grabbed her husband's tanned forearm. 'What are we going to do?' Her vision swam unsteadily before her.

'Oh relax, Mim, for chrissakes. I know money has been a complete stress but it'll be fine. I'm working on a new client at the moment, the one from Tokyo. The commission is big bickies, it'll be fine. Honestly, it will all be fine.'

But his demeanour told a completely different story. She now realised why he'd been deliberately avoiding her since he'd arrived. She knew him so well. He bloody does this all the time, she thought. I know he's just as freaked out about money as I am, but his ego won't let him admit that he might be failing as provider and protector of his family unit. If only he'd communicate with me rationally and calmly about the situation instead of just slinging accusations around. She slumped against the breakfast bench, her eyes closing in weariness.

James went back to his eye fillet and *BRW* and, realising that she'd been excused, Mim picked up her nearly empty glass of red and refilled it. She grabbed two Panadol from the cupboard and downed them with a big swig.

Topping up her glass again, she moved through the hallway and climbed heavily up the stairs then drew a hot bath with several drops of relaxing bergamot and neroli. Leaning back in the steam she went into a trance staring at the flickering reflection of the Jo Malone candles.

Something, she thought to herself, has got to change.

~17~

Distressed and Lippy-less

Mim stepped out of the water and plucked a charcoal Supima cotton bath sheet off the heated rack. It was toasty warm and luxuriously thick. She wound another towel around her hair, slipped her feet into marabou-lined slippers and reached for her La Prairie body moisturiser. She was massaging the cream liberally into her elbows and arms when James's voice came booming out of the house phone.

'Mim,' he shouted through the intercom. 'Phone.'

'For God's sake, James, the point of an intercom is that you don't have to bellow across the house,' Mim reprimanded him. She reached to pick up the cordless beside her bed.

'Mim Woolcott,' she said, towelling her hair gently to avoid follicular breakage.

'Mim, oh God, I don't know what to do! Everything's such a mess. I really need to talk, can I come over?' a frantic voice implored.

'Tiff, sweetie, it's okay. Calm down so I can understand you. Are you okay?' Mim asked.

'Yes. I mean, no!'

'What's wrong?'

'I'll talk to you when I get there. Can I come now?'

'Of course, darling, I'll be waiting for you. Drive carefully, though.'

Mim combed out her hair, troubled by the desperate tone in Tiffany's voice. After the rumours she'd heard about Cliff she expected the worst.

She tied her hair back into a ponytail. Now she'd have to re-wash it and style it properly tomorrow morning, but some things were more important than grooming. She hastily pulled on her honey-coloured, hooded velour tracksuit and swapped her slippers for her backless, laceless runners. Then she jogged downstairs.

'Is Tiffany okay? She sounded like she was crying,' James called from the study.

'She was,' Mim answered. 'Something's happened, but I don't know what it is.' No point letting on to James just yet, she decided. 'She's a mess, though. She's coming around to talk.'

'Okay, well I'll stay holed up in here,' James said, hoping he wouldn't be expected to offer any tea and sympathy.

'That's a good idea. I think she might want some privacy at first,' Mim said, and James turned back to his laptop with relief – nothing like a crying woman to really wreck a night of paperwork.

Hearing Tiffany's silver Lexus convertible on the drive, Mim went out to greet her friend, who was clearly distraught. Shaking and crying through swollen eyes, Tiffany was hidden under an ugly, shapeless coat that was obviously several seasons past being acceptable. Her face was pale and puffy, without a hint of make up. Mim noticed with surprise that she hadn't even stopped for a quick lippy fix. This must be serious.

Mim immediately threw her arms around her friend and

ushering her inside the warm house asked: 'Sweetheart, what's wrong? Come in.'

'I need a drink, Mim. Sorry, I didn't bring anything. You look great, love the velour.'

Mim poured the last of the Brown Brothers merlot into a large glass for Tiffany, and opened up another bottle to give herself a refill. Tiffany held the glass tightly with two hands and downed it in several huge gulps. She banged it heavily on the table and Mim quickly moved to refill it for her.

'Sweetie, have you got any ciggies?' Tiffany asked.

Mim jumped up to search in the back of her Le Creuset cupboard. 'Christ, I would have got in a carton if I knew it was going to be this kind of conversation,' she said to lighten the mood, while rummaging behind the stockpots and skillets for her emergency nicotine stash. Of course, no one in Mim's social set really smoked any more, but the odd one taken as needed for medicinal purposes didn't count.

Mim found the packet and they headed for the sandstone paved rear courtyard. Tiffany's trembling hands made lighting-up difficult, but finally she drew back in satisfaction and looked at Mim.

'What's happened, darling?' Mim asked with concern.

Tiffany's eyes filled with tears. 'Oh God, Mim, I'm in such a mess. I think Cliff is having an affair!'

Shit, thought Mim.

'Oh no, Tiff, you poor love. What makes you think that?'

Tiffany drew deeply on the cigarette, glugged down some more wine and began her story.

'We'd just finished dinner with the out-laws at their Camberwell house. Cliff finished early so he could be there, which was just lovely. We had a divine seafood banquet and they'd hired a magician for the children; so thoughtful. Anyway, the girls were to stay the night, so for once Cliff and I had a night at home together. I was really looking forward to snuggling in front of the fire and maybe opening that gorgeous French cognac he got duty-free. I had a shower and put on my new Calvin Klein trakkies–'

'Which ones, the taupe ones with the hood?' interrupted Mim.

'No,' corrected Tiffany, 'the dusky pink ones without the hood. Anyway, then he went up to his bathroom to have a shower too.' Tiffany leaned forward to butt out her cig and top up her glass. 'He left his mobile on the kitchen bench, which is unlike him, and it beeped. I checked the text, because we've been expecting a yay or nay from our solicitor on a property issue and I thought that's what it was. But boy was I wrong.'

'What did it say?' asked Mim, leaning forward in her chair.

Tiffany clutched her stomach, 'Oh, Mim, I feel sick!' she continued. 'It said, "can't wait to see you tonight x".

'Oh, Tiff. But could it have been a business thing?' Mim trailed off doubtfully.

'Well, I guess so. I mean the "x" bit could have been a typo, couldn't it? Without the "x" bit it could have been a colleague or client or anyone, couldn't it?'

'Well, maybe. So what did Cliff say?'

'I didn't tell him. I deleted the message and put the phone back where it was. But then, he came downstairs in jeans and a shirt – I mean, Cliff in jeans – can you imagine? I've always thought he was probably born wearing a suit. Anyway, cool as anything he says he's off to meet our solicitor for a drink to discuss the investment property.

'I was so calm, but inside my head I was screaming. It was so obvious that he was up to something once I'd seen the text. And there was stupid me, not even realising it till that moment. What an idiot!'

'You're not an idiot, he's a bastard, an out-and-out son-of-a-bitch bastard,' Mim cried. She was shocked that Cliff would be so obvious. And the floozy he was seeing, whoever she was, was obviously stupid as well as a home-wrecker – who would text their *married* boyfriend?

'So then he took off and I rang Barry – our solicitor – under the pretence of inviting them to that charity do next month. He didn't mention meeting with Cliff at all. The prick was lying to me, and he's probably been doing it for a while.' Tiffany sighed and sniffed sadly. 'Oh Mim, what should I do?'

'Christ only knows,' Mim answered. 'What do you want to do? You could confront him – or maybe it would be best to get more evidence first, you know, go through his wallet and that sort of thing?'

'Done that. I only had a quick glance but there were some charges I didn't recognise. Dinners at trendy St Kilda restaurants and receipts from that new groovy bar in Inkerman Street. But it could just be client dinners.'

'What about gifts or flowers?'

'Nothing that I recognise. There was a charge from Botanical Flowers back in February, but he sent me Valentine's flowers, so it could be that – not that I remember which florist they came from.'

'I think you need to be really devious for the next week or so,' Mim suggested. 'Try to act normal around him if you can: best not to stab him at this stage, though I'm sure you're desperate to inflict bodily harm,' she laughed gently. 'When he's not around go through the phone bills and check every number. Same with the Visa, Amex and MasterCard. Keep your eyes open, check the incoming messages on his phone, and his emails. Don't forget the deleted folder. That way when you do confront him you'll have all the ammunition you need and he won't be able to weasel his way out of it.'

Tiffany's head was spinning with the same painful thought – he cheated, he cheated on *me* – but she could see the wisdom in Mim's plan. 'All right, I'll do all that before I face him – but let me tell you, if this snooping confirms what I already suspect, I'm going to have the bastard's balls in a friggin' vice,' Tiffany said, sloshing red wine on her Prada loafers.

'Bugger, I love these bloody shoes,' she cried, but before she could tear up again, Mim interrupted.

'Sweetheart, you get his balls and I'll bring the blow torch,' Mim grinned, and was rewarded with a big smile from Tiffany.

They talked long into the night, drowning Tiffany's pain in merlot and nicotine. By about midnight Mim thought it was safe to gently broach the Fairy Fanny issue.

'Sonofabitch!' shouted Tiffany, when Mim told her about Cliff's lecherous advance. 'I had to give him a friggin' head job as a welcome-home present that night, and what did he give me? A friggin' bottle of vodka – I have NEVER drunk VODKA in my LIFE. PIG!'

'Shhh,' said Mim, almost hysterical with laughter. 'The kids.'

'Sorry,' Tiffany slurred with a very-Merlot giggle. 'But when I think of how I've slaved over a goddamn running machine and stepper every day; how I've deprived myself of every known carb – even saying no to the communion wafers at church, and drunk enough bottled water to drown a friggin' elephant – just to fight for some sort of figure so asshole Cliff could flaunt his trophy wife.' She paused. 'Not that it's ever done me much good,' she added with a sigh, slapping her J-Lo-esque butt. 'I'm never going to be a size eight again, I'm afraid – not like Fairy friggin' Fanny, obviously.'

'Hey, don't put yourself down,' said Mim, serious again.

'He doesn't deserve you if he's prepared to risk your marriage for some slutty stuff on the side.'

'Actually, I'm surprised he can even manage it,' Tiffany said with an evil grin. 'It's not like he's got the goods under the sheets. And he's too proud to go to the doctor for Viagra. Not that I'm that bothered. At least a quick BJ keeps him happy – it's all over in a few minutes and it saves me the bother of having another shower.

'So I can't actually understand what this little tart even sees in him.' Her voice dropped to a conspiratorial whisper. 'It's not like he's packing any serious equipment either,' she giggled.

Mim choked on her mouthful of wine. 'Christ, Tiffany, don't tell me any more, I can't stand the mental pictures,' she pleaded, rocking with laughter, tears rolling down her face.

By 3 a.m. they were eventually sipping soothing cups of chamomile tea and were well into planning Tiffany's revenge.

The stage was set for an execution!

~18~

Little Emperors

'Pricked again,' thought Mim, recoiling in pain as the sewing needle plunged into her finger.

'Mum, be careful,' Jack whined. 'That blood will ruin my costume.'

Mim leaned back on her heels, sucking her finger and quietly contemplating the string of expletives flowing through her head. 'I'm not going to ruin it,' she answered in a threatening whisper. 'I spent hours making it, so I am not going to ruin it, am I?'

She tightened the neck of his voluminous snowman suit a tad tighter than necessary and Jack gulped. 'Now stand still and let me finish this or we'll be late for the production.'

Tonight was Langholme Grammar's annual *Appreciation-and-Encouragement-of-Effort-and-Talent Night*. It sounded warm and fuzzy, but in reality it was a theatrical bloodbath where the precocious brats who'd scored bit-parts in TV commercials or soaps were given an undeserved spotlight, while 'nobodies' like Mim's children stood at the back of the stage dressed as plants or furniture. Last year Jack had been a cabbage and poor Charley had been the leg of a table.

Mim made the best of it, praising their efforts – but

really, how enthusiastic could you be about their interpretation of a vegetable or a piece of wood?

Each February the drama teacher gave the same speech: 'Our aim is to stimulate an organic process sown in the rich earth of our families which will spring anew each season and flourish with a bounty of talent and success.'

Mim had heard it all before and knew what he really meant was that parents would have to make their kids' costumes, attend set-building working bees, ferry the children to after-school rehearsals, help them learn their lines, and then pay $25 a ticket for the privilege of watching the whole agonising process unfold.

The school insisted on handmade costumes to reinforce the 'organic creation,' making Talent Night and the school cake stall the only two times a year when Mim couldn't buy her way out of hands-on mothering – though most of the other mums still managed to. Most simply ignored the rules and outsourced the task to the nanny or the housekeeper, then bribed their children to keep their mouths shut.

Mim couldn't bring herself to make her children lie, so, inept as she was with her hands, she struggled every year, producing lopsided bunny ears, lacklustre pirate suits and truly tragic dragon tails.

This year the production was to be 'The Four Seasons', set to Vivaldi's symphony, which was no surprise to anyone, as it had been the annual concert for the past twenty-five years. Somehow the drama master managed to weave a cast of elaborate characters into a simple weather allegory, but Mim despaired at the lack of creativity and imagination and couldn't see why they didn't try something different once in a while.

As Mim finished the last stitches on the now slightly grubby snowman suit, Chloe ran through the room, draped in Charley's flower costume, tripped over the long stem and gashed her lip open with her teeth.

Christ, that's just what I need, Mim thought, as Chloe threw herself dramatically into Mim's chest and revved her screams up a notch, right into her mother's left ear. It was all Mim could do not to shake her. As Chloe slumped more forcefully against Mim's body and wailed bloody-mouthed onto her new Karen Millen shirt, Mim was ready to give it all up. Chuck in this mothering lark altogether.

A deep sense of failure threatened to overwhelm her. She saw herself as though from above – sitting cross-legged on the floor, a screeching child pinning her down with snot and screams, a snowman looking at her like she was a misbehaving servant.

She'd stressed and panicked about this night for weeks, whereas James was briefly apologetic about missing the great event, yet managed to happily swan out of the door for his client meeting several hours before the concert started. 'Break a leg,' he'd yelled, heading off to The Flower Drum and leaving Mim to dress the boys and go over their lines one more time: *The chill of winter doth embrace me* for Jack and *The rays of sun warm thine heart* for Charley.

These were their first speaking parts and Mim thought they'd have a much better chance at getting them right if only they made any sort of sense.

Mim dreaded the humiliation she was set to face tonight when her desperate attempts at handiwork were revealed. The Reading Mums seamlessly morphed into the Sewing Mums at this time of the year and formed smug little sewing circles that produced beautiful creations – it didn't hurt that the former wardrobe mistress of the Australian Ballet was among their number, so of course Mim felt like a ham-fisted clod beside their displays of costume prowess.

She knew that Chloe would wriggle and fret on her

knee throughout the performance, spoiling it for her – and that the boys would hate their performances, dragging off their 'stupid' costumes and ignoring her praise with ill humour, scowls and flushed faces. Several of their mates had been chosen to portray the Soldiers of Spring and Warriors of Winter (no weapons, of course) and her boys would be angry and humiliated in their 'girly' costumes.

If all that wasn't enough, Mim knew she'd face a scathing appraisal from James's mother, who would meet them at the school hall. Again she'd be judged as too thin, tired or jaundiced. Apparently this was how she'd looked ever since she and James first met.

It's going to be such a difficult night, Mim thought in defeat, so why are we even going?

She had a brief fantasy about ditching the event, getting a movie and snuggling up in front of the telly with the kids in their jammies.

'Yeah, that'll happen,' she sighed, absently patting Chloe on the back and intoning soothing words as though she were on autopilot. 'There, there, never mind,' she said, more from habit than concern, as Chloe finally stopped bleeding and crying.

She couldn't even feel sympathy for her little princess. What was wrong with her?

The backstage of Langholme Hall was awash with anxiety and tension – and that was just the parents. One father was shouting at the drama master and pointing angrily at his son, who was dressed as a rather ashamed daisy.

'Looks like Bernard got back from overseas then,' Mim thought, as she watched Bernard Worthington III vent his rage at coming home and discovering that Bernard IV, a skinny, spotty kid with braces, was playing a flower.

The drama master finally disentangled himself from the

confrontation, leaving Bernards III and IV seething and plucking satin petals from junior Bernard's elaborate costume to macho it up a bit. 'No son of mine will be a bloody flower,' Bernard raged. 'You can be a weed, boy, but no Worthington has ever been a flower.'

Sally-Anne Armaund was loudly suggesting that her son, Michel-Jon, required better lighting for his cactus interpretation, in order for the audience to truly appreciate the veracity of his spikes. Her toddler daughter, Lilly-Jo, sat behind her, happily dumping the contents of Sally-Anne's fawn-skin purse into her lap. Mim hurried the children away as a box of super-sized tampons spilled across the floor.

She found the Grade One teacher close to hysterical tears in the Lower Primary Boys' dressing room. Mrs Clark had spent the day fielding objections from a stream of angry parents strenuously voicing concerns about their child's stage position, lack of lines or on-stage period. A group of Preps was bellowing the 'Song of Spring' at the tops of their voices in one corner; a wilted flower *sans* stem was pulling at the teacher's skirt, and another was holding her leg and threatening to vomit – again.

A tantrum was in full force near the bathroom, where Julie Simms-Walsh had discovered that her son Barkley had snuck out in his footy boots rather than the pixie boots she'd spent hours watching the nanny sew for him. As Julie jumped up and down on the spot in a fit of rage, Mim felt the corners of her mouth twitching. This was a nightmare and the only thing to do was laugh, she decided.

Mrs Clark stood on a chair and yelled to get their attention. It was time for the parents to take their seats and for the children to get in position.

Mim waved the boys goodbye, gathered up Chloe and headed for her seat. Chloe stroked Mim's face with her chubby hands and kissed her on the lips, 'I love my mummy, mummy,' she said, her angel's face glowing.

'Oh darling, I love you too,' Mim said, her heart melting.

'You're my special mummy – and you know what?'

'What?' said Mim rushing towards their seat as the orchestra burst into action.

'I've got a big poo in my bum.'

Mim froze. 'Oh darling, not now,' she said as the lights dimmed. 'Can it stay in until the end of the show?' she asked hopefully.

'No,' Chloe answered sweetly. 'It's already coming.'

Mim instantly dropped Chloe from the hip of her Ralph Lauren trousers and rushed back to the toilets.

She spied Ellie in the hall, speaking earnestly into her mobile. Ellie, who never had a hair out of place, seemed agitated and troubled, her beautiful features marred by a frown.

'Oh no, I can't believe it. I knew this would happen. Now what will I do! What if everything's still there?' Mim heard her say as they reached her.

Catching sight of her best friend, Ellie first registered shock and then immediately relaxed her face and trilled into the phone: 'Anyway, must be off, sweetie, things to do, people to see. *Ciao bella*.'

Depositing Chloe in a cubicle, Mim caught up with Ellie in the hall.

'Darling,' Ellie gushed. 'You look fabulous. What a bun fight!'

'Ellie, you seemed upset just then, is everything okay? Who was on the phone?'

'Oh it's fine, darling, just the babysitter.' Ellie waved her manicured hand dismissively. 'I've left Paris at home. My Ursula's in Sweden so I was forced to book that awful agency babysitter and the nanny-cam is on the blink so I have to ring in every half hour to make sure the stupid girl isn't drunk again. Anyway, how are the boys? All set for their big entrance?'

Chloe emerged from the toilet with her skirt back-to-front. Mim bent to straighten her out and before she could ask any more Ellie breezed off to chat with another mum.

I've never seen Ellie so ruffled, Mim thought as she rushed Chloe back to their seats in the darkened hall.

She caught sight of James Snr and they exchanged broad smiles as he waved her over to their seats in the second row. James's mother smiled thinly as Mim apologised her way down the row of seats. Mim for once escaped the full force of Mildred's critical eyes as her mother-in-law was striving for an incognito look behind enormous Dior sunglasses. Obviously the savaging Mildred had received from the nation's gossip columnists after slyly pocketing the diamond pendant at the charity lunch had taken its toll. But, Mim noticed with a start, not enough to prevent her sporting the flashy rock.

She slumped into her chair with Chloe's heavy weight on top of her.

'Hello, Mildred, hello, James,' she whispered to her in-laws.

'Darling, you look exhausted,' Mildred whispered back.

'Headache,' Mim said apologetically.

'No wonder you've got a headache, are you starving yourself again? You look like a skeleton,' her mother-in-law hissed, and her eyes went to the stage, her daughter-in-law summarily dismissed.

Mim sighed inwardly and discreetly studied her mother-in-law in the darkness. Skeletal herself, her bones were draped in a Vera Wang boucle suit, accessorised with matching Chanel bag, pumps and very big rocks. Mildred's paternal grandfather had owned a shipping company, which had been in the family for three generations before being developed into an international freight operation. When it sold several years ago, Mildred and James Snr's bank balance zoomed into an even more stratospheric zone – not that it did us much good, Mim thought bitterly.

Mind you, I guess we did get the beach house, she reminded herself, but still a wad of cold cash or assistance with the school fees wouldn't have gone astray.

James's dad leaned in front of his wife's rigid posture as she studied the stage. 'You're looking as beautiful as ever, Mim darling,' he whispered to his only daughter-in-law. Mim was the daughter James Snr had always longed for and he adored her and the amazing grandchildren she'd given him. He was thrilled that his son had married so well.

'Thanks James,' she returned and smiled at him and went to return the compliment when Mildred spoke.

'Oh dear, Mim, you've done your own costumes again,' Mildred sighed, and Mim's attention was drawn reluctantly back to the on-stage action.

~19~

Sushi, Anyone?

Mim balanced a jar of wasabi in one hand, a tin of smoked salmon and a packet of dried lentils in the other and stood in front of the pantry staring quizzically into space. Moments passed with her standing there motionless until Jack broke her trance.

'So, what are we having?'

'What? Oh, yes.' Mim shook herself back to reality and stared blankly at the foods in her hands. 'What was I saying?'

'You said, "What the bloody hell am I going to do with this crap?"' Chloe said innocently, her blue eyes wide.

'Oh . . . yes, that's right . . . dinner,' Mim remembered. 'Chloe, those aren't appropriate words for you to use,' she hastily added.

'I'm staaarving, Mum,' Jack whinged again.

'Wasabi salmon with lentils?' Mim pondered. 'No, the lentils will take forever to soften and there's not enough salmon . . . maybe eggs on toast . . . too basic . . . Oh Christ, I forgot James's dry cleaning, must get that tomorrow . . . I could do eggs Benedict but I hate making the hollandaise . . . Jack why are you doing that to your costume? . . . Maybe a salmon omelette?'

They'd spent the day recovering from last night's production. Mim had spent half the morning on the phone chewing over the PPA (Post Production Analysis) with Liz and Ellie. Then there'd been Jack's dinosaur diorama to build, a finger-painting project for Chloe and suitable educational show-and-tell to find for Charley for school tomorrow.

With everything sorted, Mim realised her cupboards were bare. Coles Online and the Just Fresh organic food delivery both came tomorrow morning.

'Okay,' Mim thought. 'Time for some lateral thinking.'

With James out golfing with clients again it might just be the perfect night to immerse the children in a culinary experience, Mim decided. Yes, this will be a rich learning experience, some quality family bonding time, and a lesson in cultural diversity, she thought happily. All her own strict parenting criteria had been met in one fell swoop, and she felt momentarily brilliant.

The designer-clad family headed to the busy Toorak Village, where the scent from various restaurants firing up their kitchens wafted tantalisingly in the air. They stood on the windy street as Mim avoided chewing her nails, and debated which restaurant to patronise.

The local Chinese was too slimy, according to Chloe; the boys didn't like the spiciness of the Thai or Malaysian (although Chloe had a very sophisticated tolerance for hot food for a child of her age). Pizza was in the banned junk-food category, as were hot chips.

Japanese was perfect, Mim suddenly decided – it helped that they were right outside the restaurant and Chloe suddenly needed an immediate 'tinkle, tinkle' and was holding herself most unattractively; and wasn't that the Morgans across the road with their new Swedish nanny, well goodness, that was just asking for trouble wasn't it, hiring a girl with legs like that – and oh dear, tinkle, tinkle on the pavement, let's get inside right now.

Besides, Mim soothed herself once the bathroom crisis had been sorted, Japanese was divine: delicately battered, lightly cooked and offering all kinds of nutritional benefits.

The children whooped with delight as they settled at a low table surrounded by cushions, but Mim quickly regretted the choice, as they turned the table – which was sunk into a pit – into a cubby furnished with the floor cushions.

'Get out of there, immediately,' Mim hissed at them. 'Remember the restaurant manners we discussed?'

The children took their places once again and Mim beamed with pride at her beautiful family. She thoughtfully perused the menu, thinking happily that any passing ad execs would quickly nab this attractive family group for their next Country Road commercial. Then she looked up again, smiling benignly at the children, to catch Jack with his eyelids inside out, chopsticks up his nose and in his ears, making terribly politically incorrect impersonations, to the delight of his siblings.

Goodbye Country Road, hello minimum security, Mim thought despondently. 'It's okay,' she said to the nervous-looking waitress, as she ordered tempura vegetables, sashimi, sushi and teriyaki chicken. 'We won't be here long, and I promise there will be no damage.'

Mim could feel the eyes of the other diners on her and willed her children to behave. Glasses of apple juice silenced them for a few minutes at least. But Mim had unresolved juice issues and spent the precious seconds of peace conducting an internal debate on the topic. Those television current-affairs shows insisted that juice was a sugar-laden, tooth-rotting ruse and that she may as well buy them those caffeinated fizzy drinks. But what else could she do? The children flatly refused to drink water, even in those trendy bottles.

Maybe this water aversion stemmed from her not drinking four litres of water daily during breast-feeding, as all the books advised? Well, juice it would have to be tonight, she finally decided, and at $4 per glass, she hoped that at least they enjoyed it.

'Can I have another one?' Jack asked, slamming down his empty glass.

'After you've eaten something, or you'll dilute your gastric juices,' Mim warned.

Finally, the meal arrived.

'Raw fish! You're joking!' Jack spat the contents of his mouth onto the tablecloth. 'Yuk!! Why didn't you tell me first?'

'Because you seemed to be enjoying it, darling, I didn't want to put you off it,' said Mim, regretting her honesty.

'Next you're going to tell me it's wrapped in seaweed or something,' said Jack, wiping his tongue with a napkin.

No, not if I'm smart, thought Mim.

The chicken teriyaki was also a failure, apparently the sauce was filled with too many unidentified 'green things' and was too 'weird'-tasting to be tolerated.

Third time lucky? Mim hoped, as the tempura vegetables made their appearance and the children hungrily grabbed them.

'Well, that was a triumph,' she laughed, until she realised the children were just eating the batter and leaving the naked vegetables on the plate. 'For goodness' sake, children, do you realise how lucky you are? Do you know that there are children in the world whose parents take them to fast-food restaurants several times a week? Can you imagine the condition of their arteries?'

The children ignored her and went back to bickering over the last crumbs of batter.

With relative peace at her table, she sat back to survey the restaurant and noticed Seth Barlow walk in with his two children. Mim waved congenially to hide her evil thoughts.

What a pig, she fumed to herself. Poor Gwendolyn had taken on night work at that twenty-four-hour hair salon (which had such unsavoury clients) to help pull them out of a financial crisis induced by Seth's fondness for a flutter – and here he was easily squandering twice what she would earn tonight!

'Good evening, Mim,' Seth said greasily. He had always been a slimy little number.

'Hi Seth, having a family night out, are you?' Mim asked cattily.

'Just doing a bit of babysitting for the wife,' Seth explained, as he shepherded his children to a table.

Mim turned away from him to prevent further conversation. Dreadful man, she thought. According to the rumour mill, Gwendolyn had been getting the kids in the car outside their (heavily mortgaged) Malvern house when two enormous tattooed beasts had approached to repossess her red four-wheel drive. Seems Seth had been secretly gambling away the repayments for months. How mortifying for poor Gwendolyn, especially right in front of her neighbours, who had hit their phones within minutes.

Bastard, thought Mim, turning her attention back to the children, who had at least managed to swallow some boiled rice along with their batter-fest.

Mim was starving and went to launch into the sashimi just as Chloe crawled into her lap, spilling her second glass of juice into the teriyaki. Then Charley insisted that Jack kept looking at him 'funny' and set Mim's teeth on edge with his squeaky Pee-wee Herman impersonation.

'Mmm, that's delicious,' Mim said, intent on ignoring her children's irritating behaviour and making the best of the evening. 'Isn't this fun? Do you know that the Japanese culture is one of the world's most ancient? In fact–'

'Muuuuum,' wailed Chloe, 'Charley's kicking me under the table!'

Cultural lesson over, she snapped, 'Charley, stop it! Jack, where are you going?'

'Toilet.'

'Me, too.'

'Me, three.'

'All right, but don't be long.'

Mim sat revelling in the sudden calm and took the opportunity to enjoy several mouthfuls of the chicken, before she suddenly realised it was too quiet and went in search of her offspring. As her stringent public-facility rules stipulated, they were all in the ladies' toilet, but not acting in any manner that made her want to claim them as hers. Her private-school-educated, well-brought-up-children-from-an-excellent-family were bellowing like maniacs. But worse, they had made huge, wet, toilet-papier-mâché balls and were aiming them at each other, the walls, the windows and the ceiling.

'OH . . . MY . . . GOD!!!' Mim exploded. 'I can't leave you alone for one minute! Clean this mess up!'

Still sniggering and hiccoughing with over-excitement, the trio made a half-hearted effort at scraping soggy toilet paper from the walls and floors; but Mim got the worst of the job, ruining her French polish and ripping off two nails altogether.

Mim couldn't breathe. She was blind with rage; this was beyond any mass destruction she could have possibly imagined her children capable of. Her mind raced with unflattering thoughts about the so-called top private schools in the city for which she and James paid an absolute fortune. So much for the best education money can buy, she thought, as she grabbed her bag and pushed her brood out of the restaurant. You'd think they could have taught her kids how to behave better than this.

Guilt at the frightening and soggy mess in both the bathroom and at the table made her drop a $100 bill on the front desk as she left, knowing she could never show her face in the restaurant again.

Chloe arched her back and screamed as Mim bundled her into her car seat and tried desperately to connect the harness. 'For Christ's sake, Chloe, I am going to throttle you.' Mim's controlled, mum-in-public demeanour slipped for an instant to reveal her much less attractive at-home self. Her heart sank as she bent to extricate herself from the car and heard the unmistakable sound of stilettos clacking against the concrete.

They were still a distance away, but even from here Mim's finely honed aural fashion sense could detect that several women were about to descend on her, in tiny shoes, with heels a good two centimetres above acceptability.

'Oh no,' she shuddered. It could only be the Triple Ds, the trio of diabolical mothers from the boys' school. Truly the perfect ending to the perfect night, she sighed, looking up to face the enemy.

Trip-trapping up the street with all the finesse and charm of the three Billy Goats Gruff came the Triple Ds, their beady eyes locked on her as if she were prey.

'Hiiiiiii, Miiiiiim,' the group sang out in unison.

'Bad night, lovey?' smirked Bindi Munt, the most feral of the group, indicating a still-screaming Chloe.

Shelby Harrison and Trixie Casey-Roxborough-Jones (a keen surname collector) lagged behind Bindi as they stopped to use the ATM. Sure they had their gold Amexes, but their dealers insisted on cash. Although it was past bedtime on a school night, Mim noticed with distaste that they were well on their way to being drunk.

Bindi was feeling particularly chuffed with herself having persuaded some rich geezer in Harvey's Bar to shout her a Slow Comfortable Screw followed by a Screaming Orgasm. It was more than she got most school nights as a single mum.

'Been out for dinner, Mim?' asked Bindi, cornering her between the car and a street pole.

'Yes, the children and I have had a delightful meal out together at Osaka's,' Mim lied, refusing to admit a less-than-perfect life.

'Oh God, you're lucky, my Minx and Devlin do my head in. Thank God they're both at their dad's places this week.'

Parenting really wasn't an issue for the Triple Ds, who had strings of ex-mothers-in-law and ex-husbands to take over when the Early Learning Centres and After School Care closed. The biggest role they played in their kids' lives was choosing their seasonal wardrobe – and then borrowing from it.

'So, the word on the playground is that Ellie's, like, next on LJ Mahoney's hit list,' said Bindi with a hint of glee.

Mim's blood froze at the mention of LJ's name. Now there was a true personification of evil. Caught hideously out of the loop, she covered as best she could.

'Ellie? I doubt it, that . . . um . . . incident . . . was nothing. Why, what have you heard?'

'Well *I* heard that Ellie went to the preview of LJ's exhibit last month and then so totally trashed it to Bryce that he, like, yanked the *Today-Live* coverage.

'LJ is, like, so furious and reckons that she's totally going to bitch-slap Ellie when she catches up with her.'

Mim was shocked. Ellie would never have got Bryce to

pull TV coverage. And it wasn't like Ellie even had any idea about art: she liked what she was told was good and ignored the rest like everyone else did. Ellie might be vacuous at times, but she wasn't nasty.

But this could become a serious issue. LJ Mahoney was a self-proclaimed artist, and megabitch, and would make life hell for anyone who slighted her.

In reality, LJ was more of a magpie than an artist. Her style was to collect other well-known artists' work and arrange or replicate it in what she called an 'arty' fashion. Her work was constantly exhibited at an exclusive city gallery (owned by her uncle) and sold mostly to young, impressionable collectors who were readily sucked in by the buzz created about her exhibitions thanks to her husband Philby's PR firm. LJ's low self-esteem and desperate need for the limelight meant nobody stood between her and a photographer. She'd cut acquaintances with a look, elbow family out of the way, bad-mouth 'friends' to reporters – anything to get her mug in the social pages. It was a bit daunting that Ellie appeared to be her next target.

'I am sure that Ellie didn't do such a thing,' Mim said loyally. 'She certainly didn't mention it to me. Perhaps Bryce simply had something else come up for *Today-Live* and LJ just got bumped. These things happen,' she said hopefully.

'Well, you should never let the facts get in the way of a good story,' Bindi cackled, snapping her gum.

Mim overtly glanced at her watch and was about to make her excuses when Shelby and Trixie scuttled over, tucking hundreds into their gaudy beaded purses.

'Join us won't you, Mim?' Trixie smirked.

'You'd make great bait – a bit of fresh meat and all that,' simpered Shelby, who'd just left husband number four.

'We're going to The Anchorage for after-dinner drinks, or, in our case, instead-of-dinner-drinks.' At this the three shrews threw back their hair extensions to cackle with brittle laughter.

Mim was hot, flustered and food-stained. She was fed up and angry and would have killed for a quiet drink in adult company – but would never be desperate enough to be seen with these overdone tarts. And anyway, with the three kids still bickering noisily in the car, the Triple Ds' invitation was only a spiteful swipe at her lifestyle.

'Well, girls, as much as I'd love to, I've got my mummy hat on tonight and I've promised the children some more quality time together,' Mim said, heading swiftly to the driver's door and away from this ugly social moment.

'Shame, Mim, maybe next time.' Bindi flashed her laser-whitened teeth insincerely at Mim, displaying for an instant her savage incisors.

'Goodbye then,' Mim said tightly as she started up the engine.

'See you later when your hair is straighter,' the trio screeched back at her as they stalked down the street.

~20~

Mother Earth

Mim didn't match. Well, obviously, given that she had a different bag over each arm and a different shoe on each foot. She stood debating which worked best with her raspberry Alannah Hill chiffon-and-lace skirt and matching three-quarter-sleeve cardigan.

She sighed deeply. The challenge of accessorising was usually so much fun, but lately she seemed to lack the spirit for it.

She'd made an initial effort to find an outfit after the invitation to the Forsythes' fifteen-year wedding anniversary arrived six weeks ago, when a delicious pastel candy-striped box had been hand-delivered by a liveried courier. Lifting the lid she had been greeted by the gorgeous fragrance of French Delbard Roses, the petals of which served as a luxurious bed for a small crystal vase. Mim lifted up the delicate object and it twinkled and shimmered in the sunlight. Engraved on the front was an invitation to the Forsythes' anniversary – crystal, of course.

The thrill of the invitation was soon replaced by the

angst of the ensemble-decision. Normally she relished the thrill of the chase: the strategic planning that went into sourcing a winning outfit balancing the variables of weather, event theme, fashion competition and setting (stilettos would not do if the function was to be set in the Botanic Gardens, for instance). But this time Mim had uncharacteristically left it until the week of the function to begin her ensemble sourcing.

She was aware of the parameters of her task: the Forsythes had invited 250 of their closest and most intimate friends to a garden party to be held at their home in Grange Road, Toorak.

Mim had known Petrice Forsythe from their uni days. However, due to Petrice's recent attachment to LJ Mahoney, their friendship of convenience had wilted considerably. Petrice had seemingly used her Arts Degree as a convenient fill-in until she snared herself an appropriately wealthy and socially well-positioned husband in her late twenties.

So what if it was politically incorrect, Petrice had told herself – wasn't feminism all about having the right to choose?

Mim and James had been guests at Petrice and Montgomery's opulent three-day wedding in the Bahamas, and still caught up with the Forsythes occasionally, usually at the yacht club over a Pinot Gris or at their famous marquee at the Spring Racing Carnival. Monty came from ancient money with tenuous links to a title. His family's strong dealings in the futures market had freed Monty up for a life of golf-course networking, beach-side 'business' lunches and weekly schmoozes with Daddy over a game of squash.

Together, Petrice and Monty made a formidable partnership based on shallowness, consumerism and shameless social climbing. Mim and James often shared a giggle over the Forsythes' latest wild extravagance: the sea-cruising yacht upon which neither would set foot; the Geelong Grammar boarding school education for their eldest children – both sent away before their tenth birthdays.

And the naming of the children – each after the exotic location in which they were conceived. Poor Morocco, Roma and Tuscany would never live it down.

Sometimes Mim felt a twinge of jealousy at the ultra-privileged lifestyle of the Forsythes. When they had snapped up a chalet in Vail, for instance, she had been shocked to find herself feeling discontented with her own life and wishing for a bit of the Forsythe glamour.

A week before the big event she had tried summoning the energy for her traditional reconnaissance trip but despite visiting all her familiar Melbourne hunting grounds – the QV, GPO, and of course Chapel Street – she found no inspiration for her mission. She traipsed from boutique to boutique, waiting for the expected fashion excitement to build, but somehow she just didn't feel the same thrill of anticipation or the familiar urgency to get the perfect outfit for the event.

In the end she'd settled on the Alannah Hill because it was there; it fitted; it was pretty and it would do. She'd hung it in her wardrobe without a thought for accessories.

Which is why she was standing there, an hour before the function began, with odd shoes and two bags.

She assessed her image in her floor-to-ceiling mirror one more time, and suddenly felt a smile tickling her lips. For goodness' sake, she'd been standing here asymmetrically for more than twenty minutes trying to decide on handbags and shoes. What was her life coming to, she wondered, shaking her head

Such essential decisions once haunted her. Deciding well in advance what or 'who' she was wearing was imperative for her enjoyment of the event. Failing to make a firm accessory decision at this stage was terribly out of character and Mim vaguely wondered if maybe she needed a vitamin supplement.

Focus, she told herself, reassessing the situation.

The Miu-Miu bag with the Jimmy Choo stilettos? Or the more decorous Stepford Wives look of new clutch teamed with slingbacks?

She gave a little shiver, and finally made the correct accessory choice – she chose not to give a shit. She tossed one bag back on the shelf and grabbed a pair of shoes at random. And, as she'd suspected, the sky did not fall down.

Petrice's tongue toyed nervously with her pinkie acrylic, her sharp incisors threatening to nibble the delicate coral. The weather was infuriating.

Petrice had refused to back down on her plan for an outdoor event despite the teeming rain; the forces of nature were no match for her steely resolve that this meticulously planned celebration of her life – oh, and Monty's – would be a social success.

She had spent weeks directing landscape renovation and outdoor furniture purchase to create a sumptuous backdrop for her garden party and she refused to accept a crimp in her plans at this late stage.

Harry the Hirer had sent a crew and another marquee around as an emergency delivery first thing in the morning and the team had still been tramping muddy boots over the sandstone-paved path at 11 a.m. They'd finished just in time for the gardening team to power-spray the pavers.

The new marquee had no walls so as not to restrict the sweeping views of the Forsythes' lavish gardens. The poles were awash with ribbons and flowers, the tables groaning under hand-carved ice-sculptures, floral art and lashings of platters boasting an array of dips, antipasto, slivers of chilled wagyu beef and insalates presented as tiny artworks of texture and colour.

The immaculately groomed guests sipped champagne and swapped anecdotes under the canvas, soaking in the glamour of the event and thanking their lucky stars they'd been among the fortunate to score an invite.

As the bubbly flowed, the boasts grew louder and more elaborate and Mim found herself perspiring from the collected heat fuelled by enormous gas heaters under the marquee. She weaved through the throng of partygoers to the edge of the makeshift room and gazed over at the verdant expanse. Mim felt detached from the milling crowd at her back and a sense of unreality settled over her. It all seemed so pointless and inconsequential and she felt disconcertingly like an actor who'd forgotten her script.

She looked back at the party. Everyone else seemed to be in the right place, comfortable with their role; it was just she who felt as if life had struck a discordant note – who seemed to be grappling with a sense of discontent.

'Mim, how are you?'

Mim turned and greeted the couple with cursory lip-grazes across their cheeks. It was awkward for a moment there because the Mortimers had just returned from three months in Europe and were currently doing the kiss-each-cheek thing, which made things a bit tricky. The recipient of the kiss would be leaning back just as the second kiss was coming in for a landing, so would have to make a last-minute direction change. It was all very annoying.

'Clive, Isabelle, how lovely to see you both,' Mim said with barely concealed boredom.

'Mim, darling, how are you?' yelped Isabelle. 'We haven't seen you guys since we got back! You look fabulous!'

'Thanks, Isabelle, how was Italy?'

'Ohmigod! Faaaabulous!'

'Isabelle!' said a bright voice from behind their little group.

'Monique! Malcolm!' said Isabelle in response.

'Malcolm, Clive,' Monique introduced the men.

'Mim!' said Clive, with a kiss and an arm squeeze.

'Mim, darling,' said Monique, when it was her turn at Mim's cheek.

'Hello Malcolm, Monique,' said Mim, trying really hard to smile and defeat the urge to walk away from these forced niceties.

'Where's Tiffany?' Monique asked, scanning the crowd behind Mim.

'Oh, she's in Portsea,' Mim replied with a knowing smile.

'Really, what's she doing there?' Monique asked, surprised that someone would be down on the Peninsula out of season.

'Not sure. The Mortimers were just telling us about their trip,' Mim offered weakly, hoping to distract Monique.

'Yes,' squeaked Isabelle, a wee mouse of a woman, who insisted on always wearing flat shoes, a habit that bugged Mim today more than usual. Why should normal-height people get a bad back from leaning over to talk to her when she should just follow fashion like a normal woman and gain a couple of inches and save the rest of them a dose of sciatica. She leaned slightly left past Clive's rounded shoulders to try to send a help signal to James, but he was involved in an in-depth debate with Bernard Worthington over the virtues of Australian Rules versus Rugby League. That'll only end in tears, she thought to herself.

'How was your little jaunt o.s.?' Monique continued.

'Well,' said Isabelle, glancing at each face to ensure everyone was enraptured enough for her to begin her well-rehearsed tale. 'Paris in winter, you can only begin to guess what an enchanted fairytale city it is!' she prattled.

Mim's concentration dropped in and out as the group compared international five-star adventures.

'. . . the trout was bone dry, honestly, it's not like it was business class . . .'

'. . . so I said, now listen here, my good man, in MY country . . .'

'. . . not a word of English, would you credit it . . .'

'. . . couldn't get a good steak for love or money . . .'

'. . . the five-series, who'd drive a five-series . . .'

'. . . there are SOOO many Italians in Tuscany . . .'

She just couldn't focus. Normally Mim prided herself on her keen conversational skills; smiling, nodding and genuinely listening to others. But today it was as if she could peer through the flimsiness of their topics and see each comment for what it really was – just a tragic and thinly veiled attempt by each speaker to grandstand and self-promote while subtly trumping their companions.

Mim just didn't want to play any more.

She glanced at the marquee frame, swathed under a cloyingly fragrant garland of roses and gardenias. Mim noticed a trail of rainwater steadily travelling from the roof down the ribbon to the pole's base where a small mud puddle had developed. It was a tiny bruise in the over-managed lawn, a fleck of reality in the intricately constructed vista.

Mim watched the mini-estuary fill the tiny dam. The mud was rich, dark and inviting. Her frustration dissipated as she admired the wet loamy dirt and imagined the cool earth beneath her hot, sticky feet.

Before she'd even consciously decided to move, Mim had slipped off her stiletto sandal and allowed her foot to hover over the puddle.

The promise of the cool, soft, earth was tantalising and Mim slid her foot quietly into the mud. The black, rich ooze squelched through her toes and she had a sudden flash of butter and Vegemite worming through the holes of Salada; simple pleasures from simpler days.

The moist earth welcomed her tired foot, and her other foot ached in jealousy.

She wiggled her toes and the mud caressed them deliciously. Her foot buried deeper, fully encased now in its nurturing dirtiness.

Mim suddenly became aware of her immediate surroundings. She realised the chatter nearby had stopped. With one foot in the mud, like a child with her hand caught in the cookie jar, she looked guiltily up at the group.

All four were staring at her in stunned silence.

'Mim, what *are* you doing?' Isabelle asked in a voice usually reserved for the mentally unstable.

'Just, well, just . . .' Mim trailed off. How could she respond? It was a stupid question really, they were all standing there, they could see *what* she was doing. She guessed what Isabelle was really asking was why. And that was a question that Mim, quite frankly, couldn't answer.

Mim turned her back on the group and stepped out into what was now a steady drizzle. She wiped her muddy foot onto the wet grass, which made quite an effective loofah. The spikiness of the buffalo grass stimulated the bottom of her foot and she giggled. The sound that burbled forth from her lips surprised her. She didn't laugh enough these days.

The rigid blades against her sole also felt a little, well, erotic, if truth be known.

James suddenly appeared at the edge of the staring group.

'Hey Mim,' he called out, 'do you want a towel?' – as if he was completely accustomed to this type of behaviour, thought Isabelle disapprovingly, with a sidelong glance at the husband.

James was in fact quite accustomed to this kind of behaviour, because this was exactly the Mim-type of stuff that he'd fallen in love with. Spontaneous acts of fountain-dancing, random busker-karaoke and, of course, his all-time favourite, her penchant for skinny-dipping.

She smiled and shook her head, so he walked out into the rain to join his wife, whose immaculately straightened hair was now all dishevelled. He held her by the elbows and kissed her on the nose as she looked up at him and said, 'I'm starving. Have you been up to the buffet yet?'

~21~

School Daze

The elaborate wrought-iron gate slammed shut behind Mim and locked fast with a resounding clang.

She shuddered at the finality of the sound – she was trapped, there was no going back on her classroom-helper duty now, and the thought of spending time in the rarefied air of Langholme Grammar filled her with dread. She always seemed to feel guilty about something as soon as she stepped onto the grounds. Her hair always felt wild and out of control, her voice too high or her vowels hideously flat. It was just like reliving her own cloistered schooldays.

The imposing century-old, ivy-clad buildings seemed to glower at her as she tiptoed around the finely manicured front lawn. The school had been secured with key-code locks since last summer when a paparazzi photographer snuck in to snap a prominent sportsman's son after the father had been involved in a nasty sex scandal involving a weather-girl and a selection of vegetables.

Conventionally the realm of bankers, QCs and the like, Langholme Grammar had enjoyed a proud tradition of educating only fine, upstanding citizens. But unfortunately, recent enrolments had been awash with the sons of media types, actors, tennis players and footballers. And now it seemed even tradespeople were managing to afford the exorbitant fee – rumour had it that a *plumber*'s child was part of the latest influx of blue-collar entrants.

Mim skirted the ostentatious fountain, which spouted water over a Greek antique statue depicting Ares, the God of War, in the centre of the main lawn. She climbed the white front steps that led up from the stone circular driveway to the grand façade of the main building. Then she slid through the ostentatious front door and made her way down the hushed corridor. Times-table chants floated out of closed doors and the tortured notes of a violin lesson reverberated down the curves of the sweeping main staircase.

A wayward student, obviously caught in the act of eating in class, was standing with his sandwich on his head faced into a corner of the hall. Mim gave him a wink of encouragement as he peeped out at her.

The rooms in the original building crouched off narrow, high-ceilinged corridors through which the bitter winter wind whistled and the oppressive summer heat sweltered. Refurbishment hadn't quite reached these Grade Six rooms where the Heritage code had to be obeyed before trivial concerns such as student comfort were considered. Besides, the hefty building budget had recently bottomed out after the completion of the fashionable Early Learning Centre and Prep areas.

As ELCs became de rigueur at all the best schools, Langholme had acted quickly to keep up with the trend toward forcing children only just out of toddlerhood into teeny ties and restricting blazers. The school now had both Montessori and Reggio Emilia learning styles offered in the purpose-built centres, greenhouses and meeting areas.

The three-, four- and five-year-olds enjoyed an enormous range of educational activities, specialised classes and school excursions. Every single sensory experience was available in order to demonstrate a highly accurate model of the outside world to the children wrenched from it.

Mim walked through the swinging door that took her from the old building into the more modern lower-primary section. These children enjoyed air-conditioning, heating, and carpeted hallways. Two Grade Six children passed by Mim in deep conversation. Obviously one was attempting to convince the other to forego his lunch-time and join the school choir: '. . . you'll be thwilled with our contempowy piece, it'th a wollicking thea shanty, thuch fun!' he lisped. But by the look of his friend's downcast eyes, the petite blond lad had not landed a convert.

The more comfortable surroundings did little to help Mim relax. She hated being here. She hated classroom-helper days. It reminded her so much of her own private-schooldays where facts and figures were drummed into the students through tedious hours of revision and rote learning. And what she'd seen of the boys' school (as little as possible, if she was honest) showed that not much had changed since her time.

Of course, schools such as Langholme Grammar were vital to her boys' future, she reminded herself. The Old Boys' network was strong, the school's reputation was impeccable and her sons would land good uni spots and jobs just by association. It was just unfortunate it was all so . . . so, well, so awful.

But the school's facilities were among the best in the country: the sculpture studio, the Olympic-sized pool, gym and sports fields, the school orchestra, symphony and choral groups, the television studio and state-of-the-art technology centre were worth every cent. And the headmaster was truly a gun salesman. During the initial school tour he'd made Mim and James feel like child abusers if they *didn't* send their boys there.

So here they were, with matching socks, template haircuts and surrounded by a thousand other boys.

Mim had never been in trouble during her own school career; she'd always been a diligent student, yet this place made her feel so naughty. She imagined that the teachers were scowling at her as she walked past them in their long black robes, with their arms full of important-looking books. And she was a parent, for chrissakes – how in the world would it make her two small boys feel?

Charley's classroom door was shut firmly, a note on its exterior scolding: 'Parents must not talk at drop-off time' in thick black texta.

Mim inwardly groaned as she saw that Hortense Mathews was to be her partner today and was already set up in the private reading room situated outside the classroom. Hortense was the ultimate suck-up, attaching herself to the movers and shakers of Langholme society like a starving leech. This year she'd decided LJ Mahoney was her best bet for soaking up some dimly reflected glory.

One could usually detect Hortense's presence by the trademark snorts and whinnies she used to punctuate her speech, well before setting eyes on her. 'MIM! How aaaaaaare you, dahhhling?' she brayed now, ignoring the Prep child whose laborious reading she had been pretending to pay attention to moments before.

'Fine, thanks, Hortense,' Mim replied, heading for the box of reading folders. 'Is this the batch that we're working from today?'

'Yes, it is. I've started at the front with dear little Jimmy here,' replied Hortense, stretching back her lips to reveal an alarmingly large set of teeth. 'You look FAAABULOUS, as always, Mim, really, you do . . . really, I'm not just saying it . . . you really really do. Really,' Hortense finished with a snort of glee, and paused, waiting for Mim to return the compliment, as one does. But Mim simply flashed her a slightly startled glance as she entered the classroom.

Mrs Keith looked up from instructing a group of boys how to cut out the photocopied rabbits they were creating. 'Mrs Woolcott,' she said, bustling over, her substantial bosom threatening to escape the buttons of a dull grey dress. She took her reading glasses off and let them swing from her neck on their gold chain.

'Good morning, Mrs Keith, is there anything you need in here?' Mim asked with fingers crossed; anything to escape the Hortense onslaught. 'Or should I simply do the boys' readers?'

'The readers are fine, but I wanted to discuss something with you first, very briefly.'

'Oh, yes?' Mim asked with concern. 'What is it?'

'Well it's Charley, I am quite worried about him,' Mrs Keith said, pursing her lips and pulling her chin onto her chest to create a most inordinate number of chins, Mim thought distractedly, before turning her attention to the disquieting matter at hand.

'Ohmigod, whatever is the problem?' she asked, her hand fluttering to her chest.

'It's his colouring-in. He can't – no, let me rephrase that – he *won't* stay within the lines. He's doing it on purpose,' Mrs Keith declared in the manner of a judge passing sentence.

'Sorry?' Mim had to ask, because she was sure she'd just misheard.

'He will not colour within the lines, Mrs Woolcott. We had a giraffe to colour the other day and instead of colouring it in orange, like everybody else in the room, he coloured *outside* the lines – quite deliberately – in navy, and didn't colour the giraffe in at all,' Mrs Keith finished breathlessly, her bosom heaving.

'Did you ask him about it?' asked Mim, feeling a sense of unreality about the entire conversation.

'I most certainly did, and he had the impertinence to say that it was an albino giraffe in the middle of the night.' Mrs Keith took a deep, shuddering breath at the memory.

'Wow, I didn't think he knew what albino meant.' Mim suddenly forgot herself.

'Mrs Woolcott, that is hardly the point.' The teacher waggled a plump finger in Mim's face. 'This is not the first time, you know – there was another occasion when his penchant for outside-the-line scribbling was particularly rampant, and do you know what he told me?' Mrs Keith was by now on a roll and Mim decided to let her just continue. 'He told me his mother told him to always think outside the lines and that's what he was doing,' she spluttered with indignation, looking accusingly at Mim. Then pulling herself together, Mrs Keith perched her glasses back onto the end of her nose: 'I said, "Charley Woolcott, there is no way your mother told you to scribble outside the lines", and I stood over him until he did it properly,' she finished triumphantly.

Mim looked over at her precious six-year-old boy, his blond hair falling gently into his eyes as he frowned in concentration at the task in front of him. His fingers, squeezed tightly around his crayon, bore the chubby reminder that he was still so little. His tongue poked sweetly through his full lips and Mim felt her heart surge with a bittersweet mix of love and regret.

'So you stood over my son until he did it your way, did you?' Mim said quietly, her eyes flicking over the teacher angrily. If James had been there he would have known that she was using her dangerous voice and would have advised Mrs Keith to tread very carefully.

'Yes,' the stout woman answered with pursed lips, 'I certainly did.'

'Hmmmm . . . well, you know what,' Mim said, a thousand inappropriate words rushing into her head, 'I've just remembered that Charley has a dental appointment, so I'll be taking him out of class for the rest of the day. Goodbye.'

Without a backward glance she swung Charley from his seat, stamped out of the room and to her son's amazed delight the two of them spent the rest of the day giggling and chatting as they painted multicoloured animals all over huge sheets of butcher paper on the playroom floor at home.

~22~

Stripper on Canvas

Ellie was a celebration of slavish devotion to brands and fashion as she breezed into the café for the obligatory Monday morning lattes with the Langholme mums, a gossip opportunity for all different factions of the parent community. Her tiny flared-leg Seven jeans made the most of her toned thighs and non-existent butt; the white Guess T-shirt stretched suggestively over her enviable breasts and her blonde and multi-highlighted tresses were held in place by her Gucci frameless sunglasses – which had little other purpose on this grey Melbourne day.

The seat at the head of the table had, by unspoken agreement, been left vacant for Ellie, and as she unquestioningly took her prime position she sang out 'Morning dahlings' and blew Mim, at the far end, a fingertip kiss.

The coffee and complaints were already flowing, though the mums interrupted their conversations to register Ellie's outfit, study her make-up and wonder how she got her hair so shiny, before greeting her.

'A latte as a matter of some urgency, good man,' she instructed the waiter at her elbow.

'And breakfast for madam?' he asked naively.

'Oh good lord, no,' she replied, tuning in to the conversations surging around her.

'. . . that's just ridiculous,' one mother cried, 'they can't make him go swimming if he has a scratchy throat, it's simply not medically appropriate.'

'Well absolutely not. I was livid. I've already scheduled dialogue with the principal, let me tell you. I trust Willie's self-diagnostic decisions now that he's in the second grade. That boy knows a malady coming on when he feels it. Goodness knows the complication that may now arise from his contamination in that bacteria-ridden cesspit. I've insisted the doctor start him on a strict course of antibiotics for safety's sake.'

'Good plan,' Ellie agreed, clapping her hands in glee, shaking a few dozen grains of sugar into her latte. She loved a confrontation, even if it was vicarious. 'When Rupert insisted on taking that awful sink plunger to school with him for weeks, at first I didn't have a problem with it really. I mean he was five and who knows what nonsense goes through a boy's head at that age. Bryce is fifty-two for goodness' sake, and he still has fixations on new toys and gadgets. He still sleeps with his mobile on vibrate, I mean what's that about?

'Anyhoo, then Mrs Hargreaves asked us to authorise an assessment for Rupert from the school psychologist: apparently he had full-blown plunger issues – which of course can be quite common in the gifted – but one hardly wants to be given such a terrible fright by a teacher. For goodness' sake, what do teachers know about children?' Ellie took a break from her caffeine-induced ramble.

'So, LJ, sweetie,' said Hortense, displaying the teeth and

laugh of a well-bred mare. 'When's the next big exhibit? Got anything in the pipeline?'

'Yes, LJ, what's happening next? Loved the last one,' piped up Rosy Glow (tragic how she'd changed her name after taking a course on aura reading).

LJ Mahoney flicked her talon-like nails and looked coyly down at the table for all of a second before favouring the other mums with an electric smile and tossing back her hair dramatically. She loved an audience and shone into life under the warm gaze of attention she was commanding.

'Well,' she began, with her long fingers splayed forward, looking left and right to ensure that every ear at the table was hers and speaking slowly to maximise the limelight. 'I have had just the most delicious opportunity float right under my pretty little nose!' She scrunched the said proboscis and giggled merrily.

Not a bad nose for $20,000, thought Ellie.

'But back to the story. Philby recently snapped up a simply to-die-for Victorian building in Swanston Street. He's going to relocate the PR firm; so much more CBD, really. When he popped in for a look-see he realised that it was the former premises of Club 22, which was that swanky little strip club back in the late seventies, early eighties. I mean, what a scream. I died with laughter when he told me. To think of all those rich old men who used to frequent it and those slutty little numbers who entertained them. It's just too fabulous.

'Anyway, Philbs found the most divine treasure-trove of original posters and advertising material from the club's heyday. It's so tits-and-arse, girls, like you wouldn't believe!'

She paused as Hortense snorted with unattractive and truly unacceptable laughter.

'So,' LJ continued, arching an over-waxed eyebrow at her friend. 'You should see this stuff – it's gold! Buxom strippers in gaudy silver platform boots, straddling poles, tiny silver stars glued to their tits. And the hair, my god, bouffed up, flicked back, it's a wonder they can hold their little heads up. The graphic design is unreal: balloon typefaces, rainbows. It's so kitsch it's cool.'

'And so retro, so *now*,' said Rosy.

'Oh it's so now it's almost tomorrow,' LJ enthused. 'Très zeitgeist, girls. You know how I love to stay ahead of the game.' She licked her scarlet lips with delight and ran her fingers through her cherry-red hair. 'Of course, it all needs an artistic touch, girls, these club promoters were hardly artists and most of the chicks in the pictures could do with their share of air-brushing.' She paused as Hortense honked annoyingly. 'Sooooo, I'm going to enlarge the brochures, lime wash some of the images, collage others. I'll be a busy little buzzy bee, let me tell you.

'And,' this last bit of news was the icing on the cake for LJ and she enunciated carefully so her words could have their intended effect. 'I have one special little piece that's going to look particularly good as the hero shot: blown up life-size, to underscore the entire exhibit. It's of a gorgeous young girl with a sad little face wearing these amazing purple cork-wedged sandals, and . . . well . . . poor love, not much else,' she tittered gaily. 'You should see it, Ellie, you'd so love it.'

'Sounds fab,' murmured Ellie.

'Oh, LJ, how amazing, you clever little pussycat,' chipped in another voice.

'How superb,' sang another.

'You are such a visual genius.'

'Aren't you the artistic one?'

LJ closed her eyes and let the gentle balm of adoration wash over her. She sighed with contentment and smiled around at these silly women who wouldn't know art if it kicked them in the arse.

'What do you think, Ellie, do you remember Club 22?' she asked serenely.

'Oh, yes,' said Ellie vaguely, sipping her latte, 'I think so, but it's been closed for years, hasn't it?'

'Oh yes, it's so passé, of course, that's what makes it so now. I mean, do those sorts of dirty little places even exist any more? With my help, the memories will be all shiny and new and given a slick millennium twist for my opening next month.' LJ smiled and turned back to Hortense to savagely suggest she try laughing with her mouth shut in future.

Ellie sat quietly as the conversation ebbed and flowed around her. Mim had had enough of the shallow chatter and one-upmanship and wondered if she dared skip next week's session. Then she noticed Ellie's vacant look from the other end of the table, and, realising that something was bothering her friend, picked up her mobile.

Ellie pulled the tinkling phone from her crocodile-skin bag and read the new SMS.

Blow this scene? My house? the text read.

GR8, Ellie texted back, and waited for Mim to air-kiss her way around the table before making her own escape.

Ellie came to an abrupt stop in Mim's driveway but made no move to get out of the car so Mim came to see what was happening.

She walked to the driver's door and saw in horror that Ellie had her head down on the steering wheel and was sobbing her heart out, which was obviously a bad sign – Ellie would never waste good make-up unless it was something serious.

'Oh, Ellie, sweetie, darling, what's the matter?' asked Mim, putting her hand on Ellie's shaking back and feeling the knotty ridges of her spine.

'Oh, Mim,' said Ellie, looking up at her friend through blackened eyes. What a day to forget the waterproof mascara. 'Oh Mim,' she repeated, and her huge turquoise-blue eyes re-filled with tears. Her cheeks glowed pink and her hair framed her face, making her look like a vulnerable waif.

Why don't I look this good when I'm miserable? thought Mim as she helped Ellie out of the car and into the house. 'Sit down, sweetheart, let me get you some water.'

Mim grabbed mountain-bottled spring water from the fridge and poured it into a crystal beaker, adding ice cubes, a slice of lemon and a sprig of mint. Picking up a napkin, she set the glass on a coaster on the mahogany coffee table in front of Ellie, who was denying her perfect posture by hunching over like a factory worker who had found the weight of the world too much to bear.

'Mim, what I'm about to tell you is something that I can trust only you with,' Ellie said moistly. 'I haven't told anybody this before, and I know that you won't judge me.' She sniffed noisily and, slightly shocked, Mim jumped up to pass her an embossed, scented, over-sized tissue.

'Of course I won't judge you,' she said, looking at Ellie with great concern. 'What on earth is happening?'

'Well,' Ellie took a deep breath, and blew it out towards the ceiling with her eyes closed. Opening her eyes again and looking straight at Mim, she said, 'I am the girl in the purple cork-wedged sandals.'

~23~

Ellie's Reveal

'THE BITCH!'

'The bitch, I know, she's a complete bitch,' replied Ellie.

'She knows it's you, she must know,' said Mim.

'I know, of course she knows what she's doing, she's doing it on purpose.'

'But . . . but . . . why? What a BITCH!!' Mim was furious. She stood up, and started pacing; she wanted to punch something, preferably a red-headed smug little bitch. What kind of community was she a part of where such nasty backstabbing was so commonplace? It wasn't a *community* at all. People like LJ were only looking out for number one and everyone in their way just got burnt. Mim just didn't want to be a part of it any more, she wanted out. She stopped and stood at the floor-to-ceiling plate glass window and stared futilely at the storm clouds forming in the distance.

'I know,' Ellie replied, sounding resigned. 'She's a nasty piece of work and she's doing it on purpose, and there's nothing I can do to stop her.'

'But you never trashed her stupid exhibit in the first place, can't you just explain that to her?' Mim asked, desperately thinking of a way to help her friend and stop this avalanche of humiliation.

'Hang on a minute,' she said, turning slowly, with a quizzical look on her face. 'What on earth were you doing in purple cork wedges at Studio 22?'

'Well, here's the thing,' said Ellie, sighing deeply, and she told Mim her story.

Ellie Fitzpatrick was trapped in a hideous life. There was no way out. She couldn't see any kind of happiness in her future. She could only see more junkie-filled parties, more strange men hitting on her and nowhere for her and her little sister Sarah to turn.

Her eventual escape came from the most unexpected source: her next-door neighbour Roxanne. Two years older than the gentle Ellie, she was a real wild child. Ever since they were small children, Roxanne had lived on the edge. Smoking at seven, hooking up with boys at twelve, dope at thirteen. Ellie and Roxanne had little in common except for the dysfunctional and violent home lives they had both endured, and thus an unlikely friendship had formed.

The whole street had witnessed constant screaming matches between Roxanne and her family. The fights usually resulted in Roxanne slamming their front door and going straight over to Ellie's house to drag her to the park, where they would sit in the bright red plastic globe at the top of the A-frame slide and smoke and talk about their rotten lives and what they were going to do when they were rich and famous and out of this place.

One day Roxanne took off, but this time she didn't stop at Ellie's house. She had just turned fifteen and no-one saw her for the next year. Ellie hadn't relied on Roxanne as much as the older girl had needed Ellie's sympathetic ear and therefore didn't miss her. Her younger sister Sarah filled the void of confidante and they grew closer as they faced the debauchery of their household together.

When Roxanne eventually returned she was different. She had new sexy clothes, a more angular, harder face. She was just back to collect her things. 'I've done it, Ellie, I've blown this scene.' They sat in their usual hang out, smoking SuperMild and drinking Tab. 'Ya gotta come and see me work: I'm in show business, I'm a real live dancer. And I get paid a fucking fortune.'

So, when her sister Sarah was safe at school, Ellie went to see Roxanne work and was not at all surprised to discover that Roxanne's job was at a strip club. To Roxanne, coming from her grey and dingy world, the sparkling mirrored disco balls, red plush banquette seating and strobe lights were as glamorous as any show-business job.

After that, Ellie would often escape the violence and misery of her life to visit Roxanne at the club. She loved the kindly Mrs Mac who worked in the 'Wardrobe Department' (this was just a glamorous way of saying she cleaned the filthy club, patched up the pieces of scrap the girls called costumes, and mended the never-ending stream of broken hearts and bruised bodies). But to Ellie Mrs Mac was a maternal figure who would listen to her teen worries and offer advice and comfort. Ellie loved being in that 'Wardrobe Department' more than anywhere in the world, and if she hadn't had to go home and care for Sarah, she'd have stayed there and helped Mrs Mac all night as well as all day.

Ellie loved the girls too: girls just like her, every one with a different sad story to tell, everyone optimistic about the future and looking forward to a time when they could escape. She'd spend hours chatting, helping them with their clothes, and giggling with them, just like the group of teenage girls that they were. It made her feel like she was part of a real family for the first time in her life.

Then the manager sprung her hanging around. Ellie had blossomed and there was no hiding her generous bust-line and long, slim legs. Cowboy Nick was a short, stubby man, whose pocked face glistened under a sheen of grease. His trademark burgundy polyester pants and pink ruffled shirt competed with his slicked hair and large side-burns for ugliness. The clink of his signature gold bracelets and oversized opal cufflinks gave away any hope of a silent approach, though he usually avoided the 'cattle-cars', as he liked to call the dressing rooms. He would just hit on the girls when they were working the bar after their show. But one day he wandered backstage and noticed Ellie sitting in the dressing room chatting to Roxanne. Her youth and innocence glowed beside his jaded, worn out old tarts in their faded sequins.

He stalked the fresh meat. He began by separating her from her pack, blocking her exit when the other girls ran on stage for the finale. He favoured her with lecherous grins, a slap on the arse or a tweak of her breast each time he passed, until Ellie was terrified and confused.

But the slime ball was after something more than merely a quick grope and poke. One day he barrelled her up in an empty dressing room, with his filthy paw up her school dress and his hot breath on her neck. He knew she would beg for mercy. She did, and he made his move with a deal: 'Go on stage and I'll leave you alone.'

Ellie stressed over the decision for weeks but finally realised that she was trapped. And the only way out of the trap was money. She needed to earn enough to buy her and Sarah's escape from their miserable existence. And she'd seen how well it had worked for Roxanne, who now had her own flat and was in control of her own life.

The offer – albeit a sleazy one – of a well-paid job was in fact a blessing, and she swallowed her pride – and her modesty – and went back to the club.

So Ellie became an 'exotic dancer'. The girls gave her a makeover to hide her youth. She stopped going to school. The money was good, but the tips she got after from 'working the bar' were unbelievable. Her wide-eyed naivety and little-girl charm had all the punters throwing the bills at her. They particularly loved the fact that she pretended to be scared of them.

Then one day, just a few months after she started, Bryce came in. He didn't usually frequent Club 22, but as the producer of a high-rating football program he often catered to the tastes of his on-screen talent.

He took one look at the fresh-faced Ellie on the stage and just wanted to protect her. He spoke to her as soon as she entered the public area after her performance. Ellie was attracted to him immediately. He was no Greek god, but in his eyes Ellie saw a warmth and honesty she had never known.

They started dating and married a few months later.

'And that's that,' said Ellie, looking up at her confidante. 'That's the real "Ellie Fitzpatrick" story. Not very sophisticated, is it?'

'Oh, Ellie,' said Mim, throwing her arms around her friend. 'What a story. You poor love. Whatever happened to your mum?'

'What you'd expect. She overdosed one day about a year after Sarah and I left home,' Ellie said with only a hint of sadness. 'She was young and stupid and so screwed up. There was really no hope for her.'

'I am sure that LJ wouldn't exhibit if she knew the real story.' Mim was back on the issue at hand.

'It's none of her damn business, Mim,' Ellie said tersely. 'There's no way I am going to bare my soul to that mercenary little social climber. Let her go for it. Good on her. I could not care less. And, Mim, you must promise me you will keep out and not even hint about this to her.'

'Absolutely, Ellie,' Mim agreed. 'I'll control myself, I promise.'

'You're a good friend, Mim, thank you. Now let's cross our fingers and hope Bryce doesn't lose it completely when he finds out what she's done.'

~24~

On With the Show

June 2000

Liz was on a mission, and she was running out of time and – quite frankly – out of patience trying to navigate her black Volvo through the grungy back streets of St Kilda.

The bayside suburbs were a bit of a mystery to Liz, who felt that one could find all one needed in High Street, Armadale, thank you very much. But apparently a new vibe had come into the area and it was becoming quite acceptable, with its fashionable boutiques and opulent stores. That was the problem with this new millennium: now that it was the year 2000 everything old was new again – it was so hard to keep up!

Besides, Liz just had to have a cashmere piece to wear to today's party – Ellie's little Rupert was turning two years old – who could believe it that all their babies were suddenly toddlers. All the best people had been turning up at casual luncheons and coffee mornings wrapped in darling little cashmere throws, twin-sets and boleros from a new little boutique called 8 Inkerman. Now Liz could stand it no longer: she wanted cashmere today, if it killed her.

Stopped in her quest by traffic lights, she drummed her fingers on the leather steering wheel and peered out through her tinted windows with interest. What a mélange of colour and activity, she thought. It's almost artistic, in an earthy, urban way – like one of those paintings one sees of turn-of-the-century peasant life.

A very young mother in a kaleidoscopic outfit of hessian, complete with turban, rocked a stroller while waiting at a bus-stop. Two young men leaned against a wall, with bare feet and torn jeans, sharing a bottle in a paper bag. Their eyes were blank, their bodies limp and lethargic with defeat. A blonde Rastafarian busked on the corner. The suited businessmen animatedly chattering on mobile phones were juxtaposed with the Aboriginal group in the park. The prostitutes plied their trade on street corners with blank faces and minimal clothing.

Soaking up the atmosphere of the streets, Liz suddenly felt an overwhelming sadness at the huge contrast of this area, where the poverty-stricken, the drug-addicted, the affluent and the fashionable walked side by side, yet miles apart.

The Volvo came to a stop at the Fitzroy Street lights, perpendicular to a laneway. With an almost perverse voyeurism Liz scanned the alley to see what this seedy side of the suburb would reveal. What at first glance she had dismissed as a pile of discarded rags against a mini-skip, Liz quickly realised was actually a person curled in the foetal position, a shabby coat pulled over the top for warmth. As if sensing the scrutiny of another, the street-kid slowly lifted her head and locked eyes with Liz for a fleeting second.

Poor love, Liz thought to herself. God, there were so many to help that some days she felt overwhelmed with a sense of powerlessness. She looked again as the child put her head back down on her knees, her matted black hair now all that was visible.

Something shifted inside Liz. Something flew, just out of sight, across her mind. There was something about those eyes, that face seemed familiar somehow.

The lights changed and Liz, struggling to reach a slippery thought at the edge of her mind, eased the car back into gear and steadied her foot over the accelerator, taking a last look into the alley. She was set to pull away as a sickening rush of realisation flooded her consciousness.

It was her. The eyes, the hair, the set of her face all told her that this was the daughter she'd thought she'd lost. Liz pulled on the hand-brake with little consideration for the traffic behind her, leapt from the car and ran awkwardly in her Chanel pumps towards the girl. 'Mikaylah,' she shouted as she ran towards the child. 'It's me! It's Liz!'

Mikaylah stared at Liz through a drug-induced haze. Her eyes were flat, her features slack, her cheekbones pronounced against the hollow face. Hardened to street life, her instant response was to flee. Few nights passed when somebody didn't chase her for sex, drugs, money or food.

She staggered to her feet while Liz was still ten metres away. Liz's shouting was indistinguishable over the car horns honking angrily at the black Volvo and Mikaylah stumbled down the alleyway to escape certain attack.

The alley danced in her heroin-haze, the cobblestones unstable under her feet. Fear drove her on, brought out her animal instincts for survival and forced her wasted body away from the enemy.

From far away across the ocean of her addled mind she heard the cry: 'Mikaylah: is that you?'

Mikaylah had reached her goal. Nestled between two wheelie bins a simple grey door was ajar. The door was at the base of a two storey wall punctuated with steel-barred windows. She staggered toward the entrance shouting, 'Mikaylah's dead!' before disappearing into the darkness.

Liz heard a door slam, and by the time she reached the space between the bins where Mikaylah had fled, the door she had gone through was shut and deadlocked.

Liz hammered on the door and yelled until her voice was hoarse.

'Mikaylah, I am so sorry! Please talk to me!' She looked at the simple hand-painted sign on the door. *St Kilda Angels. A Mission for Life.*

The honking back on Grey Street was escalating, and she looked up to see two policemen standing beside her empty car. She hurriedly made her way back to the vehicle, and after stammering an apology to the boys in blue, jumped behind the wheel to the chorus of angry shouts and horn-blowing from the throng of trapped cars late for their busy and important lives.

Barely unable to see through the tears that streamed from her carefully made-up eyes, Liz concentrated on getting out of the traffic and then parked in the first quiet street she could find. Turning off the engine, she collapsed back into her seat and let her emotions engulf her.

Wracked with sobs, she thought back to the moment that had haunted her for the past two years.

A day hadn't passed where she hadn't begged for time to turn back. To have that thirty seconds again. Regret was a heavy burden, and one she had carried alone ever since she had turned her daughter away from her door as though she was nothing more than a stray dog.

Liz hated herself for what she had done. She thought back to the dinner party that evening two years ago and wondered for the hundredth time how she'd made it through. It had been the first time she and the Mothers'

Group had ever dined together and they still laughed about how vague and distant Liz had been.

Liz could barely remember a minute of that night after Mikaylah showed up on her doorstep merely hours earlier. Her stomach was churning and her thoughts a scattered mess. The memories she'd worked so hard to deny – to bury – had resurfaced with a vengeance, and had lost none of their painful edge despite being hidden away for fifteen years.

Liz had been in emotional agony as she struggled to smile and play the perfect hostess to her new friends that awful night, while inside shards of memory kept rising to slice open old wounds. She just couldn't reconcile the scruffy teenager at her door with the little pink bundle she'd tearfully handed over to a nurse.

'It's for the best,' the nurse had said. 'Just think of the scandal, dear.'

So Liz had handed over her baby, with her sweet rosebud mouth, big dark eyes and cheeks that felt like peach fuzz against Liz's face. Afterwards she was empty, and the hole inside never really filled up. It was simply patched over as Liz swung herself determinedly back into a life that had little meaning to her any more.

Falling pregnant with Roman, her first child, had done little to heal her pain. Subconsciously she felt she had no right to be a mother to this boy, not after giving away her tiny newborn daughter. She hired two nannies so there would be round-the-clock care for her dark-haired infant, but she rarely held him or interacted with him, instead filling her calendar with inane social events that kept her even busier than before her pregnancy.

No one noticed much. After all, she had money and privilege – why should she change nappies and run baths? She was parenting in a perfectly acceptable form for a woman of her rank and position.

Everything had changed the afternoon Mikaylah stepped briefly back into her life. Not only was the wound inside her torn savagely open, another part of her came alive, and more than anything Liz wanted to be a mother to her remaining child. The next day she fired her nannies and started parenting. She quickly found that it helped to ease the pain inside her, but it also provided a bittersweet glimpse into everything she had missed the first time, with her daughter; the daughter she had first given away and now had sent away.

During the bleak year that followed, Roman and her burgeoning friendship with the Mothers' Group girls were the only bright moments in a dark period of depression that descended on Liz. Her guilt was so raw, her soul so grazed with regret, that for the longest time just getting out of bed each day required a sheer force of will that seemed too great to endure. If it weren't for Roman's happy gurgles summoning her, she would have made the Sheridan sheets and silk bedspread her permanent home.

After Roman's first birthday the fog began to lift from Liz. She could see her son changing and growing; could see what a good job she was doing and took strength from that. His unfailing passion for her; his delight at her presence and tears if she even left the room without him stunned her to the core and helped nurse her back to emotional health.

As Roman tottered into his second year, watching him grow and blossom into an adoring toddler made Liz's heart lift even more. A hard kernel of pain still sat squarely in her heart, but she could breathe and live and enjoy life again.

But now this. She had almost come face-to-face with her daughter for the second time, and she had blown it again.

Would she ever get the chance to make it up to Mikaylah?

Liz let out a few jagged gasps as her crying storm abated, then she dried her eyes, reapplied her make-up and considered her position.

At least she knew that Mikaylah was in Melbourne, in St Kilda in fact. She even knew where she had gone for help – she was sure if she turned up there now the teen would be long gone, but at least she had a place to start looking for her.

She started the engine and headed for home, her mind suddenly filled with a plan.

There would be no cashmere today.

~25~

Fun and Games

Present Day

'Darling, you know Mummy doesn't do games,' Monique sighed, waving Sienna and her Bratz dolls away. 'Go on and ask Chloe, I'm sure she'll play fashion models with you. It's Mummy's turn to talk to her friends.'

Sienna skipped away as Monique turned back to the Mothers' Group with a sigh.

'It's just never enough, is it?' she asked. 'We bring them to these gorgeous play centres with . . . with . . . well, with all this stuff . . .' she indicated in the general direction of the play area (which she had never actually set foot in), 'and still they want more. What else do we have to do?'

The Mothers' Group girls murmured sympathetically as they sipped their chai lattes, macchiatos and green tea. They were ensconced in a quiet corner of Monkey Business, the designer indoor-play centre where they met now and again.

Apart from serving great coffee and an interesting range of herbal tea, the best thing about this Malvern play-centre was that the parents' and children's areas were conveniently separated by a thick wall of noise-proof glass. 'We really should do this at home,' Tiffany had remarked in the past more than once.

And with Monique's nanny, Prudie, and Ellie's Ursula on the noisy side of the glass to deal with any tiffs, tantrums or tears, the Mothers' Group only had to wave and smile at their offspring occasionally.

'Anyway, sorry about the interruption, girls,' Monique sighed again. 'Now, where were we? Oh yes, that's right, after-school-care – well, of course they should serve an evening meal. Most definitely! They need to talk to Peter Rowland's Catering, I'm sure he could sort something. It doesn't need to be three courses, two would suffice.'

'Well absolutely,' Ellie drawled in agreement. 'The last thing I want to do when I pick them up at 5.30 p.m. is have two tired, hungry children hassling me for attention and food. Of course, Ursula normally does pick-up . . . but you get my point.'

'It would certainly help me out,' Monique said. 'In fact if they could board during the week that would be a real weight off . . .' she stopped, suddenly embarrassed by her admission. 'Oh, not that I would ever actually do it, of course, it's just that with the long hours in the shop and all . . . anyway, I think the after-school program is so rich and valuable, don't you think? Mitchell came home with the most delightful little craft thingy, which we would never have managed to make at home . . .' She petered off, running out of justifications.

'It's all right, Monique,' Ellie leaned forward to pat her friend's hand. 'We know that you'll soon be working full-time so you'll really need after-school care, you don't have to justify it.'

'It's not that at all,' Monique came back quickly, 'I just

think it's an excellent chance for the children's further development!'

'Of course it is, Monique,' the other mothers assured their friend.

'So is Tiff still in Portsea?' enquired Ellie. 'I haven't seen her in simply ages.'

'Mmmmm,' replied Mim, 'apparently having a detox month or something.' Tiffany had sworn Mim to secrecy and, as much as Mim hated lying to her friends, she was determined to keep Tiff's plan quiet.

'Nice for some,' said Ellie as her mobile trilled 'Dancing Queen', bringing a welcome interruption to the topic of child-care. Ellie listened for a moment then sang into the phone, 'No worries, lovey, see you then.'

She flipped the Motorola shut and, fluffing up her hair where the phone had slightly flattened it, announced sarcastically, 'You'll never guess.'

'Liz's running late?' Mim asked.

Ellie nodded with pursed lips as she dropped the phone back into her Gucci handbag. 'She's hopeless!'

'You can't talk!' Mim said playfully as Ellie grinned.

'She's up to something,' said Monique, 'I'm sure of it. She's always off to secret meetings and she's so hard to get on to during the week.'

'I know, it's weird,' agreed Monique. 'Even I don't know what's going on.'

'Now that is weird, I've never known you not to have your finger on the pulse!' Mim laughed, but for once wasn't envious of Monique's traditional command of gossip.

The girls discussed the interesting topic of Liz and what on earth could keep someone so rich and well-staffed so busy. Surely they'd know if it was a lover, they speculated. And really, Liz was not the type at all for a tawdry love affair.

'Maybe she gambles,' Mim was suggesting as Chloe

came up and tugged at her mother's pristine white sleeve. 'Hmmm?' Mim said distractedly, caught up in the deliciously naughty conversation. 'Oh yes, darling?' she asked, glancing briefly at her sleeve to ensure Chloe had not left grubby fingerprints.

'Come and see the shop Paris and me made,' Chloe said, beaming at her mum. 'It's a supermarket!'

'Oh,' Mim said, torn between the intriguing chat and being a good mummy.

'Come on,' Chloe tugged at her insistently and Mim gave in.

'All right sweetie,' she smiled, then bent towards the other mums. 'Say nothing without me, girls,' she warned.

Mim inspected the makeshift supermarket in the home corner and dutifully admired the 'specials' and the 'check-out', amused to note that her daughter was the shopkeeper and Paris was the 'lady'.

'Lovely, girls, well done,' she said extricating herself as quickly as possible to head back to the table before the others started talking about her.

Ellie had left the table to take a call on her mobile and was standing at the far side of the patisserie counter. Monique wandered over to order a third macchiato (her biorhythms were a tad flat today), but as she got within earshot she could tell from Ellie's tense body language and urgent tone that this was no ordinary chat.

Monique was startled to hear Ellie's normally breezy voice edged with hysteria. 'Look, I can't calm down,' Ellie was saying shrilly. 'The place has been sold. It's all still there, I just know it is. What am I going to do? Who can help me out of this? What if everyone finds out? . . . I really need to see you.'

Monique was torn between wanting to comfort her obviously upset friend and feeling embarrassed about eavesdropping. She decided to move discreetly away as she heard Ellie finish the call.

'I can be there tonight, Sarah. Absolutely, I have nothing on tomorrow, Ursula can take the kids to school . . . Okay, I will leave here at seven and should be with you by nine . . . Mmmm, okay, thanks so much . . . see you then . . . love you.'

By the time Ellie slammed her phone shut and gathered herself together, Monique was back at the table fussing in her handbag at the table to cover her guilt. Monique tried to read her immaculate complexion for clues. Ellie caught her stare and smiled back.

'Love that turtleneck, darling. Is it cashmere?'

'Naturally,' Monique scoffed. 'You know I wouldn't wear anything else.'

'We love a natural fibre,' Ellie said breezily and sat back on the café chair, crossing her ankles.

'So what's on tonight, darlings?' Monique asked.

'Homework, dinner, bath, bed, ho hum,' offered Mim.

'What about you, Ellie, what's on at your place?' Monique leaned forward enquiringly.

'Oh, you know how it is, Bryce has a work do on, and I am quite looking forward to a lovely soak in the bath and an early night,' Ellie said smiling over at a toddler in head-to-toe Baby Gap, oblivious to Monique's blank stare.

My God, thought Monique, it must be serious for her best friend to have just told her such a bare-faced lie.

'Oh God, look at that,' Ellie suddenly said, inclining her head toward the monstrous brightly coloured adventure playground area.

'What?' asked Monique, staring blankly at the frenzied children swinging, running and sliding through the garishly coloured tubes and tunnels.

'Oh good Lord, I see it,' Mim sighed. 'Look out, girls, first-time mother at three o'clock.'

Monique looked in the direction of Ellie's subtly pointing pinkie (nicely varnished in Espresso, just the thing for a coffee morning).

A rare sight was being played out in the playground as an obviously enthusiastic and yet-to-be-jaded mother was climbing into the colourful slide with her toddler.

'Only child!' Ellie and Monique muttered in unison.

'Oh, God,' said Monique, shielding her eyes in mock horror, 'she can barely squeeze into the tube; that is so not a good look. Do you think one of us should tell her?'

'What? That she's too fat to play?' Mim asked, arching one finely plucked eyebrow, daring Monique to openly admit to her bitchy comment.

'No, of course not,' Monique nervously laughed. 'No. I mean tell her that parents really don't have to play here; I mean she's making the rest of us look bad, isn't she?'

'The kid obviously loves it, though,' said Mim, watching the mother-and-child moment. 'He's squealing with laughter.' Mim was fed up with playing their usual criticism game, it just made her feel shallow and empty.

'She's just trying to show us all up,' Monique moaned.

Some mothers at nearby tables had also noticed the 'interactive' mother and were nudging each other and whispering. A couple of them even, reluctantly, got up to pat their offsprings' heads and whisper encouragement.

'Oh, I can't stand it a minute longer,' said Monique, 'I will not be shown up at a play centre, for God's sake!'

The others stared. Jaws dropped. Monique was going to play? This was unprecedented.

Stalking briskly into the play area Monique found Prudie tying on Sienna's tiny pink Nikes. 'Prudie, darling, could you please take Sienna up for a slide on your lap?'

'Muuuuuum,' whined the affronted Sienna, 'I'm six! I don't need helping to get down the slide!'

'Just do it for Mummy, darling, then you can have a skinny babycino and a choco-lo-fat muffin with me after!'

'O-KAY!' the child relented begrudgingly, and stomped off with her nanny in tow.

Monique returned triumphantly to her seat, mission accomplished. A few minutes later Sienna came to claim her promised reward and sat spooning babycino froth into her mouth and giggling with Paris and Chloe.

'They all play so well,' Mim smiled at the trio. 'We really need to organise a girls' night for them to sleep over together.'

'That would be gorgeous,' Monique agreed, 'We could get that company, what's it called – Fairy Facials I think – to come and do mini makeovers on them, how fun!'

'Yeeess,' agreed Mim, and continued sarcastically, 'then we could throw them on the modelling circuit and have them pouting and strutting before they hit puberty.' Mim was immediately hot-faced and shocked with herself for being so nasty.

Normally the idea of a home beauty salon for the little girls would have struck her as charming and fun too, but lately she'd been worrying that maybe all the attention to appearance might not be such a good thing and she hated to think of Chloe under constant pressure to look 'right' as she grew up. It had struck her recently that maybe she wasn't providing a very good role model for her daughter. Monique shot Mim a shocked look, but decided she was probably just premenstrual and let the matter drop.

As the mothers around them began packing up children and paraphernalia, the Mothers' Group girls also started making noises about leaving. Paris slurped up the last of her drink and Ursula started packing up her dolls and crayons.

'Oh dear, it must be time to go.' Ellie looked enquiringly

at her nanny, who was bundling Paris into her Madeline-style coat. 'Do we have to go?' she gave a mock whine, 'can't I have one more latte?'

'Sorry, Mrs Ashcombe, it's Paris's quiet time,' Ursula answered smoothly.

'God, it's all about the kids nowadays, isn't it?' Ellie moaned. 'Sometimes I could really do with a break from motherhood you know.' She stood and flung her wrap stylishly over her shoulders. 'Anyhoo, ciao bellas – gorgeous to have some quality play-time with the kiddies. Speak soon.' She blew them a group kiss and led her mini-entourage out to the car park.

Monique was getting herself organised to leave as Liz rushed in with Hubert.

'So sorry to be late, girls – you're not all going?'

'Sorry, I have to, I've got to get these disgusting nails sorted,' Monique moaned tapping her gleaming manicured fingers on the table.

'I'm good,' offered Mim. 'Work is madness, I have thirty-two flyer options to pdf and email this evening, but I can't do a thing till the cherubs are in bed so I can stay for another hour. We could have lunch.'

'Fab!' exclaimed Liz. She plopped onto a chair, sent Hubert off to play with Chloe and eagerly scooped up the menu with the standard 'I shouldn't but . . .' as she scanned the menu choices. 'You sound under the gun at the moment, darling,' Liz said with concern. 'Heaps on?'

'Yes,' groaned Mim, 'I'm so busy!!! Working from home sounds great – you know work and mother at the same time and all that – but it's really just a nightmare and I'm over the whole thing right now.'

'Really?' murmured Liz. 'That's no good, sweetheart.'

'The concept of working for yourself is great: work your own hours, be available for coffee with the girls, school emergencies or sick children,' Mim began, aware that Liz, with her indulgent lifestyle, would have no concept of the effort of juggling work and home.

'It sounds ideal,' agreed Liz.

'But it's hell, Liz, it really is!' Mim said, panic creeping into her voice. 'I already had two client calls before the others got here today. I had to rush out to the courtyard so the unprofessional background noise of screaming children couldn't be overheard.'

'Surely the client would understand?' asked Mim.

'Oh God no, not Taylor's Tarts! And they are tarts, both of them: two sisters, no children, in their late twenties with high expectations and no clue of what I'm trying to juggle to keep up with their unrealistic demands.' She paused. 'Oh, Lord,' she said with both hands over her eyes, 'I sound like such a complainer. I should just give it up, right? It's not like we need the money . . .' Mim halted at this point and dropped her hands and her voice to a whisper as she looked at Liz. 'It's just that we do need the money, Liz, it's all getting so tight at the moment.' She paused.

'Oh, Mim,' said Liz with surprise, 'I had no idea!'

'It's just so difficult to keep up, you know,' Mim continued. 'There's Langholme's winter soiree coming up; that's a new outfit. I had to promise to cater a luncheon for the fund-raising committee – otherwise they'd be gossiping about me all year; then we've got the golf-club membership and racing club memberships due, and there's a Gucci handbag on sale like Tiffany's and you know the sort of pressure there is to be up-to-the-minute with everything. You'd think I'd be past peer-group pressure by now,' she laughed uncertainly. 'But somehow it's an even bigger issue now, there just seems to be so much to prove . . .' she trailed off.

Liz's thoughts had wandered as the reality of Mim's

money woes became clear, but she looked up as she realised Mim had stopped talking, and gave what she hoped was an encouraging murmur.

'Thanks,' Mim sniffed to the waiter as he put down the smoked salmon and caper foccacia at her place and a blackberry muffin at Liz's.

Mim nibbled the edge of the foccacia and quickly made a face and dropped it back on to her plate in disgust. 'For God's sake, can't this place get a simple meal right? I wouldn't feed a street-kid this rubbish, the salmon's dry on the edges.'

'Mim!' Liz cried. 'What an incredibly spoilt brat you are sometimes!'

Mim's face crumpled with hurt and confusion.

Liz sighed. It had been a brutal morning at the mission and sometimes stepping back into her other world was difficult. She was exhausted with the effort of keeping her two lives separate. But that was no excuse for speaking so harshly to Mim. It was time to come clean, she decided.

'Mim, I'm so sorry, that was a terrible thing for me to say,' Liz began. 'It's just that, well, I haven't been entirely honest with you girls, and I think it's time I started being more truthful.'

Mim pushed her dry salmon foccacia away and stared wide-eyed at her friend. 'What is it?'

'I got upset with what you said just now about street-kids because since 6 a.m. I've been at a mission in St Kilda serving up scrambled eggs to homeless teenagers,' Liz told her with a serious look on her face. 'I'm not normally rostered on for breakfast, but they were desperate.'

'Normally rostered on? Is this, like, a regular thing then?' Mim asked in disbelief.

'Yes, it is. I've been doing it since Roman was two years old.'

Liz told Mim her story. She held back the personal

details, of course, but her volunteer work at the St Kilda Angels was revealed, and Liz felt incredibly relieved to finally share this part of her life.

Mim drove home, astounded after the long talk with Liz. Who would have thought that Liz, of all people – with all her money – would be leading such a giving, selfless double life. And, more importantly, why was she doing it?

Everybody in their social set attended money-raising functions for various causes: children, whales, rainforests – they donated by buying tickets to fabulous do's and winning expensive items at charity auctions, and therefore felt truly benevolent because they were 'giving to the poor'. But to actually be hands-on – well, it just wasn't done!

'What on earth is in it for her?' Mim found herself thinking, and then abruptly realised the selfishness of the thought.

Oh God, no wonder she sounded like a spoilt brat – or princess, as James would say.

She thought hard for a few minutes. What did she actually do for anyone else?

Nothing, she realised, her face hot with shame. Somehow labels, the right invitations, fashion and keeping up with the Smith-Kline-Joneses had become the causes closest to her heart.

Shit, I think maybe I am a Private School Princess, she thought. Maybe it's time for a change?

~26~

The Big Old House in the Country

Ellie drove the Porsche through the Langholme Grammar circular drive and picked up Rupert, who was wrestling with another Grade Two boy on the lawn.

'Hi, possum, hop in,' she called from the window of the car. 'Oh shit,' she said under her breath as Rupert's teacher strode toward the car, 'it's Mrs Creighton. Quick, darling.' Rupert chucked his bag on the back seat and Ellie pressed the accelerator to escape the unwelcome onslaught.

'So, how was school?' She glanced over at her first-born as he gazed out the window.

'All right,' was the unenthusiastic reply.

'What was the best bit?'

'Lunchtime, but there wasn't enough food. Can I've two packets of chips tomorrow?' he whined.

'We'll see. And the worst bit?'

'Art.'

'How could you not like art? It's meant to be fun,' Ellie said.

'It's so boring. He makes us all do the same thing and I

got in trouble for punching Tarquin. But he started it. He called me Fatty Boombatty.'

'Oh, sweetie,' she stroked his chubby little cheek, 'he doesn't understand you've got a gland problem.' At least Ellie now knew the reason Mrs Creighton had wanted to bail her up.

With the Porsche double-parked outside TJs, Ellie rushed in and grabbed Paris. She really wanted to have a minute to talk to Miss Haughton about Paris's social skills (or lack thereof) but the parking situation forced her to grab and run. Next time, she promised herself.

Pulling up into their four-car garage, the children jumped out and ran for the house, leaving Ellie carrying the bags and following the trail of discarded items they left in their wake.

Stepping over socks, shoes, jumpers, school notices, craft and an unidentifiable pink bit of goop with beads stuck onto it, which she skirted as if it was radioactive, Ellie made her way to their Italian marble kitchen. 'Rupert, sweetie, out of the cupboard. Paris, what happened to your beautiful new stockings?' She eyed the huge hole torn in the stockings lying on the floor.

'George happened,' Paris replied. 'I HATE him,' and she stomped off to the TV room.

With the children snacked-up and in front of the television, Ellie went upstairs to pack. She opened her overnight bag and threw in jeans, runners, windcheater and T-shirt, and a tracksuit to sleep in. It gets cold there, she thought. She momentarily picked up her silk robe, and lay it back on the bed. No, she thought, that's inappropriate.

She grabbed her overnight Louis Vuitton case and headed back downstairs to check on the children, greeting Ursula in the kitchen. What a little treasure. She was already starting dinner and had the children up at the bench eating a second snack of carrot sticks and dip.

'Oh, hello Ursula, thanks so much for getting the dry-cleaning.'

'No problem, Mrs Ashcombe, it's my pleasure.' Ursula smiled at Ellie while simultaneously removing a dip-coated carrot stick from Rupert who was threatening to stick it into Paris's hair.

Ellie went into the office to make a couple of phone calls and then ducked back upstairs to get changed into black wool pants, a cream turtleneck and flat black ankle boots. Grabbing her quilted cream jacket, overnight case and black Prada sac, she headed to the car.

'Bye kids,' she said, kissing them on the way past. 'You behave for Ursula now, see you tomorrow.'

And she was out the door.

As Ellie zoomed down the highway, heavy clouds that had been threatening all day finally unleashed their fury and the Porsche wipers were going full pelt. She was anxious to be there, yet apprehensive, and wished she didn't have to go at all.

She started reflecting on who she was about to visit and the past they shared. Ellie's past was not exactly as she made it out to be. She felt dreadfully guilty misleading most of her friends, but, she justified to herself, they loved her, the today-Ellie, not the twenty years ago Ellie. That Ellie was a very different person.

Ellie had been a normal girl, who thought, like all little girls, she was probably a princess. But, as she looked out of the only skinny window letting grimy light into her cell-sized room, she thought, how could a princess live here? Unless, of course, it's a princess who has been locked in a tower by a wicked stepmother and is guarded by a dragon.

Only it wasn't a stepmother, it was her real mother, who was being chased by demons of her own. Addictive, terrible demons.

Every night Ellie walked her sister home from school to their three-room workman's cottage. The front door was barely a metre from the street, joined at each side to other cottages so close that the fights and shouts of desperate and often dangerous inhabitants permeated the lathe and plaster day and night. The cottage was on the edge of the city, years before the edge of the city became trendy and started pumping out litres of latte and mountains of foccacia. This was a suburb originally built in the 1800s for the working-class poor, and it had gone steadily downhill since. The first architects to discover the wonders of 'warehouse space' and 'urban living' were years away from Ellie's little patch.

She had been a very quiet girl. She had discovered early on in life that if you stay as quiet as possible, you won't draw attention to yourself. She had become a master at making herself invisible. She made lunch for herself and her little sister Sarah every day and then the girls walked to the local state primary school, and years later to the high school across the road.

Ellie loved her sister and would help her with her homework each night, talk to her about her friends and problems, and make her dinner. Ellie tried really hard to keep her own grades up, but found it very difficult. She had little time after maintaining their household, as pathetic as it was.

Often her mother would party long into the night with the strangers she brought home. On those nights the girls would shut the bedroom door and lie in bed together in fear as they remembered the terrible night when one of the 'guests' had come into their room with probing fingers and an evil laugh.

Returning abruptly to the present, Ellie shook her head. She didn't want to go there. She didn't want to think about that right now. She left the freeway and before long was on the quiet road she knew so well. Great tall ghost gums lined the driveway as the Porsche made its left-hand turn and crunched up the gravel towards the big, old house.

The porch light was on and a figure waited in the doorway. Another blonde, long-haired beauty with legs that went on forever stood with the light shining out around her, making her glow like an apparition. With her arms folded, blocking out the cold, she hugged the woolly cable-knit cardigan around her. The baggy cords and ugg boots did nothing to belie her angelic appearance.

Ellie parked the car and, grabbing her bag and case, strode across. The women were of equal height when they embraced.

'You're here,' said the woman.

'Thank God,' Ellie replied.

~27~

Sanctuary

Ellie's feet echoed on the ancient floorboards in the draughty hall. Dozens of memories – some sad, some joyful – flooded back as she breathed in the familiar smells of the house. She dropped her bags at the foot of the imposing timber staircase and looked around for anything new, but it was all as it had been for decades.

From above came the soft sounds of a woman weeping. Ellie gave her companion a wry smile and they moved together into the huge, toasty warm kitchen. They sank into a pair of threadbare, overstuffed club chairs pulled up close to the open fire.

A pot of tea sat brewing on the heavy oak table between them. Sarah poured the tea and handed a steaming cup over to her sister.

'Mmmm,' said Ellie appreciatively, 'you still make the best cup of tea in the world.'

'It's all in the brewing,' smiled Sarah. 'That, and warming the pot first.'

'Quiet night tonight?' Ellie asked.

'Yes, we had a full house all week but most of them have moved on,' Sarah explained. 'There are only two here who are seeing the counsellor tomorrow. I don't know how long they'll stay,' she mused.

'As long as they want, I should imagine,' said Ellie with a smile, knowing her sister very well.

'When they're ready, there's plenty of time.'

The women relaxed back in their chairs, warmed by the flames, tea, and just being close to each other again. Ellie's thoughts finally stopped swirling through her head as she sat mesmerised by the dancing flames. She could feel her face glowing with heat as she revelled in the peace of being here: being with Sarah.

'So,' her sister eventually broke the quiet, 'what's actually happened?'

Reality hit Ellie hard. For a few moments she'd escaped the horrible facts, but now she had to face it all again. Tears spilled down her face as she leaned forward to grasp Sarah's hand and begin her story.

'Bryce rang me in the middle of the school production last week. I could hardly hear him over the noise, but finally I realised what he was trying to tell me. The building – *that* building,' she looked at Sarah meaningfully, 'has been sold. But worse than that, apparently it's like a time capsule inside. They sealed it up in 1984 and nothing's been touched since.'

Sarah clutched Ellie's hand harder, turning pale in the firelight. 'So are the photos still there then?' she asked.

'Yes, they are, and one of the other school families has bought the property and now has all the promotional material – the posters, the flyers, it's all there!'

'But surely it will just get thrown out?' Sarah asked.

'The stupid woman has decided to exhibit it as some kind of wretched retro exercise in self-promotion or something!'

Sarah gave a sharp intake of breath.

'I know, it's such bad luck. We had been trying to buy the building ourselves for years so we could torch it and get on with our lives. I just knew that something like this would happen if we didn't – and now it has.

'So now it's too late and I'm ruined, there's nothing I can do. And when word is out, I'll be a social pariah. Plus I've lied to my friends all this time – except for darling Mim, I told her last week – but how will the others ever trust me again.' Ellie sobbed hard, leaning in to her sister.

'Come on, sweetie,' Sarah comforted her, tucking Ellie's tear-soaked hair behind her ear, 'We've been through much, much worse together and survived. And we'll make it through this, *together* – I promise.' Sarah smiled, giving her big sister a hug and moving into the kitchen to make another pot of tea and grilled cheese sandwiches.

'But Sarah, you don't understand: no one will speak to me, no one will want to know me. I'll be publicly shamed,' Ellie sniffed, her head leaden from crying.

'Okay, so tell me the worst thing that can happen,' Sarah answered in her calm way.

'Well, I'll be the laughing stock of the whole school and the whole city. I'll be dis-invited from all sorts of fabulous events. I'll be hideously humiliated and I'll never be able to show my face again,' Ellie sobbed.

'Okay, so is that all?' Sarah asked simply.

'Hello? Isn't that enough,' Ellie snapped sarcastically.

'But what about your life – your real life? Will that be affected?'

'Excuse me, that *is* my real life.'

'No it's not, that's all just surface stuff: what the mums at school think of you; what the social set says you did or didn't do; who likes you or doesn't like you; whether they gossip about you or not – it won't be pretty, I know, but it's not the end of the world.'

Sometimes Ellie could strangle her pragmatic sister. 'Okay then, you tell me, Miss Straight-and-Narrow, what would be the end of the world then?'

'Losing Bryce, Paris or Rupert,' she answered. 'Is that likely to happen?'

'Well no,' Ellie hesitated, realising she'd been outsmarted. 'But what if the kids get wind of it?'

'So? Just be honest with them, the truth will never hurt them. It'd do them good to have a small dose of reality in that perfect little synthetic world they live in.'

Ellie visually flinched at that and Sarah quickly apologised. 'Oh sweetie, I'm sorry, that was mean of me. But your kids could be a lot tougher than you think; and it's true, it would be good for them to know that actually very little in life is perfect, everyone has hard times – it's not all designer labels and fancy parties in real life, is it?'

'I suppose not,' Ellie conceded. 'It's just after what we went through I really want to keep them in a safe bubble of perfection for as long as I can.'

'But Ellie, is it worth it for the work you have to do maintaining it? Keeping secrets like this will destroy you eventually.'

'I know. Anyway, it won't be a secret much longer.'

The sisters talked on for hours, and by midnight Ellie was almost starting to feel as if everything would be okay after all.

'Sarah, you're a marvel.' She smiled at her sister. 'I haven't had a moment's peace since this began, but then I came here and you've put it all into perspective for me. Like you said, "what's the worst that can happen?" I mean, maybe I'll be ostracised by some and lose my social status – but I'll have what's most important to me: you, the kids and Bryce. And that's all that really matters in the end.' She breathed her first deep breath in days and reflected on the amazingly therapeutic power of the house. Much of it had to do with Sarah, of course, but it was also the peaceful bush setting and the sense of comfort and serenity that the house itself offered.

It wasn't the first time she had called on its soothing powers.

One night many years ago, a night that was seared forever into Ellie's memory like a deep scar, she had woken up in the early hours during one of their mother's many parties to become instantly aware of another presence in the pathetic little room she shared with Sarah. Her eyes adjusted to the dark as quickly as it took her to sit up and realise what was happening.

A man was on top of her sister. Sarah's bright eyes were staring in horror over the huge hand that was muffling her screams. Her stick-like white legs were spread and looked like they were threatening to snap under the weight of the man. Ellie picked up the only weapon she had on hand, her science textbook, and whacked him over the head with all her might.

He roared and leapt up, swinging a powerful arm back that connected with the side of Ellie's head. She went down and whacked her head on the bed leg. When she came to, seconds later, Sarah was leaning over her, calling her name. The stranger was gone.

Ellie had never forgotten the look of horror and pain on her sister's face. They'd left that night, run to Mrs Mac for help and been referred to this house in the country – a refuge, a place where young girls could seek care and support while they got themselves on their feet. It had been a godsend for the sisters, a balm for their troubled and damaged souls. The fiercely independent Ellie stayed a week with her little sister but, determined to support them both, returned to the city to earn the money for their future.

In those days Mrs Lovell ran the house, and she cared for Sarah like she was her own, seeing that she got the quiet therapy she needed. After their mother's overdose, and with no other family to turn to, Sarah was given the chance to regain a normal life by going to the local school and grow up in this untraditional, yet loving, surrogate family. She contributed by helping out with the guest meals and housework and Ellie sent her money whenever she could.

After high school, Sarah completed a psychology course at an adult education centre and continued to work with Mrs Lovell. And when the older woman retired, Sarah took over the running of the hostel: her home. She could empathise with the lost souls who found their way there. The girls who needed little more than kindness and understanding; a warm bed and some nutritious food. She doled out all in generous proportions. Sarah was careful to never actually break the law, although sometimes she sailed pretty close to it in order to protect girls terrified of being returned to abusive parents or partners.

Now, as the fire turned to glowing embers and the sisters drank their way through a final pot of tea, Ellie's anxiety was soothed. They had decided on a course of action. At last it was time for sleep.

'I've put you in your usual room,' Sarah told her, leading the way upstairs. 'Sorry it's so freezing, but the heater's on the blink. I've left lots of blankets in there and tucked in a hot-water bottle for you.'

'Thanks, gorgeous,' said Ellie, giving Sarah a hug as they reached the first landing. 'I'll be fine.'

Sarah went into her own room and Ellie continued up the next flight of stairs to the top floor. Sarah was right, the house was freezing away from the warmth of the kitchen fire. From outside Ellie could hear the familiar sound of the gum trees swishing against the slate roof, possums moving around in the ceiling and, from far away, the sea murmuring to itself. They were all sounds that Ellie now associated with safety.

Creeping slowly down the hall on the Persian runner, she found her way to Room 11 by the soft glow of the antique wall sconces. The house was silent, sighing softly to itself as its timbers and beams adjusted themselves into a more comfortable position.

She jiggled the old key in the temperamental lock until it finally gave way and she was standing on the threshold of her own little haven. This was somewhere that Bryce had never been, a place that her children didn't know about and that was kept secret from even her closest friends. This was a part of Ellie that was truly her own.

Little of the simple decor had changed since her first night in the room all those years ago when she had been a frightened big sister desperate for Sarah's safety and the hope of a better future for both of them. She flicked on the light and sat on the beautiful worn chintz armchair to pull off her boots. She threw them carelessly (forgetting what they had cost, who had designed them and the reverential treatment they normally commanded) onto the threadbare carpet and turned back the covers of her wrought iron bed.

A white waffle cover that Mrs Lovell had made for her still covered the sheets, which were the kind of simple, soft flannelette that Ellie hadn't slept under for years. Welcoming and warm, the bed swallowed her problems and lulled her to sleep to the sound of the wind in the eucalypts and the secure thought that her sister slept in the room beneath her.

~28~

Tiffany's Revenge

'Here's to another balls-up,' said Ellie, raising her glass of bubbly in greeting to Mim. 'Of course, it's not technically a disaster yet, but this early in the evening it could still go either way,' she laughed.

Ellie, revived from her secret country retreat, looked stunning in an impossibly snug, ankle-skimming, blue-velvet Donna Karan number. She was a picture of elegance and old money – which was perfect given the *Richly Royal* theme of this year's Langholme Grammar Winter Soiree.

The Winter Soiree (held in autumn, before it got too cold for skin-baring eveningwear) was a must on the school social calendar. It was intended as a friendly mixer, but was actually an intensive networking opportunity for mothers jostling for position on the Langholme Grammar social scene, and for dads keen to schmooze business contacts. The right outfit, an amusing anecdote and the occasional shrewd observation could cement invitations to all the best children's parties and mean the difference between being relegated to the fairy-floss machine or serving high tea in pretty starched linen aprons at the school fete.

As soon as the Spring Racing Carnival ended the mums packed up their feathered millinery and began plotting the ultimate fashion statement for the Winter Soiree – well, at least the smart women did. Each year the Langholme Grammar social committee announced a new theme for the ball – heralding cries of complaint and joy from the school community. For the week following the announcement, cafés across the suburbs were abuzz as mums sipped their lattes and planned to extract the maximum glamour from any given theme.

Last year's *Provincial Picnic* theme had made the wearing of diamonds, silk and furs difficult to justify – but several mothers had pulled it off with aplomb and reaped the social-status benefits for the past twelve months.

This year's theme made everyone happy. With the recent ascent of 'our Mary' to European royalty, the school's social team had conjured up the *Richly Royal* theme and sent mums into a frenzy of historical fashion research (reading old *Vogues*).

Somehow the Triple Ds had managed to work leather and multiple piercings into their regal ensembles, and the CPM came as J-Lo and Christine Aguilera (pop royalty), while the Mothers' Superior were in their element as Anne Boleyns, Anna Kareninas, some Joan of Arcs and a smattering of Mary Queen of Scots. The bigger the martyr, the better.

The glittering event was always held at an exclusive inner-city South Yarra function centre. For weeks beforehand the social committee was in a tizz arranging decorations. This year the room resembled a rich fusion of Versace meets Versailles.

'Christ, Mim, I can barely walk in this frock,' moaned Ellie, struggling to inhale.

'But it's worth it, Ellie. You look unbelievable,' said Mim.

'True,' agreed Ellie. 'And if one must suffer in life, at least let it be for fashion!' She glanced around. 'So, James a no-show this evening?' She asked while keeping one eye on the action over Mim's shoulder.

'At a work thing again. It was last minute, of course, always is,' Mim sighed. 'He promises he'll drop in later, though,' she added, not holding out much hope. 'I don't know, Ellie, I'm starting to think he's intentionally avoiding us. Surely he could have ditched the meeting, he knows how important tonight is!'

'Mim, darling, what's happening?' Ellie said in concern, her voice dropping to a whisper as she noticed Hortense Mathews at a nearby group distinctly put her head on one side trying to catch the gossip.

'Oh, it's James, sweetie, we're just at loggerheads constantly at the moment. I'm beside myself with worry,' said Mim. 'But seriously, this is neither the time nor the place for such misery: we're supposed to be having a ball!'

'So the invitation said, darling, but I'm yet to see the evidence. Let's talk tomorrow,' Ellie suggested.

'Thanks, sweet, that'd be great,' and with a massive effort Mim plastered her very best social smile on her face and serenely looked out at the room. Standing atop the wide marble staircase on the top floor of the centre, they were in a perfect position to people-watch.

Mim was thrilled with this year's theme: with her dark locks and slim build, a Mary Donaldson tribute had been easy to conjure. The silk bridesmaid's dress from her sister's wedding was perfectly royal and hadn't been seen among this set – it was full-length, charcoal with a white bodice and white Chanel Camelia under the bust-line. And really she couldn't be bothered to go to any more trouble than recycling a frock; the effort of pulling another fashion trick out of her hat for every new social function was wearing her down. Most of the other Langholme mums seemed to have the stamina for it, but lately Mim had felt a growing sense of unease about the extravagance of new outfits and the showing off that went along with them.

As they made their way down the stairs, Mim could just catch the heavenly tones of the string quartet above the cacophony of shrieked welcomes and 'hello dahlings' as the night really got underway. All around them smartly uniformed waiters with laden drink trays attempted to navigate the ocean of frocks while being buffeted into silk eddies and swept along by sequined currents.

'Where's Tiff, are they here yet?' Ellie asked.

Mim smiled to herself, thinking of Tiffany's big surprise. 'No, I haven't seen her, she's been in Portsea for the past six weeks, but she's definitely coming. I don't think we will miss her big entrance.'

'What big entrance?' Ellie asked, face aghast. 'She's not wearing that horrible salmon-taffeta puffy skirt again, is she? I realise she thinks it hides her chunky butt, but someone has to tell her. Eighties fashion may be retro and dead trendy right now, but there are definite rules: if you wore it then, you're too old to wear it now!'

Throwing back the last of her champagne, Ellie spied a perfect example of tragic design sense just behind her. Indicating the fashion victim to Mim, she said, 'Case in point at five o'clock. What was she thinking?'

Mim spied a look at Bunny Burroughs, who was resplendent in a diamond tiara, and a mauve silk evening gown that was way too much flounce and far too much lace. Her 1980s Farrah Fawcett 'do' topped off the look.

'Don't be such a bitch, Ellie, maybe she's paying homage to Lady Di,' said Mim, nudging Ellie, who was staring quite openly.

'Darling, the only thing she's paying *homage* to is the look she found in 1982 and hasn't strayed from since. She hasn't moved a fashion muscle in well over twenty years, poor love.' Ellie was distracted by a new entrant. 'Hmmm, look over there, that's interesting,' she said, pointing with her chin in the direction of the door and managing to deftly swipe two more bubblys from a waiter who floated by.

'What? Oh, isn't that Charmaine and Edward Heatherington? He's a surgeon, isn't he? Love her look, very Russian Royal family; very Romanovs – *such* a tragedy. So what's the big deal?'

'Well, yes, he is a surgeon, and it is a bit of a tragedy. Look at what he's wearing.'

'It's just a suit, big deal! I don't get it.'

'*He* would much rather be playing the Russian princess, if you know what I mean.'

'No way!'

'Way, darling, way!' Ellie smirked over the top of her glass.

'I always thought he was a bit lecherous, the way he looked women up and down, but maybe he . . . oh . . . I see . . .'

'That's right, sweet, he's coveting their frocks!'

'Oh dear.' In the past such a juicy snippet of gossip would have been readily shared with the nearest circle, but now Mim and Ellie swallowed their giggles and instead simply shared a knowing look.

Suddenly Ellie cried, 'Darlings, over here!' From her statuesque six foot vantage point, she was able to spot the other women arriving. Liz and Monique entered the room arm-in-arm with their husbands trailing obediently behind them.

Then it happened. The big moment; planned for just that precise second. Ellie saw it first. She grabbed Mim's arm.

'Ohmigod! Check it out!'

Tiffany, solo, stood grandly at the entrance, handing her wrap to an eager attendant. She smiled graciously around the room until her gaze caught her girlfriends. Ellie, Monique, Liz and Mim stared in amazement.

The Mothers Superior, in their pearls and stoles, stopped judging for a minute to stare. The CPM stopped smoking and looked in wonder. The Triple Ds took a break from eyeing up the dads as all eyes rested on the new arrival.

Tiffany looked unbelievable in a figure-hugging, full-length (size eight at least, Jennifer Gowrie-Smith thought crossly) Oscar de la Renta sequined silver gown. Her hair was coloured golden and cut in a shaggy, layered crop – *à la* Sharon Stone. Stepping into the room, her elfin face beaming with excitement, everyone noticed that she suddenly looked a good fifteen years younger. The crow's feet were gone; the jowls were gone; her eyes were enormous and unhooded; a plane could land on her cheekbones. Her forehead was completely wrinkle-free and the weird little frown mark in the centre of her forehead had disappeared. Every ageing mark, line and sag in Tiffany's face had been erased.

She stood in front of her friends and gave a languid catwalk-model turn. The paunch – gone! The bottom – gone! The tricep-bags; the eye-bags; the saddle-bags – gone, gone, gone.

Goodbye old Tiffany. Hello silicone-collagen-botox-enhanced Tiffany!

'OH . . . MY . . . GOD!' Ellie and Mim squealed in unison, grabbing Tiffany in a group hug – feeling for themselves just how firm her new butt was.

'You look amazing! You shifty little operator, is this where you've been for the last six weeks?' Ellie demanded.

'Yep, I've just notched up a cool $100,000 worth of

bod-mods! And boy, did I deserve it. The sleazy bastard is so racked with guilt he won't say a word when the bills hit him. When he leaves me I'll happily take this little number for a spin,' she said, launching her new body into a sexy shimmy.

'Tiffany, you are the modern face of women's lib,' Ellie cried. 'You should give talks in all the girls' schools. You're my hero. And where is the sleazy bastard, anyway?' she asked. 'I didn't see him come in with you.'

Tiffany picked at imaginary fluff on her gown.

'He's probably in the dining room,' she said nonchalantly. 'I volunteered him for the decorating committee; hopefully he's swinging off a chandelier as we speak. Oh, and by the way, I hired a private detective. I know who the other woman is.'

'No way . . . Who?'

Mim and the girls held their breath and squeezed each other's hands as they waited for the next bit of juicy gossip to be revealed. This was a great night.

'You know Keith Crabtree, our accountant? Well . . .' she paused for effect. 'It's his daughter, Clarissa.'

'Holy shit.'

'Holy fuck.'

It was better than the girls could have hoped for.

'How old is she?' Mim asked.

'Twenty-seven,' Liz replied coolly.

'Holy shit.'

At that moment a set of large doors slid open to reveal a glittering dining room. Each place boasted five silver settings of cutlery: one for each course. Monogrammed china, gold presentation plates, five different wine glasses – again, one per course. Each table groaned under the weight of crystal and silver condiment sets, gravy boats, salt cellars, pepper grinders, every culinary whim of the guests was pre-empted. White lilies reached for the ceiling, and violets crept across the crisp linen. Waiters stood at each table to seat the guests on chairs that were better dressed than any debutante – in flouncy white skirts with silver bows cinching in their little chair waists.

The decoration committee was putting the finishing touches on the stage. Cliff was heading towards the entry as his wife entered, flanked by her support team. His eyes narrowed as they fell on Tiffany as though he was trying to place a familiar face. Then they widened; then widened further.

'Jesus, is that you, Tiff? What have you done to yourself? You look . . . well, you look friggin' gorgeous! Christ, that Portsea air's done you wonders. Have you just got back today? You look ten years younger.'

'Really, isn't it amazing what six weeks' break will do for a girl,' Tiffany said breezily as she sailed past. 'Oh, and Cliff?'

Cliff nodded eagerly.

'Your fly's undone.'

The Mothers' Group girls could barely control their chortles as they made their way to their table.

Mim flounced out her napkin and laid it on her lap. 'Wow, this is an incredible development. You're handling it very well,' she said with concern to Tiffany. 'Are you sure you're okay about it?'

'Well, of course I'm not okay,' admitted Tiffany. 'I was really floored when I found out. But the one redeeming thought I keep having is that I can't wait to see what Keith Crabtree does when he discovers who's been sleeping with his daughter.'

~ 29 ~

Power Talk

'Slow down, Mim,' puffed Tiffany as her little legs struggled to keep pace with Mim's long strides. Albert Park Lake was a mirror and there were hundreds of other joggers, power-walkers and pram-pushers out enjoying the bright autumn day.

'Sorry, sweet.' Mim slowed her pace fractionally.

The hangovers from last night's Winter Soiree were waning in the fresh air, and Mim was keen to pump Tiffany for information now that she had her to herself.

'So,' said Mim, 'what's the update?'

Tiffany's new body looked svelte and sexy in her navy Adidas flared-leg tracksuit pants, and Guess red, white and blue windcheater. Since her emotional night with Mim she had fluctuated between feeling miserable and used, to feeling vengeful and powerful. She had been thorough in her research and, with the help of a private-eye, all evidence pointed to the fact that Cliff was indeed having an affair.

The detective had followed his paper trail down a sordid path. It led to restaurants (when Cliff had told Tiff he was at business meetings), to hotels (instead of the office), and in one case a Gold Coast resort (not the bemoaned conference in Sydney).

The email trail was the most obvious, though. He was so stupid if he thought his password was going to stop her from accessing his laptop. It had taken one guess. Tiffany typed 'BIGMAN' and was in. Sure enough, as per Mim's advice, there were the emails in the deleted folder; a long list of them dating back to October of last year. And all of them signed 'Clary'.

Tiffany found it difficult reading the emails. Some were almost pornographic, as she'd expected, and quite intimate, so she was almost embarrassed to be reading this personal correspondence – until she shook herself and remembered that she was married to the recipient.

'Well,' said Tiffany, 'I told you about this "Clary" woman, didn't I?'

'Yep, Keith Crabtree's daughter?' Mim said.

'The very one. I read all their emails. It would seem they got together last October at the Awards function. Sophie had the flu that night and I had to cancel at the last minute. I remember Cliff was annoyed because he thought he'd look like a loser sitting at a table with an empty chair next to him.

'Then the emails started. She seemed, initially, like a bit of a stalker, which surprised me because I thought Cliff would hate that kind of thing. But he got right into it and there are lots of references to meeting at romantic locations. The prick even took her to the same restaurant he took me to on our first date.'

'Ohmigod, has he no shame?'

'No, apparently not, but I think we knew that.' Tiffany shot Mim a sidelong glance. She sighed deeply and continued, 'Then there were the weekends away, once even at the beach-house. I remember that weekend. God, I can't believe I was so STUPID! I had picked the kids up from school on a Friday afternoon and decided on the spur of the moment to head off to Portsea for the weekend. I *thought* Cliff had a golf day on so I wouldn't be seeing him at the beach-house till late that night.

'We arrived at Portsea and there was Cliff's car in the driveway. I wasn't even the slightest bit suss! We went in and he came walking down the stairs with a huge smile on his big, ugly mug. When I asked what he was doing there he told me that the golf day had been at Moonah Links and he had popped in for a shower and change before heading out to meet the lads at the nineteenth hole. It all seemed so feasible at the time! He seemed happy to see us and said "great minds think alike". Then we had the most wonderful family weekend away together. You know, on my way down, I probably drove past the little slut on the freeway.'

Then Tiffany filled Mim in on the rest. Another realisation that she had had, through her traumatic journey of discovery, was that Cliff was probably planning on leaving her. At least the momentous decision to break up the marriage had been taken off her shoulders, she reflected ruefully.

So now Tiffany had to decide on the best way to protect herself and her children. Obviously the assets would need to be liquidated and split up; the Mason-Jackson family home, the cliff-top beach-house in Portsea and the chalet at Falls Creek. But before a single thing was said or done she'd shouted herself a cosmetic fling on Cliff's tab – it was the least the bastard could do.

Next on the list was a divorce attorney – she was going to screw every last cent out of him.

Stopping at the exercise station, both women pushed their way through fifty gruelling sit-ups and some leg-presses – Tiffany, somewhat gingerly, given her delicate state.

Mim threw one of her long pins up on the stretching bar and released the strain in her calves.

'Oooooh, that's better,' she groaned.

They wandered down to a bench at the water's edge and sat, watching the ducks flapping about in excitement as a child fed them popcorn.

Mim looked at Tiffany as she stared out over Albert Park Lake. The fine scars from the recent surgery glowed pink around her hair line. She wondered how long Tiff's makeover would satisfy her; Mim knew her well enough to know that she always felt just one more beauty treatment away from happiness. That's how I've been too, she thought regretfully, but God it's exhausting, and I never want to go as far as Tiff has. I wish I was brave enough just to let it all go; all the facials, manicures and hair appointments. She turned her attention back to Tiff.

'So?' asked Mim. 'What next?'

'Well,' Tiffany stared at a peacock preening its feathers on the other side of the lake. She ran a fingernail along her newly defined jaw. 'Look out world!'

That night, post-cleansing, Mim stared in the mirror at her naked, nearly forty-year-old face and saw a time capsule. There were the laugh lines from screeching at Monique's great sense of fun, the crow's feet from years of smiling at the children playing at the beach, the freckles across her nose (aka facial age spots) from her sailing days. And the frown lines? They were the most valuable of all her age marks. Only a mother had frown lines like that.

She was pleased to see her history on her face, not erased by chemicals and misguided vanity.

She rubbed her hands over her eyes and face and looked once more in the mirror. This time she looked into her own eyes. Hello? Is anyone in there? Who are you? I don't recognise you. You're no longer the idealistic uni student hoping to save the world, you're not the adventurous spirit ready to fly off to the Galapagos Islands and be amazed by a giant tortoise, or the awestruck new mum, euphoric and dedicated.

Where did those women go and who's left behind? She had no answers.

~30~

The Big Blue

Mim decided it was time for an emergency cigarette. She looked at her watch yet again. Almost midnight. She'd tried James's mobile numerous times but it just rang out. At what point should she start ringing the hospitals? Her fatigued mind started to wander and before she knew it she'd imagined everything from the police arriving at the door to choosing her outfit for the funeral.

Then the garage door sounded. Thank God he's safe, she thought. Now I'm going to kill him. She remained seated in the armchair in the living room and waited for him to enter. James was heading into his study with another overloaded briefcase when she startled him by speaking.

'Long day at the office, honey?' she said without a smile.

'Oh, Mim, you startled me,' said James as he turned to face her. 'Yeah, I had to get this report finished for a client meeting first thing.'

'Did it occur to you to ring me?' Mim asked.

'Well, I did try at around seven but it went to Message-bank, then I kinda got distracted and kept on working. You should have called if you were worried.'

'I tried your mobile and it rang out and I tried your direct line and you didn't answer,' said Mim, getting up to follow James who had walked into his office.

'Oh, sorry darling, we were working in the conference room. I must have left my mobile on my desk,' said James as he started unpacking his briefcase.

'We?' enquired Mim.

'Lauren, our new account executive, and I. We were going over the PowerPoint presentation.'

With Tiffany's recent drama fresh in her mind, Mim was overcome with paranoia. She put her hand up to her throat to settle the stronghold.

'Lauren? I don't remember you mentioning her?'

'Oh, didn't I? She's new to Melbourne, we must have her and her husband over for lunch one weekend – their three are the same ages as ours.'

Her paranoia momentarily settled, Mim moved on. 'James, I have been worried sick. I was about to call the hospitals,' she began.

'Mim, you really do overreact sometimes. You know I am hellishly busy at the moment, where else would I be? When have I ever just gone out and played up? I am either here or at the office.'

'Tuesday.'

'Hmm?' he was distracted again.

'Last Tuesday, remember? The business lunch that went until 1 a.m. and you didn't call me.'

'Oh, yeah, that. Well that was a one-off, wasn't it – we all had to blow off some steam after working so hard to win that automotive client.'

'Fair enough, James, but I am sick of the excuses. I am so over these ridiculously long hours. I am sick of being a single mother and I am sick of explaining to the children every night that they probably won't be seeing Daddy before bedtime.' Mim stood with her arms crossed and her pale grey silk and cashmere robe wrapped tight to her neck.

'Now look here, Mim,' said James, finally paying full attention. He pointed a finger at her. 'Do you think it's easy for me? I am working my balls off to keep up at the moment, and all I get when I walk in the door is another screaming match! I am sick of your attitude, I swear to God it's always about you!'

Mim spluttered in indignation. 'Me? My God, James, it's about us! Don't you see where this marriage is headed, don't you see that it's falling apart and that we're both too busy to even realise? I'd much rather have a husband at home being a hands-on father and support team than this ridiculous show of wealth.'

'Then why don't you fucking well take your little tail out there and get one of those magnificent husbands,' he said nastily, and headed off to the kitchen.

James was pouring himself a double scotch by the time Mim flew angrily into the kitchen and stood opposite him, the limestone bench a barrier between them.

She was furious. Blood pounded in her ears as she forced herself to calm down.

'How dare you!' was her strangled cry.

'How dare I what?' he retorted, playing the innocent, a familiar fight strategy that drove her crazy.

'How dare you speak to me like that!' she screeched at him. 'I am genuinely worried, James. I am constantly juggling funds, I am sick of being broke. I lie in bed at night doing the maths and it scares the shit out of me.'

'Me too! I'm working as hard as I can to make the money!' said James, taking a gulp of his drink. 'How about you stop spending it all?! For chrissakes, I make a friggin' fortune.'

'That'd be right, blame me,' she countered, 'but it was you and me together as a team that made these decisions. We spend *more* than a friggin' fortune just keeping up, and now we're in a hole. How do you suggest we pay the $20,000 we owe in school fees? The $10,000 land tax? God knows what else we owe the tax department, then there's $25,000 in credit-card bills. The bloody mortgage payment has just been wrenched from the bank account which barely leaves me enough for staff and groceries. And we owe so much on this place that I can't see when we'll ever pay it off.'

'Yes, we did decide on this life together,' snapped James, 'but it means I'm the one who has to work to afford it. And then you get pissed off when I'm never home. Look, I've got a new client biting at the moment – I know, I know, it'll mean more travel, but think of the commission. It'll be fine.'

'IT'LL BE FINE!?!' Mim spat out. 'FINE! How on earth can you say that? Aren't you even a little bit worried? Don't you care? Don't you even miss us? You're so wrapped up in your own grand high-flying world you don't even seem to notice the children. You miss the big events, you don't even ring them!'

'Oh, really? Is that what you think? I was at the fete. And, as a matter of fact, I emailed Jack today, and I have been emailing him regularly . . .' James returned.

'That's just great, James, a really solid virtual relationship you've got going there with your son. If you'll remember, however, HIS PC IS STUFFED! You were supposed to upgrade the virus software two weeks ago! Anyway, this isn't about email, this is about you, James. When are you going to wake up and realise that there is more to life than work? That we are in strife? I can't live like this any more!'

'What are you trying to say, Mim?' James' voice dropped several octaves, his eyes boring into hers, just daring her to say it.

'I am saying that we need to take a good hard look at ourselves, at where we're going, because the future scares the shit out of me. I didn't want this, James; I didn't want to be stretched so tight. I don't like the person I have become. Hung up on labels, no time to be a decent mother, shoddy work, horrible clients. I feel trapped, like I'm in a vortex and you're never around to help.'

'Goddamnit, Mim!' James exploded, crashing the glass onto the benchtop. 'Do you think I like what I've become? You know this was never my dream. You know I wanted to start my own business, work from home, be a great dad, instead of chasing the next big break.' He took a breath and continued in a sarcastic tone, 'But first came the private school babies, then came the flash house with the right postcode, then the beach-house. It's never-ending and you always want more!'

'That's bullshit! I'm the one holding this all together day after day. Don't you dare put this on me! I'm stressed out of my mind as it is. I can't handle it any more! I am about to explode, and all I want is a happy family. Something has to change, I can't live like this any more!'

'Well then friggin' well don't,' finished James, and stormed out.

~31~

The Search Begins

It was six years since Liz had caught sight of her daughter. Six years since she had started her desperate search – beginning the day after she had seen her living on the streets. At first she went regularly to the mission to look for Mikaylah, but despite constantly questioning the staff, no one remembered the forlorn girl with the dreadlocks, and she never returned. She had simply disappeared.

Despite the constant disappointment, Liz continued to visit the refuge weekly, and eventually she realised it had become a small lifeline for her: the tiniest connection with her absent daughter.

She was back for her fourth time when one of the staff suggested she pick up a broom and lend a hand if she was going to stand around all day scanning the faces of each kid who walked in. Liz initially baulked at the idea, but was too embarrassed to say no. She self-consciously slid the broom over the tattered lino and then decided to find the mop to get out some of the uglier stains.

The next week she came back with the donation of a

new industrial broom and mop and found they did a much more efficient job of the floors.

The week after she brought her own pink rubber gloves and started work on the dirty basins in the communal bathrooms. After that it was some carpet pieces for the office and then some warm blankets for the kids' beds.

She'd been coming for six years now but felt no desire to stop.

It had initially been a shock for a woman who lived such a sheltered and privileged existence to see how tough life could be for those who were forced to make the streets of the city their home. And as one who outsourced all the less-desirable aspects of her life to others, suddenly *choosing* to mop, change beds and peel vegetables was a huge turnaround.

In her first months as a volunteer, Liz teetered about on her ridiculously impractical heels, and although she'd tried to dress down, she soon found that 'work clothes' were something her wardrobe was just not equipped with. She'd had to go shopping for her first pair of jeans and basic tops, and eventually found her work uniform quite liberating. After six months at the mission she stopped wearing jewellery on her volunteer days, and by the end of the first year she'd even stopped worrying about her hair.

What surprised Liz most was that the job she had taken on out of guilt and despair had actually become enjoyable once she got the hang of it. She initially shied away from the dirtiest tasks, but it wasn't long before she forgot about keeping clean, about protecting her French manicure and the fear that she might catch something.

In her second year she began exchanging smiles and small talk with some of the shelter's regular clients and soon found herself making great friends with the staff, including Tracy March, the young and enthusiastic counsellor who headed up the mission. At first she had been intimidated by the rough veneer of the kids, but she soon came to see how much of that was bravado and a kill-or-be-killed instinct that these world-weary youths used to survive on the streets.

After her days at the shelter her body ached with tiredness and she would sometimes carry the sadness of the kids she had met, yet she always felt happiest at these times, driving back home through St Kilda's colourful streets and alleys, and feeling for the first time that she was truly a part of life, someone who made a small but meaningful difference.

She told no one about her secret days volunteering in St Kilda. No one needed to know; she did this for herself, and for Mikaylah, and that was all that mattered.

As she became more accustomed to working at the mission, Liz found that she wanted to do more to help the endless stream of damaged young people who flowed through its doors looking for comfort, food and warmth. At times she felt ashamed of her own luxurious life and longed to contribute more to these troubled kids.

Already she donated money to the mission each month and was the first to reach for her purse whenever the oven needed fixing or the fax machine died. But she wanted to do something more tangible; something lasting that might help one of these kids change the direction of their life.

She thought about it for weeks, lying awake in bed at night and considering the best approach. Then she met with Tracy and the mission committee members to put forward a plan. She wanted to create a trust fund to finance education scholarships for the kids. Any of them could apply for the scholarship as long as they had a willingness to learn and a determination to kick their drug habit.

The committee seized upon the idea (particularly the promise of financial support), on the stipulation that it be coordinated by trained youth workers. Liz spent months working with Tracy to get the program up and running, and finally, six months after she first came up with the plan, the scholarship was launched.

At first it drew little interest from the kids who drifted in and out of the mission, until one day a seventeen year-old who'd only just hit the streets recognised it as his ticket out of a downward spiral. Nathan Cooper had no serious drug issues and a few scattered years of high school, and was deemed a prime candidate. He'd always had an interest in woodwork and chose a carpentry apprenticeship. Liz's scholarship supplied him with books, public transport, a clothing allowance and any other education-related costs. The mission youth workers helped him find accommodation, took him to Centrelink and counselled him through his studies.

Liz cried with joy when she heard of young Nathan's first tentative steps towards healing.

After a shaky start, Nathan began to shine. After his first year he returned to the centre to volunteer on his days off from TAFE. With his positive example and the time he spent encouraging other kids, it wasn't long before another three decided to give the scholarship a go, and after that the programme bloomed. So, a new guideline was introduced. Scholarship winners had to promise to return to the mission to talk to the kids about how their life was going and how they were managing to stay clean and off the streets.

The talks became so popular they were shifted to an old hall out the back of the church every Friday night. Although many were enticed by the free cups of soup and bread rolls, Tracy was still delighted at how many street kids came along.

'It's like they've found something, some kind of interest,

some teeny glimmer of will!' Tracy said to Liz in amazement.

Local comedians and performers heard about the talks and offered their time as 'support' acts, which created even more interest. The talk-and-show would only last an hour but it gave counsellors an opportunity to make contact with the troubled youth and offer assistance.

Liz continued working with the mission; organising fancy fundraising events to raise scholarship money and also regularly dipping into her own trust fund. There was no cap. Every single child who showed a determination to stay clean could win this chance of a new start. Thanks to her personal family trust, Liz was a wealthy woman in her own right, and Sebastian had no idea how much money she was secretly donating.

Liz's happiness grew and she began to feel at peace with herself. But no matter how much of her time and money she gave, there was one hole inside that just couldn't be filled – the one left by Mikaylah.

~32~

Home to Mother

Mim didn't throw the bottle of scotch in her hand at James, but it took all her willpower to relinquish it to the safety of the bench. It was as if the world had suddenly tilted after their vicious argument and Mim was struggling to stand upright. The room seemed muted and blurred.

She took careful, deliberate steps up the stairs to her bedroom, where she fell on her bed and gave in to great wrenching sobs. Somewhere, even in this pain, she remembered her sleeping children and tried to muffle her cries with a pillow.

God, why was it all going so badly? What the hell was she doing so wrong that her life was such a mess? Who was there to look after *her*? To help *her* sort out this mess? She felt utterly alone.

Finally, worn out from crying, she lay on her back and watched her thoughts spin.

James had basically just told her to piss off. What a fucking bastard. But did he really mean it? Surely they were just words shouted in anger? But the words had come so easily. Maybe he'd been considering ending their marriage?

Mim gave a post-sob shudder and nestled deeper in her goose-feather cocoon.

Self-pity overwhelmed her. *Poor me!* She wanted to shout. *Poor Mim. Who's looking after poor Mim?*

'Oh God, you're pathetic,' she muttered under her breath, and even managed a grim smile at her indulgent thinking.

Mim was never one to wallow for long, so she soon turned her thoughts to problem-solving and damage control. Right, she thought, staring at the crack in the blinds. Where to from here? First things first, James and I need some space. We need some thinking time, time alone to sort out our feelings about this relationship. Then we need a communication opportunity.

She mulled over her strategy for another half an hour before triumphantly announcing her first move to the empty room.

'First thing tomorrow, I'm going home to Mother.'

'Darling!' her mother threw open the door and reached to hug Mim in one efficient move. 'Come inside out of the rain. Children, look at you, you've all grown so much. Don't touch that, Chloe. Come on into the kitchen, everyone.'

Mim's mum was the ultimate power-woman. It was for her and her contemporaries that the phrase 'super-mum' was coined.

Entering the workforce in the misogynistic 1950s, Julia Jones had to be everything to everyone and do it extremely well. After a remarkable career in stockbroking (remarkable for anyone, not just for a woman), she finally had the respect of all the big men on campus. She had smashed the glass ceiling with a perfectly executed karate roundhouse kick, without ruining her Chanel shoes, and managed to simultaneously sugar a French teacake and supervise the household staff.

Julia never relinquished her shoulder pads, never wore trousers, and only wore pearls on Sunday.

'Cup of tea, darling? Or a chardonnay?' she asked Mim.

'Mum, it's 11.30 in the morning,' protested Mim.

'Oh, of course, tea it is then.'

The children hit JJ's toy cupboard (JJ is what Julia insisted they call her, she was far too young to be someone's grandmother), and were soon entrenched in constructing the elaborate Brio train-set.

Mim's parents lived in the affluent outer suburb of Donvale. Pristine English gardens bordered huge haciendas and were surrounded by gum trees. They had never felt the urge to 'downsize' their five-bedroom home. They enjoyed a weekly game of tennis on their court and would frequent the local club for a game of golf or the occasional cards night.

'Where's Dad?' asked Mim.

'Oh, somewhere, off tinkering, I don't know what he's up to. He mentioned a trip to the hardware store,' Julia said vaguely as she placed the tea service on the coffee table. 'I must say I was quite surprised with your phone call. You haven't stayed the night out here for quite an age.'

'Yes,' Mim murmured. 'I had to get away. James and I needed to have a bit of space.'

'Oh dear,' said her mother sympathetically, 'sounds like a little trouble in paradise?'

'Well, yes, I guess you could say that.'

Mim sat in her mother's immaculate sitting room and told her the whole story: her fears for her marriage; the money worries; the stress she was under and the continual sinking feeling that enveloped her that perhaps this path she was committed to was not, in fact, the right one.

'Mum, I think I'm going insane,' she whispered. 'You know how your housekeeper had that breakdown last year – I think I'm headed for the same thing. I can't seem to keep a thought in my head, or put a sentence together. I think I'm losing the plot.' Tears welled in her eyes and she brushed them away with a shaking hand.

Julia could manage tea and feigned sympathy, but was so damned balanced and capable that she couldn't really empathise with Mim's confusion. 'Darling, are you sure you're not over-analysing everything?' Julia said kindly. 'I mean, thinking you're getting depression is a bit dramatic, isn't it? Why don't you just have a good brisk walk and blow the cobwebs away? It's amazing the power of a solid constitutional.'

Mim rolled her eyes and sighed. 'Christ, Mummy,' she began, grappling for a way to explain herself. 'It's just not fair. It's all his fault, how come I have to do everything?' She realised too late that she sounded like a petulant teenager. What was it about being around her mother that made her regress?

'Darling, let's just look at this in a clear-minded way. I'll just nip into the bar and open a bottle of wine and we'll really nut this thing out–' The phone interrupted their conversation. 'Just as soon as I deal with this . . .' Julia changed direction, grabbed her mobile and headed for the office.

Julia had been a terror on the trading floor in her day and still wielded mighty clout as a broker. Her clients made big money, and therefore so did Julia, though now she worked from home part-time. Mim watched her mother through the double-glass office doors. Julia smoothed a stray brunette lock into her sleek chignon, fiddled with her chunky gold chain and frowned into space as she listened to her client.

Funny kind of mother, really. Not exactly the apron and jam-sandwich sort, Mim thought.

Mim knew her mother loved her family, but she preferred a certain distance. She coped with visits from the grandchildren – but only in small doses.

'I've already done my time with children,' she'd tell Mim whenever the babysitting word came up, and eventually Mim got the message and stopped asking. Julia overcompensated with generous gifts and shouted wonderful holidays (as long as she didn't have to go too).

Mim was massaging her earlobes to fight off the sensation of a headache (Ellie swore it worked wonders) when her father wandered in. 'Hello, Midge,' he greeted her with a bear hug. 'How's my baby girl? I just saw my beautiful grandchildren in the rec room. Aren't they all getting tall? Gee that Jack's as smart as a whip. And Charley, what a build on that little guy, he'll be a formidable full-back one day. And precious Chloe: every bit as beautiful as her mother.'

Mim returned her father's warm greeting with a smile. 'It's so good to see you. I haven't seen you since lunch at Lynch's last month. How have you been?'

'Grand, my dear girl, simply grand. Absolutely loving life. This retirement caper's all it's cracked up to be, let me tell you.' Donald Jones hitched up the leg of his Ralph Lauren Polo chinos and sat with his ankle resting on his knee and linked fingers supporting his head. His steel-grey hair was as thick and wavy as twenty years earlier. 'Where's your mother . . . Oh, don't tell me: client call?' he smiled with the well-worn patience of a man married to a workaholic.

'Dad, how come you never minded Mummy working so hard?' Mim asked, suddenly curious about her parents' relationship. 'Didn't you care that there was never a home-cooked meal on the table in the evening?'

'Well, Midge, I knew what I was getting into when I married the woman. In fact, it was what attracted me to her in the first place. She wasn't like all the other girls, all insipid and just out to please their man.' Donald shifted in his chair and crossed his legs, keen to indulge in his favourite role as raconteur. 'Of course, after the first few years of marriage, the novelty of having this career woman as a wife wore off a bit and I started getting sick of dining at the club or coming home to a dark, cold, empty house. I put my foot down!'

'You didn't!' said Mim, amused at the thought of anyone standing up to her mother.

'A lot of good it did me!' Donald guffawed at the memory. 'But we needed to meet in the middle somehow, to find a system that suited both of us, so I whisked her away for a surprise getaway to a lovely little rooming house in Lorne, which was just a sleepy little coastal town in those days.' Donald started to go off on a tangent. 'I remember it as if it was yesterday. It was next to the Pacific Hotel, overlooking the pier. We spent the day walking on the beach, looking for fossils, and talking. We sorted out all kinds of issues. We found out where each of us stood in the relationship, what we needed and what we were prepared to compromise on. We sealed the deal that night on the Pacific's front veranda with a Pimms and lemonade. Or was it a Gin Sling? I don't know. I know it had mint leaves in it though. We shared the most delicious fisherman's basket that night and then I had chocolate mousse for dessert and your mother had crème caramel. Or apple crumble. I don't remember.'

'So did it help when you got back to town and your real lives?' Mim asked, trying to get her dear old dad back on track.

'Absolutely, my dear, best thing we could have done. Oh, we've had our ups and downs, every couple does, but a lot of good came out of that week in Lorne. For a start, nine months later your brother arrived. HAH!' He took in the look of distaste on Mim's face and barked a laugh. 'What, did you think the stork brought you?

'Anyway, we made it a regular thing; time away together to think and plan our lives – rather than just battling through every day without any direction, we planned what we wanted and took it from there.

'I wanted a wife at home more often; your mother wanted a high-falluting career – so we discussed, made compromises and it all worked out.'

'How?' Mim asked, vainly hoping to hear the meaning of life.

'We got a housekeeper! I got home-cooked meals and ironed shirts, and your mother had freedom.' He slapped his thigh and chuckled. 'At least then when she was home she was all mine and not in the kitchen!'

Mim should have known better.

He meandered over to the bar as Julia swished in. 'Oh, there you are, Donald. Could you open a bottle of that 2003 Stonier chardonnay please, dear?'

'Certainly, darling, coming right up.' Donald whipped out a cork and brought over three glasses. He rested his hand on Julia's shoulder as he reached forward to place her glass on the marble side table, and just as Mim was thinking that her mother treated him a bit like a waiter sometimes, she noticed her bejewelled hand reach up to give Donald's an affectionate squeeze.

'Now, where were we?' Julia sipped her chardonnay and assembled her best listening face.

'Well, I think I've got it all out of my system, Mum. Since I've been talking to Dad I've decided you're right. I think I'll just go for a brisk walk.'

'Oh, brilliant, darling, I am pleased.' Julia sat back relieved, then suddenly gasped: 'You are taking the children with you, aren't you?'

~33~

Reality check

'Mum, we're back.' Mim and the children spilled into the house through the garage door, warm packets of fragrant fish and chips in their arms.

'Mim, thank God . . .' Julia was grey with shock.

'Mummy, what is it?' Mim cried, dumping the food on the table for the children to squabble over like greedy seagulls. She had never seen her mother so agitated.

Julia led her into the office out of the children's earshot. 'Darling, I'm so sorry to be the bearer of this news. It's James.'

'James, my God, what is it? What's wrong? Is he okay?' Mim was immediately wild-eyed and panicked.

'He's at Epworth Hospital; he's had a heart attack.'

'What?' Mim felt as if she had been punched hard in the stomach.

'Darling, listen,' her mother held her, 'he's stable now. It happened on the sixteenth hole at Royal Melbourne. His golf partner just called your mobile.'

'Oh Jesus,' Mim whispered, the colour draining from her

face as she slumped against her mother. Her mind whirled with fear. 'Not James, oh please not James, let him be all right.'

'Look, you must get straight to the hospital, darling,' Julia said, taking charge as always. 'Dad will drive you, you're in no condition to drive yourself. I'll take care of everything here, just go.' Her eyes were filled with tears as she hugged her daughter.

'Okay, yes, that's the thing to do. I must see him, must make sure he's okay. Oh my God, oh my God, how could this happen?'

Mim lay her palms flat against the window of the Intensive Care Unit. The glass was cold and unfriendly and offered little comfort. She gazed at her reflection, at the blur of neutral tones from her Saba striped jersey, and that was all she could manage for a few seconds. Then she forced herself to look beyond this, to look at the beds and the bodies behind the glass.

It was all so alien and sterile. Machines beeped and thrummed with cold, clinical purpose as the grey bodies they were attached to lay motionless – lifeless it seemed – on their crisp, white sheets.

Quickly scanning the faces, Mim saw no one she recognised; these were mainly elderly men, worn and battle-scarred. But then she looked again and slowly realised that the man in the corner with the sunken eyes and bloodless lips was James.

James, her vital, fit husband of just forty-two, looked as though he were made up for Halloween. His face glowed with a ghoulish pallor under the savage fluorescence and his skin hung slack in creases around his jaw.

Mim stifled a sob, biting hard on her lip to swallow the emotion that threatened to spill from her.

As Mim prepared herself with a hospital gown and covered shoes in the sterile anteroom, she also prepared herself emotionally. This couldn't be her life; this was like a bad movie. Husband and wife argue; husband dies; wife lives with guilt and grief for life.

She shook herself. No, her husband was alive; she had been given another chance to erase the awful things they had said to each other and start again.

She swallowed the bile that rose in her throat as she realised how close they'd come to losing everything. She couldn't even remember any more what they had fought about; all remnants of blame or petty differences were banished. It was time to see the big picture.

She crept slowly to his bedside.

James opened his eyes and looked into hers. There was life there, thank God. He made a half-hearted attempt to smile but was thwarted by the oxygen tube in his nose.

'Oh honey,' Mim couldn't hold back the tears that spilled down her cheeks.

'Mim, the other night. I didn't mean it,' James rasped urgently, his words punctuated by the machine monitoring his damaged heart.

'Shhh, James, don't.' Mim leant forward to kiss his forehead. 'It's all okay, it's fine, it's over. But what about you, how do you feel?'

'Rooted. It happened on the sixteenth hole. Just like being shot. Someone started CPR, apparently, thank God. Thankfully a golf-course is the second-best place to find a doctor,' he smiled wanly, attempting a quip.

'And what did the doctor say?'

'Pretty straightforward heart attack.' He gave her a rueful look. 'Sorry, love.'

'Oh James,' she took his hand in hers and kissed it tenderly.

'Mrs Woolcott?' A tall, good-looking doctor walked briskly into the ward. 'Good evening, Kenneth Williams, cardiologist. If you'll excuse us, your husband needs some more tests, including an ECG and an angiogram. He's going to be fine; and bar any concerning results you can take him home in a few days. But if you would just wait outside that would be greatly appreciated.'

Mim left them to it and went to sit on a hard bench in an unwelcoming waiting room, drinking something that only remotely resembled coffee.

James could so easily have died today – today, just a regular day on the calendar, could have been his last day. She shuddered and attempted another mouthful of the disgusting beverage.

He could have died and the last things we said to each other were screamed in anger, she thought to herself.

She wiped her hand across her face, her make-up long gone.

How would I have told the kids, what would we have done without him? I had no idea he was under so much strain.

She gazed down at the cracked linoleum and noticed a mark on one of her Chanel loafers. 'Ohmigod,' she cried, sitting up in shock, anxiously scrubbing the offending spot with her thumb. Luckily it came off easily and she sat back in relief. These were her favourite shoes, she couldn't cope if they were damaged.

Then it hit her.

She looked again at the $1200 designer shoes, which she had lovingly coveted for six months before treating herself to a pair. Wearing them had sent a thrill through her. Even seeing them neatly lined up in her wardrobe gave her joy.

Shoes.

Not love or life or moments shared.

Just shoes.

Not her children, her husband, or a close friend.

Fucking shoes!

She stood and looked again through the window of Intensive Care. She saw the relatives, their faces crumpled as they sat beside their loved ones. She saw the nurses bustling efficiently as they monitored their patients, concentrating on their well-being.

She wiggled her toes in her loafers. Her feet felt sweaty and cramped. She was disgusted with her greed.

They're just damn shoes.

She saw James being wheeled back into the room and for an instant caught his eye and smiled at him. Then she strode down the empty corridor to throw the stagnant remains of her pseudo-coffee in an overflowing bin, crushing the Styrofoam cup triumphantly as she hurried back to see her husband.

Sometime later a harried nurse at the end of her shift was stunned to find a practically brand-new pair of Chanel shoes discarded under a chair in the waiting room.

'Bugger me,' she exclaimed. 'I've hit the jackpot!' Swooping them up, she rushed home to sell them on eBay.

~34~

Cliff Gets It

Cliff's meaty paw clutched the roof of his new Maserati GranSport Spyder as he hauled himself out of the low seat with an old-man grunt. He'd traded his conservative BMW 760 Li for this new phallic-compensator and was rapt with how it now caught the fillies' attention as he sped down Chapel Street. He saw those hot bits of stuff eyeing off his powerful machine and imagined their panties getting damp from the roar of his Spyder. If he hadn't been in such a hurry he'd have stopped and done a couple of them a big favour in the back seat.

He hitched his new Jagmen jeans over his flabby gut, and decisively zipped up his black leather jacket.

I am *so* the man, he decided arrogantly.

As he headed toward the gym, beads of sweat sprang to life on his hairy back and his butt muscles tightened with anticipation. He'd arranged to meet Clary tonight and his dick had already sprung into action like a divining rod, pulling him in the direction of his mistress.

'Fuck that Viagra's good stuff,' Cliff thought to himself smugly. He'd taken a double dose tonight, so Clary had better be up for some serious action. She was getting the goods today – not just the sizzling package in his pants – but also the news that from tonight he was free; free to be hers, unburdened from the suffocating shackles of family life and that dumb bitch Tiffany.

Mind you, he corrected himself, she'd gone all silicone now. But her desperate attempt to win him back was too little too late – anyway, underneath all that work she was still almost forty.

He'd told her earlier tonight. The moll, she'd just laughed at him. How dare she laugh? Didn't she realise she'd be fucking nothing without him?

He should have gone with his first plan and just texted her. Oh well, it was done now.

He snuck in a side door of the gym and spied Clary packing up the equipment from her after-school gymnastics class. Christ, her hard titties and hot little arse look fucking fantastic in the lycra leotard, Cliff thought, licking his lips. With so much blood rushing to his crotch it was all he could do to think clearly. He came up behind her as she bent to retrieve hoops from the floor, grabbing her hips and grinding savagely into her pelvis.

Clary looked up from under her straw-like bleached mane as her head dangled upside-down, and grinned at her man; the one she had so cleverly lured from his fat wife and ugly kids and would soon be married to, with complete bank-account access and a full set of credit cards. Now that made her wet.

It was more than enough to make up for his tragically small and often soft cock, Clary thought with satisfaction, happy with the compromise she had struck for herself.

'G'day, stud-muffin,' she purred. 'You've taken your time

to show.' She stuck a finger in her mouth provocatively and sucked it noisily.

'Well I'm here now, gorgeous,' he said by way of foreplay, and, pulling her upright, pushed her hard against the pommel horse, smashing his teeth against hers in a battle of tongues and saliva.

Her tits were unreal, he thought as he groped them roughly. So firm and high.

Clary peeled off her leotard and stood naked before him. 'So, big man, what have you got for your little Clary?' It was always best to get things over with as quickly as possible so they could go shopping, she'd discovered.

Cliff's mottled red hands were shaking as he fumbled with his YSL belt buckle and pushed his jeans and Y-fronts down around his hairy ankles. 'How do you like my weapon of mass erection?' he asked proudly, flipping his mistress towards him as she threw one leg over the pommel horse.

He grabbed her shoulders as he went to work, giddy with lust and excitement.

Oh fuck, oh fuck, how good am I? How fucking good am I? his thoughts thumped in rhythm with his inept thrusting. Look at the hot little unit I've scored.

The moonlight reflected off his fleshy white arse as his performance heightened then quickly died. He gave one last dramatic thrust, just to prove some kind of point, and heard the dreadful crack beneath him as the pommel horse gave way.

Lithe gymnast that she was, Clary had the dexterity to leap away. But Big Man Cliff, with his jocks around his ankles and more blood in his member than his brain, didn't register the danger in time. The fifty-kilo pommel horse fell forwards, and Cliff, bare-arsed and panting, fell with it. Tangled by his own trousers, he fell awkwardly, twisting his back and landing square on one steel leg of the equipment, noisily snapping three lower vertebrae.

By the time the ambulance arrived, Clary was respectable and had, at his insistence, dressed Cliff, causing immense pain and further spinal damage.

Delirious with pain as he was strapped to a gurney and loaded into the back of an ambulance, Cliff was in too much agony to notice his now-former girlfriend making eyes at the strapping young paramedic.

~35~

Art-show Aftermath

Ellie shut the car door with a solid European 'whumph'. She tugged her multi-coloured striped Eugenie sweater and took a deep breath. A heavy rain had fallen last night and the landscaped gardens and playing fields of Langholme Grammar seemed relieved at this momentary break from the drought.

Damn, what a morning to be on reading duty, Ellie thought as she helped Rupert and his school bag, library bag, sports bag and violin case out of the car. But I refuse to ditch, I will not sink to their level.

She walked past the CPM standing in their usual spot at the playground edge like a group of vultures waiting to attack. As Ellie passed, they angled their bodies away and she was sure she overheard one say, 'There she is.'

Her resolve strengthened. She was determined to see this day through. With a sigh Ellie made her way into the school and into the den of the Mothers Superior.

LJ's exhibition had opened last night. Just when Ellie thought she was going to be sitting at home, wallowing in the humiliation, Bryce had whisked her to Aria at 1 Macquarie Street in Sydney, a world-renowned restaurant overlooking Circular Quay. They'd got back to Melbourne by 1 a.m. and though she was a little tired this morning, she was grateful for Bryce's thoughtfulness.

She walked towards the Reading Mums, who were in a tight group, gossiping excitedly, and Ellie didn't need to guess too hard what the topic was as they suddenly fell silent at her approach.

'Hang up your bag, sweetie, reader in the reading box and into class.' She guided Rupert off to his morning chores, then, steeling herself, she approached the reading box to select the first victim for the morning. Naturally, the Reading Mums guarded the box as their own personal domain and she had to break through the group to get on with her duties.

'Morning, Ellie,' said Mary, turning her head over her shoulder. 'Good night last night?'

'Yes, it was fabulous actually.' She briefly filled the ladies in on her evening.

'Really, that was kind of him,' said one of the other mothers in a disbelieving fashion. 'Special occasion, was it?'

'No, not really, he just wanted to surprise me,' Ellie said, taking the next reader.

'We actually attended LJ's opening last night. Very glamorous affair,' boasted Trixie.

The mums had all been rather chuffed when they received an invitation to LJ's exhibit. She normally excluded most of the school mums, except for those on society's A-list. When the parents had arrived at the glamorous event, they were shocked, and a little insulted, to discover most of Langholme Grammar was in attendance. Even the principal and his little wife were there.

'Really, how was it?' Ellie asked with little enthusiasm.

'Oh, weren't you invited, darling? Sorry, put my foot in it. I presumed you would have been . . . *everyone* was there,' said Trixie.

'I was invited, but declined,' said Ellie, wishing Trixie would dry up and go away.

'Well, it was unbelievable. The photographers; the canapés; the exquisite champagne. She does it so well. But the art, Ellie, the art! Truly spectacular, she's really outdone herself this time.'

'Yes, she has,' agreed Ellie, thinking, Just kill me now.

'There was the most amazing piece at the entrance of the gallery, Ellie, you really should pop along and see it,' Trixie spoke with insincere wide-eyed innocence. 'This girl was a dead ringer for you. Really, could be your twin. Of course, I haven't seen quite as much of you as this girl was displaying.' Trixie was truly enjoying this ridiculous charade.

'It *was* me,' said Ellie in a flat voice.

'Sorry?' said Trixie and all the women stopped smirking and looked at her, open-mouthed. They were flabbergasted. They hadn't expected a confession. It took all the fun out of the game.

'I said, it *was* me.'

'Oh, really, well . . . um . . . there you go then,' Trixie's intention had been thwarted and she was at a loss as to how to continue.

Ellie saved her the trouble, turned sharply and went into the classroom to begin reading with the first boy. Just out of earshot she heard one of them, she couldn't tell which, say to another, 'I always knew she was common.'

'So how'd it go?' said Mim after the waiter had left their lattes and moved away.

'Oh – my – God,' Ellie's face was drawn, her shoulders reflecting her defeated mood. 'It was hideous. The stupid bitches were loving it. How am I going to face the rest of the year at that school? The principal was there last night, for chrissakes.'

'Oh jeez, I hadn't thought of that,' said Mim as her hand flew to her mouth. 'Did you see him this morning?'

'Yes, as a matter of fact I did; you know how normally he rushes past to show he's very busy? Well, today as he passed me in the hall I got the benefit of a huge toothy grin – slimeball.'

'Oh, Ellie, he's such a sleaze,' Mim said in shock. 'So, what now?'

'I'd love to just change schools, move cities, change our names and start all over, but obviously that's ridiculous,' Ellie said, stirring her latte thoughtfully. 'I did have one plan that I think could be quite wonderful.'

'Do tell,' said Mim, pleased to see Ellie was thinking positively.

'Well, Bryce and I have always dreamed of doing the Italy thing – you know, living in a little village, kids at the local school, learning how to cook fabulous pastas and things like that. I thought this might be the perfect time to do it. I don't want to appear to be running away, but if I can last out till the end of term and leave with a bit of dignity, in twelve months surely it will all have blown over.'

'Ellie, how marvellous! What an opportunity for the children, they'll pick up the language in no time. And you and Bryce will absolutely love it!' Mim was thrilled at this idea.

'Yes, it's quite exciting, isn't it? And with all the planning and packing, I won't have time to dwell on other things.' Ellie looked up with a tired smile. 'So, tell me the worst, how was it really?'

'Oh, well it was quite tacky. All the usual suspects, two-bit actors, has-been comedians, tired old socialites who attend the opening of a paper bag. Everyone was very critical of LJ's "artistic" endeavours, unless it was to her face, of course. The shot of you is actually quite beautiful, you know, Ellie. It really is. Killer bod.'

'Thanks, Mim,' Ellie smiled. 'Not something I intend to hang above the fireplace in the formal living room. I barely remember it being taken and I never actually saw the photo.'

'Well, pretty much everyone you know has seen it now, unfortunately, darling,' Mim said as gently as she could. 'It was actually the only image the media was interested in.'

'Oh God, can it get any worse?' Ellie moaned into her latte. 'Those bloody journalists are such vultures.'

'I know, darling. All the society photographers were there, and it will be on Kerri-Anne today, too. So I am afraid it's going to get worse before it gets better.'

'Never mind, Mim, it will all be fine. I've been through worse than this. It's a real bugger, though, I thought it was all behind me. I guess you can never really escape from your past.

'Now, enough about me, even I'm getting bored. How about you? How's it all going? How is poor old James? That gave me a scare when you rang and told me. Is he going to have to have a bypass?'

'Well, he's out of hospital on Thursday, then we see the specialist and have tests in two weeks' time, but obviously he's been told to take it very easy between now and then. I was planning a weekend away for just the two of us and I think I'll extend it into a week and really give him a quiet, restful time in the country – no phones, kids or work stresses.' Mim smiled with exhaustion at her friend. 'But thanks for calling me so often this week, you've really given me strength.'

'Oh, don't be daft,' said Ellie with a flick of her manicured fingers to dismiss the unnecessary gratitude. 'So, where are you thinking of going?' she asked.

'I hadn't really thought about it yet, maybe down to the Peninsula. I was thinking of the beach-house but it's such a long drive and also I think we both need to be looked after. I'm not feeling a hundred per cent either and my nerves are absolutely shot.'

'Would you consider Moorooduc?'

'Moorooduc? Why Moorooduc? It's just a sleepy little country town, isn't it? I don't really know anything about it except you drive past it at a hundred kilometres an hour on your way to Portsea.'

'Isn't that what you're after? A sleepy little town?'

'Well, yes, I guess so. Do you know a place we can stay?'

'As a matter of fact I do,' Ellie smiled. 'I know the perfect place for you both. Let me just make a quick call.'

~36~

R & R in Mooroodue

Sarah straightened up from raking the leaves as she watched the black Mercedes coast down the sweeping gravel driveway. She leaned the rake against the big old ghost gum and walked up to meet her guests.

Mim was helping James out of the passenger seat when she saw Sarah approach. She was astounded. It was Ellie: a countrified version, but Ellie nonetheless. The corduroy clad legs strode out in the same coltish way as Ellie's, and the long blonde hair was just as thick but up in a ponytail.

Before Sarah even said a word she embraced first Mim and then James. They were both taken aback at this intimate greeting from someone they'd not met yet, but took it in their stride.

'Mim and James, welcome to Springhill,' she said, standing back to appraise the couple. She reached for their bags. 'Here, let me take those, you both look as though you could use a cup of tea. Do come inside.'

Despite the bright sun, the chill in the air left no doubt that winter was well and truly on its way, and the Woolcotts gratefully followed Sarah from the front hall into the drawing room to stand before the roaring fire.

'I'll just take your bags up and will be with you in a moment with afternoon tea. Please make yourselves comfortable.'

'How could we not?' James wondered as Sarah left the room. 'Look at this place.'

They surveyed the room, marvelling that every little creature comfort had been considered. The overstuffed Laura Ashley upholstered furniture was worn but invitingly comfortable, and was arranged cosily about the large room. Heavy drapes, dropping down to finish in a luxuriant heap on the floorboards, framed elegant French doors. The doors led to a picturesque courtyard furnished with wrought-iron antique patio furniture and then fell away to the sweeping front lawn, dotted with old gum trees.

'Mmmm,' agreed Mim, 'it's gorgeous. I feel relaxed already.' Mim's mind was at ease knowing that the children were safe in the care of Ellie's reliable Ursula for the week.

'Ahhhhh,' James sank into one of the wing-backed leather armchairs flanking the fireplace. 'I'm exhausted. Just that walk from the car has me out of breath. This is ridiculous.'

'Well you just take it easy,' Mim warned. 'We don't want to end up at Frankston Hospital.'

'Mim,' said James, looking over at his wife with an outstretched hand, 'I can't tell you how sorry I am for the last few weeks; I've been such a prick.'

Mim took the two steps to her husband and held his hand. 'Oh, darling, I'm sorry too. I haven't been thinking of you; of course you've been under a lot of pressure too, I understand that now. I'm just so sorry it had to get to this.'

'I'll be fine, honey. We'll both learn to start living life again, won't we?' He smiled up at her and she answered by bending down and hugging him tightly.

'We'll have to,' she said.

Sarah brought in the tea-tray, groaning under the weight of a charming old teapot, complete with hand-knitted cosy, mismatched cups and saucers, and a huge plate of straight-from-the-oven scones accompanied with jam and cream. Mim's mouth watered and she realised she was starving. It was the first time in weeks she'd actually felt hungry.

'I thought you might be peckish,' said Sarah as she placed the tray on the leather ottoman between the two chairs.

'Your guest-house is lovely, Sarah, very special,' Mim said as she broke all her own nutrition rules and helped herself to a scone. 'Ellie has never mentioned it before.'

'Oh, it's a special place all right,' said Sarah. 'Ellie probably didn't feel you needed it before now. Sugar?'

The ghost gums seemed to be up-lit, but Mim quickly realised, as she admired them from their second-storey window, that it was simply the full moon reflecting off their smooth, white trunks. She closed the curtains and turned back to talk to James when she heard his gentle snores. Their snug little room had welcomed them into its sanctuary and, after a quick wash in the corner sink, James had fallen into bed and off to sleep.

Mim smiled sadly at the heavy blankets and bedspread moving up and down with James's breathing. She was so worried about the impending tests and was relieved that he was sleeping comfortably.

She kicked off her calf-skin, high-heeled boots and pulled on her Peter Alexander ugg boots and quietly slipped out the door.

The warm kitchen was in the final stages of dinner clean-up. The roast lamb and baked vegetable meal that Sarah and her kitchen help, Molly, had served earlier had been gratefully accepted by the table of ten.

Sarah was just polishing the stainless-steel sink. 'Tea, Mim?' she asked.

'Lovely, but you finish up, I'll put the kettle on.' Mim took the heavy kettle over to the sink, being careful not to splash any water on its shiny surface.

'We've had such a beautiful afternoon on your property,' Mim said once they had made the tea, gratefully sinking into an old armchair beside the kitchen fire. 'We wandered around, we found the orchard, and there's such a sweet sitting area hidden behind the hedge back there.'

'Yes,' agreed Sarah, joining Mim at the fire with her mug of tea, 'that spot is one of my favourite places at this time of year. It captures the sun and keeps the wind at bay.'

The women sat in silence, staring at the fire and nursing hot cups of tea. Mim felt odd at first, accustomed as she was to asinine chatter filling in any gap in the conversation. She couldn't bear it for much longer and was about to ask Sarah to give her the history on the house when Sarah looked her straight in the eyes and said, 'How are you?'

'Me?' said Mim. 'Oh, I'm fine. It's James who's ill, he really needs this rest week.'

'I am sure James will be fine. He looks fit and the doctors will sort out his problem. It's you I'm worried about.'

'Me?' repeated Mim. 'I don't have any problems at all. I'm a coper, you see, I have to be. If the mother falls apart, well, then, where would we be?' Mim laughed away the questioning light-heartedly.

'You've had a lot on your plate lately, Mim,' said Sarah kindly, 'and if the mother needs to fall apart then she should be given the opportunity. There's no point sacrificing your needs for everyone else. Now, how are you?'

'Look, it has been a bit tough lately, we've had a few issues, and the drama with Tiffany, then Ellie and then the hospital catastrophe last Saturday night,' Mim attempted to give Sarah the *lite* version of her issues. 'Well, I guess I've just been feeling a bit stretched lately. A little over-taxed.'

'Feeling the weight of the world on your shoulders?' asked Sarah.

'Yes, and I keep getting this tight feeling in my chest,' said Mim, frowning and indicating her chest with a splayed hand.

'Anxiety can do that,' said Sarah, gently poking the fire.

'Yes, anxiety mixed with anger and an overall sense of hopelessness.' Mim's face was tight with tension. 'I can't see where it's all going to end, but I really want it to.'

And before Mim knew it she was sharing her story with Sarah, telling her absolutely everything. Every personal detail about her and James, about their financial struggles; how she was sick of the competition for superficial things and, most importantly, how it was affecting her physically – the stress, the feeling of depression, the headaches. Before she knew it, floods of tears came and she was barely coherent, sobbing and snotting all over the place.

Sarah got up and brought over a box of tissues, then resumed her gentle listening. Mim kept on talking through the weeping, kept unburdening herself and Sarah kept on listening, carefully guiding the outcry with subtle questions.

Sarah was doing what Sarah was destined to do. Her gentle nature and generous spirit made her a born counsellor. Hundreds of women before Mim had sat in the same chair, talking in confidence to a kind person, a trained psychologist and, ultimately, a good friend.

Eventually, Mim was worn out. She stared at the now blurred flames through damp eyes.

'That's a lot to wear, Mim. You're a mother of three little children, you're having relationship issues, then, in a time of crisis, you have to spring to the side of the man you're experiencing conflict with when he has a heart attack. Not to mention putting your clients on hold, which I am sure wouldn't have gone down very well.' Sarah leaned forward, speaking earnestly to Mim. 'I know you want to work miracles, Mim, but you also need to give yourself permission to collapse if you need to.'

'Thanks, Sarah, sorry to burden you,' sniffled Mim.

'Don't worry about it, Mim, that's what I'm here for.'

Exhausted, Mim bid Sarah goodnight and made her way upstairs. She felt numb. She no longer felt so futile, but she still didn't have any answers. However, her cathartic outpouring had had an anaesthetic effect, and when Mim lay down next to her husband she immediately fell asleep.

~37~

Nice Place to Visit

'You can't be serious?' Mim stopped with the coffee cup halfway to her lips and stared at her husband in amazement. They were sitting in the courtyard of a little tea-house in Red Hill, enjoying the sun's thin warmth.

'Well, think about it for a minute,' said James. 'It's just an idea to toss around and see where it takes us.'

Mim couldn't believe what James had just suggested. She struggled to keep the excitement from bubbling up from where it was simmering in her gut. Move here? What a concept!

They were enjoying the last day of their retreat, and although they were anxious to see their children they were unusually hesitant to return to the city. They'd had such a wonderful week. They had stayed with friends in Portsea many times in the past, but their experience of the Mornington Peninsula was limited to Portsea back beach, Sorrento Main Street and Baxter Hungry Jacks. And once they had endured the Rye Carnival, but it was 'hideous', Mim had later told friends.

This time they had discovered the Mornington Peninsula hinterland. Meandering drives along dirt roads led them to hearty English fare at quaint little pubs, cellar-door tastings at picturesque vineyards and farms offering delicious organic local produce.

Mim had even spent an hour horse-riding along Gunamatta Beach.

It was when they were sitting together and looking out at the expansive view over Port Phillip Bay at Seawinds National Park that the idea had first crossed Mim's mind. *Why couldn't we live down here?* she'd thought. She quickly dismissed it as holiday-itis. This was surely a common refrain from holidaymakers approaching the end of their vacation.

But the little voice in her head wouldn't go away. From that moment forth, every experience they had, Mim viewed from the point-of-view of a local.

This is where I'd buy my fruit and veg, she'd think. This lovely rural school with the excellent reputation is where the children would go to school. This is my post office; over there is our local café.

She'd start to get excited and contemplate it as a future, then she would come crashing back to reality. There was no way James would do it. He loves his job, it's too far to commute and he needs to be much closer to the airport.

So to hear her husband voice her exact thoughts had left her absolutely gobsmacked.

'We could buy a few acres, maybe with a dam. Perhaps a great old weatherboard farmhouse, with a big veranda,' James said excitedly.

'What about your job?' asked Mim. 'It'd take you over an hour and a half to get into the city every day. Two hours at peak.'

'I'd quit,' said James, quite pleased with himself.

'What!' cried Mim, floored that he'd even suggested it.

'Yep, quit. Who needs it? I've always wanted to start up a dot-com business, and it would be perfect down here. I could build a home office on our property. With what we'd make on selling the city house and the holiday house we could buy something outright here and still have a bit to set up the business.' James started to go off at quite a pace. 'The kids can go to school just over the road there – no private school fees! And they'd love living on a farm. We'd have ponies, and chickens – Chloe would love chickens. What do you think, Mim? Do you think you could do it?' In his eagerness he appeared years younger.

'Oh, James, yes, it's exactly what I've been thinking all week, but I didn't want to say anything,' Mim gushed happily, but then the grin suddenly dropped. 'But it's so far away from everything: you know friends, families, the good schools . . . great shopping.'

'But Mim, it's only an hour for visits, and it's the people who matter. Isn't the rest the shallow stuff we're trying to escape?'

'You're right, of course,' she said, shaking her head. 'Yes, yes, I want to change, I really do, it's just going to take me some time to get used to the new us.'

'Excellent. First step is to bring the children down here over the next few weekends and see what they think. Then we'll start looking at properties. Say, why don't we pop into Mornington and see what the real-estate agents have on their books?'

Mim laughed inwardly and shook her head as James rabbited on, flipping through his paper to get the Coast and Country section out.

His father had been right. 'Now that you're married to James,' he'd warned Mim on their wedding day, 'life will never be boring.'

★ ★ ★

'Yabbies! You're kidding, it's got yabbies! Awesome!' Charley and Jack hurtled down the hill, racing each other to the dam.

'What are yabbies, Mum?' asked Chloe, walking through the paddock in her shiny new Disney Princess gumboots, clasping Mim's hand.

'Um, they're kind of like mini crayfish.'

'Ohhh, like in sushi,' said Chloe. Mim smiled at the agent, from Satchwells, Balnarring, apologetically. 'City kid,' she explained.

'That's cool,' he said. 'I'll tell you how to catch yabbies if you want,' and he walked ahead with Chloe to where the boys were standing at the water's edge.

'Well, what do you think?' James asked Mim.

'It's perfect,' said Mim. She smiled up at James as they walked towards the children, who were listening to Roy's explanation, when she stepped squarely into a cow pat. 'I will need more appropriate footwear, however,' she said ruefully as she tried to wipe the cow poo off her brand-new suede high-heeled boots. 'For some reason, I thought Country Road was the perfect choice for today's expedition.' She laughed at herself and gave up the futile task.

James had given notice at work and the Woolcotts had put their house on the market. And, although they currently had no income and would soon have no roof over their head, they both felt strangely liberated by shedding the burden of city living.

They turned to look up at the old farmhouse. It was eighty years old and had been renovated several times, resulting in a warren of little rooms and corridors. Charley had already discovered 'the chamber of secrets' hidden under the stairs. It would do while they planned their own renovation, and the original façade could easily be retained, Mim noted with her keen designer eye.

The boys screamed in delight and Mim and James looked up to see them running towards the back of the property. 'Kangaroos, Mum, look!'

Sure enough, a small mob of greys were heading away from the wild male Woolcott children in graceful leaps.

'Kangaroos! Well, that seals the deal for me,' said Mim, hugging James around the waist as he put his arm around her shoulders.

The boys, having given up their kangaroo chase, were screaming playfully at each other, hollering at the tops of their lungs, and it didn't bother Mim one bit. For a start they were about 200 metres away by now, and also they were boys, they were supposed to be a bit wild and crazy from time to time, and now they could go for it – at a safe distance – thanks to all this glorious space.

'Well, Roy,' said James, putting out his hand to shake the agent's, 'we'll take it. Good work, you found a place that suits us perfectly.'

'It's my pleasure. When you outlined what you wanted I thought of this straight away,' said Roy smiling broadly.

The three children came running over to their parents, breathless with excitement, flushed cheeks glowing. They were covered in cow manure and dirt from the rolling-down-the-hill race they'd just enjoyed.

'Have a look at you lot!' said Mim. 'Looks like I'll be trading ladies' lunches for laundry!' And not minding one bit, she thought, as a lump rose in her throat, and she watched her happy, beautiful children take off at full pelt once again.

~38~

The Wait Ends

Present Day

Mikki Cooper was the luckiest woman alive.

She really believed it was true. Coming home to her one-bedroom flat in Carnegie (her flat, her very own) she said a quiet thank you to the universe for her good fortune.

Even better, as she stepped through the door, there in the poky hall was their wedding photo, and she couldn't help but smile again at how blessed her life felt.

She walked into the living room, past the blue modular couch, and tossed her keys into the fruit bowl on the bench of the galley-style kitchen. She opened her canvas handbag and rummaged to the bottom to find the present she'd bought Nathan that day. It was their seven-year anniversary – even though they'd only been married six months, she wanted to celebrate the day they first met.

She smiled at the memory as she dug some wrapping paper out of the bottom drawer.

Nathan had been at the mission for one of his regular

meet-and-greet sessions. Mikaylah had been so fucked up; man, had she been fucked up. She still got a chill down her spine when thinking how close she'd come to dying anonymously on the streets in those days.

At that stage it had been more than a year since she'd been into the St Kilda mission. After that encounter with her so-called mother she'd given it a wide berth. She'd found a crew over in Smith Street, Collingwood, who had a squat and a good supply – and that was all that ever mattered in those days.

Then she'd hooked up with a dangerous crowd who lived precariously on the edge. One day she scored some evil shit with them and found herself dumped in an alley over the other side of town. They'd left her for dead in a street not far from the St Kilda Angels, so when she finally came out of it, Mikaylah had staggered into the mission for some food and shelter.

She scuttled in the back door, like a scared bug, lined up for a steaming bowl of tomato soup and found an empty seat away from everyone else.

It was a miserable, comfortless Melbourne day and the centre was packed. Mikaylah huddled at the edge of a table and concentrated on hunching over her bowl. A dero sitting next to her shouted out in the midst of drug-induced hallucinations and lurched towards the front of the room yelling incoherent obscenities.

Mikaylah drew his vacant chair in with her feet, creating a barrier between herself and the rest of the room. Her eyes were on her soup, her arm around the bowl, her legs clutched at the vacant chair when it was tugged. She grabbed the chair tighter – 'Get the hint, cock-head,' was her response. The chair was tugged with more force until it was pulled out of her leg-grip.

She glowered and shrank down further.

'Hi there,' said a bright, male voice.

Oh, Jesus, a fucking counsellor, Mikaylah thought to herself, and grunted in response.

'I was wondering if I could talk to you for a minute please?'

Mikaylah glared back at the placid brown eyes that were fixed upon her.

Nathan edged the chair over closer to the corner so that he was adjacent to her. The bowl of soup was between them so he sat on his hands for lack of anywhere to comfortably rest them.

'How are you doing?' he asked kindly.

'Awright,' she lied.

'We haven't seen you here before, have we?' Nathan asked.

Mikaylah shrugged in response. Her hands rested one atop the other behind the soup bowl and the fingers of her right hand pincer-gripped the rim of the over-full dish.

'I was hoping to tell you about a scholarship program that we're running at the centre,' Nathan continued. 'It's a wonderful opportunity for smart kids like yourself. I was the first recipient of the scholarship and . . .'

Nathan was on a roll, his eyes were darting around, his face mobile, and his enthusiasm for his story was obvious.

Mikaylah kept her eyes fixed on his face and Nathan mistook this for interest. She was in fact, slowly tipping the bowl away from her so that a thin, hot stream of tomato soup ran over the bowl edge into Nathan's lap. She was fascinated with how much he was into his story and how long it took him to respond. At least ten seconds, she estimated.

Suddenly he leapt up as the heat of the soup penetrated the denim of his jeans.

'Holy shit, what'd you do that for?' he yelled as he ran for a cloth.

'What'd you sit down and bother me for?' she'd replied, and slipped out to the alley before he had a chance to return.

Mikaylah's lips had curved into something like a smile for the first time in years.

She was soon lining up for dinner at the centre most nights. Nathan's infectious sense of humour and enthusiasm gave her hope for the future. It was Nathan who had given her the nickname of Mikki and it was Nathan who eventually convinced her to join the Salvation Army methadone program. After many months of interminable struggle and many setbacks she had finally beaten her addiction.

She laughed, comfortable in her own lounge room, as she wrapped the mini Andy Warhol print of a can of Campbells Tomato Soup. What kind of guy marries a girl who pours soup on him?

'My kind, that's who,' she said aloud, a girl deeply in love.

Christ, she'd better hurry, she was speaking tonight at the church hall and she still had to read over her notes.

It had been an exhausting year for Liz. To ensure her anonymity as the generous patron of the scholarship fund, she had cut back her hands-on time at the St Kilda Angels and instead devoted her time to running the scholarship programme from home.

The programme had ballooned into an enormous business, with the scholarship being offered at missions and charity groups all over Melbourne. While the counsellors at the mission looked after the recipients of the programme, Liz was in charge of the book-keeping, fund-management and fundraising.

In her role as patron of 'Street-Smarts' she hosted many glittering affairs to extricate surplus dollars from Melbourne's affluent. The wealthy flocked to her events – any excuse to attend an affair hosted by the glamorous Liz Munroe and her famous husband.

She was worn out from the amount of luncheons, black-tie functions and soirees that she'd thrown in the last twelve months, but the outcome had been sensational: the funds were rolling in and the children were being educated.

It was almost a year since Liz had spent any amount of time at the mission and she missed it terribly, although she kept in contact with Tracy via emails and occasional phone calls. But tonight Liz was treating herself. Both children had gone off for sleepovers at friends' houses and she was taking herself out to her favourite place.

She smiled at the irony as she headed towards St Kilda. Who would have thought eight years ago that her favourite Friday-night destination would be a church hall in St Kilda listening to an ex-junkie talk to street kids.

Mikki jumped on the 67 tram that travelled along Glenhuntly Road, then down Brighton Road, and read through her notes. She was all a-jitter tonight, though this was something she'd done plenty of times before.

The soothing movement of the tram calmed her nerves and she put her head down to read.

The speech outlined Mikki's last few years on the streets: How desperately she'd been living; foraging in garbage bins for food; stealing anything she could get her hands on; spending everything on drugs.

Then, after she'd got clean, how the amazing opportunity of the scholarship at the St Kilda Angels had come up, how this incredible anonymous philanthropist was offering free education and resources to anyone who could get themselves straight enough to take advantage of it. She wanted to instill in the audience tonight what an awesome gift education was. You could turn your life around with such an opportunity; something that was incredibly rare when you were living on the streets.

Mikki's speech went on to talk about how she had returned to night school to complete Year Ten, then her VCE, through the support of the mission staff and the generosity of the scholarship that supported her. She'd then moved on to tackling a teaching degree and felt that her life had finally begun.

She stared out blindly at the Glenhuntly Road shops. Of course, other kids weren't as lucky as she was. Nathan was the sole reason she was alive today. He was the one who had believed in her, who had shown her a way out of the vortex that was sucking her down and pulling her away from hope. Why he kept supporting her when she did everything in her power to push him away was beyond her.

She thanked God for him every day. Even though most of the work, the sheer desperate effort, had been hers alone. Something in her had recognised that this was her last hope: this mission, this man and the future they promised. Every day of her recovery was gut-wrenchingly hard as she struggled to believe in herself enough to let go of the habits that consumed her life and fought against the physical hold they had on her.

It was the hardest work she had ever done: fighting back from nothing and nowhere to somehow reconstruct her shattered self and battle to be whole again.

She knew that she could never really afford to get too smug or complacent. There were still plenty of big issues that dogged her, but with the help of her therapist, who she still saw once a week, she knew she was winning her battles – and that's why she had finally agreed to marry Nathan – he had first asked her two years ago, but she hadn't said yes until she'd known she was truly managing her issues, taking responsibility for her destructive behaviour and was in control of her life and addictions.

She raised her hands and rubbed her trademark short cropped pixie haircut and remembered the two crazy streaks of red that she'd stripped in this morning. She grinned. Nathan would love it.

Liz was early and pulled into the alley behind the mission to duck into the kitchen. She had two cartons of tinned salmon that she'd picked up today for the traditional weekend fishcakes. She helped the cook load bags of fresh bread rolls and stockpots of soup into her boot and headed over to the church hall.

Mikki alighted at the junction and walked down Fitzroy Street. Nathan was setting up the chairs and she greeted him with a smile and a hug. After enjoying his admiration of her new hair colour, she went into the kitchen to greet the other helpers.

The hall began to fill and Mikki started to get pre-public-speaking butterflies and nipped into the ladies for a nervous wee.

Tracy stood at the front door to greet arrivals and weed out potential trouble-makers. A couple of off-duty police often volunteered their time and loitered in the audience to protect the vulnerable group. She looked back to assess how the hall was filling up and saw Liz striding towards her.

'Liz,' Tracy smiled, and greeted her friend with a hug and a kiss. 'We've missed you, how have you been?'

'Oh, flat out Trace, so busy, and I've really missed being here.'

'You must have been, but it's all for a great cause,' said Tracy with a reassuring smile. 'Want to have a drink after?'

'Love to,' Liz said. She glanced at her watch. She still had time for a quick toilet trip and she made her way down the narrow corridor that ran alongside the kitchen wall.

The toilet door was locked, so Liz knocked.

'I'm in here, I won't be long,' came the voice from within.

'That's okay,' Liz sang out, and leaned on the wall opposite the toilet door to wait.

The dial flicked from engaged over to the green vacant sign.

Her wait was finally over.

~39~

On the Move

Mim shut the garage door and turned inwards to face her house. The scene of devastation that lay before her knocked her for six. Her arms, full of Officeworks bags, dropped; her shoulders slumped. She sighed and just wanted to give up.

Her house, her beautiful house, was a wreck. She'd taken such pride in maintaining a showroom standard for their living space ever since the painstaking renovation had been completed six years earlier, and to see it in such a shambles was heart-breaking. Open packing boxes lined the corridor and every available surface. Kitchen cupboards spilled their guts onto the floors and benches. Stacks of butcher paper waited to wrap precious ornaments. And she didn't need to go into the bedrooms to know what lay in wait there. Mountains of clothes, bed-linen and accessories towered ready to be allocated to the various bags; op shop, eBay, friends, tip, new house.

So much sorting! So much organising! Then there was the fridge to clean out, the pantry to go through, but they still had four more nights here so only half of it could be done now.

Mim slumped onto the stool at the kitchen bench, shoving aside a partially completed 'to-do' list, a tape measure and a wrapped Wedgwood teapot. She dumped the shopping bag in front of her and rolls of masking tape and black markers spilled across the bench, joining the jumble.

Where to start? She'd given up writing the list because it was just so long. Whenever she thought of how much she had left to do she started to freak out. Everywhere she looked, all she could see were more jobs. She gazed towards one of the most daunting tasks: the laundry. It was an exercise in frustration: she needed the clothes clean to pack but as soon as she finished one lot another lot would hit the hamper. And what with the cupboards' contents all over the benchtops there was no room to do any washing anyway.

Her gaze wandered back from the laundry and was arrested by the door frame.

'Oh no!' her hand flew to her cheek. She hadn't thought of that, her children's heights were recorded down the edge of the frame. At the start of each term the Woolcotts religiously measured their little ones, usually with much laughter and good-natured competition. They couldn't take the frame with them . . . could they? Mim wondered momentarily before she dismissed the thought as foolish sentimentality.

But how could she leave those memories, that record of the kids' growth? Then she remembered the three-year-old hand prints decorating the back of Charley's door; the hallway where her babies had taken their first steps; the big oak tree that had served as cubby house, picnic spot, camping ground and school project aide.

It was so much more than a house. It had been their family home; her first real 'grown-ups' house . . . the place she'd brought her baby girl home from hospital.

This wasn't the first time she'd felt like this since the family had made the decision to move. The sense of loss often overwhelmed her anticipation. But she couldn't possibly voice these feelings to her mother or her friends; they would think she'd had a change of heart and the last thing she needed to hear was 'I told you so'.

She was still excited about the new life awaiting them in the country, but she couldn't shake this niggling worry that she was doing the wrong thing. It was a massive decision to inflict on the children: to take them from their schools, their friends, to turn them from urban kids to rural ones. Of course they were excited now, it was all still a novelty, but what about when they realised that their friends weren't a bike ride up the street; that sports and activities would be greatly limited; and that their school wouldn't be anything like the one that they were leaving.

James seemed fine. Since resigning from his job he hadn't looked back and had revelled in the packing and organising. In fact, he was currently down at the new place doing what he quaintly termed 'odd jobs' around the farmhouse. Cute, thought Mim, but quite frankly you'd be more useful here.

She was worried that he also might find being stuck out in the sticks a tedious way of life six months down the track.

And what about her? What was she doing to herself? She was leaving her friends; her support network. Who could she turn to in an emergency? Well, she reassured herself, James, of course, that's the point – he'll be around now.

And of course they'd make new friends.

But it's so far away from the culture of the big city – Melbourne's theatres, art galleries and museums, she pondered, scratching some dried Weet-Bix from the kitchen bench.

Don't be stupid, she scolded herself for sitting there and

working herself into a state. You never went to the theatre or the museums anyway. And the peninsula is renowned for its artists and galleries: there'll be plenty of culture around every corner!

She steeled her resolve, grabbed the markers and tapes and went back to work. Tackling the laundry first, she picked up a Tuscan vase, a gift from Ellie. While she wrapped it she thought of her friend and her family swanning their way around Italy. The Ashcombes had left by ship almost immediately after the nude photograph incident. The thrill of the art exhibition scandal sank without a trace in the wake of their departure. It was no fun if the gossips couldn't bear witness to Ellie's shame, and Mim and the others had heard little of the event since.

Mim moved to the enormous linen press and started piling mismatched towels into a box marked *St Kilda Angels*.

Ever since Liz had told the Mothers' Group about her newly found daughter the women had done their utmost to help the Mission with funds and household donations wherever possible.

Of course, the scandal had been absolutely delicious to the other Langholme Grammar mums, and Liz had been ostracised by the various cliques with the utmost enthusiasm. Outstanding invitations had been reneged; she was no longer called for casual coffee mornings; and even the exclusive tennis club to which she and Sebastian belonged had mysteriously declined to renew their membership.

It was funny, Mim mused, how important all that stuff had been to Liz and, admittedly, to herself in the past, and now there were just so many more important things to concern oneself with.

Liz had taken Mikaylah and Nathan away with Sebastian and the boys on a family bonding holiday to give everyone a chance to get to know one another. I can't wait to hear how that's going, Mim thought, as she wrestled an enormous glass vase down from the highest laundry shelf.

The house slowly started to get past its tsunami stage and gradually began to take on some order. Mim had a section of the living room devoted to the items needed for the crossover week when they were going to stay with her parents before the new house was ready. She tossed onto the pile a suit-bag containing outfits and accessories for both her and James to wear on Saturday to Derby Day.

She was still amazed at how little she cared now for events such as these. Derby Day had once been a social highlight; details meticulously planned down to colour of pedicure polish and size and shape of brazilian wax. But now she had so many more issues far greater weighing on her, and so much to do! The only reason she didn't cancel was that the tickets had been bought months ago. Besides, it was a lovely opportunity to say goodbye to her true friends. Quite a fitting farewell, really.

Tiffany would be there on Saturday: stag, of course. It is quite strange to see one of us out on the prowl again after years of marriage, Mim thought and smiled. She somehow felt that Tiff would take to the situation like a fish to water. Still, it was always such a shame for the children, not that they'd be in the minority at Langholme Grammar: half the year level's parents were divorced.

Mim was shocked, but not surprised, when Tiffany had given her the update on Cliff. Apparently three months after 'the accident' he had recovered enough to be pushed around the grounds of the rehabilitation home. But there was no hope that he would walk again, or even pee normally, having lost all feeling below the waist.

Tiff had joked that having the pretty young nurses bathe him or change his colostomy bag was probably the highlight of his day. The children visited occasionally, but their schedules were hectic and they had few windows of time available.

Clary had left for a journey of self-discovery to Kathmandu and no-one had heard from her since.

Mim sighed to herself as she finally developed the knack for the hand-held sticky-tape dispenser. Poor Cliff, she thought, what an idiot though. As boxes were sealed and stacked at a rate of knots, she began to feel more organised and more together, and with this came a resurgence of anticipation and excitement for the move.

It's going to be fantastic, she thought, as she threw away piles of redundant household items. The fresh air, the beaches – and the mums at the school looked really down-to-earth and lovely. Darling Mocha will have to get a couple of the local canines to teach him how to dig holes, he'll enjoy being a country dog. Maybe we could train him to round up cattle? Oh no, that's right, we don't have cattle. But anyway, Chloe can start pony club, the boys can get trail bikes, they're going to be so happy. They will – I am sure they will.

It really is a perfect situation: to start afresh, to simplify. I can't wait. I wonder how you make scones? It can't be that hard.

~ 40 ~

You're Going Where?

'Darling, I know the whole "Tree Change" thing is so the go at the moment, but moving to Red Hill? Isn't that a tad extreme?' Monique tilted her head to peer from under the brim of her stunning Melissa Jackson hat.

'Surely you want to hold on to Malvern just in case it gets a bit, you know, tedious,' Tiffany suggested with a big smile and just a hint of bitchy undercurrent.

Right! Game on, thought Mim.

'It's actually Malvern that I'm finding a bit tedious, Tiff, and all the snobs that go with it,' Mim grinned happily back, not interested in being anything other than honest.

It was Derby Day and the women sat in a prestigious marquee on the 'The Rails' at Flemington Racecourse, which was filled, like a teeming aviary of exotic birds, with delicate creatures of every hue and style, proudly preening and flaunting their wares. Flemington's famed roses were a blooming mass of fragrance, the carpet of lawn was manicured to the last blade, and cheerful bunting sailed atop celebrity-packed marquees.

'It's not a temporary move,' explained Mim, patiently keen to get the conversation back on friendlier ground, 'it's a lifestyle choice. We need to simplify. We've sold the beach-house, and Malvern. It's quite liberating really. We will miss you guys but it's only an hour away and you must promise to visit us.'

'Sounds a bit Buddhist to me,' Monique said, '. . . but then I suppose that's not a bad thing . . . I mean Richard Gere's gone a bit that way, hasn't he – and he's gorgeous!' She sipped her pink piccolo through a colour-coordinated straw while keeping a shrewd eye on the passing parade of fashion.

Derby Day is quite possibly the biggest fashion moment in Melbourne every year. Blow this one and you could forget about invites to the next season's best soirees. Therefore the Mothers' Group girls all started working in earnest on their Derby ensembles a good two-to-three months ahead of time. There were appointments with the city's best milliners; outfits to be chosen; accessories perfectly matched; and the right Nancy Ganz underwear bought to suck in any excess rolls. One year Tiffany had flown to Sydney because she'd heard an exclusive lingerie boutique had an all-in-one undergarment that actually made the wearer appear taller.

Precisely five days before the day, hair salons and beauticians in Melbourne's best suburbs were booked solid as body maintenance became an obsession for the frenzied fashionistas. Spray tans were booked for the Friday. This crucial job needed to be done twenty-four hours before to allow the tan to darken marginally before the big day.

It was essential that blonde locks were highlighted on the Thursday; anything more than forty-eight hours of regrowth would require a last-minute emergency dash for a crown touch-up. It didn't matter that most heads were hatted – one could potentially make an eleventh-hour decision to swap to a fascinator, so foregoing foils was just playing with fire.

Manicurists and pedicurists whipped up an emery frenzy across the suburbs, and if one could book both hands and toes simultaneously, it was truly a time-management coup. Fat-free bodies were buffed and exfoliated to a newborn softness, all unnecessary hair ripped, lasered and waxed to oblivion, eyebrows shaped and lashes tinted, and slight tummy bulges remedied by manipulation of the pill or colonic irrigation. Monique had an annual standing booking for the first week of November at Maison Merdon, and swore by their famous Bowel Burnish treatment.

Amid a flurry of fittings, numerous panicked phone calls and credit-card damage, the big day had finally arrived. The much-phoned weather number had threatened rain, but had, thankfully, been wrong and the sunshine burst its way through morning drizzle just in time for the first round of Fashions on the Field.

Hollywood-taped and cellulite free, the flamboyant hordes teetered and fluttered through the Flemington gates, alighted from chauffeur-driven vehicles, spilled off the train platform in cheap knock-offs with too-high shoes and too-silly hats or – in the best cases – emerged like butterflies from the flock of helicopters landing on the centre of the racecourse.

The lip-sticked, hair-sprayed and Botoxed masses took their places in the caste system of the course. Distinguished members in morning suits linked to immaculate wives in George Gross or Escada headed straight for the Champagne Bar or The Chairman's Club. Robbie Williams lookalikes eagerly followed scantily clad gaggles of twenty-something girls who screeched hysterically while balancing on pencil-like heels and flaunting thigh-baring skirts while enjoying

Mum and Dad's $1500 car spot in the Nursery carpark. The corporate marquees were the plum pick. An invite to the Emirates, Myer or L'Oréal marquees in the prestigious 'Birdcage' area was social gold.

Each year, favoured Langholme Grammar parents were invited to the Forsythes' car spot on The Rails. The most prestigious of each of the available carparks, The Rails was situated right at the edge of the action. Flanked by the Birdcage on one side and the home straight on the other, it was an excellent, and envied, position.

The Forsythes' carpark was more lavishly styled than their own wedding: silver buckets iced dozens of mini bottles of French and Crown lagers, trays of sushi and crustless chicken sandwiches garnished with roses competed with other cutting-edge delicacies. Pristine white-linen napkins and white china leapt from the hot-pink tablecloth. Bunches of fuschia roses in floral vases complemented the table, carefully placed under the huge white market umbrella, which was also draped in garlands of pink roses.

But for Mim, this year's Derby Day preparation had lost its thrill and she had simply pulled her hair in a low pony at her neck and, with relief and little care, stepped into last year's Lisa Ho outfit and matching hat.

'Love your frock, darling,' LJ Mahoney had commented, then added nastily, 'Isn't it lucky that pastel is still in, it looks just as good on you this year as last year!'

Mim had just smiled at her. 'I don't care what anyone says,' she told her assembled friends as she related LJ's catty remark, 'we're broke and I couldn't afford a new outfit this year.'

'Shush, Mim,' said Monique, glancing over her shoulder. 'Someone will hear you.'

'I don't care,' Mim repeated with a self-satisfied smile. 'James has finished up at work and until we settle on the house we are broke and I really couldn't give a stuff who knows.'

'Can't you just say you're budgeting,' insisted Monique. 'Broke sounds so . . . well . . . poor.'

They all laughed but were easily distracted by the sight of a group of young women sauntering past with breasts barely contained in their halter tops, and flippy skirts hardly covering their bottoms.

'Will you just look at that,' Tiffany indicated to Mim with her piccolo of pink champagne. 'How ridiculous.'

'I know, it's such a shame, no class any more, no sense of style. And they're not even wearing hats!' said Mim, with more than a touch of sarcasm. 'Alert the media!'

'How on earth they get into the members' is anyone's guess,' moaned Monique.

Tiffany nudged Monique as she spied well-known hotel-chain heiress Anastasia Sebleton escorting a woman in a stunning sequined gown complete with chiffon diamanté-studded wrap. 'Check this out,' whispered Tiffany, 'who'd wear *Collette Dinnigan* to Derby Day, I mean really!'

'Careful, Tiffany,' whispered Monique, 'that *is* Collette Dinnigan!'

'Collette, darling!' Monique gushed and tilted her head a full ninety degrees so that she could air-kiss the bronzed cheeks of the fashion designer from under her mammoth hat.

Tiffany, horrified by her fashion faux pas, waited chastened for an introduction to the international haute couture creator.

After a quick show-and-tell session . . .

'Love your bracelet – platinum is it?'

'Have you been in the Emirates marquee yet – gorgeous!!!'

'Love the shoes – Manolo?'

'Yes I got them in LA for the event.'

'That hat is the most!'

. . . the two celebrities continued on their way, leaving the girls to their banter.

'Boys, we're here,' Mim sang out to their husbands, who were heading towards the carpark from the bookies, somewhat distracted by a slinky nubile duo that was passing them by.

James and Malcolm grinned sheepishly when they realised they'd been caught out.

'Ladies, looking lovely,' said James, and the men stood next to their wives and bestowed the required attention before they could break away, get a cold Crownie and discuss their next wager.

Petrice Forsythe floated over, decked out in a flamboyant haute couture floral chiffon layered dress topped with a Peter Jago hat in a rainbow of pastel, as her husband Montgomery joined the group.

'So James, old chap,' said Monty, 'what's this I hear about you taking the family up bush? Won't you all be a bit isolated?'

'Hardly up bush,' said James. 'We're off to live on the Mornington Peninsula. It's only an hour from town, it's hardly Flying Doctor country.'

'Well, I suppose you'll be close to some halfway decent golf courses, at least it's got that going for it,' conceded Monty. 'It all sounds a bit feral, though, and what about the Gentlemen's Club? We expect members to attend the monthly breakfast meeting, how will you make that?'

'I'm letting my membership lapse, old man, don't think I need any of that pretentious crap any more,' said James.

'What!' Monty turned puce with indignation. 'But it takes years to get admitted into the Club, you can't just let it lapse, what will people think?'

'I really don't care what people think, I might join the CFA instead!'

'Well, it's all a bit too pedestrian for me,' said Monty, storming off, his sensibilities highly offended. He loudly whispered to Petrice, 'Time to cull the guest list yet again. The Woolcotts are no longer *our* kind of people.'

James turned back to put his arm around Mim and said quietly, 'What a wanker! I can't believe I've ever aspired to being part of his golfing four.'

'Darling, you don't need to rub his nose in it, his Gentlemen's Club is his life, you know,' chided Mim.

'Well, he should try to get a more interesting life then.'

James and Malcolm headed off to find cold beer and help out a neighbouring carpark that was having trouble with its market umbrella. Tuning back in to the conversation, Mim heard Petrice crowing, 'Can you believe the news about Liz Munroe? It's just too tacky to be true! LJ phoned me yesterday morning, and obviously I rang Liz immediately to uninvite her today but her machine said she'd gone away.'

Liz's best friends shared a glance and said nothing.

'Fancy just flitting off like that without letting me know she couldn't honour her invitation,' Petrice continued, fingers splayed across her chest. 'How rude! I thought she had more class than that! Of course *I* thought she had more class than to have an illegitimate daughter too . . . *honestly*, you think you know someone. Suzanna! Dahhling!'

Her attention was captured by Suzanna Smythe sweeping in, wearing a frothy Show Pony dress. It was obvious by the blinding sparkle of her ring finger that her cheating rat of a husband was back. Every time Barry Smythe upgraded Suzanna for a younger, prettier model, he bought his way back into the family home and her affection with a bigger, more impressive diamond. This one was at least five carats and, judging by the clarity, it had cost a bomb.

'Suzanna, it's gorgeous.' The women crowded around Suzanna's ring finger exclaiming loudly.

'Just incredible. Kozminsky's?' Monique asked.

'Naturally,' replied Suzanna, holding out her hand and admiring the token of renewed affection. 'I just love it. Barry will be here shortly – he's so generous, so thoughtful, he's taking me out tonight to Silks to celebrate our twelfth wedding anniversary.'

Somehow, Mim thought, every time the bauble got bigger, Suzanna's self-esteem got comparatively smaller. Big price to pay for a ring.

LJ glanced over her shoulder as she slipped into the anonymity of the crowd. She had left Philby and his desperately boring PR cronies at the Terrace on the pretext of having 'a bit of a wander'. She was safe out here away from the Members'; no one would recognise her in the Public Area, mingling with the great unwashed.

She wandered over to one of the bookies and made a pretence of staring at the odds. But behind her enormous Gucci sunglasses she expertly scanned the crowd.

There, over by the bar: six foot two, dirty blond hair pushed back by silver wrap sunglasses. Earrings. His suit was cheap, his shoes were scuffed and his physique powerful. He was comfortable in his own skin, slouched against the bar, draining the last of his plastic tumbler of Jack Daniels and Coke.

He was laughing at something his weedy, pointy-nosed companion had just said. Three other equally grubby punters joined them and began to discuss the form guide.

Then he glanced up, almost as if he sensed her gaze upon him. Their eyes locked. A languid smile crept across his face. He knew.

LJ held his gaze as she prowled past the group; a predator stalking her prey. She strode along the perimeter of the building, picking her way through the flotsam of sun-faded tinnies and cigarette butts until she reached the rear wall. Her Prada mules daintily tiptoed past the dumpster where she was obscured from the crowd.

She stood, legs akimbo, arms folded, and watched a large, black spider weaving its web on the rusted corrugated iron-guttering.

She didn't have to wait long. The broad figure cast a long shadow across the alley as he paused to stomp out his ciggie, taking a few measured seconds to grind it under his heel before moving towards her.

'G'day,' he flashed imperfect teeth. 'What's your name?'

'Do you care?' LJ breathed seductively, hooking one manicured talon into his belt and pulling his large frame over her skeletal body. His powerful forearms, scarred with indiscriminate tattooing, pounded the shed as his mouth firmly opened hers. The dirty taste of nicotine thrilled LJ and her tongue greedily searched for more as she thrust her cleavage into his chest.

His rough hand kneaded her breast as she efficiently dispensed with his belt and fly. He forced his hand under her designer skirt with little deference to the $500-per-metre silk.

Finding her naked under her skirts, it was a simple matter for him to hoist her scrawny leg up around his waist for easy access.

He grabbed a handful of the flame-red hair and pulled back her head.

She came violently, twice, before swinging her leg down and leaving him with barely a backwards glance as he fumbled with his strides. She sauntered away, pulling her dress straight and tucking her breast back into its push-up bra.

She was hot and flushed with satisfaction as she strutted back toward the Members', so self-absorbed with her own pleasure that she walked within a few steps of Philby, who stood, grey-faced and swaying with shock, obscured by the dumpster.

'Girls . . . you are simply NOT going to believe this.'

Vivienne Heatherington, a meringue of pink tulle and embroidered floral, rushed up as fast as her strappy pink sandals could carry her. Her baby-blue eyes peeped out from the dual assault of a frosted fringe and enormous rose-laden hat.

'Why, Vivienne,' said Tiffany, her glass arrested in its trip to her newly plumped-up lips, 'whatever is it?'

'Well, you know I'm not one to gossip.'

'Of course not, darling,' reassured Mim, her curiosity piqued, 'but do tell, we won't say a word!'

'Well, I was just talking to Charisma, you know, the one who owns the boutique in Flinders Lane?'

'Yes, yes,' encouraged Tiffany, 'go on.'

'Well one of her customers is Dotty Silverberg who just bought an incredible Azzedine Alaïa piece.'

'Really?' enquired Monique. 'Is it the ruched silk wrap? I saw it there last week, you should see it, Mim, you'd look great in it.'

'Monique, shush! Go on, Viv,' said Tiffany.

'And she was over at the stables chatting to Sir Rupert, who says, by the way, that Vacuous Maiden is a sure thing in the next because she's on a new diet.

'Anyway, Sir Rupert had just been dining with his ad agency MD, David Bentleigh, who had just been in the men's room cubicle. I think I know why, don't you? Hmmmm, those advertising types, hmmpph.' Vivienne turned her nose up with a superior say-no-to-drugs sniff.

'Yes, Viv, then what happened?' Mim gently prodded.

'Apparently, David Bentleigh was standing at the sink when Philby Mahoney came in and lost his lunch. He told

David the whole thing. Philby had followed LJ because she'd been having mysterious disappearances lately and apparently he was getting a bit suspicious. He followed her into the *Public* Area.'

'No way!'

'Ohmigod!'

'I can't believe it!'

A chorus of women gasped in shock. Vivienne's audience had increased considerably.

'No, no,' said Vivienne, 'that's not it, it gets worse!'

'Worse? What could possibly be worse than being caught in the Public Area?'

'Well,' Vivienne was reaching the climax now, and revelling in the pleasure of it, 'Philby caught her having sex!'

'NO!!!'

'Oh . . . my . . . God!' breathed several stunned women.

Vivienne paused dramatically, then, when every eye was on her, she completed her coup:

'With a bogan!'

A collective intake of breath silenced the immediate vicinity of the carpark as shockwaves rippled throughout The Rails.

LJ sauntered through the stables, waggling her fingers prettily as she passed Sir Rupert, deep in conversation with Dotty Silverberg. She slipped minx-like through the turnstiles back into the Birdcage. As she passed by she considered popping into Charisma Heidelberg's marquee for a champers but quickly dismissed the idea. After all, shopkeepers were a bit below her.

She felt sexy and confident, able to bring to stud any handsome young buck she might spy. They were at her beck and call.

The hot pink beacon of the Forsythes' carpark was easy

to find. She nipped in the back way and helped herself to a piccolo. She sat gingerly on a chair, grinding herself ever so slightly against its rough fabric. Christ, not a third one, she thought with smug, post-coital satisfaction.

She touched up with a dab of lippy and removed her sunnies. As she looked around to find someone to chat with she saw Mim, Tiffany and Monique. The beginning of a smile froze on her lips. Their body language was unmistakable. Her eyes skimmed past them and rested on that vacuous non-entity, Vivienne Heatherington, who was standing with another woman she recognised from tennis. They wore similar looks of shock.

The next group was the same, and the next group. She looked past the Forsythe carpark and, with increasing horror, realised that the surrounding carparks were full of people silently staring.

Her heart fell. Her confidence plummeted to be replaced by an impending sense of doom.

She didn't know how, but they knew. They all knew.

Fuck.

~ 41 ~

Back to Basics

Mim cradled her mug and blew on her tea as she stared out the window past the backyard and down the hill at her two boys whooping with delight as they played cowboys. She turned around, leaned against the sink and surveyed the daggy old kitchen. She was feeling sentimental about it now and, as old as it looked, it was still functional so she'd decided to delay the renovation for a few years.

She remembered with an inward laugh some of the kitchens in which she'd been a guest in the old days. Showcase kitchens. Tiffany's in particular, with its honed marble benchtops and the latest technological gadgets, self-closing drawers and state-of-the-art sliding mechanisms, was particularly amusing as she'd never actually used it.

Tiffany had felt a working kitchen was an eyesore, with dirty pans and food out and about, yet she felt the open-plan element was so important to her architecture. In a dilemma she'd opted for the butler's pantry off the kitchen: this small room housed her microwave, dishwasher and sinks, and she had therefore ended up with an unusable tiny kitchen and an unused display kitchen.

Life was so much easier and freer now, Mim thought as she wandered through to their eating area. Not big enough to be classified as a dining room, it was more of a hallway with a table in it: a great big rough-hewn table with fifty years' worth of nicks and marks and paint spatters. She'd found it in the old shed on their property just after they'd moved in last year. It was a brilliant discovery, she'd been so excited to sand it back and bring it into the house. It was huge, it seated ten, so family and friends could all be comfortable, and they'd already seen it fully occupied many times. And because it was so worn it didn't matter at all if the children had their scissors, glue or train set on it. It doubled perfectly as a craft table, and spills didn't seem to bother Mim so much any more.

She wandered out to the back veranda and from the top of the wide steps she called down to her daughter, who was in the yard. 'Chloe, put your hat back on please, sweetie.' Chloe had discovered the delights of worms and was methodically turning the soil in the garden beds looking for the slimy little creatures to deposit in her bug-catcher. 'Sure, Mum,' she called back and picking up her Hi-5 cap, she slapped it on her head without hesitation.

Unbelievable, thought Mim. A year ago I would have had an absolute battle on my hands. Back then the kids took every opportunity to argue with me. Now all of them are being so much more reasonable and helpful. Of course they weren't perfect, what kids were? But Mim was sure the country air was doing them good.

Of course, she reasoned, it probably also had a lot to do with the fact the family now spent so much time together, and she and James were so much calmer and happier. They had plenty of time; time to wander down to the dam; time to watch the horses eat their dinner, time to sit on the back step and brush Chloe's hair and watch the sunset.

Mim no longer spent hours shopping for items that used to seem so crucial: the latest video games for the kids, fashion items, or the perfect gift. She no longer wasted time swapping her handbag to match each day's outfit (her new Succulent Designs bag was perfect with everything). She didn't waste time applying a full face of make-up and change of clothes just to do school pick-up. There was now ample time to meander at the farmer's market and chat to Jan, the nice lady who worked the till, instead of flying through Safeway glancing at her watch, trying to squeeze so much into each day.

The children's school was an absolute gem with its joyous approach to learning and life. It was so much better than they ever could have imagined. It had such an incredible sense of community. The teachers were actually interested in the students as children – small people with potential, not scores to be achieved or problems to be rectified.

It had taken Mim some time to get used to the more relaxed style of education, however – some habits were hard to part with – but now, a year later, she was thrilled to know that her children were learning life skills, not just grammar and fractions.

She smiled when she remembered her first efforts at being a 'country mum'. She'd started with what she thought would be the 'right' look, buying herself a complete outfit of brand new R.M. Williams riding boots, moleskins and chambray shirt (she'd baulked at the Akubra, but only just), but when she'd turned up at school to deliver the children to their class rooms she'd felt a real twit. The other parents wore a variety of outfits, jeans mostly, but some of the working parents wore normal suits, shirts and skirts and anybody who actually worked their 'land' did so in old cords, slickers and work-boots. She laughed at herself when she thought about it. That'll be a funny dinner-table story one day, she thought. Not quite yet, but one day.

She was still learning to concentrate on the inside of herself rather than the outside, but she was getting there.

She wandered back inside the house, letting the flyscreen door slam casually behind her. A delicious ray of sunshine fell through the window onto the comfortable old armchair that she'd found at a local second-hand dealer.

Mim picked up the other cup of tea and walked through the cosy sitting room and into the wood-panelled study.

'You star,' said James, turning from his handyman attempts at one of the cupboard doors. 'You're a mind-reader.'

She leaned down with the tea and gave him a kiss. He was as excited as a child with his new tool set and was constantly looking for odd jobs to practise his new DIY skills.

James sipped the tea and told her excitedly about the latest clients who had responded to his recently launched website. James was selling the local art and craft online and the response had been phenomenal. The community artists were in full support of his project: 'Sure beats Balnarring Market at six a.m. in the rain,' one had said.

A New York boutique had recently placed a large order for the Eucalyptus and ti-tree scented candles and there was interest from a department store in Bristol for a big shipment of corrugated iron bird-houses.

Mim made her way back to the veranda to check on the children.

Jack and Charley had adapted their game from being cowboys to now being the cowboys' horses and were leaping 'fences' made from bits of the bonfire planned for the following weekend.

Chloe's worm farm had doubled in size since she discovered what happened when she chopped them in half.

Mim sat on the steps of the veranda and surveyed the scene, marvelling at what a lovely time her entire family was having. She stretched out her legs to enjoy the winter sun and noticed she still had on her beaten-up old Blundstone gardening boots.

She looked at them, stunned. They were truly ugly, chunky and in no way fashionable.

These were not the boots of a happy person.

Yet she was happy. Fancy that.

Acknowledgements

The authors would like to thank the many people who have helped to make *Gucci Mamas* a reality.

Thanks so much to the wonderful team at Random House for treating us so well every step of the way; particularly our incredibly insightful and clever publisher, Larissa Edwards, who saw the potential in the original manuscript and helped to steer it in the right direction. Thanks also to our editors, Jessica Dettmann and Sara Foster, and to publicity manager Briony Cameron.

We'd also like to express our gratitude to the wonderful Selwa Anthony, literary agent, without whom this book would not have flourished. Thanks for always being at the end of the phone with good advice, Selwa.

We must also thank our children:

Harley, 16
Ruby, 13
Darcy, 10
Connor, 9
Oliver, 8
Francesca, 6
Elliot, 4 and
Lucas 2

for letting us work sometimes! And also our wonderful husbands, Rob and Ian, for their unflagging support.

And we can't end without sending a huge thank you to everyone at Penbank School. The staff, students and community have been with us every step of the way, delighting in every new development and snippet of news. From working in the spare office to having impromptu meetings in the school kitchen, Penbank has been at the heart of this book – and bears absolutely no resemblance to Langholme Grammar!

Michelle would also like to thank: My beautiful friend Tracey for once again standing beside me every step of the way in life and work; my gorgeous sister Kelly, for sharing the past and the future; and Mum and Dad, who always knew I could.

Lisa would also like to thank: All those patient people in my life who indulged me by listening to the never-ending impromptu author readings as each new page hummed out of the bubble-jet; darling Ian of course (whose encouragement is limitless); the patient and kind Sam Westle; Melita; my sister Deb; Nean; Prudie; and of course my generous and loving parents, Bev and Doug Barlow.

About the Authors

Michelle Hamer and Lisa Blundell each have four children, one husband and assorted pets, including a rabbit, blue-tongue lizard, turtle, cat and dog. Lisa sometimes even has koalas in her backyard, but Michelle thinks that may be taking the notion of a tree-change too far.

As with the characters in their book, both women have been Reading Mums; they sometimes get caught up in Carpark Mafia gossip, but they have never been Mothers Superior – well, not on purpose anyway.

Michelle and Lisa take shopping very seriously – whether it's at a posh boutique or the local St Vinnies. They both appreciate the importance of a well-brewed latte and don't mind being Gucci Mamas every now and then, as long as they can get home and pull on their trakkies afterwards.

Michelle is a prolific freelance journalist who has written for newspapers and magazines such as *The Age* and *FHM* for the past twenty years. She is also the author of three non-fiction books published in four countries.

Lisa comes from a varied media and advertising background that included doing voice-over work, advertising and copywriting.

Hotel Heaven
Matthew Brace

Matthew Brace has been a happily helpless luxury hotel addict from an early age and became so hooked that he gave up a lucrative career as a Fleet Street journalist to become a professional travel writer.

Hotel Heaven is the fascinating, glamorous and hilarious account of more than a decade of relentlessly posh travel, painstaking research and an awful lot of fun.

In *Hotel Heaven*, Brace takes you inside the hallowed walls of the world's most fabulous luxury hotels. He walks you through their corridors and lush gardens, lets you plunge into their pools and luxuriate in their best suites. But things do not always go to plan for the jet-set travel writer and Brace recounts hilarious and humiliating incidents which have almost ended his career as a professional bon viveur.

So dust off your Prada in-flight satchel and come on a truly fabulous round-the-world glamour trip with an incurable luxury hotel junkie. Come to *Hotel Heaven*!

The Shoe Queen
Anna Davis

1920s Paris. The 'Crazy Years'. English society beauty Genevieve Shelby King parties to the utmost with the artists and writers of bohemian Montparnasse. She has a rich husband, a glamorous apartment and an enormous shoe collection. But there is something hollow at the centre of Genevieve's charmed life.

When she spots a pair of unique and exquisite shoes on the feet of her arch rival one night, her whole collection – indeed, everything she has – seems suddenly worthless. The exclusive designer Paolo Zachari, renowned for his fabulous shoes and his snobbish eccentricities, hand-picks his clients according to whim. And Zachari has determined to say no to Genevieve.

As her desire for the pair of unobtainable shoes develops into an obsession with their elusive creator, Genevieve's elaborately designed life comes under threat, and she is forced to confront the emptiness at its heart.

Night O' Shite
Amy Cooper and Debra Taylor

It's Saturday night, there's nothing on television, you decide to rent a DVD from the local video shop. The problem is, you can't find anything good, which leaves you faced with choosing the mediocre or the truly awful.

The truth is, Hollywood churns out more bad than good, but don't just resign yourself to it, embrace it! Don't get out a bad movie, get out the worst movie. Don't go for poor, when you can go for appalling. Why not make a real night of shite of it?

Night O' Shite isn't about the worst movies ever made, it's about the ones they told you would change your life, be the best experience you ever had, were something you couldn't afford to miss . . . and then turned out to be shite.

Now, at last, there's a guide to Hollywood's worst, and not just a guide, it's a celebration. Don't have a disappointing night in watching *Gigli* alone. Invite your friends over, learn the worst lines, eat some themed food, worship Ben and Jen for what they are – just plain awful.

Alice in La La Land
Sophie Lee

A series of disasters in her home town causes Australian actress Alice Evans to flee to Hollywood, where she finds life is not the glittery stuff of dreams. It's the Hollywood nightmare. She is forced to navigate her way round the city in a cheap Japanese rental car, lurching from one audition to the next. She has no money in the bank, no friends, and her auditions aren't exactly setting the town on fire. She shares an apartment in the decidedly non-glamorous Miracle Mile district with an out of work swimsuit model and two bellicose cats who have a habit of invading her suitcase when she's not looking.

Alice begins to suspect she's come to the worst place on earth to turn her luck around, but she's hell bent on her mission to succeed. One day she has a chance meeting with an Irishman called Nick, who encourages her to think carefully about holding onto long-held dreams when life could open up many new possibilities.

Mim Woolcott was once a down-to-earth girl who loved her freckles as much as sailing with her carefree husband. But one day she woke up to find she was keeping Prada, Louis Vuitton and numerous day spas in business and her life had descended into a merry-go-round of shopping, backstabbing and snobbery.

Welcome to the world of the Gucci Mamas, where every day Mim has to negotiate the Carpark Mafia and the Mothers Superior as she drops her children off at the most prestigious school in Melbourne. But in between keeping up with the Joneses – or in this case the Mason-Jacksons – cracks are starting to show in Mim's perfect life as money gets tighter and her husband works ever longer hours. If her two best friends have similar problems, Mim would never know – the Gucci Mamas are far too busy picking their outfits for the races and having manicures to notice each other's troubles.

Something's got to give, and it will take a catastrophic, life-changing event to bring Mim to her senses. But will it be too late?

Wryly funny and sharply observed, with characters who are all too real, *Gucci Mamas* will have you hooked from the first page.

FICTION

Cover design www.saso.com.au
Cover illustration based on originals by Nick Monu and Pink Tag

ISBN 978-1-86325-565-3
9 781863 255653